The Blue Ribbon

- Ron Hevener

On With The Show.

Ron Hevener '03

Ladies and Gentlemen . . .

In a pivotal scene from this romantic novel, one of the characters plays her favorite love song as she looks back on her life. For your listening pleasure, the publisher has produced a fully orchestrated recording of "ANYTHING FOR LOVE" arranged by talented composer Andy Roberts and beautifully performed by the Author. To order your CD for $5.00 each plus $3.00 shipping and handling, please call Pennywood Press at:

Phone: 717.664.5089
Fax: 717.665-4651
Email: Pennywood@dejazzd.com

The Blue Ribbon

Who wins the Ribbon
. . . And who wins at Love?

By RON HEVENER

Pennywood Press
1338 Mountain Road
Manheim, Pennsylvania 17545
USA
Telephone: 717.664.5089
Fax: 717.665.4651
Email: Pennywood@dejazzd.com

The Blue Ribbon

A novel by Ron Hevener

Copyright 2003 Ron Hevener
Edited by Ron Hevener and Maxine Bochnia
Cover photo by Henry Kielblock
Cover design by Raintree.com

This book is a work of fiction. Any resemblance of the characters to persons living or dead is purely coincidental.

ISBN 0-9679514-8-8

MANY THANKS TO . . .

As with all good stories, a writer pulls in friends and others of special talent to help round out the characters, debate the overall direction of a novel and make its plot more fun. It's a team effort, and our work includes everything from developing a book's story line, to rendering the illustrations it may inspire, designing collectible merchandise; writing the screenplay for television or film adaptation and producing a theme song in the recording studio to set the story's mood. Considering that all this is done while caring for and training the animals on which our stories are based, novels are quite an undertaking here at Pennywood.

That being said, I would like to thank the production staff here for everything they contributed to the making of THE BLUE RIBBON. Many thanks to my researcher, Maxine Bochnia, without whom this story would not have taken on its authentic tone and sense of humor. Certainly, my own isn't always what one would call "fine-tuned." I must thank my business partner, Ken Zook, for his patience with my many gambles and risks that have swooped him into more escapades than he ever dreamed of or wanted. Thanks must go to my dear and loyal friend, fellow artist, Bonnie Stepp, who is the greatest painter of the collectible Hevener figurines in the world and to

Sandy Adams, my twin, two years apart. I would like to thank my handsome brother, Duane for being true to himself. It sets a good example. Thanks go to our ever-youthful and spirited mother, Jeanene, and to our wise and noble father, John, who always has time for those he loves; to the late Jacqueline M. Kauffman, who so lovingly founded the Lochranza Kennels in 1945; Ruth Hamilton, who has always been there for me; Shirley Hunter; Dr. Marianne Fracica, the greatest vet in the world; and to a certain mysterious woman who shall, at her request, not mine, remain nameless. She has no idea how much her letters have meant to me.

Special thanks go to the following list of friends and relatives who, in their own, individual ways, remind me how spectacular life is, and who keep me going.

Look how many it takes!

Avvie and Guy Hoffman; Wendy and Gardner Hamilton; Jim Roche; Trudy and Russ Neely; Joe Birch; Joe Trudden; Deborah Hahn, Russ Diamond; Ed and Regina Zeroski and the boys; Susan and Rod Richardson; John and Sharon Sensenig; Bruce and Julie Hamilton and family; Mary Anne, Jessica and Laura Hevener; Joshua Hevener; Tonya Hevener and her kids; Eric and Dave Adams; Crystal and Marlaina Hevener who I think of often and to whom I wish the greatest love; film Director Rupert Hitzig; Kim Criswell, who will always be my favorite star; the inspiring Joyce Turley and Fred Nicholas; Charlotte and Skip Kresge; Rob, Roz and Ben Hunter;

Ralph Moore; Vicki and Bob Swayne; Megan and Tom Petry; Joe Eckenrode; Farrah and Tom Morrow, Jane Sohns with whom I have ridden many times on the mountain trails talking about life; Record Producer extraordinaire and my dear friend Bolden Abrams, Jr. together with all the rest of his Philadelphia family who took me in to their lives so generously; the brave Bruce Davis, quite a survivor; the inventive Paul J. Cappielo, DVM, together with his wife, Susan and their children, Michael and Christina; the smiling Julia Fracica and Victoria, special to me for many reasons; Linda Mitchell and the entire staff of The Peaceable Kingdom Animal Hospital; Jill Parker; Meredith Moore; Richard Zook, whose laughter and jokes lift me at times he doesn't even know; Jill Tipton; Charles and Verna Hevener; Karen and Lester Livengood; the independent John Horning; Cowboy Bill Mitchell and his beautiful family of horse lovers; Kevin White; Matt Comp; Ramesh and Shashi Kaushal; Gita Sebastian; my uncrowned professor, Richard Busch; the professors of the North Museum who showed me the intellectual world in all its glory; and Mrs. Shober, who believed in me and let me daydream in school.

Champagne for everybody! We've got ourselves a novel.

And now?

On with the show!

FOREWORD

Certain animal characters in my stories are real. In THE BLUE RIBBON, "Kane" is one of those characters.

I was lucky enough to meet this gentleman of a dog during the height of his illustrious show career, when he came to live with my friend, Jacqueline M. Kauffman. I had purchased my first AKC registered puppy from this interesting woman many years before and occasionally handled her dogs in the show ring.

After her death in 1994, Jackie's beloved Lochranza Kennels was moved to a beautiful estate named after one of the first Collies she ever bred. There, according to her wishes, the bloodline continues as she directed.

On a warm day in June, 1997, in my arms under a spreading Maple tree, Kane took his leave and crossed the Rainbow Bridge to rejoin his friend, Jackie. Together, they exemplified the rare quality called "Class" that raises certain individuals among us to the lofty stature of legendary champions.

Ron Hevener
Lochranza Kennels
www.ronhevener.com

Prologue

Across the lawns of Lochwood, safe in his spacious kennel behind the boxwood hedge, the old dog lay stretched in a patch of sunlight. Once magnificent, his golden coat was now a matted tangle of rough, dusty fibers; his stained eyes defying the world to keep him one day longer. Choice morsels of food presented on a shiny platter for the great Collie whose trophies adorned the sandstone mansion outside of Havenburg, Pennsylvania, lay untouched. Temptation could stir his primal heart no more . . .

"Every morning I feed him, and every night I just take it away," the kennel man said to Doc Taylor, kneeling beside the weary dog.

"I've never seen him like this before, Jack," the vet said, pressing his stethoscope to the noble champion's leonine chest.

"You won't be hearing much in there, Doc. Ol' Kane's made up his mind."

"How long has he been this way?"

"Since Esmeralda disappeared," Jack said.

Silence from each of them, but at the sound of the familiar name, a delicate collie ear twitched ever so slightly, then drooped. *It was hopeless. She was gone. She would never come home. He would never hear her voice, never hear her laughter again.*

"Two weeks can be a long time for a dog."

"She's been gone longer than that before. Only, not without Kane, here."

"He's her favorite, all right. You know, dogs can waste away if they lose the one they love. I've seen it before. I've seen 'em just give up and quit. At the clinic, if a dog's been hit, I just cross my fingers and hope it wasn't a Collie. I hate breaking somebody's heart, and they're the one breed I know that'll just give up the ghost. Like there's no fight in 'em."

"No fight? Maybe they just figure if it ain't gonna be fun no more, they're out of here! And I can't blame 'em."

"Well, you do have a way of putting things," Doc Taylor said, folding up his stethoscope and placing it in his bag. "Does he get out to run?"

Jack wrinkled his brow and stepped back. "You know better than to ask me that! In fifty years I can't think of a day the dogs in this kennel don't get out to stretch their legs."

"I wasn't criticizing you, Jack. Anybody knows the runs are big enough here even if the dogs were never turned loose a day in their lives. I was just thinking if he'd get out for a change of scenery, it might - ."

"Stop right there, Doc. This is Kane! The king! He's got the run of the house, the fields, the woods; anywhere he wants. If Esmeralda ever got the idea people think any different - well, let's not get into that!" he said, stroking the collie's beautiful head as twenty kennel mates paced and circled with curiosity. Nearby, a sable and white female lifted a paw against the fence and tilted her head sideways. *What were these men talking about? Why was Kane so sad?*

"She don't understand," Jack said. "None of 'em do. They remember the good days, when Esmeralda would say "Come on, Jack! Brush 'em up and get ready. We got a show to do!" Never told me 'til the last minute. Nope, that way the dogs always looked great. I guess there ain't a whole lot of kennels left that can fill the classes like we used to. We'd decide to make a champion, and enter enough dogs to make sure at least one of 'em would get the points! But, I guess that's all over now."

"You know it isn't. You could round up some of the other kennels and get a major any time you wanted. They listen to you, Jack."

"Yeah, they listen all right. Long enough to find out what show we entered and break the major at the last minute."

"Dirty pool."

"The kind nobody wants to swim in."

Dr. Taylor took a pocket sized notebook out of his shirt, jotted down a few things, and headed for his truck. "We'll give him a shot," he said, handing Jack a list when he came back.

"What's this 'we' shit?"

"Oh, that's right. You're the one who can't stand needles," the vet said, neatly administering a shot of vitamin B-12.

"What's that for?" Jack asked.

"Just a little something to perk him up a bit. What do you say about the rest of my prescription?"

"This, here?" Jack said, reaching for the glasses inside his coat. "Vitamins? Broth? Long walks?" he read out loud. "Already tried all that stuff."

"How about what I underlined," Doc Taylor said with a grin.

"Oh, *that!* Well, that's something Kane already took care of himself before Esmeralda left." Smiling, he walked to the next kennel run, opened the gate and called out. "Annie! Here girl!"

In an instant, the elegant Collie so nosey just minutes before leaped for joy and followed him to Kane's lair.

"Want to see for yourself, Doc?"

Running skilled hands along the young Collie's sides and gently palpating her abdomen, the vet searched for signs of life. "Been a long time since there were any Kane litters around here, he said, feeling several developing puppies. "Esmeralda must have been thrilled when she found out."

"Would have been," Jack said. "But, she doesn't know."

In his cottage later that night, Jack and Nancy, trusted housekeeper at the Lochwood estate, tried making sense of things over supper.

"I can't believe it," Nancy said, fiddling with spinach and potatoes. "I can't believe this happened."

Jack set a glass of water down on the scarred kitchen table, reached for a napkin, and dabbed his mustache. Looking around the small room where he and Esmeralda had so often discussed pedigrees and combed through Collie magazines, he said, "She's still hanging in there. That's the important thing." *But, for how long? How long could she hold on to life if life wanted her no more?*

"Is it really true they're going to put the dogs to sleep if she doesn't make it?" Nancy gripped her cup with both hands. Tension mounting in her voice, her forehead creasing with uncertainly, she said, "If the dogs are put down, what happens then?"

"Where did you hear that?"

"She mentioned something about it once. I just wonder if she ever changed that part of her Will."

Jack smiled gently and covered her hand with his. "I wish she had. The Will says unless Esmeralda finds somebody to carry it on, the kennel ends with her."

"What about us? Don't we count?"

"I think she was hoping for a child," he said.

Wondering why Esmeralda would show her Will to Jack, but not to her, Nancy started to ask, but changed her mind. It was because of Steven, she decided; the love of her life and the biggest mistake. Funny thing about love; it could be so different with someone else.

"How many others know about the Will?" she asked.

"None that I know of," he said. "Ready for bed?"

"Soon," she smiled, gathering up the dishes. "Soon as I'm done here. Warm it up for me?"

"Deal," he said, giving her a kiss and heading up the stairs.

Alone in the kitchen now, unable to shake the question growing inside her, she wondered: *Had Esmeralda, usually so private about her business affairs, told anyone else about her Will?*

That night, as the moon rose high, the old dog lifted his head and gazed down the lane, longing for Esmeralda's return. White and glowing, the haunting light dripped through feathery trees onto the lake. Where was she, he wondered? Why had she left him alone like this? Beside him, his sable and white companion stirred.

Throwing back his head, in the moan of wolves centuries before and after him, he howled.

A light flicked on in the cottage. Careful not to disturb Jack, Nancy, unable to sleep, slid from underneath the covers and found her socks beneath the bed. Pulling herself into a terrycloth robe, swishing back her hair, she carefully sneaked down the creaky stairs. If she could remember where each creaking board was, she might be able to reach the door. "Uh!"

It was only a chair she had bumped. On she went, one step and then another. Finding her coat and boots, she felt in the darkness for the smooth, round handle of the porch door. Careful not to arouse the other dogs, she high stepped over the stony lane, rushed through the nearest chain link gate and made it to the kennel.

There he stood, a silent, lonely sentinel.

"It's OK, boy," she said, messing up his thick ruff. "I know you miss her. We all do. But, isn't Annie keeping you company?" At the sound of her name, Annie came over, wagging her tail.

"You want a hug?" Nancy asked, wrapping an arm around the Collie's belly and pulling her close. "Hey, wait a minute. What's this?" she asked, her hands pressing against Annie's belly and feeling the bitch's swollen nipples.

"Kane?" she asked. "Do you know anything about this?" Wondering if Jack knew; impossible to believe that he didn't; his silence about Esmeralda's Will suddenly made sense. In the manner of one to whom grooming is an automatic reflex, almost second nature, she began breaking apart the small tangles, remnants of play and courtship, behind the dogs' delicate ears. Tugging and pulling, she scratched the itchy skin beneath as their throaty moans of pleasure and fun encouraged her to go on.

"Wait here," she said. Disappearing into the kennel building, she found the drawer marked "Grooming Supplies," retrieved a brush, scissors and folded terry cloth and returned to Kane's run. "Here, big fella," she said. "Let's show them what a champion looks like. Let's make Esmeralda proud!"

As she worked, her mind locked into saving the litter of puppies she now knew were on their way, a path of moonlight beamed from the frozen lake to the cloud-less sky. Hoping the woman on whom all life at Lochwood depended wasn't ascending that stairway to the heavens tonight, she whispered, *"Wherever you are, you crazy, love-sick fool . . . hold on!"*

Chapter 1

They were friends.

Blanche and Esmeralda were the kind of friends few of us will ever know or understand. They were good friends; true friends; the very, very best of friends; the gawky blonde wise cracker, and the shy, but richest girl in town. In the savvy realm of pedigrees, stud service and bloodlines, these two powers behind the famous Blanche' and von Havenburg Kennels were destined to become household names. To the rest of the world they were nobodies.

It was 1942. America had been attacked and the military draft was making soldiers of every able bodied man. The Andrews Sisters were singing "Boogie Woogie Bugle Boy," Greer Garson in "Mrs. Miniver" and James Cagney in "Yankee Doodle Dandy" were filling the movie palaces and Wall Street was plotting its next move. America was at war, and in the midst of it all, upholding a genteel tradition of culture and civility, a saucy

17

West Highland White Terrier by the
princely name of Ch. Wolvey Pattern of
Edgerstoune had just won Westminster.

The Encounter . . . "Just how perfect
does this fake have to be?" Blanche
asked, tossing a bolt of cotton on the
measuring table and snapping her pinking
shears with a flourish. "I'm a whiz," she
winked. "I can make *diamonds* out of
rhinestones!"

"Don't you mean a silk purse out of
a sow's ear?" said the elegant young
woman in black.

"Oh, no, Honey!" Blanche laughed at
her. "You gotta save the *silk* for your
dresses!"

Amused by the cheerful retort;
hiding what she knew; the chic young lady
studied the kingdom of the witty retail
queen. *Dorothy's Dress Shop*, at the corner of Broad Street and Main, was neat,
tidy and the only place in town to buy
ladies' hats and finery. Her attention
rested on the scuffed rungs of an old
wooden ladder rising to the dimly lit upper levels where the most expensive fab-
rics were shelved, and the amused shopper
smiled to herself. Blanche Jacobus was
entirely different from what she had expected. She was totally and completely
refreshing.

"I'm going to the Mother's Day dog
show in a few weeks," she said in
finishing school tones as she noticed the
homemade display of what appeared to be

hundreds of colorful spools of thread in an ink stained printer's tray hanging on the wall. "A very important dog show. Going to Paris now for my wardrobe is out of the question," she said. The War, which had lasted longer than anyone might have guessed, was taking its toll in more ways than a small town shop girl might appreciate.

"My mother sent me some magazine clippings from London," she went on. "I worry about her being over there, alone. As soon as I can, I'm booking passage. I brought along one of the pictures to show you," she explained, as Blanche raised an eyebrow and nodded quietly. "Isn't this the most wonderful jacket you've ever seen? Wouldn't it be wonderful?"

"Honey, I can make anything wonderful from a picture," Blanche said. "It just costs a little extra, that's all." *Fascinating, the kind of people one met in the world of fashion, she thought. What movie did this one step out of?* "And how is London this time of year?" she asked, deciding the movie was *"Wuthering Heights"* as she played along with the Merle Oberon wannabe.

"Well, the weather there never changes." The Merle Girl said with a mist of longing in her voice. Other than that, it's as good as can be expected." She smiled bravely. "It's been a long time. Too long. But, I used to visit my mother there every year."

"Good place to keep a mother," said Blanche, aiming her voice in the direction of the back room. "Matter of fact," she said loudly, "I'm thinkin' of sending MINE off to the *NORTH POLE!*"

"WELL, I can't WAIT!" came the unexpected retort over the sound of a sewing machine from behind a curtained doorway. Both sets of eyes quickly darted toward the voice.

"Sharp as a bat!" Blanche whispered under her breath with a smirk.

"*I HEARD that!*" came the rough but playful answer as if attached to the first remark in a game honed by a razor's edge and family love.

Shaking her head, Blanche just laughed and tucked the picture in her smock; bright pink like most of her wardrobe. It wasn't easy being a big diva in a small town, she thought, reminding herself that important people like Hedda Hopper and Jimmy Stewart had come from Pennsylvania, too. Yes, a star had to come from someplace and Havenburg was as good as any. For now.

"Well, you just keep stitchin' back there and don't get so uppity!" she whipped back, tossing her head in the direction of the curtain; waiting for a smart crack.

"*You work me like a slave! A SLAVE, I tell you!*"

"Don't you worry about her," Blanche said to the customer whose cosmopolitan allure drew her like a magnet. "Half the time, I can't tell if it's her or one of those birds of hers yakkin' away back there. 'Course, if I could get them birds to run a sewing machine, maybe I could take over this place and *THEY'D* work for peanuts!"

"*I HEARD that!*"

"YOU DID? Well, I guess that means I don't have to get you that *HEARING AID* I've been thinkin' about!" Blanche fired back with all the assurance of one who knew who she was, where she was and exactly where she was headed. Already visualizing her own improvements on the jacket, she said, "You know, it ain't always the material you start with that counts." She rolled her eyes toward the back room, sighed and chuckled.

Stretching the cloth alongside a yardstick with the grandest flair she could portray, she smiled her best-selling smile. "No, it's what you do with your material that matters," she explained. "Now, take this," she offered the cotton and rubbed it between her fingers. "Every bit as good as wool for most people, wouldn't you say? But, speaking for me, *myself*," she winked and clicked her tongue with a sense of fun, "I prefer something more glamorous!" She pointed to the bolts of cloth along the top shelf. "Of course, that's because *I'm* a *designer!*" she said, making the final cut.

"Which is why I've come to you. My housekeeper has told me all about you."

London and a maid, too, now, Blanche thought. Other than the local hotel, the only place she knew with a maid was Lochwood, the von Havenburg estate outside of town. Twisting her neck for a peek, she couldn't see any limousines parked along the street. Well, it didn't really matter, she decided, folding the cloth and pinning it together. A sale was a sale and, these days, even she was living her own movies. *But, I know that face from somewhere*, she said to herself, trying to remember her classmates before she had dropped out of high school.

"So, you got yourself a maid, do you?" she heard herself saying. It was really just a way of making friendly conversation, though laced with curiosity as to what "Merle's" next *la-de-dah* claim to fame would be.

"Yes; Mrs. Harrington?" she asked, as if Blanche should know the woman.

"Hey, wait a minute! You mean the English lady?" Blanche asked, genuinely impressed now for the first time. "She comes in here all the time! She works at - " her face went slack and she took a quick breath. "Oh, don't tell me you're one of the *von Havenburgs!*" she said, laughing at the very idea that her powers of observation, usually so sharp, could have missed the familiar, recently ordered black dress in front of her.

"Esmeralda, yes," said the one who would never match Blanche's curvy style and streetwise manner no matter how hard she tried.

"*Esmeralda!* That's right. She talks a lot about you," Blanche said, squinting for a closer look as she wrapped the cloth in tissue and the image of Merle Oberon dissolved in dancing rays of sunlight. "Sorry to hear about your father, Kid," she said, referring to the untimely demise of the town's biggest employer. "Excuse me for saying so, especially in your grief and at a time like this, but that's a mouthful of a name he stuck you with, ain't it?"

Composure melting, Esmeralda fished in her purse and felt her ears getting warm. "My mother named me," she said, paying the bill. "It's from a story she used to read to me when I was a lit-tle girl. And I'm not a kid."

"Sure you are. And I'll bet you an' me got a lot in common. Say, I like you! I'm gonna do you a big favor. Yes, I am. Now, you can't be going around with a high falutin' name like that. No, sir! Every time you go shoppin', the prices'll shoot right through the roof! Why, you'll show up an' they'll be ten times the price!"

"You think so?"

"*Think* so!" Blanche stepped back in awe. "Honey, these may be bad times, but, in business, take it from me, it's *always* bad times. Why, you gotta squeeze every nickel you can out of strangers and take good care of your *friends!*" She glanced around. "See any price tags around this place?" she whispered, as if being spied on. "Up here," she said, with a sneaky look, tapping the side of her head. "Every last one of 'um!"

"You mean you have all the prices for all these items memorized?"

"Sure! I'm great with numbers."

"Well, I find it absolutely amazing that you can stand there and say you just

23

cheated me!" Esmeralda said, with a cool stare.

"Oh, no, no, no, Honey!" Blanche fluttered her hands, as the sewing machine in the back room stopped cold. "*I'd* never do *that!* No, what *I'm* talking about is all the *other* stores in town. No, in here, we just don't have price tags 'cause we never know from one week to the next what our supplies are going to cost us, that's why. Saves all that wear and tear on our pencils, ya know, havin' to change around the prices so much, and all. Yeah, them erasers are expensive!" Was there a nervous edge to her chuckle when she said that?

"Naw, I'd never cheat you!" Blanche laughed, looking from side to side. "Not with us bein' the same age an' all," she added, confident she'd talked her way through that one.

"I see," Esmeralda said, nodding politely and having a much better under-standing now of the brassy shop girl she had come to see. Mrs. Harrington was right. She was quite a character.

"Yes, well," Blanche managed to say, when "*Phew!*" was what she was think-ing as she wiped both hands on her smock and got back to the business that was never far from her mind. "Now. About that *name* of yours!"

She had always done this; trans-formed her world and everyone in it into exactly what or whom she wanted them to be. "Momma" sewing away in the back room had become "Mamba." After Mamba, there was "Popsy." And, as her brothers and sisters could testify as they joined the Jacobus household in various shapes and sizes, they were stamped with names like "Jolly-Boy," "Sally-Girl" and "Little Sis" in that order. Any of which monikers could change at any given moment.

For Blanche, the asbestos shingle house the Jacobus family called home was really a marble castle in disguise, pink of course, just as easily as her brown, shoulder-length hair had suddenly turned bright blonde one day, "From the sun." That others could see the hair, but only she could see the castle, made no difference whatsoever to her.

Taking a look outside now at the rusty black Ford that Popsy had won for her in a card game when she turned eighteen, she smiled and nodded. Yes, life was good when the world was your oyster.

"*EZ!*" she said, making a grand pronouncement like the knighting of a member of the Royal Order about which she knew not a thing. "I like the sound of it. Now you've got a name that suits you," she said, taking out the magazine picture and unfolding it on the checkout counter again.

"If you're speaking to me, my name is Esmeralda."

"Too late," Blanche said, aiming all her powers of concentration at the English model pictured beside a fine Thoroughbred racehorse now. "From now on, you're Ez. Like it? I think it fits you about as good as this outfit we're lookin' at, right here," she said, tapping her perfectly manicured red fing-

25

ernail on a classic combination of hunting jacket and slacks tucked neatly into boots of fine leather.

"*Oh, no!*" she exclaimed in surprise tainted by a bit too much practice. "This is *NEVER* gonna work!" Shoving the picture away; she pressed the back of her hand to her forehead as if every artistic sensibility in her being had just been offended.

"But, why?" Esmeralda asked, alarmed by this sudden, dramatic metamorphosis.

"Why? *Why you ask?* Because it's a *wool tweed,* that's why! *Can't you tell?*" Blanche asked, sneaking a peek between her fingers.

"But, didn't you just say the material shouldn't matter? For Heaven's sake, you're a seamstress – "

"Fashion designer," Blanche said straightening up to her full height of five-eight.

"Pardon me, I stand corrected," Esmeralda apologized. "But, exactly why can't it be made of cotton? If you don't mind telling me, that is. I mean, if it's not a trade secret or anything."

Blanche gave her a look of utter disbelief. "Because, my dear, this is *fashion!*" the shop maven said. "High style! What *you* want is something warm enough so you don't have to wear a coat and cover up your pretty figure! Didn't you say this is for a dog show or something like that?" she asked, setting the scene.

"Yes, I did," Esmeralda said, intrigued by the plot unfolding right before her eyes.

"Well, aren't they important places for you to go? Aren't you going to be outside in the cold with lots of men standing around looking?"

"Yes, of course," Esmeralda said, slightly embarrassed.

"Well, Honey, excuse me for saying so, but on a chilly morning in May aren't your little puppies gonna be awful perky if we make this thing out of something as light as cotton?" she laughed, staring at Esmeralda's petite chest and enjoying her own wit. "*Tell you what,*" she said, lowering the boom as Esmeralda's cheeks deepened to a shade of natural rouge. "I just happen to have a nice bolt of warm wool on that top shelf back there," she purred, reaching for the ladder and her measuring tape. "How about you go and take a look, and I'll be right with you."

Ka-CHING!

The curtain to the back room parted.

"What was *she* doing here?" Mrs. Jacobus asked, looking out.

"I got us a new customer, Mamba!" Blanche boasted proudly, holding up the cash. "I'm makin' her a new outfit and she paid me in advance."

Dorothy Jacobus, her black hair fading into silver, ran a chapped hand along her lined neck and sagging throat. "Hush, birds!" she said to the screeching parakeets spewing seeds on the floor. So it had finally happened, she thought, as Esmeralda crossed the street and slid into a waiting car.

"Be careful," she said, looking around the empty store, knowing she had to take in laundry, clean houses and do sewing for the neighbors to make ends meet. Had all that work been for this dreaded moment?

"Oh, I will Mamba!" Blanche shoved the drawer of the cash register shut and headed for the back room to help. "The way that girl talks about dogs, I'll bet they've got a whole pack of 'em out there just waitin' to rip my nylons!"

The Merger . . . And so it began. The poor, but proud, salesgirl driving out to the grand von Havenburg estate for fittings; Mrs. Harrington serving English tea on translucent Wedgewood china; Esmeralda in pearls and furs, glorifying the exhilarating world of dog shows. Not that Blanche was much interested. For Blanche, what mattered most was the cost of a movie ticket, the latest shade of lipstick and a certain emotional playground called love. In the meantime, VH Belting Company, maker of fan belts for cars and the only factory in town, had survived the tragic loss of its president and founder, Jason von Havenburg; everybody's paychecks were secure for the moment and Blanche Jacobus, future designer to the stars, was happily making *dresses for the factory's new majority stockholder . . . .*

"So, just what is it you're looking for, exactly; when you go to these shows," she asked. "I mean, what are you after?" Blanche wanted to know, surrounded by racks of the latest Paris fashions in a dressing room the size of her own living room at the row house Palace.

"A new puppy," Esmeralda said.

"A new puppy? Well, how many do you have?" Blanche asked, wondering what might be hiding under the white canopy bed with its feather quilt in the adjoining room.

"None right now," Esmeralda said. "Since my last dog, Foofie, died, I haven't even been able to think about getting another dog until now."

"What changed your mind?" Blanche said, opening her sewing kit and threading a needle.

"Collies!" Esmeralda sighed, stepping up on a small hassock. "I saw them for the first time a few months ago and I've been studying the breed ever since," admiring all of her selves in a three-way mirror.

"Lassie? That orange and white dog with the big hair?"

"Sable and White," Esmeralda corrected her. "And, yes, with the hair, only we call it 'coat'. Don't you read? Haven't you seen Eric Knight's book, *Lassie Come-Home?* You, know he's from Pennsylvania, too. Just like us. I'm surprised at you, Blanche. Really I am."

29

"Pardon *me!*" Blanche said, pretending to care. "Hold still! You're messing up the hem!"

"Well, a *real* designer might seize the moment and turn that crooked hemline into a whole new fashion statement. An entire collection with crooked hemlines protesting crooked politics and sexual repression! Stand up women of America! Let yourselves go! OUCH! You stabbed me!"

"You deserved it. Dressmaking is serious business, like painting pictures or working in clay. It's an art."

"That makes you an artist," Esmeralda nodded in agreement.

"And a good one," Blanche agreed a bit too fast. "I'm an artist makin' her own way in life."

"And where is this artist going?" Esmeralda asked, admiring herself in the mirror again, "this artist who doesn't even know about a novel written just a stone's throw from here?"

"Hollywood," Blanche said, sitting up straight and leaning back for a better view. Maybe her Mom was right. Maybe she'd have to start wearing those glasses.

"Maybe they'll make a movie of the book. Would you go see it then?"

"Depends on who's in it," Blanche said, fluttering her hand. "Turn around, I want to see it from the back."

"Who cares who's in it? *It's about a dog!*" Esmeralda sighed, as if there was nothing more important in the world.

"Nice!" Blanche said, bypassing the remark and turning things back to herself. "Blanche J, you've done it again!"

"Blanche J?" Esmeralda asked.

"Yeah. Like it?"

"Well, it's . . . OK . . . "Esmeralda said, making a face.

"What do you mean, *OK?*" Blanche made the same face right back at her.

"I don't know . . . "

"What do you mean, *you don't know?*"

"Well, it's just - well, if you really want people in the fashion industry to take you seriously, you need a name that sounds high society. International, you know? Like you're from Paris or Milan or - "

"Well, I ain't French."

"No, you definitely aren't," Esmeralda said, crossing her arms in thought.

"Although, I do know a thing or two about doing things the French way," Blanche added.

"I'm sure you do," Esmeralda agreed. "And, you're every bit as talented as a Rodin or a Matisse or a Chanel."

"Talented, am I? Yes, I've been told that."

"Oh, very much so. Anybody can see how talented you are."

"I knew I liked you!" Blanche brightened. "The minute I saw you, I said to myself, you know, there's something about this girl I like!"

"What's your middle name, Blanche? Tell me," Esmeralda asked, grabbing the chance to get even for the undignified label, "Ez."

"Why, it's Anne."

"Anne?" Esmeralda asked, in the flat tone of "Oh. Gee. *Just plain Anne . . . .*"

"*Hey!*" Blanche snapped. "My mother gave me that name!" she joked, remembering this same conversation in reverse.

"The one in the North Pole?" Esmeralda asked, right with her. "She'll be glad to know I'm looking out for you. A great designer like yourself can't go around expecting to attract the best clientele with a name like that. Nobody would be willing to pay what you're worth. No, what you need is flair! You need a little mystique! We've got to find a name that's special. Why, restaurants would charge you *twice as much* to put on a fashion show if they thought you were just plain, old simple Blanche Anne Jacobus," she said, wearing a path across the Persian rug. "I've got it!" she said, snapping her fingers.

"What have you got? The flu?"

"Blanche A, that's who you are!"

"Blanche A?"

"Only, we'll spell it *Blanche'*... French; got it?"

"Oh, I '*got it,*' all right. I just don't know if I can *live* with it, that's all. This whole town had a bad enough time when I went blonde. How am I gonna live up to a high-falutin' name like Blanche-ay?"

"You will, Esmeralda said. "And after a while, it'll feel as natural as your roots. Promise! Oh, I love it, don't you? I love it as much as I love this riding suit! Tell me, should I wear a

32

man's shirt and tie with it? Should I? Oh, I could feel so indecent, like that German film star."

"Dietrich!"

"*Blue Angel!* Men falling at my feet! *Vimmen luff me, too, dah-ling! Oh, I'm falling in luff again!*"

"I'm going to design costumes for Dietrich," Blanche said. "You wait. I'll get to know every one of them. The minute I get myself to Hollywood, they're gonna love me. Move over Edith Head - I'm showin' the movies how to *really* dress a star!"

She believed it. All her life she had believed there was something; a force, a guide, a *knowing* bigger than she was, herself. The shape of a necklace; the color of a gown; the curve of a man's cane could stir responses within her that she couldn't explain. How could she be expected to explain them? What could she know of the power of such symbolism when it had been hidden so well by the Egyptians for centuries? What did a woman such as Blanche Jacobus, from a small town in rural Pennsylvania know of this wisdom? Only what she, herself, could sense from somewhere within; perhaps the remnant of a life long ago.

"An artist just knows things," she'd say, unable to explain why her creative ideas evoked more universal response than her personal experience or training should have permitted. "I can just feel things."

"And are you going to Hollywood alone?" Esmeralda asked, somewhat protective in her question. "An artist as good as you, Blanche, might need someone to look out for her."

"Yeah? Well, I'm a big girl and I might take offense at that."

"Oh, you're a big girl all right."

"*Watch it!*" Blanche said, defensive about her weight; clawing the air between them with the sewing needle clenched between her manicured nails.

"You know your way around here, well enough," Esmeralda said. "That's for sure. But, let's be realistic. Outside of this cozy town you've grown up in, I mean, well, it's a whole different world out there, isn't it. Have you ever been to the City?"

"Lancaster? Sure! Lotsa times."

"I meant New York."

Out of her league and knowing it, Blanche shook her head, but jutted out her chin.

"Well, it's a whole lot closer than Hollywood and, trust me, it's no picnic getting around there alone," Esmeralda said, knowing she would help this young woman in life; knowing it as surely as she had known it when she walked into Dorothy's Dress Shop after her Daddy's funeral. Strong as she was, proud and talented as she was, Blanche Jacobus needed - would always need - someone to pave the way and clean up the mess that would follow her around just as sure as a pack of dogs sniffing a bitch in heat.

"OK, maybe you've got a point," Blanche conceded, surprised at herself for giving up so easily. "Maybe, when it comes down to it, I can see people wanting to buy from somebody who really knows the business. Hey, who am I trying to kid, huh? We both know the closest I've been to a fashion house is a magazine."

"Exactly where I come in," Esmeralda smiled sweetly. "I've been to all of them."

"Pushy, all of a sudden," Blanche said, squinting for a better look. "You sure you ain't a Jacobus?"

"I couldn't afford to be," Esmeralda smiled again, this time running her fingers along the lapel of the new tweed jacket and shaking a gold bracelet.

"Well, truer words than *that* were never said! So, is it my eagerness to get ahead or do I hear the makings of an offer jingling somewhere?" Blanche asked.

"More than an offer, my friend" Esmeralda said, deadly sure of herself now. "What *you're* hearing may be the chance of a lifetime!"

She had done it. She had found a way to right the wrong; she had come up with a way for each of them, so very different, yet so much the same, to hold on to her own identity.

And so it was that Esmeralda got her first step up. In exchange for introducing Blanche to all the "right circles," she would have a magnificent wardrobe copied from all the top fashion houses of Europe together with fifty percent of the newly-formed Blanche' Creations for as long as the business would last.

Ka-CHING!

Great Minds . . . As soon as their deal was in place, Esmeralda sprang into action. Working Daddy's fan belts like sling shots, she landed her new discovery smack-dab in the center of all the right parties; all the right places, at all the right times.

"But what do *I* want to go to the dog show for?" Blanche asked a few weeks later. "That's *your* thing, not mine."

"For the same reason we went to the department store in Philadelphia," Esmeralda said, "We're meeting people! Expanding our horizons! Aren't you glad we went there? Didn't you like the buyer, Blanche? You're very lucky having a whole department store asking for your dresses for their Fall Fashion Show. By the way, I've got a present for you," she said, handing over a beautifully wrapped package.

"For me? Oh, I just love presents!" Blanche giggled, tearing open the paper to find an autographed copy of *Lassie Come-Home*.

"Great," she managed to say, her face wilting. "Now, I've got something to read in my spare time."

"Between sketching out your new designs and bringing your creations into the world, I'm sure you won't get to it. But, that's OK," Esmeralda said, amused. "I can read it to you. And when we're done with that one, I can read you "*Lad:*

36

A *Dog.*" That's my favorite. You know, the author really does raise Collies and he's from Jersey. Maybe we can go sometime and visit. Would you like that, Blanche? Would you like to go to Sunnybank with me?"

Blanche rolled her eyes. "Well, I wouldn't want to deprive you of my company. Sure, I'd go. What if you get a flat, then what? Anyhow, if I don't know by now there ain't no stoppin' Ez von H when she makes up her mind, then I ain't been paying attention. And, just between you and me, attention is what I'm all about, right?" She laughed at herself as only one who knows every move she makes, and knows them well, can do. "So if we get a flat, you just let everything up to me. *I'll* get somebody to fix it! I could get a man to fix a flat if we were stranded in the Sahara desert! Thanks for the invitation and the gift," she said, sweetly, giving Esmeralda a polite kiss on the cheek. "Hey!" she said, pulling away. "How many dresses did you say that store wants?"

"Three," Esmeralda smiled, touching her cheek, certain Blanche knew exactly how many, what size and what style, but just wanting to savor her good fortune again. "And that's just for starters," she added. "If the buyers like what they see, you'll have three more to make for the Spring collection. Which means, we have to circulate in the right places now, so you'll be seen by all the right people."

"Such as," Blanche asked, "Hoity-Toities parading a Beagle around, with a piece of liver in their pocket? Don't they know liver stains?"

"Maybe if they win the Blue Ribbon, those Hoity-Toities don't care," Esmeralda responded with a wisdom beyond her years. "Blanche, the fashion show's in Philadelphia, and so is the dog show tomorrow. Don't you see? We could meet some of the Biddles or the Kellys or maybe even the Colemans. There could be reporters and photographers roving around all over the place."

Blanche smiled happily. "Cocktail parties?"

"Forget the parties and get some rest," Esmeralda cautioned. "You're picking me up at seven in the morning."

"Seven! I'm not even brushing my teeth that early."

"Seven, sharp," Esmeralda reminded her. "We don't want to miss the Collie classes."

True to her word, Blanche arrived on time with a toothbrush in her mouth.

"Nice touch," Esmeralda said, answering the door and noticing the garment bag in Blanche's arms. "What did you bring?"

"A surprise!" Blanche laughed with a sparkle in her voice, swooping Esmeralda under the crystal chandelier and into the study filled with overstuffed armchairs, sofas and a baby grand. "Remember all that cotton I made you buy when we first met?"

"Yes, and I'm sure you found a use for the extra change."

"Well that's what I call it!" Blanche said, breathless. *"Extra change!* I got so excited about the idea, I stayed up all night!"

"Doing what?"

"Making these!" Blanche said, unzipping the bag and laughing. "I figured if you're gonna end up getting a puppy today, like you said, well, chances are, knowing you, that little son of a gun is going to get his muddy feet all over your blouse and you won't even have the sense to care. I mean, because you'll probably love him so much and all, you know. And you won't have the heart to put that puppy down on the ground where he belongs, like I would. So, what I went and did was make you a blouse for under that suit of yours."

"Well that was very nice of you," Esmeralda said, with genuine surprise.

"But, that ain't all!" Blanche said, tossing the first blouse aside to reveal another and another. "I got you five blouses out of that material – every last one of 'em the same. Now you can just take 'em all with you and if you mess one up, all you have to do is hurry off to the nearest powder room and change!"

"I love it!" Esmeralda laughed. "What a clever idea!"

"Oh, I've got lots of ideas," Blanche said. "And most of 'em 're naughty," she grinned, her brown eyes dancing with mischief.

"Naughty can get a lady just about anyplace she wants to go!" Esmeralda laughed again.

"And a few places she don't!" said Blanche, shaking her head. "You like the blouses?"

"Love them!" Esmeralda said, gathering them up and putting each one back on its hanger. "Need some coffee before we go?"

"No, I'm OK," Blanche said, becoming thoughtful now. "You know, I just want to thank you for all you're doing for me, Ez."

Perhaps it was the tone of her voice that made Esmeralda stop. Curious, she stood; cotton blouses folded against her chest. "It's no bother, Blanche. We're in business, remember?" Should she tell her, she wondered? Should she tell her why she went to the shop that day; why she couldn't stay away no matter what? No, she decided. Not now. It was too soon.

"Well, nobody's ever cared enough to help me out like this before," Blanche said. She meant it.

"Hey, lady," Esmeralda smiled, rubbing Blanche's arm up and down briskly. "I'm on your side. Remember?"

"Whew!" Blanche suddenly whooped, shaking off a moment of rare sentimentality. "Glad I got *that* off my chest. I was getting worried. I can buy my bra a whole size smaller now!"

Parking spaces weren't easy to find at the Mother's Day dog show outside of Philadelphia.

"Over there!" Esmeralda pointed, as they drove past row after row of cars from New York, Maryland and New Jersey.

"Where's the calliope?" Blanche quipped at the sight of yellow and white striped tents, vendors hawking everything from brushes and dog food to cages and porcelain figurines. "This place is a circus! Look at all these people – there must be thousands! Are they really here to see dogs?" she asked, astounded at hundreds of canines in every size, shape and color being carried, walked and ig-nored.

"And each other," Esmeralda smiled, pleased that her friend was giving it her best effort. "I'm so glad the weather's with us. Did you ever see such a clear blue sky? Blanche, can you open the trunk so we can get our things?"

"Where are we headed?" Blanche wanted to know, her voice having a spe-cial ring to it, as she carried their picnic basket and a lawn chair a few min-utes later.

"First, we've got to find the Ter-rier ring," Esmeralda said. "I heard the dog who won Westminster is here."

"And you expect him to buy a dress from us?"

Esmeralda laughed. "Blanche, your business acumen amazes me."

"Acumen. Now, that's a good word. Somehow, I can tell this is leading up to something," Blanche said, studying the spectators sitting politely outside the ropes along the perimeter of each show ring.

"Yes, it is," Esmeralda concluded. "Because, purebred dogs - the really top show dogs - the kind traveling *all over the country* to win - well, it's like I said before. Quite often, they belong to the very kind of people the proprietors of Blanche' Creations should know."

"Proprietors. Now, there's another good word. Well, I'm willing to meet any-body who is going to help the business," Blanche quipped.

"Oh, it's not all just business to-day!" Esmeralda smiled as they found a nice spot in the grassy field and spread out their blanket. "We're here to have a picnic, show off my new suit and buy a puppy!"

"A Collie, right?" Setting out two plates and a pair of forks wrapped in white checkered linen napkins, Blanche admired her manicure. "You know, you're right about that Eric Knight fella. He ain't the only one writing about dogs. I found the other one. The one you told me about?"

"You did?"

"Yeah. I saw his book about a dog named Lad. I found it in Mr. Hubley's book store over on the corner of Main and Linden. You know where that is?" At Es-meralda's blank look, she withdrew the question. "You know, Ez, now that you're in charge of the factory and all - "

"Which I'm not," Esmeralda correct-ed her.

"Well, as far as everybody else is concerned you are. So, you'd better get to know the town they live in."

"And why must I do that, when I have you?" Esmeralda teased.

"Well, sure, I know the town. I know every house and every alley." Why did that sound almost dirty, she asked herself? "'Course, I don't want you getting the wrong idea about that."

"*Oh, there he is!*" Esmeralda suddenly whispered, clapping her hands with delight.

"A dog?" Blanche asked, paying her no mind. "Look around, Honey. There's a million of 'em."

"Over there! Ring three!" Esmeralda gestured, her eyes bright.

"Ring three? Where's that?" Blanche asked, buttering a piece of bread.

"Oh, Blanche, the numbers are right there," Esmeralda indicated a pole on which a large sign had been taped. "Where are your glasses?"

"And mess up my whole look? Please!" Blanche growled, putting down a piece of friend chicken, licking the tips of her fingers, drying them on her napkin and fussing in her purse. "Somebody ought to coordinate glasses to a lady's outfit," she moaned. "Or to her shoes. There's an idea! I'd have myself a whole drawer full of 'em."

"Blanche, hurry. I'm sure you don't want to miss this."

Finding a fancy, hand-embroidered case, Blanche pulled out a pair of opera glasses and fanned the air with a grand-iose gesture.

"Ooo-la-la!" Esmeralda teased play-fully. "When did you start using those?"

"Like the color?" Blanche asked, not bothering to give details. "Bright Red, to match the shade of my lipstick. You wait. When we get to Hollywood, I'm gonna set that town on *fire!*"

"Well, right now we're in Phila-delphia," Esmeralda said, adjusting her hat. "*Ring three,*" she nodded, with a glint of mischief.

"Why . . . Ez . . . " Blanche almost sang, steadying her gaze. "I do believe that's a well-defined male *backside* you're staring at." Curling her brightly painted lips into a satisfied smile, she said, "Why didn't you tell me you were talking about *a man!*"

"And miss that look on your face?" Esmeralda asked.

"You're bad!" Blanche said. "Look!" she said, her face lighting up. "Col-lies!"

"*Gorgeous!*" Esmeralda sighed.

"The man or the dogs?" Blanche teased.

"Guess!" Esmeralda sang back. "You know, it must be terribly difficult being a judge. So much responsibility to han-dle."

"From the looks of it, I'd say a man like that could handle just about anything," Blanche commented slyly.

"Prematurely gray, don't you think?" Esmeralda asked.

"From all those important decisions he has to make," Blanche speculated, plunking an olive in her mouth after poking out the pimento with a fingernail.

"What you're looking at is Robert Sheffield," Esmeralda explained, as one who had done her homework. "He was born in Ontario, and he's been raising and showing Collies most of his life."

"How come you know so much," Blanche asked.

"Because I've been studying the Breed," Esmeralda said, reaching for a drumstick and potato salad. "I never make an investment without doing some research on the people I do business with. Good chicken. Yummy."

"Well, I'm no expert," Blanche said, acting as if she were, "but, if it was me in there instead of him? I'd be throwin' half those dogs out. Look at 'em! *The Breed's ruined!*" she said, licking off her fingers once more. "Did you try the coleslaw?"

"*Ruined?* Whatever would make you say something so vile?"

"Well, I just heard somebody back there sayin' the very same thing! The way I figure, if the breed's *ruined*, you might as well not be wasting your money." She seemed so proud of herself, sitting there, in her pink dress and broad-brimmed hat. "Did Mrs. H. pack anything to drink?"

"Looking out for me, are you?" Esmeralda grinned. "Well, you might as well know people at dog shows say that kind of thing all the time - of course she did;

45

soda pop or iced tea?" she asked, looking in the basket. Turning to the ring again, she said, "Don't pay any attention to them."

"Sounded pretty sure of themselves to me," Blanche said, looking back at the ones she had overheard. "Iced tea, please."

"Blanche, the very first thing you learn at a dog show is, *everybody's an expert!*" Esmeralda said, offering a thermos. "Here you go."

"Well, ruined or not, being a judge an' all, that man's gotta make a big deal for whoever it is that's hired him. Now, if you ask me, *that's* the *real* show."

"And Robert's damn good at it," Esmeralda said. She liked swearing sometimes, but only for special effect. It worked better when people didn't expect it of her.

"*Robert*, is it?" Blanche said, ignoring the profanity and raising her opera glasses again. "I *see.*"

"*Breathtaking* . . ." Esmeralda sighed.

"Oh, yes," Blanche said. "Packaged in navy blue pants, a white blazer and a whole lot of muscle. Ouch! I hurt just looking!"

Esmeralda choked and nearly sneezed as she sipped her soda. "*Whatever* are you thinking!"

"If you only knew." Blanche smiled. "If you *oooooonly* knew. But, then, how *could* you?"

"What's that supposed to mean?"

"Sheltered princesses living in grand mansions don't have a clue, that's what."

"Is that so?" Esmeralda said, unable to admit Blanche might be right. "Well, who's he going to pick, Smartie?"

Tucking a loose strand of Harlow-blonde hair behind her ear, Blanche narrowed her eyes. "Right now, I couldn't guess," she said. "But, if you ask me," she snickered, "from this point of view, it'll be *damn* fun finding out!"

"In other words, *you* don't have a *clue*," Esmeralda pressed. "Well, I'll tell you who's going to win. It's the dog from Jersey. Are you done with your plate?"

Blanche scoffed, handing over her plate with a pile of discarded chicken bones and a small pile of pimentos. "Oh, it's *dogs* you're talking about!"

"Pay attention," Esmeralda said, scraping off the plates into a paper bag.

"Oh, I'm paying attention all right." Blanche smiled, folding up the blanket. "I pay attention all the time."

"See the man with the hat? That's Mike Kennedy. He handles the Bellhaven Collies," Esmeralda explained, opening their lawn chairs.

"What's the dog he's got with him?"

Esmeralda checked her catalog, "That would be Ch. Laund Liberation of Bellhaven."

"Nice looking," Blanche said, appraising the Sable and White Collie with her artist's eye.

"Only the top winning Collie in the Breed right now." Esmeralda said with an air of authority. "He belongs to Mrs. Florence B. Ilch."

"Is she good for business?" Blanche wondered aloud.

"If she buys in Philadelphia, she is."

"Where's she at?" Blanche asked. "I want to get a look."

"Well, she won't be in the ring, herself. She won't be anywhere near it. That's what she's got Mike Kennedy for. She's probably off hiding somewhere. Of course, she might not even be here at all."

"Too good for all this, huh."

"Actually," Esmeralda explained, "A smart owner doesn't want to distract the dog from what the handler's trying to do."

"Well, if I was in that ring, I tell you all *I'd be lookin' at* is that judge. What'd you say his name is? Robert?"

Making no comment, saving Robert for herself, Esmeralda reached over for the fancy glasses. "Give me those things," she said. Was it something about how he moved, she wondered, leveling her gaze? How he carried himself? It was his smile, she thought, sure now. Yes, it was his expression.

"You'd throw out the dogs and give all your attention to the judge," she said, keeping her eyes on him. "Blanche, did anyone ever say you've got the Devil in you?"

"Oh, I've got the Devil in me, all right."

"Precisely what makes you so much fun!" Esmeralda smiled, handing back the glasses as Robert lined up the entries. "Are you enjoying your first dog show?"

"Never thought the scenery could be so interesting," Blanche smiled.

"Oh, there's plenty of scenery. All kinds of it. Aside from that, don't be fooled. This is a tough game. To win, a dog has to be perfect. Not just physically, but mentally, too. But, I guess, for me, a dog is beautiful just because it's all clean and brushed and happy."

Blanche crossed her legs and twirled her foot in little circles of worldly wisdom. "If this business is the same as all the rest I know, darling, happiness has nothing to do with it. It all comes down to *who* you know, *what* you know - and how low you'll go."

"Blanche!"

"Fact of life, Ez. Smooth your feathers and don't get so riled up. Oh, yeah!" she remembered. "And who *KNOWS* you know what you know - don't forget *that!*"

"Well, if it's blackmail you're after, then you'd better add *how you found out!*" Esmeralda said.

"Ooooo, Ez, you and me are gonna make out just fine in the fashion industry. You're starting to think *Hollywood*."

"Land of Big Pictures," Esmeralda said. "Well, I get the big picture, all right. That's why I think the lady from Jersey is going to win. First of all, she's smart enough to get herself a good handler and she takes care of him."

Licking her pinkie finger, Blanche ran it over the arch of her eyebrow. "Mike over there, you mean? Oh, he's good. I'll bet he could make a mutt from the pound look like it's a whole new Breed. But, what I want to see is what the judge says. This Robert of yours looks like a man who can make up his own mind."

This Robert of yours, Esmeralda thought, liking the sound of it. "He's lining them up," she said. "Look how nervous the handlers are. I'd be, too. Wouldn't you? Wouldn't you be nervous?"

Robert Sheffield, bearing the weight of the crowd's expectation and handlers' angst, stepped back with an air of authority to study the nine Collies in front of him one last time.

As the crowd stared in suspense, he crossed both arms. Propping his chin on one hand, he smiled inside, loving the power. One, two, three and four he pointed; decision made, class over.

"I don't *believe* it!" Blanche said, taking a deep breath. "Here, I thought we found ourselves a man who could make up his own mind and he goes and gives it to the big winner after all. What about the rest of the dogs? Ruined or not, some of them looked pretty darn good!"

"But, didn't you see how Laund Liberation moved, Blanche? Did you ever see such freedom? It was beautiful to behold, wasn't it? If you ask me, I think Robert picked the most exciting dog in the

50

class. Let's go over and congratulate the winner."

"Over my dead body! Ten to one, he picked that dog because of how famous it is."

"Well, if you don't want to congratulate the winner," Esmeralda said, with a look of mischief as she handed back the opera glasses, "then let's just go over and meet *Robert.*"

Giggling, the young ladies folded up their lawn chairs and hurried across the grass to where a cluster of admirers were gathering around the most popular judge on the dog show circuit.

"Isn't he handsome?" Esmeralda whispered.

Blanche ran her hands down her skirt and straightened up. "If you like 'em tall and dark, maybe."

"I just love his wavy hair."

"Shirt's wrinkled," Blanche tattled, pursing her lips at the thoughts that kept flitting through her mind.

"Did you ever see such a smile?"

"It's what's behind a smile that counts, Honey. A lady always knows."

"Mr. Sheffield?" an older woman was asking him. "Did I hear you say you have a new litter on the ground?"

"Yes, Mrs. Browning. Beauties!"

"That must be Elisabeth Browning, of Tokalon Kennels, in New York!" Esmeralda whispered. *"Smile!"*

Smiling as brightly as she could, Blanche noticed a pleasant-looking man standing patiently, waiting to speak.

"Nice dog," she said to him, of the Sable and White male at his side.

"That's Steve Field," explained Esmeralda, nodding to him politely. "I think he's a school teacher."

"Never too late to start over," said Blanche, smiling as Robert invited everyone to come and see his new litter.

"I'm having an open house on Saturday," he announced in warm, comfortable tones. "Right after handling class. The kennel's going to be open from two 'til five for anybody who wants to visit. I live just a few miles outside of Hershey on Boch Road. There's a sign out front and a Collie painted on the mailbox," he said, charming everyone with a big smile and crinkly lines around his eyes.

Esmeralda raised her hand and stepped up on her tiptoes. "I'm looking for a puppy!" she said. "Are we invited, too?"

Sheffield smiled and laughed goodnaturedly. "Of course! As long as there are Collies on this Earth."

Acquisitions . . . *It was just a small farm outside of Hershey, Pennsylvania: Maple trees, yew bushes, and neat red barns with white board fences. Canadian by birth, Robert Sheffield had moved here to be closer to the budding sport of dog shows and had fine-tuned his breeding program until Sheffield Kennels was home to some of the finest Collies around. He lived alone, except for an occasional overnight guest, and liked it that way.*

Collies in baritone, tenor and high soprano announced the arrival of a black Ford; Robert looked up from washing the feed bowls. . . .

"Quiet, everybody! Settle down!" he called out.

Braking hard, Blanche skidded her old Ford to a halt on the gravel, as Esmeralda rolled down a window and waved. "Are we too early for Open House?"

He smiled. "First to arrive!"

Inside, she whispered to Blanche. "*Cuuu-*ute!"

"If you like a ladies man," Blanche said, the corners of her mouth turning down.

"I'll be right with you!" Robert hollered, hurrying to finish up his kennel chores.

"Take your time!" Blanche hollered back, eyeing the freshly painted buildings, the trimmed lawns, the shiny car. "Nice," she said, under her breath.

"And he lives alone, I found out," Esmeralda said.

"Now, why would that be, I wonder."

"Well, I'm sure he has girlfriends," Esmeralda smiled. "But, nobody steady, as far as I know."

"I *see*," Blanche cooed. "The man likes *variety*."

"Maybe he just hasn't found his true love, yet," Esmeralda suggested as Blanche primped her hair.

53

"What makes you think he's worth it?" Blanche wanted to know, looking in the mirror.

"Besides being gorgeous? Dig out those red opera glasses of yours and look around this place!"

"I have, Honey," she said, rendering her judgement. "Rented."

"Rented! How would *you* know?"

"I've got a natural feel for such things," Blanche explained, reaching for her lipstick now. "It was born in me. I can spot a fake a mile away. Especially when it comes to diamonds."

"Diamonds? What do they have to do with anything?" Esmeralda asked. "Do you even own a diamond?"

"No, but I'm going to. One of these days, I got a hunch I'm gonna have the biggest diamond anyone around here ever saw!"

"Ladies?" It was Robert, taking off his hat with a deep bow, low at the waist. "Welcome to Sheffield Kennels. Sorry to take so long," he smiled, as they both melted.

"Oh, don't apologize," Esmeralda said. Why did her cheeks feel so warm? It was those brown-green eyes of his, she decided; the way they twinkled at her. "We were just talking about how nice your place is," she said, deciding, no, it was the way he moved; easy, loose; as if nobody was looking and there was hungry flesh under those clothes. Was his chest hairy or smooth, she wondered? Glancing at his watch; running her eyes back up to his face; she knew. He was hairy.

"Thanks," he said, aware of the inspection. "I rent it from the family that owns the farm down the road."

Was that a cough Esmeralda heard behind her back?

"It's nothing," Blanche said, holding back a smirk.

"They take care of everything for me," he said. "They even look after the dogs when I'm away." His clean smile wrapped itself around all three of them.

Realizing they hadn't been introduced, Esmeralda blushed deeper. "Remember us? We met at the dog show."

"I remember," he said.

"I'm Esmeralda von Havenburg," she said, extending her hand.

"Very nice to meet you." Taking her hand in his, he asked, "Didn't you say you're looking for a puppy?"

"Yes! The best Collie puppy in the world! I've been learning as much as I can about them."

"Well, raising a puppy is like painting a house," he said.

"You know a thing or two about painting houses?" Blanche observed, stepping up to the bat. "I may need an estimate."

"The family trade," he replied.

"In that case, Honey, you can paint my house any time," she smirked. "In fact, you and me can paint the whole town." *Was that a silent kiss she just blew him?*

"Paint it red, you mean?" He asked coolly. An avalanche of ice couldn't have crashed between them more suddenly as he turned his back. "And how did you like the dog I picked for Winners?" he asked Esmeralda.

"Ah! Yes! Well, I liked him very much," she said. "He was the prettiest dog there."

Was that a cough she heard again? "Just getting over a cold," Blanche mumbled, to no one in particular. Robert didn't look.

"Blanche and I have been studying the standard," Esmeralda said, trying to be professional. "I thought the dog you picked was breathtaking."

"Purely an act of grooming expertise," Blanche said, with a sudden air of authority from out of nowhere. "But, then, you'd expect that from somebody of Mr. Mike Kennedy's caliber. I know I would. Being a *designer* and all."

"A *designer*," Robert nodded, appreciatively.

"Fashion," she added, going on. "is my game. Being a designer and all, I notice just how much a thing like good grooming can do."

"I've heard Mr. Kennedy takes a horse brush to the Bellhaven dogs every day - only a natural bristle, so it never breaks a hair," said Esmeralda, not to be outdone. "And I'll bet that's no easy task, considering how many dogs they have to take care of."

"Well, now, packaging ain't everything," Blanche said, standing with one hand on her hip and the other gesturing in the air, "Although it matters a lot. I'm the first to say packaging can cover up a multitude of sins. Yes, indeed. Now, to me, from *my* point of view, that dog was *missing* something. I could see it from clear across the field, I could. Still, I have to admit he moved a whole lot better than anything else in the ring. Didn't you think so, Ez?"

"Yes, I believe I said so."

"Yes, I sure do like a dog that *moves!*" Blanche clicked her tongue. "It'd be a shame to have one that couldn't."

"I'm impressed," Robert said, hiding a grin as Esmeralda bit her lip at Blanche's show of pretense.

"Why, thank you," Blanche said, maintaining her charade. "I can be a very impressive lady when I want to."

"And what did you say your name is?" Robert asked.

"*Blanche,*" she smiled grandly. "Just like Vivien Leigh in *Gone With The Wind.* Blanche Jacobus, spelled j-a-c-o-b-u-s."

"*You mean like Blanche in* Streetcar Named Desire, *don't you?" Esmeralda would have said if the play had been written yet. And, didn't Vivien Leigh play Scarlett in "Gone With The Wind?" she might have pitched in for good measure . . . .*

"Well, Blanche Jacobus," he said, his eyes twinkling as he took her hand. "Would you like to see my puppies?"

As they made their way to the horse barn where the Sheffield Collies lived, Esmeralda wondered why everything around Blanche always sounded so suggestive. "Mmmm, I love the smell of a clean stable," she said, as they entered the barn. "Are they your horses, Robert?"

"They belong to the farmer," he said about the pair of Belgians stalled at the end of the row. "I can't think of a better place to keep the dogs than with horses, can you? Lots of room for them to play in here," he said, sliding open the bolt of a nearby stall to reveal a litter of excited, wooly puppies.

"Oh, they're so sweet!" Esmeralda laughed. "Aren't they, Blanche?"

"If you like 'em soft an' fuzzy," came the flat reply.

"Who wouldn't?" asked Robert, hoisting up a pair of Sable and White pups with dark hair just beginning to frame their faces and intelligent, trusting eyes.

"I just want to hug them!" Esmeralda clapped her hands. "Can we pet them, Robert?" she blushed quickly and looked down. "I mean, *Mr. Sheffield!*"

"Robert's fine," he laughed, accustomed to people from dog shows treating him with extra respect. Tipping his hat back a little, he said, "We're Collie people, right?"

Unable to speak; not understanding why; she could only nod.

"Ahem!" choked Blanche, drawing attention to herself. "Darn cold again."

"Nasty things, those colds," Robert said, every bit the game player she was. "Well, Miss Jacobus, maybe you'd like to help us pick the best puppy for Esmeralda, here. That is why you came along, right?" he asked, knowing nothing could be further from the truth.

"Oh, yes," Esmeralda nodded, answering for her. "Blanche? Would you like to help me pick a puppy?"

"Oh, I couldn't possibly," Blanche demurred, her former air of authority on the spot now.

"But, you did very well at the dog show," Esmeralda challenged. "She did, Robert. Really. Why, by the end of the day, she was picking more winners than I was. Go on, Blanche. See if you can pick the best one."

"Beginner's luck," Blanche said, begging off, suddenly humble.

"It's more than that," Esmeralda said. "An artist is naturally gifted at such things."

"Well, now, if you're gonna put it that way," Blanche said, perking up to her normal braggadocio. "All right, let's have a look." Gently, she reached for one of the pups in Robert's arms and felt the man resist. "Hey, what're ya scared of?" she teased. "Let me have the little son of a gun."

"Sorry," Robert said, loosening his grip.

"For what?" she asked, taking the puppy and looking Robert in the eye. "For not trusting me or 'cause I found out?"

"Of course I trust you," he smiled, holding her gaze; clearly wanting her to take the puppy he still held. "It's just that *this* one," he said, offering the puppy to her now, "is more used to people. Forgiven?" he asked, wrinkling his brow and tipping back his hat with a finger.

"Well, I don't know," she said, discreetly pushing his pup away and hanging on to her own. "I think, in a manner of speaking, you may have just insulted me, sir."

"Something I would never want to do," he said.

"Well, I think maybe you have, in spite of that" she said, her cool, streetwise confidence back in full swing now. "In a manner of speaking, Mr. Sheffield, you just said I'd be mean to this puppy I'm holding here. Or else that I'm not good enough for him." Smiling like the cat who got the canary, she said, "Just how do you propose making all this up to me?"

"Maybe we can make a deal."

"Smooth operator," Blanche said, looking over at Esmeralda. "What, exactly, do you have in mind?" she asked him, still looking at Esmeralda, but making sure her rear view was in full sight.

He thought for a minute, or appeared to. "Well, maybe I could teach you, as they say, the ropes of the kennel business if you like. Since Esmeralda is looking for a puppy to show, I could help her."

Blanche looked at her nails. "I was thinking more like an adjustment in the price department."

"*Blanche!*" Esmeralda scolded.

"Price?" asked Robert.

"Well, I guess you're asking a pretty penny for these dogs of yours, right? Well, these are hard times now. Me and Ez, we're just starting out in business, and you know how tough that can be, you having your own kennel business an' all. Ez takes care of the money and I'm the talent," she explained.

"We're partners," Esmeralda explained. "We have a fashion business. Or, rather, Blanche does and I'm helping her. Blanche' Creations. All we need is a few good references and we're off to Hollywood."

"I'm not so sure I like the idea of money that ought to be spent on the business ending up in dog shows and all that," Blanche interjected. "Why, with how good these puppies are, their quality an' all, Ez might have to spend her whole life's savings just buyin' the dog! Well, gettin' him is one thing, but taking care of what you got is a whole something else."

"But, Esmeralda and I have already agreed – " he said.

"Agreed to what?" Blanche said, taking charge with a 'let me handle this' look to Ez. "I'd say, all you've agreed to is, she wants a puppy and you want to sell one. Come on, Ez," she said, grabbing Esmeralda's arm so hard they both almost tripped. "We'd better go." Brush-

61

ing off her skirt as if to rid herself of dirt; staring Robert in the face; she said, "I know a shyster when I see one!"

"Shyster? You're calling me a shyster?"

"I'll call you more than that if you don't watch out!" Blanche said, raising her voice now. "Nobody takes advantage of my friends. *Nobody!*"

Taken aback by her sudden fury, Robert stood . . . looked at them carefully . . . and burst out laughing. "You're good," he said to Blanche, his eyes filling with certainty. "You're *very* good."

"So I've been told. Lotsa times." Pleased with herself, she tousled her puppy's fur and rolled him over on his back, "I do have to admit, this one, here; he's the best." Proud, she sucked in her cheeks to accentuate her cheekbones, cursed the cake she'd had for breakfast, and asked, "Where's the rest of the family? We've gone this far, you might as well take me home to meet Momma!"

"You're sure you want to see any more of my worthless dogs?" Robert asked, silently handing the other puppy to Esmeralda with a quiet nod.

"Sure I'm sure, Honey," Blanche smiled, back in charge. "Lead the way." She sure loved watching the scenery from behind. She could watch that scenery of his all day long, imagining right where she'd build a campfire . . . .

"Their mother; their dam," he explained, to spare his guests any embarrassment in the event Blanche launched into another one of her tirades of expertise that wasn't, is Sheffield Duchess, over there" Robert said, unruffled by their brief exchange. "There she is," he pointed.

Both women looked out the barn door to see a gnarled silver maple tree from which hung a long-abandoned rope swing, swaying gently in the breeze. Under a bright blue sky, a broad canopy of pale green leaves created dappled shade. Resting in freshly mown grass, was a regal Collie staring back at them.

"My gracious, what a beauty," Esmeralda sighed.

"My very best bitch."

"*What did he just call her?*" Blanche whispered in Esmeralda's ear.

"*A female dog,*" Esmeralda whispered back.

"*Damn? Bitch? . . . sure likes to throw around those four letter words,*" Blanche said, speaking louder.

"*Shhh!*" Esmeralda hushed her, embarrassed.

"She's the mother of three champions so far, and hopefully," he gestured to their pups, "two more.

"Is that right?" Blanche asked, cuddling the little Collie in her arms as Duchess raised her head and perked her ears forward. "And where's your Daddy, fella?"

"Come with me and I'll introduce you," said Robert, leading the way to another building.

At the sight of her young being carried away, Duchess trotted over and looked up anxiously. "It's OK, Girl," Robert assured her. "They're friends."

Duchess quieted down, but kept watch nearby.

They approached a converted chicken coop made into a row of kennels where three fine specimens scrambled to their feet and barked with excitement. "These are my stud dogs," he said.

Blanche just shook her head. "Hadda be a man who came up with that one."

"Baron!" Robert called. "Here, Boy!" Immediately, an immense, lion-like Collie stood at the gate to his kennel and held himself at attention.

"Ladies, meet Ch. Sheffield Baron, the best dog I ever bred."

"A Duchess and a Baron. Royalty," said Esmeralda, holding her puppy tight.

"You can say that again," echoed Blanche. "Any chance these boys are going to turn out like Pops?"

"If we're lucky," Robert answered. "We line breed on Baron's great grand-sire."

"Line breed? What do you mean?" asked Blanche.

"It means breeding dogs that are related by a common ancestor," he explained.

Her face went blank.

"Didn't you take science, Blanche?" asked Esmeralda. "Genetics? Mendel? The monk who studied plants? You know, picking out certain individuals and criss-crossing their descendants until, after a few generations, they all start looking like the one you first started with?"

"Must've been busy doing my sketches in art class."

Inrigued, Robert asked, "You draw?"

Blanche looked him in the eye with mock disbelief. "How else do you think I come up with my creations? I may have movie star looks, but, I ain't dumb."

"There I go again," he said, feigning apology. "Insulting you."

Esmeralda laughed. "Keep it up and you'll owe Blanche a whole lot more than a puppy!"

"Exactly what I'm starting to be afraid of," he smirked.

Blanche tossed her head and squared her shoulders. "Surprised?"

"No. I'm not surprised; not at all. Meeting you, I'm sure you will go as far in life as you set your mind to. Hollywood or anywhere else."

"Why, thank you," Blanche said. "See, Ez? We found ourselves a gentleman."

"You said you need references," Robert said. "Do you mean references or clients?" Struggling with a possibility, he asked, "Can you describe the type of customer you're looking for? I might be able to help."

"People who want only the very best," said Esmeralda.

"The very best. You mean they must *discriminating*, correct?"

"Oh, yes. They have to be *very* discriminating," Blanche said. "They have to know *quality*."

"*Quality*. And what else? What else must the perfect customer know?"

"Well, they have to know lots of other people and be able to spread the word." Blanche went on.

"*Spread the word*. You mean, tell everyone else? *Gossip*?"

Esmeralda chipped in. "Well, I wouldn't exactly say *gossip*, but, yes, they do have to be able to tell others what they know."

"Very important when building a reputation," Robert agreed.

"*And,*" Blanche added. "This is important; they have to be sure and remember the *designer's name*."

"In other words, they must be the kind of people who don't forget a thing," Robert surmised.

"Exactly!" Blanche said, happy that he got the idea.

"But, then I have the *perfect* clientele for you!" Robert said, as if solving a mystery.

"You do?" Blanche commented dryly, sure that nothing he could suggest would reach the 'right kind' better than what they were already doing.

"But, your perfect clientele goes to dog shows!" he smiled.

Dog shows! Blanche's face dropped. "Look here, Robert, this ain't no joke! Me and Ez have plans. Big plans! We can't go around gettin' ourselves side-tracked on rinky-dink stuff like dog shows. Sure, it was fun and all. I mean, who doesn't like a circus, right? An' it was a real hoot, some of those frumpy get-ups the gals wear. Personally, I wouldn't be *caught dead* lookin' like that," Blanche shook her head. "No, you're barkin' up the wrong tree, Mister," she said, laughing at her own wit. "Me an' Ez, we ain't the dog show type." But, Esmeralda had nothing to say.

With an air of patience, Robert straightened up. "Perhaps not," he said. "But, if you were a dog lover shopping for clothes, wouldn't you rather patronize a designer who shows dogs, too? Someone who understands your life? Your world?"

"Oh, *Blanche*! I think it's a *great* idea!" Esmeralda said, unable to hold back. "Can't you see what Robert is saying?"

"I see what he's saying, all right. He wants to get his dogs out there, the same as we want our name in the stores." Winking at him, she said, "How right am I, Smoothie?"

"Very astute of you, Miss Jacobus."

"You remembered the name," she said, flattered.

"Of course. Blanche Jacobus. Future Collie Breeder."

Shooting him a hard look, she said, "I thought I just explained to you – "

Esmeralda put a soothing hand on Blanche's arm.

"Well, he's trying to confuse me," Blanche said, shaking her off.

"I would never presume to do that," Robert smiled, enjoying the torture.

"You wouldn't?"

"I'm only suggesting how we might work together," he said, his brown eyes looking to Esmeralda for support.

"See that?" Blanche said, still not satisfied. "A typical man! Sniffs out a good thing and now he wants to be part of it!"

"She's right, Robert," Esmeralda said, putting all the cards on the table. "We really do have to stick with our plans. I'm sorry, but, when it comes to her career, nobody knows better than Blanche what she's talking about. She makes all the clothes for her family – she made this blouse for me – you can't even tell I didn't buy it in a store. She can look at a picture in a magazine and make the same dress the very next day. She works all night if she has to, just to get it right."

Noticing a thread sticking out of the seam at her shoulder, Esmeralda gave it a quick tug. To her astonishment, the thread began to unravel, quickly separating the whole sleeve from the blouse. "Oh, my!" she said, trying to hide her embarrassment. "Oh, dear!"

"Let me help you!" said Robert, not knowing what to do.

"*Bla-anche!*" Esmeralda blushed, shooting an accusatory glance at her friend.

"Nice doggie," Blanche said, petting Baron and paying them no mind, however difficult that may be to believe. "Having trouble, Ez?" she asked sweetly.

"My new blouse! It's – it's falling apart!"

"I'll see if I have a needle and thread in my purse," Blanche offered.

Look at that, Robert thought to himself, as he watched the self-made heroine sashay off. "Quite a woman," is what he said.

"Quite!" Esmeralda answered, not fooled for a minute.

"Crafty," he added.

"Very." Esmeralda said.

"What if this had happened on a movie set?" he asked.

"Trust me. It wouldn't," Esmeralda assured him. "She only made this for me last night - after I told her we were coming to see you."

Robert looked off to the truck, where Blanche was fussing through her purse without letting go of her puppy. "How lucky."

"Blanche can be very . . ." Struggling for the word, Esmeralda bit her bottom lip, "entertaining," she finished. "If I had one ounce of her talent, there's no telling what I could do."

"Is that so?" Robert roughed up Baron's harsh coat and the dog groaned with pleasure. "That's why you're helping her get started in business?"

"Not entirely."

"Blanche Jacobus doesn't seem like the type that needs help from anybody," he said.

"Sometimes life isn't fair," she went on, setting her puppy on the ground to play with its brother. "Sometimes, things aren't the way they seem. Sometimes, those who are less fortunate need someone to look after them. A fashion designer is an artist and all great artists need someone who can give a little push when they need it," she said. "That's where I come in."

"You mean, you can sew?" he asked.

"Oh, I wouldn't say that," she laughed. "No, I wouldn't say that *at all*! I find other ways to inspire and teach."

"Tell me more about yourself, Esmeralda."

"What's there to tell? I'm a spoiled, little rich girl who nobody is ever going to feel sorry for, and nobody would understand."

"Except Blanche."

She nodded. "Except Blanche. Some day she'll understand me very well."

"That makes her one of the fortunate ones, doesn't it?"

There was something warm in the way he said that. Wondering if she would hear that tone in his voice again, she went on as if any deeper intentions had rolled off her. "She's had a hard life, Robert. When the man of the house lost his job at the fan belt factory, Blanche left school to help the family. She was only fourteen and she had a long way to go. She helps run her mother's shop, and they clean houses and take in laundry, besides. She's always clean and fresh."

"I've noticed," he smiled, with an evil glint in his eye.

"Oh, not the way you mean. Underneath all the flirting, Blanche is pure business. You'll see. She knows all the clothing manufacturers, all the fashion houses, which materials hold up best and what colors are smart to wear. She loves silk. That's her favorite. And I know she loves cashmere and mohair because she's raided my closets a hundred times now. But, I don't mind. You should see her squeeze into my sweaters like all the starlets wear them; tight. When Blanche goes to the ice cream parlor, she can make all the guys forget about their sundaes."

"I'll bet she can," Robert said, watching the topic of their conversation strutting back to them in her finest Mae West imitation. "But how is she going to prove herself in the movies?"

"With her talent, that's how. And I can get the connections to pull it off. By the time I'm finished, everybody's going to know Blanche Jacobus and her creations."

"Is she serious about her work?"

"You'd better believe it. Oh, Blanche can have fun, but she dreamed up all the costumes in her portfolio by herself. Pulled them right out of thin air, like magic. She's always making notes for all the colors and all the accessories. We have it all planned. First, we're getting ourselves a little apartment and I'm going around to the stores and talking to buyers. Blanche doesn't know this, but I'm looking for something spectacular - a billboard; a big advertisement of some kind that everybody'll notice! By the time I'm done, everybody's going to want to wear a *Blanche'* original!"

"I believe you."

Chattering with excitement, Esmeralda spun her tale. "After a while, we'll meet up with some handsome actors at the studio where Blanche is under contract," she said, "Paramount or Universal, most likely. We'll get married – double wedding – and live in big houses right next door to each other. We'll have fancy cars and lots and lots of kids."

"Sounds like an Oscar winning story to me."

"It was!" she laughed, giving him a playful shove. "I saw it at the movies!"

"Playing with me, are you?" he smiled. "What happens if your handsome princes never show up? Think how lonely you'll be!"

"Oh, we'll never be lonely. Blanche will see to that. Too busy? That's something else."

"Too busy for a Collie puppy?"

"I hope not! I love them."

"They'd love you, too," Robert said, almost softly. "I can tell."

Her blouse felt hot. Why was it so hard for her to take a compliment?

"Here ya go, Kiddo," Blanche said, back again, with the puppy trotting at her side. "Stand over here in the light. Take off that jacket and give me that sleeve." Handing her puppy to Robert, Esmeralda obliged as Blanche skillfully threaded the needle and began stitching.

"Right here?" Robert asked, surprised. "Wouldn't you like to go inside?"

Blanche raised her eyebrows. "In the movies, you gotta work on location.

And, by the way, Mr. Sheffield, that blouse is stayin' right where it is, so don't you go getting any funny ideas. Anyhow, you and me got business to discuss."

"Business," he said.

"That's right. Now, I've been thinkin' about these puppies of yours," she smiled, blowing him another kiss.

"On your way to the truck and back," he said, bracing himself.

"Yeah," she said. "I walk slow. And don't think I couldn't feel ya lookin', 'cause I did!"

Robert wrinkled his brow in mock surprise. "Esmeralda and I were busy talking!"

Blanche sighed and shook her head. "Sure you were. And cows don't give milk." With a tug, she worked her thread along the shoulder seam of the blouse. "Now," she said, "About these Collies."

Esmeralda brightened. "Aren't they cute, Blanche? Don't you just want to take one home?"

Blanche smoothed Esmeralda's sleeve. "Oh, they're cute, all right. But, what do a couple of beginners like you an' me know about any of this stuff? It's one thing takin' in a mutt you find runnin' along the road and a whole different story raisin' somethin' like Robert, here's got. These dogs are *registered*. They're *pedigreed*."

"The *very best* pedigree," Robert pitched in. Was he egging her on, Esmeralda wondered?

"There ya go, Ez. The very best," Blanche said. "Hold still, now, or I'm gonna jab you with this thing!"

"Not again!" Esmeralda winced, but Blanche ignored her.

"Well, as I was saying, Robert, me an Ez, we have ourselves some pretty big plans. Just as soon as we can, we're leaving town an' heading for California."

"So I've heard," he said.

Blanche shot a glance at Ez. "And what did you think about that?" she asked him, knotting her thread. "When you heard it, exactly."

"I think it's a great idea," he said, noticing Esmeralda quietly pick up Blanche's puppy as it was about to squat. "Until then, you can raise these pups, get them started in the show ring and build a name for yourself all at the same time. What do you say?"

"Hold on a darn minute!"

"Oh, say yes!" Esmeralda pleaded, pushing the puppy into Blanche's arms. "Isn't he adorable?" she asked, winking at Robert.

As she stood there, cradling the pup in her arms, Blanche, for once in her life, looked like the picture of mother-hood. An instant later, she was screaming.

"Ez! You dirty, rotten BITCH!"

"Me?"

"I'LL GET YOU FOR THIS! Take him away! He's peeing all over me!" Blanche bellowed, dangling the puppy at arm's length as a large wet spot dribbled down the front of her chest.

Ever the gentleman, Robert stepped forward and saved the fuzzy culprit. "I have a clean shirt hanging in the bathroom if you would like to freshen up," he whispered. "I apologize for my," he searched for the right word, "puppy," he said, looking directly at Esmeralda, who was beaming with delight.

"Pretty gutsy of you," Robert said, as Blanche stomped off, all traces of Mae West forgotten.

"She had it coming," Esmeralda grinned smugly. "Like I said, I find other ways to teach."

Laughing at such unexpected audacity, Robert countered, "But, I thought you were friends."

"The *best* of friends," Esmeralda corrected him. "There's a difference."

This time, it didn't take long for Blanche to return. "That was very nice of you, Robert," she said, standing his collar up with a sense of feminine victory. "Do you mind if I wear it home? Otherwise, I'll have to drive stark naked."

"My loss," he couldn't resist saying and both ladies felt it. "But, perhaps this will make the drive home more pleasant." Reaching into his jacket, glancing at Esmeralda with a sense of conspiracy, he presented two sets of AKC registration papers already filled out.

"What's this?" Blanche asked, with a suspicious look at them both as Esmeralda smiled broadly. "Wait a minute! This whole thing? This whole thing was a set up? *Esmeralda von Havenburg, you DIDN'T!*"

"A Best Friend from *your* best friend," Robert said. "I hear Collies are quite the rage in Hollywood."

"I've never been so *embarrassed!*" Ez huffed, as Blanche started up her car and flicked on the radio to the melody of "Flying Home" by Lionel Hampton and his Orchestra.

"Well, I didn't feel so hot myself, getting pissed on like that," Blanche said, smiling nicely for Robert as they waved good-bye.

"You deserved it. I don't think I'm ever going to forgive you," Ez pouted.

"Sure you will, Honey. It's just a silly joke. I wouldn't waste my time kiddin' ya if I didn't care, *would I?*"

Esmeralda moaned.

"Aw, quit your moanin' and say what's on your mind or I'll call the cops and have you arrested for holdin' up traffic."

"You do have a way of getting to the point," Esmeralda said, kissing her new puppy.

"And you got a way of wearin' it down," Blanche shot back.

"We have puppies to raise now, Blanche. Children! We're responsible women now."

"Not if we sell 'um, we ain't! I'll bet we could get a good price for Collies like these, more than you paid. Two tickets right out of here."

"You *wouldn't!* Not Collies from Robert Sheffield!"

76

"Yeah, well my respect for Mr. Sheffield went down a notch or two back there, whether you know it or not. Anybody selling two perfectly good puppies to a couple of rank beginners like us is asking for trouble - an' if you ask me, it don't have nothin' to do with Collies!"

"*Blanche!* How can you say such a thing!"

"I tell ya, *I know men!* And they don't give nothin *nice* away unless they want somethin' *nasty* in return."

"I have a mind to go right back to Robert and say you don't want the puppy."

"Oh, I want the puppy all right. I gotta do SOMETHIN' to get out of this town or I'll be washin' laundry and cleanin' houses the rest of my life. I got places to go and things to see!"

"Then it's all settled?"

"Not so fast! I still gotta figure this out."

"But can you believe it, Blanche? Can you believe we have Collie puppies of our very own? I never thought of having a kennel of my own before."

"What's this about a whole *kennel* now? I'm just getting used to the idea of *one* dog."

"Father always had his Greyhounds, but I never thought of a Breed for my very own. Collies are so beautiful. Aren't they, Blanche?"

"They're beautiful all right, but all I see is Robert Sheffield getting rid of a couple of extra mouths to feed and, on top of everything else, now he says we gotta take classes, too. I'm done with classes. I left all that behind me in High School. When did he say those classes were? Saturday? Saturday's the busiest day in the shop. My mother'll throw a fit!"

"You can be finished and back in the shop by noon. And it won't be for long. If your puppy is as smart as mine, it'll only take a few weeks."

"Who said yours is smarter than mine?"

"Well, I don't know," Esmeralda teased, snuggling her face against her puppy's neck. "You've got to admit this little fellow looks pretty smart in his gold suit and white shirt."

"What do you say, Mister?" Blanche asked the one pressing against her side as she drove. "Are we gonna take that?"

"It'll be fun!" Esmeralda said. "We'll *make* it fun. We'll get up early and get all dressed up, and we'll go to the classes and everybody'll just love our dogs. They will, Blanche. I know they will!"

"I can see you don't know a thing about human nature," Blanche said. "Well, I'm a student of it. These dog show people of yours like competition. I can tell. And, like you said, every one of em's an expert. Why, you should of heard the way some of them talked! If words were knives, there'd be blood all over the place!"

"But our dogs are every bit as good as theirs!"

"Maybe better. But, it ain't all about dogs, Ez. You gotta *know* people. You gotta know them how I do. Right now, at that show we went to, you and me were just two nice girls watching things, smiling at everybody and everybody's smiling right back. Then all of a sudden, we're fighting for that Blue Ribbon you talked about."

"I don't want people to hate me," Esmeralda said, hugging her puppy, as musical strains of Tommy Dorsey's orchestra playing "I'll Never Love Again" for Frank Sinatra filled the car.

"Oh, they'll hate you, all right. They're gonna hate you and me and both our dogs. Next thing you know, they won't enter a show if they think we're gonna be in it. What do we do then? Stand around waving at the crowd?"

"We'll work as hard as we can," Esmeralda said. "They'll like us, we'll make them like us! We'll pay special attention to everything! You can make us pretty dresses to wear with matching collars and leashes if you want to. You can, Blanche! We'll be beautiful! Who knows? Maybe a Hollywood producer will see us, and ask if you want a job in the movies! It's a chance. It's a chance!"

Regaining her composure, Esmeralda watched the trees and houses for a while as Pennsylvania farmlands turned into small towns and back again. "You said yourself how tough things are; how hard it is to make a go of anything. Don't you want to try?"

"Sure, I do, Kid," Blanche said, sorry now she had been so tough. "I was just testing you, that's all," she coaxed. "Come on, Ez. Perk up, OK?"

"I can't."

"Now what is it."

"Tell me how you know so much about dog shows all of a sudden."

"Quick study. I knew we were coming here and a lady's gotta know the game. I figured somebody might pull a fast one, so I made a few phone calls from that catalog you forgot to pick up when we went over to see Robert at the show. You'd be surprised what people will tell you over the phone, especially when they think you want to buy a dog. By the time I was done, I'll bet I could be a judge myself, if you want to know. Anyhow, you were smart getting both of them. Thank you by the way," she said, sincerely. "And if I wouldn't have studied up, how else would I know Robert tried holding back the best pup?"

"He did not!"

"I tell you, he did. *Here, this one's friendlier.* Bull! He wanted to keep *this* puppy, right here, for himself!" Turning to her puppy, not exactly the love of her life, but working on it, she cooed, "Didn't he, Sweetie? Well, I guess we fixed him!"

"Oh, you fixed *him*, all right," Esmeralda said, realizing now what Robert had done for her.

"I'm not sure I like the sound of your voice when you say that."

"Blanche — *that* isn't the one he was trying to hold back. *This one* is."

"*What?*"

"I remember. I remember because the puppy you took away from him didn't have a full white collar."

Checking her puppy's neck on both sides, seeing a slash of Sable, Blanche hissed, "*That slick-assed cheat!*"

Esmeralda grinned. "Figured you out, didn't he?" she said, kissing her puppy again.

"Well, that's it!" Blanche said, slamming the dash with her fist and making everybody jump. "If he thinks I'm gonna help him get his name out there, he's got another thing comin'. *We're going back!*"

"Careful with the dash. You might hurt your hand, and we're going to need it."

"I tell you, we're going back!"

"Oh, no," Esmeralda said, taking charge in a way that left no doubt she wouldn't budge. "Going back is something we most definitely are not doing. We're moving up, Partner. Don't you see?" she asked with an intensity Blanche hadn't noticed before. "It doesn't matter who has the best puppy. It doesn't matter if these puppies ever amount to anything at all. Robert gave us a million-dollar idea! Blanche, get your sewing machine ready. We're selling your collection at dog shows!"

"*Dog shows!* But, my work belongs in the fashion houses of Europe! On movie screens all over the world! I can't be

81

dragging my dresses around in the dirt, getting all kinds of clingy dog hair all over them!"

"But, you see how they dress at these things. It's not because they want to - it's because nobody has ever cared enough to design just for them! Think about it, Blanche."

"*I am thinkin'!* A minute ago, I was a poor wash girl. Stuck in a little town in Pennsylvania, countin' up towels and shirts for my neighbors an' cuttin' cloth in the store at night. Now, I got myself a puppy from a champion litter. I don't know about you, Honey, but I see a one way ticket right out of this town and you want to hold me back! You're crazy!"

"But, Blanche, you can't go now! What would Robert think?"

"I don't care what he thinks. He suckered me in with the worst puppy."

"I'll trade you!" Esmeralda said, thinking fast. "Here! Take mine!"

"An' for the rest of my life I gotta hear about how you sacrificed your shot at *dog show fame? No THANKS!*"

"I'd NEVER do that! I wouldn't!" Esmeralda sobbed, swooping up both puppies in her arms; loving them.

"Oh, no, you don't!" Blanch snapped. "You keep your grubby hands OFF my puppy! I don't care what you or that house painter Robert Sheffield or anybody else says - *I'm gonna make my dog a STAR!*"

Boot Camp . . . Back in the 1940s, the William Penn Kennel Club held handling classes every week for those needing to sharpen their ability. Contrary to what the public may think, success as a handler in the dog show ring, as in any of life's competitions, requires a finely tuned arsenal of skills; not the least of which is the ability to cast insult with a smile. If you had a new pup, the Armory was the place to go. But, as those lucky enough to frequent the higher altitudes of the dog show world can attest, "Ring skills" come in a smorgasbord of diversity . . . .

"OK, everybody, line up your dogs so we can go over the AKC Standard for our Breeds," Robert, in white shirt and khakis, called out to the handlers and their dogs.

"This ought to be good," Blanche said, smoothing her skirt and staring down the competition. "Come here, Hon. Don't you be scared," she said to her puppy.

"Hon?" Esmeralda raised an eyebrow.

"Yeah. Don't you think it fits?"

"I think you should change it."

"What's this about changing names all the time? He's a man dog, ain't he? Well, I gotta make my life easy. His name's Hon."

As Robert walked up and down the row, he greeted owners eager to please and dogs excited to see each other. Was he walking slower the closer he got to them, showing off something, emanating some invisible kind of power? "Good morning, Esmeralda," he said, deeply. "You've done a nice job of grooming. How does he like his new home?" Were those brown-green eyes sparkling extra bright, she wondered?

"Oh, he loves it," she smiled back. "Jack - he's our kennel man - gave Barry his own run."

"You have a kennel so soon? And someone to run it?"

"My father had a racing kennel - Greyhounds - and I've been wondering what to do with it since he passed away a few months ago."

"I'm sorry to hear about your loss," he said. "And have you and your kennel man decided what you are going to do?"

"I'd like to try raising Collies," she smiled. "Starting with Barrymore, here. Do you like his name?"

He nodded. "Quite fitting for a dog headed for center stage," he said, ignoring Blanche's sour face.

"Yes, I like it, too," Esmeralda said, pleased that she had crossed the first hurdle in an important show dog's career. The right name could make or break a dog. "Jack says I have to keep Barry outside if I want him to coat up."

"He's right," Robert agreed.

"But, I do so much want to keep him in the house with me."

"Ez, all you gotta do is move into the kennel an' you can be with

'Barrymore,' there, as much as you want," Blanche butted in.

"And Blanche," Robert smiled, knowing by now that being ignored was the one thing this woman couldn't stand. "How are you this morning?"

"Wishin' I was somewhere else and tryin' to make sense out of this drama club," she said, scoping out the crowd. "See that woman with the Great Dane and the guy with the Bassett Hound over there? That broad actually stepped on his foot for getting too close to her dog and laughed in his face."

"And what did he do?" Robert asked.

"Apologized. *He* goes and apologizes to *her* for steppin' on HIS foot. You're crowding me, the lady says to him. What's she think she is? A queen?"

"She might as well be," Robert said. "That's Connie Bentley, president of the club." Something about his manner gave the hint that, just like the dogs she had chosen with which to be identified, Connie Bentley was accustomed to towering over others.

"Well, tell her there's two queens on the chess board now," Blanche smiled, raising her chin. "What do you say about that, Hon?" she asked her little golden pawn.

"I think he says the drama's just beginning!" laughed Robert, with a side-glance to Esmeralda. "Would either of you like me to introduce you to Connie?"

"No need. We've got radar. Anyhow, I like taking my time when it comes to things like this." Looking him in the eye, Blanche handed her pink satin lead to him and asked, "Smoothie? Meet Honey. This, here's, your Breeder," she said to the happy, wiggling pup who danced around at the familiar sight of Robert. "He's got a thing about his tail," she said, making conversation with double meaning. "Can't seem to keep it still," she smiled.

"Runs in the family, I notice," smiled Robert, equally proficient, kneeling down and running his big hands over Honey's sides and belly.

"Something about the way you do that gives me chills," Blanche said, throwing a girlish look at Esmeralda. "You'll have to try out for one of my fashion shows sometime."

Pretending not to hear, Robert stood and considered his next move.

"*The underwear division,*" Blanche whispered to Esmeralda.

Making no comment, but hearing very well, Robert faced her, winked, and moved on.

"I like that man," Blanche said, watching him walk away. "There's something about him."

"You'll have to keep trying if you want to get anywhere with Robert," said Esmeralda, when what she really meant was, you'd better get in line.

Skillfully, Robert continued down the row, checking teeth, running his hands over ears and backs, all the way to the tips of tails. Stepping to the front of the class, his voice bouncing off gray cinder-block walls and a shiny cement floor, he addressed the group.

"Any one of these dogs could probably win something in a show," he said. "But, our purpose in these classes is to do better than that. Much better, if we're lucky."

As Blanche shifted her weight to one side and crossed her arms in boredom, somebody coughed and someone else chuckled. How much better could a lady do, she thought, than to snag a man like Robert?

"Let's pick ourselves a Blue Ribbon winner," he smiled, clapping his hands together.

Already done, Blanche thought.

"Keep in mind, the same dog doesn't necessarily win all the time," he said. "At a show, the judge is only selecting the best dog on that particular day. And we all know, dogs, just like us, can have their bad days. Tell you what," he said. "Everybody who thinks their dog has a good *stop,* raise your hand."

Immediately, a few hands went up.

"What's he mean?" Esmeralda whispered, looking at her puppy. "I don't know what he means. Should I raise my hand?"

"Don't wrinkle the blouse, Ez. I'm trying to sell it. By the time we leave here, I'm going to have us a new customer or two."

"Well, shouldn't we ask?"

"What for? As you know, I take myself seriously. I take everything I do seriously. You know how you said you check things out before you invest? Well, you know those phone calls I made?"

87

Blanche reminded her. "What he's getting at, if I remember right, and I have a very good memory, is the place right between a dog's eyes. Does Barry, there, have any space between his eyes?"

"Well, of course."

"Then raise your hand now. See? Nothin' to it. This dog show stuff is simple. You got yourself a champion."

Pleased, Esmeralda did as she was told and Robert congratulated the group. "Good," he said. "Now, all of you know the *slope* of the stop is something that varies from Breed to Breed. For example, A Chihuahua in the arms of band leader Xavier Cugat is going to have a much more pronounced stop than, say, one of General Patton's Bull terriers. But, what about the rest of a dog's head. What about the things that give it balance? Breeding good dogs, and developing them according to an ideal goal, is all about balance. It's about discipline, too, for the Breeder. But, it's really about balancing the forces that affect the dogs we're bringing into the world."

"That's what I like about Robert," Esmeralda said. "He's so smart."

"It's the gray in his hair, Ez," Blanche whispered. "I've never met a gray haired man who doesn't think he knows a thing or two."

"And if we're not improving the Breed," Robert asked, "then what are we doing all this for?"

"*Money!*" a heckler said.

Robert nodded, with a sense of good sportsmanship. "Well, you're right. If a

Breeder takes care of his dogs, and upgrades his stock with each generation, they should be good enough for people to want them. And the prices they bring should, in return, keep the bills paid. Don't you agree?" he asked, to a round of amens.

Of course they did. They were dog people; a special Breed of their own; a community of souls who, no matter how they might occasionally treat each other, believed in right and wrong, in beauty, and trust. In a world of bombs and bullets, falling stock markets and war none of them had started, none of them could stop, they were the last dreamers, looking ahead for that next winner. They were the last bastion of American sentimentality. As long as they had their dogs, things were OK; as long as they had their dogs and each other, they weren't alone.

"Balance," Robert said, not realizing how far his simple teachings might go that day; "The one thing we need in this life. In our dogs, balance is more than a physical thing. It's mental, and spiritual, too." Lovingly, he said, "I know there are lots of people out there who say a dog doesn't have feelings, or doesn't have a soul. But," he looked around in a way that left every one of them sensing he was speaking just to them, "I doubt if there is anyone in this room who feels that way."

Smiles, and introspection passed through them all, like a calming and gentle wave. They were different from oth-

89

ers. He understood that, and he was letting them know it was OK.

"Balance." He said it again. "Physical balance. Starting with the head, why don't we all take a look at our dogs and see what we think? Being fair, looking at your dog like a stranger would, does your dog have a balanced head?"

"OK," Blanche said now, before Esmeralda could ask, "I got this figured out. It's like measurin' for a hem. We know what the 'stop' is, between the eyes, right?"

Esmeralda stood her puppy beside Blanche's. "Well, now he's talking about the distance from the stop to the very back of the skull being the same as the distance from the stop to the tip of the dog's nose. That's what they call balance. 'Cause it's equal, you know? At least, for Collies it's supposed to be."

Once again, they raised their hands and Robert counted. "Eighteen out of eighteen. Not bad," he smiled. "OK, now let's check ears. The dogs' ears," he added, to a round of chuckles. "Again, everybody's Breed has a different standard, but, remember, the judge is going to be looking for *foreign substances* - like weight, for instance, in some breeds. Most of you know my breed is Collies. Well, let's talk about Collies. They're supposed to have what's called a 'Tulip' ear. Don't ask me who came up with that word for an ear that flops over at the tip, but, that's what it's called; tulip. Anyway, in Collies, we know a lot of handlers rub powdered lead into the outer fur on the tips of the ears. Why do they do that? Because the dark color of the lead doesn't stand out, and the weight of the lead," he explained, "pulls the tip of an ear down just enough to give it the perfect shape. And yet, the rules say if you're caught putting weight - or any foreign substance - in your dog's ears to make them tip over, then you can be disqualified and told to leave the ring. A judge has that right if he wants to use it. So, OK, we've got some Collies here today. How many have natural ears?"

The hands of each Collie owner shot up like rockets.

"Impressive," he said. "A room full of dogs with perfect ears."

Like a Sergeant inspecting his troops, he paced up and down in front of the line, explaining the attributes of a purebred dog's head. "It's a subtle thing, judging purebred dogs. Not everybody agrees on the elusive combination of features that create what we call the dog's all-important 'Expression.'"

"Just exactly how much of this has to do with the expression of the handler?" Blanche wondered out loud, pushing a curl behind her ear and batting her eyes.

"Is it the slant of the eyes?" Robert continued, addressing his remarks to her now. "Their shape? Their depth of color?" Hers were a deep shade of blue he had noticed.

"Is it the dog's markings, maybe the shading of color on its face, or the placement of its ears?" he asked, looking at hers. "If the conformation is correct, and if you have a good-moving dog, then everything else is subjective."

Striding confidently to the center of the ring, he spread his legs, folded both hands behind his back and announced, "Dog show in five minutes!"

"Five minutes!" said a heavy-set wo-man in a pleated wool skirt and white blouse. "I can't even pull up my zipper in five minutes!"

Blanche laughed. "You need a Blan-che' Creation, my dear!" Handing her a card, she said, "Blanche Jacobus, fashion designer."

"Nice to meetcha!" said the woman, hurrying away. "Gotta go brush my dog!"

A few minutes later, Robert called the group together once again. "Everybody get an entry number!" he said, clapping his hands. "All you first timers, find somebody to help with your arm band and let's get started!"

Taking a rubber band, Esmeralda took a paper with a number on it and slipped it over Blanche's arm.

"Careful, Ez. These sleeves are get-ting a workout today."

"There you go," Esmeralda said, pat-ting her on the back. "Just like a real dog show."

"Kinda tight," said Blanche, flexing her arm a few times and looking around to make sure she looked right.

"OK, line up by number. Dogs around once!" hollered Robert. "First handler, come back around and stop here when

you're through. The rest, follow him!"
Sternly, he narrowed his eyes and eval-
uated each dog's way of going as dogs and
handlers trotted out, came to a halt and
took their positions.

"Down and back," Robert said to the
first handler after examining his German
Shepherd from head to foot.

"Straight down?" the man asked.

Robert nodded; man and dog trotted
away and Robert studied the dog's placement of every foot. "A Shepherd is what
we call a single track dog," he explained
to the group. "He moves like a wolf, or
an Indian in the woods, each footprint
falling into the next, single-file, getting closer together as the dog picks up
speed. Other herding dogs have the same
characteristic," he said. "See how this
dog moves? Very nice," he said, to the
dog's owner.

Facing the group; demeanor serious
now, he said, "Next, please?"

Turning quickly to Blanche, Esmeralda said, "It's my turn - oh, I can't!
I'm going to faint!"

"Ez, ya ain't got time to faint.
Lover boy's waiting."

As Esmeralda self-consciously led
her puppy over to Robert, a hush seemed
to descend upon the room. Was it her
imagination or was there a special light
in Robert's eyes once again? Taller somehow, almost regal, he smiled as she felt
her ears getting warm.

"We meet again," he said, softly,
but she was sure every word echoed off
the walls.

"I'm nervous," she said. "I don't know what's the matter with me."

"Take a deep breath," he said.

"I'm dizzy."

"Stage fright. Try to stay calm. Pretend no one is here but you and your dog. Think about him, not yourself. Make it fun for him."

Trying not to unsettle her, wishing he could erase everyone else but this sensitive, hesitant woman whose image had burned in his mind from the moment he first saw her, Robert cleared his throat. "Down and back, please," he said.

"What the Hell are they talking about?" Blanche asked, with a hand on her hip. "I thought he's just supposed to look at the dogs and keep this show moving."

"Oh, the show's moving, all right," a woman's husky voice behind her said. "Like a head-on collision."

Ambushed, Blanche said, without turning around, "Pretty sharp. Who, may I ask, is reporting the accident?"

"Connie," the woman said, as Blanche spun on her heels to face her. "Connie Bentley. 'The Lovely Danes of Lamour.'"

"Pleasure meeting you," Blanche said, with a nod. "Is this one of your pups?" she asked, of the Fawn Dane stomping a paw on Honey.

"Lamour Lolita. I bred her myself."

"Next!" Robert called out.

"Well, would you mind teaching her some manners?" Blanche asked.

"She's just playing," Connie said, making no effort to stop her dog.

"Well, I'm not," Blanche said coldly, lifting Hon up in her arms and making her way over to Robert with an assurance that hadn't been there the day they first met.

"You can let him walk by himself," Robert said, when she got there.

"Yes, I know," Blanche said, politely.

"Very slick of you, leaving an earring in my bathroom like that," he whispered.

"Gave me an excuse to see you again, didn't it?"

"Careful," he warned, under his breath. "They're watching us."

"In that case, you need to help out me an' Connie over there. See, we've been talking and we've got a question or two about some of the finer points when it comes to this whole handling thing. You know, like how to get the judge to notice what you really want him to, so he can give you the *prize*?"

"Well, no matter what you 'do' . . . with whom . . . or how often," he said, as she looked up at him with mock innocence, "the *prize* is supposed to go to the best dog on that particular day. Do you really think you can sway a judge's mind?"

"Oh, Honey, I can sway more than his mind if I want to," Blanche winked, reminding him of their visit after she had come back for the earring that day.

"Is that so?" he asked.

"Oh, yes," she said, stepping closer. "In fact, I'm sure I can. I'm very observant, you know, and I'm getting the hang of it. If you'll let me demonstrate," she said, checking to make sure Connie was watching and turning around to rotate directly into Robert's crotch, "I *think* I might be able to prove my *point!*"

Blanche proved her point all right, and almost got away with it right in front of everybody. But, Robert wasn't exactly what they call an easy catch. Stepping back, he neatly appraised Hon . . . and sought out Esmeralda . . . .

"You're right about Blanche," he said later, testing the waters. "She's a lot of fun."

"Yes, she is," Esmeralda said, unable to look in his eyes. "A lot of fun."

"Would you like a soda?" he asked. "We always have refreshments."

"No, thanks," she said. Why did she say that, she wondered? The truth was, she was starving!

"Are you sure? Some of the ladies make great sandwiches." He indicated a cloth-covered table stacked with plates and cups.

"I'm sure," she nodded, mad at herself now.

"Well, if you're not the type that likes to eat, then I can't very well ask you out to dinner, can I?"

He was asking her out? Asking her out to dinner? She knew she should have said yes to the refreshments!

"Well, I guess I messed that up," she said.

He liked when she blushed. It was nice, knowing he had that affect on her.

"Can I visit you sometime?" he asked. Alone?"

Force of Nature . . . There is no love more powerful than a love that is meant to be. For Esmeralda, the days had been endless deserts; the nights, swirling blizzards of ice and stinging needles since he had asked to be with her, and her alone. Was he The One? The one meant only for her; in all the world, the one for whom she had been born? Every inch of her body radiated with feeling, pulsing with a life of its own! They were together; together as they should be; as they would always be; as she knew they must be forever.

Wildflowers along the path had never seemed so bright; the sky had never seemed so blue. "It's my favorite place in the whole world," Esmeralda said, as they walked along the woods at the edge of the field. "I ride on this path whenever I can."

"Do you take Barry along?" Robert asked. "It's good for him. The exercise would give him a great advantage in the ring."

"Oh, yes. He likes to come along," she smiled, picking a daisy. "Jack uses this trail for the Greyhounds, too."

"Your father's dogs."

"They were, yes." she said. "Now they're mine."

"They're very beautiful when they run," he said, somewhat familiar with the sport of Greyhound racing. "They're a very old Breed."

"Yes, and my father always believed in having the best he could afford."

"Did they make him wealthy?"

"The factory did that for him, but the dogs helped," she said. "Even when they didn't win, he seemed to get something important just by being around them; seeing them grow up. He met a lot of great people in the sport. He loved seeing his dogs run; so free. Throwing all their heart and soul into it. Esmeralda, he'd say; whatever you want in life, go after it with the same passion as a Greyhound. And look at me," she said, laughing at herself. "I've gone into Collies! Am I bad?"

"Just say you're expanding the business," Robert said, taking her hand. Her breath almost stopped. Was it true what the stories said, she wondered? Would bluebirds and butterflies dance around them? Would there be music? She listened and heard none.

He kissed her hand and held it to his mouth. "Collies have passion, too, Special One," he said. Yes, she saw, his dark hair was turning silver just at the temples. Did that make him wiser? Yes, his eyes; his haunting eyes, seemed to be asking for permission. Permission for what, she wondered, knowing she would let him do whatever he wanted; whatever it was; as long as he didn't leave her.

"Esmeralda, I think you might be the most amazing soul I've ever met."

Had he really just said that, she wondered? Did her really find her amazing? Nobody had ever said something so nice to her before. But, it was more than that; much more. This man; this handsome, independent man had just said she was the most amazing woman he had ever met. Oh, please let me remember this day, she thought; let me see the sky, feel the sun all over me; feel the heat under my sweater . . .

Filling the awkward silence as they walked on, he picked up a stick and tossed it aside. She hadn't answered him, he thought to himself. Had he offended her? If he had; if he had in any way insulted her, or frightened her, he wouldn't forgive himself.

"Does all this belong to Lochwood?" he asked, when what he really wanted to say was, is there anyone special in your life?

"Two hundred fifty acres," she said, finally speaking up. "My father pieced it together from three different farms. When the family first came over here from Germany, they lived over there," she said, showing him the tin roof of an old sandstone barn almost hidden by a wooded hill. This path we're on, is the trail the neighbors used when they worked the fields. Can you hear them?" she asked.

He listened, perhaps to amuse her; perhaps because he, too, could still believe what children know. "The work horses," he said.

"And now they live in your barn," she told him. "Do you ever wonder if you lived before?"

"Somewhere else, you mean?" he asked.

"Yes," she said, stopping now and standing closer to him. "Did you ever feel like you knew someone from a long time ago, but you had actually never met that person before. And you had no reason to make you feel that way except the possibility that maybe, somehow, it might be true?"

"An interesting thought," he said, asking himself why he didn't admit he had sometimes felt the very same way? What was he afraid of? Was he afraid this intriguing woman, a student of philosophy thrust into the harsh world of business now that her father had died, would reject him? Laugh at him? Scream at him, when she, herself, had just said they may all have lived before? All he could say to her was, *an interesting thought?* What was the matter with him, he asked himself? Where was his courage? This beautiful spirit had just revealed to him an outlook on life that set her worlds apart from everyone else around her. How isolated she must feel at times; how lonely.

"My mother believed that," she said, looking at him now. "She believed my father and she had known each other in another lifetime."

"Your mother?" he asked, knowing he hadn't met anyone fitting that role at dinner.

"She lives in London," Esmeralda said. "She hides from the Blitzkrieg in a shelter under the garden house on her estate. She hasn't lived here since I was a child."

"Really?" he asked, not knowing what else to say about such an unusual arrangement.

"Oh, it's OK," she said. "I'm used to it. They had a fight when I was little and Mother went back home to her family."

"So much for predestined lovers," he said, sad that the story didn't have a happier ending.

"Mrs. Harrington has taken good care of me."

"She's very devoted to you."

"She was my mother's maid."

Wondering why a mother would leave without her child, he decided not to pry. There would be other times for such questions, he decided. It was a decision tinged with hope.

"Please tell Mrs. Harrington her chicken cutlets were delicious," he said.

"Thank you." She seemed pleased. "She'll be happy to know that."

"Who helps you with all this?" he asked, speaking of the open fields and woodlands around them. "It's so much to manage."

"Jack and Faye help me," she said.

"Faye?" he asked.

"Jack's wife, yes; she's great. I didn't like her at first. I guess I was jealous; I had a terrible crush on Jack for the longest time. But, he loves her and Faye's one of the family now. I can't imagine the place without her."

Sticking both hands in his pockets, he asked softly, wondering if he dared to just yet, "Is there anyone special?"

"Oh!" she said, surprised at herself for understanding the direction of his conversation. "You're asking if I have a *boyfriend!*" Her mouth went dry. "Well, no," she said. "I don't. Most men are intimidated by me."

"Intimidated?" he asked.

"Well," she said – if her ears were any hotter she could have melted both earrings and the good luck necklace Blanche had given her all at once – "you know, because of the family business; the factory and all. I'm a woman in a man's world now. I deal with bankers, trustees and accountants."

"Since your father, you mean?" It was hardly a secret.

She nodded, unable to answer. Even now, her father's death was almost impossible for her to bear.

"The factory employs most of the people in town," she said.

He had never met a woman with such responsibility.

"See what I mean? Even when I said it just now, I felt a change in you."

She was right; but, what she would never know is that, far from intimidation, what he felt for her was the deepest respect.

"Don't you know love doesn't see such things?" he asked.

Love, she thought? *I can hardly allow myself to think of it.* "Love is something I have yet to find," she said, her eyes questioning his, "or even to consider."

"Will you consider this?" he said, folding their hands to her chest between them, and kissing her. It was a long kiss; wet, slow, deep; his tongue gently parting her lips and pushing into hers. When he finished, he looked deep into her eyes. "Delicious," he grinned, studying her embarrassment.

"Robert," she said, wondering if he would do more; what would he do to her; where? How often? "It's OK, Robert," she whispered now, her voice thick, her throat tight. "It's OK."

"Let's go back," he said, knowing instinctively she was his; remembering every detail of this moment. There would be other times, he knew; other times to explore each other's bodies, and learn about their souls. Looking up, he saw a sky filled with gathering storm clouds. No, he would not accept them as a sign of what waited ahead for them, around the corner. Theirs could be a good life, he told himself, knowing something would get in the way, as it always had for him. "It's getting dark," he said, picking a small bouquet of wildflowers and placing them in her hand. "I'm falling in love with you, Esmeralda."

"Love?" Mrs. Harrington asked, later that night. "My dearest child, he won't be the last to say such a thing to a young lady like you."

Like me? What does she mean, a young lady like me, Esmeralda wanted to know?

Instead, she said, "He picked these for me," and handed the guardian of her happiness the wildflowers.

"I'll get a vase for them," Mrs. Harrington said, taking them and heading for the kitchen.

Love, Esmeralda thought, alone in the study, surrounded by shelves of books with their warm leather bindings; the comfortable, wing-back reading chair and the portrait of her father over the fireplace. The very idea of it, the sound of it, the very possibility that anyone might really, truly *love her*, made her feel as light as a tuft of bulrush seed floating high across the water ripples of a lake. Please let him kiss me again; hold me again; smile like that – please let him want me like I know he did. I could feel it, she thought to herself. I felt it pressing against me. He loves me. *He must!* He said so.

But, wasn't there supposed to be music?

RrrrrrRRRRRRUMBAH!

"Come on, Mamba, *dance with me!*"

"Child, what's got into you! You've been acting like this for days!" Dorothy hollered over Xavier Cugat. "Turn that thing down! You're scarin' my birds!"

"I can't, Mamba! I can't!" Blanche yelled, turning the radio louder and swirling around the shop.

"Well, stop it! You'll knock something over!"

Dancing on, fever-hot, Blanche swung her hips, threw out her arms and tossed her head back as if she had been born Spanish. "Take me to Brazil, Mamba! Take me to Brazil!"

"I'll take you to Brazil, all right! If you don't get hold of yourself I'll –"

"You'll what, Mamba!" Blanche twirled to a stop, her eyes bright, her skin pink enough to match the silk bandanna in her hair. "What will you do? Congratulate your daughter?"

"Well, I'd be happy to congratulate you if I knew what it was I'm doing it for. What is it, Blanche? Something good for the business? Did you get another customer? Another store, maybe?" Blanche' Creations was the only thing she could imagine stirring up her daughter this way.

"Better, Mamba – better!" Blanche sang, dancing off again.

Turning off the radio with a snap, Dorothy Jacobus stood, her face expressionless, hands at her side. "What is it, Blanche? What do you want to tell me."

"*I'm going to be married* – I know it! *I know it!*"

"But, who? How did this happen?" her mother asked.

"He's the most gorgeous man you've ever seen, Mamba – tall, shoulders so

105

broad I'll bet he could do all the worryin' for both of us. And you should see his - " she glanced at her mother and thought better of saying how much she liked his ass.

"Mamba, I feel - I feel so - "

"Foolish?" her mother asked, stopping Blanche cold.

Why did she do that? Why did she always have to ruin the happy times? "Mamba," Blanche said, placing all her attention on the sad woman who had raised her and by whom she had never felt loved, "For once; *for once in your life*, I'd *think* you'd be happy. You're getting rid of a daughter. You're gonna have one less mouth to feed!"

"When? How soon? Is that a promise?" It was a clumsy joke.

"Just as soon as I can get him to ask me," Blanche said, accustomed to her Dorothy, the killjoy.

"You mean he hasn't asked you yet? Who is this man? Do I know him or is this another one of your secret admirers your too ashamed to introduce me to? Where did you meet him?"

"It's Robert Sheffield. You know, where I got Hon? At the sound of his name, the young dog looked up. "Robert loves me - I know he does!"

"But, Baby, you've got a future ahead of you. You got to think about yourself!"

"Oh, but I do, Mamba," Blanche cooed with a wisdom beyond her years. "I think about myself all the time!"

"There you go with one of your smart cracks. Isn't this man older than you?"

"I like him that way," Blanche said, primping her hair.

"How much older?"

"Who cares?" Blanche asked, eyes wide.

"Well, some day you might," her mother said. "Some day, it could matter very much."

"Mamba, if the business takes off like me an' Esmeralda are plannin', I'm gonna be so rich it won't matter. *Mamba!*" she said, grabbing her mother by both hands and swinging her around, "Oh, Mamba, *let's have fun!* Let me buy you fur coats and pretty hats and white gloves - let me make you happy! Don't you want to be happy? Please say you do!"

"Happy?" Mrs. Jacobus asked, a distant look in her eye. "I thought I was, once." More than that, she wouldn't say; had never said. "The important thing, Baby, is that you're happy, not me."

"Oh, I am! I am!" Blanche said, searching her mother's face for something - a glimmer of hope; a spark of approval withheld for as long as she could remember. "Oh, Mamba," she said. "Don't worry. You'll like Robert. You will."

But, not nearly as much as Blanche did.

If her husband had been around, Dorothy might have asked him what to do that night. She might have said, "Bill, I'm worried for her. I'm worried she's getting too close to the von Havenburg girl."

"What for?" he might have asked. "What is it you have against the von Havenburgs? At least Blanche is getting something started for herself."

She couldn't say. No matter how often she had tried, no matter how much she wanted to, she had never been able to say why she prayed her daughter would never walk the primrose paths of the von Havenburg estate.

"Blanche is special," she said, knowing she had never told her so. "She can go far. I guess - I guess I'm - "

"Scared she'll make a mistake? Fall flat on her face? Make the wrong choice?" he would ask, as he always did. It always came down to that, she thought; always came down to making the wrong choice.

"She'll be all right," he would always say, not touching her, not daring to intrude on her private misery. "Blanche is a survivor. She's got a head for business and she knows where she's going."

"And, she loves you," he would say, like he always did.

He would have said that, if he had been around for her now; if there wasn't a card game, or a horse track, or a Bourbon and water at the neighborhood bar. Like so many other out of work husbands, Bill Jacobus, skinny, defeated, understood about choices; especially when you didn't have any.

"I've figured it all out," Blanche said in her usual way as she put the finishing touch on a dress for Watt & Shand in Esmeralda's parlor. "If we fold the skirt like this," she said, draping the shiny cloth to one side, "and place the buttons here," she pointed to the hips, "we can show a little leg. And, a woman can feel real good about those new shoes she just bought over in the shoe department."

"Clever," said Esmeralda. "I'm sure the Buyer will like that."

"And don't forget the jewelry," Blanche said. "Are we supposed to supply it, or will they?"

"Oh, they have a big jewelry department," Esmeralda said. "They'll have the perfect compliments for our dresses."

"Do you like the color?" Blanche asked. "I thought ice blue was right for this one. Who's gonna model it, do you know?"

"Well, I think Miss Lancaster County is one of the models."

"Never met her."

"You will," Esmeralda assured her. "There's a cocktail party after the show and the models are going to be wearing the dresses."

"Well, they'd better not spill anything," Blanche frowned. "Like my sketch for the house wife number? What do you think of the red and white checkers and the bandanna in her hair?"

"Nice feel."

"I'm going to ask if the guy who makes the window displays can put up matching curtains, and maybe a table cloth, to give it some extra *oomph*, you know?"

"I can see it. I like it. How soon are we going to be ready?"

"Another week at the most," Blanche said. *"I'm so excited!"*

"And you should be," Esmeralda said. "Watt & Shand is a big account and it'll give us practice before the Philadelphia show."

"Oh, we don't need practice, Honey. What we need is customers!" Blanche laughed, her eyes twinkling extra brightly as they had been for the past several weeks.

The best weeks of Esmeralda's life.

Robert!

Six feet of man with brown-green eyes and a wicked sense of humor when he put his mind to it.

Robert.

His voice; sensual, manly . . . her name spoken from his lips like their own private mantra had never evoked such erotic desire. She remembered those wet lips, his hot mouth, his demanding tongue. *Esmeralda*, she heard him saying; *Ez . . . mur . . . ahl . . . da!*

Hold me, Robert, she thought. Right here - right now! On the path in the woods; in your car; in the barn; on the sofa; in your bed - I want to show you everything! *Everything! I love you, Robert. I love you!*

But she hadn't shown him everything. Not yet.

110

Deadly Seige . . . Studying the puppy's walk the next day, Robert knew something was wrong. His keen sense of observation, honed after years of diligent animal husbandry, detected something off balance in the young pup's way of going. "What's the matter, Girlie?"

Checking her feed bowl, he saw that she hadn't cleaned up her breakfast. "That's not like you, Molly. Don't you like my cooking?" Usually, she liked it very much. Usually, Molly was on a diet, but not now. Now; for the past few days; he had been trying to get her to eat. Checking for worms, he noticed none in her stool; her warm, dry nose and sad eyes told him she hadn't recently touched the fresh water bucket he so religiously kept filled for her and for every other dog in the kennel. Resolving to try cooked hamburger and rice, he decided to check her temperature after making the rounds and moved on to the stud kennel.

"Baron!" he called out.

Why hadn't Baron come running outside to greet him?

"Baron?" he called, entering the building he had transformed from a deserted chicken coop into a respectable kennel facility. "Baron!"

But there was no response. The beautiful head of the dark champion with the faint white blaze between deep and curious eyes did not appear. Was he gone? Had he somehow disappeared during the night? Searching, walking faster now,

Robert checked the kennel gate; still latched. Inside the building, his chest becoming tighter with each step, he searched out the stall on which the gold nameplate bearing the name "Ch. Sheffield Baron" was nailed.

Please be here, my friend, Robert thought to himself. *Please don't leave me.*

It had always been like that, he thought. Always, when he really began loving something; when it really mattered, it was taken away from him. A whimper brought him back to the matter at hand.

"Is that you, Boy?" he asked, falling to his knees beside the listless Collie. "What's wrong, fella?" he said, gathering the luxuriously coated animal in his arms, knowing whatever had stricken the puppy had reached Baron, too. There's no time to waste, he told himself – *hurry!*

"What is it?" Esmeralda asked, when his call came.

"Distemper," Robert said, hardly able to believe every dog in his kennel must fight for its life now against the deadly virus. "Oh, God," he said, his voice hoarse, like a man struck with disbelief; a man facing the impossible. "I'm losing them; *everything I've worked for!*"

"But, how?" she asked. "How did it happen?"

"I don't know," he sobbed, unashamed; "*I don't know!*"

"But, Robert - how serious is it?"

"It's the most deadly virus they know. There's no cure."

"But, there has to be! You can't just lose your whole kennel like this - you can't!"

"But, I am," he sobbed. "I am!"

"No! I won't let you - I won't let this happen!" she said, pacing side to side, reaching for a paper - "Where are you, Robert? Tell me!"

"No!" he said, fighting for his pride; for the right thing to do. "Stay away. You have one of my good puppies. You have to stay away. Both of you. You and Blanche."

"But, I can't, Robert! You can't be alone right now, don't you see that? You need help. Who's going to help you with the dogs? Who's going to help you take care of them?"

"The neighbors," he said, grateful for her words; her comfort. "I've already asked them."

"The people who own the farm?" she asked.

"Yes," he said. "You have to stay away until the vet says it's safe."

"I will," she said, desperate for him, wishing she had told him so, wondering why she hadn't by now, when she knew he loved her; despising herself for being so afraid. "I will," she said, twisting her necklace; hanging up slowly as the young neighbor and his dog hiked up the road to Robert's place.

In jeans and flannel shirt, he was a typical farmer; his muscular body more appealing than his face would ever be, even with the help of a beard to hide the scar. It was a scar that set him apart from others; embarrassed him.

"Seen you had company last night," he said to Robert, later, as they scrubbed floors, feed dishes and water bowls with disinfectant. "Pretty?"

Detecting a certain underlying tone, perhaps too much interest behind the question crafted by one getting the most out of every word, Robert just clicked his tongue and tilted his head. "A gentleman never tells," he said.

"You get yourself lots of company," the neighbor went on, as Robert soaked dog combs and brushes in hot soapy water.

"Just lucky," Robert said, feeling the neighbor's eyes on him as the man boldly compared them.

"They like you, don't they" the young man asked, careful with his words; wanting to know more.

"I guess so," Robert smiled, offering nothing.

"*Pussy,*" the young man licked his lips, saying no more. Nodding, he let the thought dangle between them; the scent; the feel of a woman.

Brushing it off, Robert paused and asked, "Can you hand me those leashes and collars on the table over there? The vet says we have to disinfect anything the dogs touched."

Standing up, crossing the room and returning in almost one, smooth motion, Nathan Miller was one whose way of carrying himself stood out in a crowd.

Surely, this young man would never be alone, thought Robert, feeling somewhat insecure as Nathan squatted directly in front of him and dropped the leashes into the water. "They like you," he said, looking directly into Robert's face.

The dogs, you mean? Robert wanted to ask, knowing it wasn't what Nathan wanted to hear. No, he didn't want to hear that at all. Again, Robert just smiled and, for a moment, thought of Esmeralda. If Nathan thought of a woman like Esmeralda strictly as *pussy*, then he had no comprehension of what else adorned her soul. If men like Nathan thought, even for one moment, they stood a chance with a woman like her, they would have to grab him by the shoulders, throw him bodily against the wall and kick the last drop of blood right out of him.

"If you ever want to share," Nathan said, with a wide nasty grin, "let me know."

"Right now, the only thing I want is to know how the dogs got this," Robert said, bringing him down.

"*Sheee-it,*" said Nathan, as if to mean *what's more important than women?*

Ignoring him; washing, scrubbing, wiping down walls, floors, windows; Robert asked himself how it was possible for the dogs to come down with distemper when none of them had even left the grounds? How was it carried, he wondered? Could he have brought distemper into the kennel himself? How long was the incubation period?

He thought back. Had he noticed any dogs showing signs of illness at the shows? As a judge, roving his hands over their bodies, checking their mouths, moving from one dog to the next, had he inadvertently spread the fatal disease? Pray, no, he thought, his stomach queasy.

"Nathan," he asked. "Have any of the farms around here ever had an outbreak like this?"

"None that I know of," Nathan said, his mind centering on the task at hand.

Wondering if perhaps people hadn't recognized the symptoms, Robert asked, "Snotty noses? Sneezing?" His question drew a blank. *Where had it come from?*

"The dairy down the road had a cow that didn't make it," Nathan said.

Not sure if cows could carry the disease, Robert asked, "What about any cats? Dogs?"

Nathan shook his head. "The only thing I can think – "he finally said, then stopped, as if remembering something that hadn't seemed to matter before this.

Robert dreaded what might come; what he might hear; what might be the missing clue.

"Well," said Nathan, as if it didn't matter; couldn't possibly matter; "our dog, there" he nodded in the direction of a matted spaniel sniffing around the yard outside, "well, she might of had herself a cold for a while. But, she got over it, then. Do you think maybe she might have died from it, too?"

As the full impact of what he had just heard washed over him; swirled through his brain and sunk in, Robert's hands dropped as far as his heart.

Fourteen of the Sheffield Collies had been affected; most would not make it and six were dead; as dead as soldiers never knowing what hit them, in the war spreading all over the world; the war no one had ever believed could happen.

Chapter 2

It was 1945. Germany had surrendered and the War in Europe was over. As Johnny Mercer sang "Ac-cent-tchu-ate The Positive," John Rait bowed to standing ovations in Broadway's "Carousel" and Joan Crawford won her Oscar for "Mildred Pierce." Those who could were rushing to their loved ones, those who couldn't were writing letters and a Scot-tish Terier named Ch. Shieling's Signa-ture had just won Westminster. . . .

Stock Exchange

. . . Some of us are lucky; some aren't. Esmeralda was one of the lucky ones. After her mother left town, for reasons best kept behind locked bedroom doors, Jason von Havenburg had continued to run the flourishing fan belt factory, smoking cigars and betting at the races; flashing hundred dollar bills at a time when Americans stood in bread lines. Wearing tailor-made suits and

spit-shined Italian shoes, the self-pro-
moter doting on his only child never
missed a beat, never missed a chance to
flirt with shady ladies, never missed a
trick in building his empire. Unfortun-
ately, Jason von Havenburg did miss a
doctor appointment or two along the way
and met an untimely death half-way
between New York prime rib and champagne
while being tickled with a feather boa.
Exactly where he was being tickled, we
shall never know; who did it remained a
mystery. Who would have guessed Big
Jason, so careful to provide for the
management of the factory in his daugh-
ter's best interests; and a generous
allowance for her mother as long as she
stayed abroad; was allergic to birds?

"It's from your mother!" Mrs.
Harrington said, waving the telegram for
Esmeralda to see.

From London? Hoping; frightened;
Esmeralda hurried from her desk.

"*She's safe!*" Esmeralda cried, with
relief and tears. "She wants to see me!"
she screamed, holding on to the telegram;
the only link to her mother. Eyes wide,
she looked to Mrs. Harrington as if for
advice. "I was so scared!" she said, falling to the sofa, exhausted from worry;
"I have to go to her."

"Can I do anything to help?" Mrs.
Harrington asked. "Do you need help making the arrangements?"

"I don't know," Esmeralda said,
sitting up. "It's been so long since I've
traveled abroad. I haven't thought - ."

119

A month wouldn't be nearly long e-
nough to make all the arrangements, she
realized. Securing passage by ship,
catching up on everything her mother
might want or need to say, and then returning to the States. A month would
hardly be enough time at all. *Robert . .
. Robert!* She would tell him tonight,
after everything was arranged, when it
was too late for him to change her mind.
He would understand. He would understand
her need to see her mother. And when she
returned, they could finally plan their
wedding.

"Blanche can run the fashion business herself for a while . . . " she
said. *One down, she thought.* Blanche
would love being in charge. She could
deal with the buyers directly and they
would like her.

"Jack'll be in charge of the farm
while I'm gone," she said. *Nothing to
think about there.*

"And, of course, you'll be in
charge of the household."

"You'll be missed," Mrs. Harrington
said.

"I'll be all right, Janet," Esmeralda said, returning to her desk. Ships
would surely be crowded by people wanting
to reunite with their loved ones. If she
was to leave, she must hurry, she
thought, picking up the phone as, busy in
her shop, Blanche pulled the thread once
more and knotted it discreetly behind the
button. *Classy*, Blanche thought to
herself, imagining the model on the
runway as the fabric swayed with her walk

and the row of dark buttons drew attention to her thigh.

Joan Crawford could pull it off, she thought, picturing a matching set of earrings and a dark hat. Oh, yes . . . Joan would know how to work this one.

Assuring herself that, one day, she would have the chance to meet the great star, Blanche answered the call batting her eyes with a dreamy, " . . . *Hello? . . . Oh, it's you, dahling . . . how absolutely divine . . .* "

"Blanche, I've heard from my mother."

"All the way from London? What a voice!"

"She sent a telegram," Esmeralda said, not laughing. "She wants me to come see her."

"What! You can't do that! We've got a show to get ready for. Say, what is this? You skippin' out on our deal or something?"

"No," Esmeralda said. "I'd never do that."

"Then, why don't you stay?"

"Because I haven't seen my mother since before the War, and who knows when I might ever see her again."

"What about the business," Blanche asked. "Who's gonna take care of the books and make all the arrangements?" she wanted to know.

"I've already taken care of that," she said. "You and Robert can look after the business while I'm away and when I get back I'll be the happiest friend you ever saw. How's that?"

121

About as good as putting a cat in a cage with a canary, Blanche thought. "Don't you worry, Hon. I'll take care of Robert," she smiled. "How soon do you leave?"

"I was able to book passage on the first ship out of New York. I'm packing now; there's no time to waste."

"Well, don't forget anything. Oh, what am I saying?" Blanche fretted. "I'll be right over!"

The next half-hour was spent calling the vet, the pharmacy and various tradesmen in order to assure the estate would run smoothly while she was away. "One last call," she sighed, as the doorbell rang and Mrs. Harrington admitted Blanche into the room. If she was to be gone for any length of time, Esmeralda must allow Kenneth Gehman, at the office, to know. As its largest stockholder now, there might be important papers for her to sign and he must be kept apprised.

"Mr. Gehman's office," the secretary answered, as Blanche held up a dress for Esmeralda's approval before putting it in a traveling bag.

"Maria? May I speak with Kenneth, please?" Esmeralda said, giving Blanche the nod to the evening gown. Knowing Mumsie, she would need an ample mix of casual and formal both. "Pack as many Blanche' clothes as you can," she whispered, holding a hand over the receiver.

Recognizing Esmeralda's voice, Maria DePerot, a slim, Brethren woman in her perpetual thirties, smiled. "Of

122

course, Miss von Havenburg. If you hold a second, I'll put you right through."

"Kenneth?" Esmeralda asked, almost able to smell his cigar.

"Esmeralda!" the president of VH Belting Corporation exclaimed with surprise. "How are you today? Is everything all right?" he asked, in his Bostonian accent.

"Oh, I'm fine, Kenneth. I wanted to call and let you know I'm leaving for London."

"Are you sure that's wise?" he asked.

"Oh, yes," Esmeralda answered. "I'm going to see my mother," she said, as Blanche wrapped a blouse around her head like a turban and acted high style.

Clamping a hand over the receiver again, Esmeralda whispered loudly, *"She's not like that at all!"*

"Are you planning to be back in time for the stockholders' meeting?" she heard Mr. Gehman ask and returned to him.

"I'm not sure when that is," she said, reaching for a calendar and turning away from Blanche to avoid laughing.

"The Fifteenth of next month," came his answer.

"The Fifteenth? Oh!" Esmeralda said, disappointment showing in her voice. Behind her back, Blanche made a sad face; then went around and stood right in front of her to make sure Ez saw it.

"Of course, if it would be easier, I can vote for you by proxy," he offered, knowing Esmeralda, like her father, would think it over before making any decision requiring her to put faith in someone else.

"I haven't seen my mother since the war," she said weakly, turning away from Blanche, considering what it might mean if she were to entrust her holdings in his care. "Is there anything important to vote on?" she asked, shooshing Blanche away with her hand.

"Well, there's always something important," he said. "We had a loss every quarter for the last two years," he reminded her. "but, most companies in the car business believe we're on the verge of a real boom once people start buying again. Not that new cars are the customer for us," he added. "But, if they aren't buying new cars, where are the old ones that need a belt coming from?"

"What else, Kenneth?" she asked, sensing his concern; knowing he'd tell her.

"It's some of the employees," he said. Was he lowering his voice or was something wrong with their connection, she wondered?

"Is it anything I should know?" she asked. "Can you tell me?" At the seriousness in her voice, Blanche turned her full attention to packing. When it came to Esmeralda's other business, she stayed out of it. Unless she couldn't resist.

"Of course I can," Gehman said, reassuring the little girl he had seen grow into a responsible young woman building her life and her future. "They want more money."

"Why? Aren't we paying a decent wage?"

"Sure," he said.

"But?" she asked.

"They want more."

"Fire them," she said. "Give the jobs to people who appreciate what my Daddy built."

"It's not that easy," he said. "When your father took the company public to raise money and keep us afloat before the war started, it left us wide open for a take-over."

"Take over? From another company, you mean?"

"That's always a possibility," Kenneth said, inhaling and holding it a moment while considering his next statement. "But, right now, not likely."

"Then, what are you concerned about?" she asked, wrapping the long phone chord around her finger as she began pacing the floor.

"Some of the employees have been buying stock and they hired an attorney. They're going to be at the meeting. And I think we may be in for a fight."

"Never!" she said. "*Never*. Call their attorney and offer to buy the stock back," she said.

Surprised by her sudden determination; by the fact that she hadn't even stopped to consider her decision; he asked, "Do you know what you're saying?"

"I believe I do," she answered, resolved.

"I didn't say how many shares we're talking about."

125

"I didn't ask," she said.

"Will you be calling your banker?" he wanted to know.

"Yes," she said. "Good-bye, Kenneth. I'm calling right now."

"What's wrong?" Blanche wanted to know. Until now, she had never seen Esmeralda so purposeful; driven by a force bigger than herself that no one else could comprehend.

"It's the factory," Esmeralda said. "I don't know if I should leave right now."

"But, you've got to," Blanche said. "Mrs. Harrington got your tickets and the ship leaves tomorrow."

She had to make a decision. She had to save her father's company from any chance of a take over. Did he know, she wondered. *Daddy, did you know that by going on the stock exchange you could lose control of the whole company?*

Of course he didn't. He would never have allowed such a thing to happen - and neither must she. Anxious now, fighting back the impulse to hide behind the team of advisors and financial experts with whom she was surrounded; knowing her father would never have done that; she dialed her banker, then hung up.

"Blanche?" she asked suddenly, catching the budding fashion maven holding a row of straight pins between her lips. "If your father had started a business, and it grew into a big company, and it was in trouble, what would you do about it?"

"Depends on what kind of business and what I had to work with," Blanche answered, speaking as best she could. "If it was my father, that wouldn't be much."

"What if it was a fan belt factory and you had plenty."

"In that case, I'd pull out all the stops, that's what I'd do. Nobody'd get their hands on what my Daddy built!"

Picking up the phone, Esmeralda dialed again.

"It's Esmeralda von Havenburg," she said. "I'd like to speak with Mr. Kraybill."

"Mr. Kraybill is in a meeting," the woman said.

"I see. In that case, can I speak with someone else in the Trust Department?"

"Certainly," the woman said. "I'll transfer you to Mr. Shelly's office; that would be Mr. Kraybill's assistant."

"Thank you," Esmeralda said, scribbling on a piece of paper, knowing she had never met the man, wondering if her message would get through.

"George Shelly speaking," a cool voice said. "What can I do for you, Miss von Havenburg?"

"I'd like to buy some stock," she said.

"All right," he answered, ready to take a note. "What are you looking to buy?"

"VH Belting," she said.

Silence. "May I ask what for?" he said, putting down his pen.

Knowing he wanted to know why she would buy stock in a company she already controlled; unwilling to impart that information, she said, "For twice the value."

"Twice the value?" he asked.

"Yes."

"How many shares do you want to buy?" he asked.

"Every share authorized by Kenneth Gehman," she said, hanging up. The decision was made. It was final. She would go to London; Kenneth would look after her interests.

A month, possibly more, without Robert, she thought now. Would he miss her? What would he say when he found out? She had to tell him; she would let him know tonight, after the movie.

"Blanche, are you staying over?"

"Sure, Honey. Everything OK?"

"It will be," Esmeralda said. "Robert and I are going out this evening; an opening at a gallery. I'll tell him about the trip over dinner. Can you help me pick out something special to wear?"

"A month?" Robert asked, his eyes questioning hers as they parked along the lake that night. She hadn't been able to tell him over dinner.

"Probably longer," she said, knowing that to mislead him would be unfair.

"Esmeralda," he said . . . "I know I don't have a right to ask. Not yet, anyway," he smiled. "But, don't go."

If eyes could plead any more deeply than his she would fall to her knees, her face to the cold floor and never move; never even breathe for a hundred million years. They were alone. Dinner and the opening had been wonderful; she might have told Blanche about it, if she had thought such things would interest her. . . . but not now. Now, she just wanted to feel Robert's arm around her, making her feel safe . . . the feel of his hand on her leg making her feel wanted . . . the heat of his fingers moving under her skirt . . . .

"If you go," he whispered, skimming the tips of his fingers along the inside of her thighs. "I won't ever sleep. How can you sleep without dreams? . . . I won't hear you laughing," he said, kissing her hair, "or feel you next to me like this . . ." He loved the smell of her hair, her skin. He kissed her ear, ran his tongue along its edges, sucked it. A pleasant chill went through her . . . . "Mmmmm," she breathed, relaxing into him, feeling safe here, in his car.

"Hmmmm," he answered, nibbling at the back of her neck . . . sending shivers down her spine. "I love you, Esmeralda . . . *love you.*"

"Are you sure?" she wanted to know, playing with the buttons of his shirt. "What if I'm a monster? What if, under these clothes I'm ugly?" He had never undressed her.

"I love you," he whispered. "You would be beautiful every minute, every hour, every day of my life." She loved the way he smiled when he was kissing her; like it was their special, playful secret.

"Maybe I'm really a man," she said, teasing. "I feel like one sometimes."

"You're not a man," he said, guiding her down on the seat. "I'd better find out," he smiled. Yes, she loved the crinkles at his eyes.

"And if I was?" she asked, looking up at him.

"I'd love you anyway," he said, easing himself on top, sliding both hands under her skirt now and pulling off her panties. His hands; knowing what they wanted, where they were going; palms and fingers under her ass, thumbs slipping up and down her vagina . . . . Was it wrong? Was it wrong to be doing this? How did he know what to do, she wondered? Was a man born knowing? Is that what he meant just now?

He was smiling; not about her; not at her, like at some private amusement in which one might take pleasure. No, he was smiling . . . *with her*. Again, she looked into his eyes; this time, instead of holding back, worrying what he might think, what she might think, what anyone else might think if they should ever find out, she let herself feel. Simply . . . feel.

His lips on her face, her mouth; his tongue skimming across her teeth as she felt that smile again and met it with her own . . . . No words were said, yet she felt as if she understood him, and she was sure; yes, she was sure he

130

understood her. He did. She knew he did. She knew by the feel of him against her, on top of her; she wanted to see – *oh, she wanted to see* – how could it possibly fit into her? She reached down and touched his penis, bigger now than it ever looked when covered by his pants. How could a man walk like that, she wondered? But, he isn't walking now, she told herself. He's with me. Spreading her legs, she ran both hands up and down his back, pushed under his belt and felt his ass. Her arms were long enough to reach the whole way and her touch excited him. Lifting her hips, pressing her melting vagina against his hot erection, she could feel him at her . . . pushing . . . hesitating . . . pulling back. His eyes; she looked at his eyes in the shadows of the car and it seemed as if their souls had found each other in a sea of loneliness; a sea as wide as the one that would take her away from him now. *I want to remember this,* she thought, feeling him enter her again, pushing into her; sure of himself now; deeper; deeper – how deep? – falling into her; taking the leap of faith into her arms. *I want to remember this as long as I live!* Shoving her hands up under his shirt, digging her nails into his back, scratching, thrashing her head side to side as he forced himself farther – deeper, harder – she sank her teeth into his shoulder and found his rhythm. Rotating in tight circles, he pressed against her clitoris and kept the pressure firm; his fingers, smooth and wet from the natural lubrication of her own body, played with her in a way she had never felt before. Don't stop - *don't you dare stop!*

Moaning, hissing, breathing hard like a proud stallion - afraid of nothing - laughing with delight! - he flew out of himself, into the heavens. And she . . . she was with him. For that one, electrical instant, as time stood still for them, she was truly, eternally, beside him, around him, above him, inside him, all over him . . . *she was with him.*

The Takeover . . . *Of course being with someone and being "with" them are two completely different things. Music of the night has a way of vanishing under the harsh spotlight of the morning sun. Nevertheless, as she took her place at the breakfast table, different now in a way she knew there would be no way to turn back, Esmeralda wondered if anyone might notice. Did she walk differently; talk different? Was there anything about her that Blanche or Mrs. Harrington might notice? If there was; if men had the power to transform a woman in such a way that others could see it; she must know . . . .*

"How's the gallery district these days?" Blanche asked, over orange juice and toast.

Mrs. Harrington set a plate of eggs in front of Esmeralda, saying "Just the way you like them."

132

"Thank you, Janet," Esmeralda said. The world was a beautiful place today, she thought to herself. It would be good to see London again; good to hug her mother.

"Oh, it was fine!" she smiled to Blanche.

"See anything interesting?" Blanche asked. "Any new artists I might want to meet?"

"Not really . . . " Esmeralda answered, biting into a blueberry muffin, resisting the impulse to tell about the most incredible night of her life.

"We got most of the packing done," Blanche said. "Me an' Janet."

Esmeralda nodded and finished her orange juice.

"The rest, you're gonna have to do yourself," Blanche said.

Again, Esmeralda nodded, secure in Robert's love; hoping Blanche would forgive her winning this battle.

"Are you scared?" Blanche wanted to know, hating to admit she would miss the friend she had met just a few short years ago.

"I don't have time to be scared," Esmeralda said. "I have to be at the train station in Lancaster in just a few hours."

"Well, I don't think we forgot anything; we followed your list, and, I guess, you can buy just about anything else you really need, once you're over there." Why was the corner of her eye stinging, she wondered, touching it; a gesture not unnoticed.

"Why, Blanche," Esmeralda smiled, pleased. "Is that a tear?"

"Who, me?" Blanche said, acting surprised. "Honey, I can't wait to get you out of my way so I can start livin' again," she lied.

"I'll go upstairs and finish packing," Esmeralda said, leaning over and kissing Blanche on the cheek as she left. "Janet can help me with a few last-minute things. Why don't you come up after you're finished with breakfast?"

"No, I gotta get back into town and help with the shop."

"This is good-bye, then?" Esmeralda asked.

"Well, don't put it like that," Blanche said, as they hugged. "Or, I'll really start bawlin'."

It didn't show, Esmeralda thought to herself, relieved, as she went upstairs to throw last minute things into a traveling bag. No one could tell.

Outside, Blanche tossed her things on the seat, revved the engine and turned on the radio to the woeful wail of Billie Holiday's "Lover Man (Oh, Where Can You Be)." If she stepped on it, she would be at the shop just in time to turn on the lights and unlock the door. Driving out the tree-lined driveway, away from the life becoming more important to her than she had ever thought, she slammed on her brakes.

Robert!

With a quick look at herself in the rear view mirror, she called out, "How ya doin', Hamdsome?"

Pulling up beside her, obviously on his way to the mansion, he said, "I thought I'd wish Esmeralda a *bon voyage!*"

"Too late," Blanche thought, quickly. "She packed last night and she's already gone. You're wasting your time - I was just there, myself." Well, at least *most* of it was true, she reasoned with herself. If he believed her, it was his own fault, she thought. "Hey, don't be too sad about it," she said, trying to sound as comforting as she could. "She said I was supposed to tell you good-bye," she added, feeling just a bit guilty and wondering where that sensation ever came from.

"Hey, I know!" she sparkled. "How about you an' me go back to your place and you can tell me all about Collies? You know, I've been thinkin' about it, Robert, an' I've decided you're right. I could make a real go of this thing. Why, I could set up my own kennel, just like Esmeralda if I had the place and knew the right stuff. Even better! I'll bet I could make all kinds of champions if I had somebody smart like yourself tellin' me what to do . . . ."

Paul Shelly finished shaving, put on a fresh white shirt and knotted his tie. Assessing himself in the mirror, he might have passed for a millionaire. Assessing his bank account; well, he'd rather not think about that.

Twice the value, she had said. Feeling a bit uneasy for not telling his boss right away, he totaled up the face value of VH Belting shares he'd just bought and multiplied by two. By the time Esmeralda's letter arrived at the office, authorizing the bank to buy from her trust fund, he'd be on Easy Street.

"This is interesting," Walter Kraybill said, a couple of days later. "A message from Esmeralda von Havenburg saying she's going on a trip and she authorized us to release the funds to buy up VH Belting shares. It came in yesterday."

Setting aside the papers he was working on, Shelly leaned forward, curious. "How high are we supposed to go?" he asked.

"Twice the value, it says."

"Twice the value? Are you sure?"

"That's what she says," Kraybill answered, reaching for the phone. "Whatever Ken Gehman wants. I think I'll call Gehman right now and see what's up. We've got a Hell of a lot of money in that trust fund."

News of the Day . . . As atomic mushroom clouds billowed up from Hiroshima, polluting mankind forever, Esmeralda came back from London to find two slick bank employees gone on early retirement; an assembly line of smiling new workers at the factory; her portfolio bursting with shares of VH Belting and her trust fund gravely depleted. But nothing - nothing in the skies of Heaven or the oceans of

136

Earth - could have prepared her for the devastating news from Mrs. Harrington. While she was gone; while she was so far away nothing she could have done would have stopped it; the most fragile thing in her life - more important than money, a mansion, or any city in the world - had been lost. Blanche and Robert, in an effort to beat the stork . . . had married.

NEWSREEL: 1946 . . . . The United Nations is official; the world's first computer is created and Ethel Merman heads the Broadway cast of "Annie Get Your Gun." Frederic March takes home an Oscar for "The Best Years of our Lives;" and to the sound of The Dixie Hummingbirds singing "Amazing Grace," a Wire Fox Terrier named Ch. Hetherinton Model Rhythm wins Westminster . . . .

Back in Havenburg, Blanche' Creations reverts to sole proprietorship; The Havenburg Gazette cries "Local Heiress Opts Out: Says, 'My Heart Belongs to Daddy.'"

NEWSREEL: 1947 . . . . Jackie Robinson breaks baseball's color barrier; Ella Logan and David Wayne star in "Finian's Rainbow" and ticket buyers line up to see Elia Kazan's "Gentleman's Agreement." To the Author's delight, E. P. Dutton & Co. renews the copyright for Albert Payson Terhune's "Lad: A Dog;" Sarah Vaughan's jazz single "If You Could See Me Now" spins on everybody's record player and a classy Boxer named Ch. War-

lord of Mazelaine is strutting his way to victory at Westminster . . . .

In Southeastern Pennsylvania, the papers scream, "Local Designer Submits Costume to Mae West For Upcoming Movie Project. Ex-Partner von Havenburg Says, 'If It's Good Enough For West, It's Good Enough For Any Body.'"

NEWSREEL: 1948 . . . . The Soviets stun what remains of international sensibilty and erect a wall through the heart of Berlin. Laurence Olivier wins the Oscar for "Hamlet;" Edward R. Murrow releases the spoken word album "I Can Hear It Now;" and a graceful Bedlington Terrier named Ch. Rock Ridge Night Rocket charms Westminster . . .

The Havenburg Gazette says, "Local Heiress Heads to London To Visit Ailing Mother. Hopes To See The Queen. Dog Show Maven And Ex-Partner Jacobus Quips, 'If It's A Queen She Wants, She Should Have Stuck With Me!'"

NEWSREEL: 1949 . . . . Mao Tse-tung launches the Peoples Republic of China and Nationalists flee for Taiwan; Broderick Crawford and Olivia deHaviland each win Oscars; Broadway applauds "Kiss Me Kate." On the jukebox, Hank Williams sings "I'm So Lonesome I Could Cry" and another Boxer Ch. Mazelaine Zazarac Brandy wins Westminster. In Philadelphia, society pages scream: "They're Back!" as Esmeralda poses for photographers in a Blanche' Original.

Chapter 3

It was 1950. America sent troops to defend South Korea; Judy Holliday won Best Actress for "Born Yesterday;" and Bette Davis was starring in "All About Eve." "Guys And Dolls" was cramming every seat on Broadway, and, to the Country sounds of Hank Snow strumming "I'm Movin' On," another Scottish Terrier, this one named Ch. Walsing Winning Trick of Edgerstoune, took the honors at Westminster.

Another Opening, Another Show

Life in Havenburg, Pennsylvania, blurred into a smear of color like oil paints thinned over a canvas of many layers and Blanche' Creations, once the bright dream of two young women, didn't quite happen. Exactly how Esmeralda managed to keep her friendship with Blanche going in spite of losing Robert was just as much a mystery to some as her reasons why. Maybe that's all there was to it; they were her rea-

sons, no one else's. Then again, maybe it was just the only way she could still see him. The factory rolled on, the town prospered, and on the world stage, dog shows embraced their clowns, their actors and lovers every weekend.

"*Oh . . . my . . . GOD!*" a short-haired woman in loose fitting clothes shrieked with laughter. "I don't BELIEVE it! Did you see what just happened!"

"*Hoooo-weee!*" a man whistled. "I've heard of using BAIT, but this is WILD! *Those buttons popped right off!*"

"Did you see that lady flash her tits!" somebody said loudly.

Hiding her breasts, Esmeralda bravely fought back tears and tried holding her dog in one hand while keeping her blouse shut and baiting him with the other. "Please, *PLEASE* be the kind of man who doesn't care about this, she thought, of the young Ring Steward scrambling to pick up buttons for her in the grass.

"Are you OK?" he asked politely, with an unmistakable breathless quality as Esmeralda blushed and he handed over what he could salvage. Speechless; unable to look him in the eye; she offered her dog's lead.

"*Get me out of here,*" she whispered hoarsely, thankful her prayers had been answered.

"Sure," the young man said, offering his jacket. "Right this way."

On the way back to Blanche's "Show Biz" truck, where Esmeralda kept her Extra Change, they passed a row of vendors hawking wares.

"Whatsa matter, Ez?" a familiar voice called out from behind a table stacked with leashes and collars. "Falling apart again?"

"I've never been so embarrassed!"

"Sure you have. At Robert's place, remember? Our first time there. Aw, come on, Ez; just harmless fun. You don't need any more points on that dog anyhow. How many times can you make the same dog a champion?"

"I want him to be the best in the country."

"Yeah, well you gotta make it past Blanche' Kennels first - and that ain't easy."

"Are you saying your dogs are better than mine?"

"Ez, I don't have to," Blanche smiled. "I got a judge at home who tells me so every night. Oh! *You're good*, Baby." She imitated Robert. "You're *real good!*"

Stung, Esmeralda hurried to the back of the truck, flung herself inside and buried her face in her hands.

"What am I going to do! How am I ever going to live this down?" she cried, looking around for her suitcase. Snapping it open, she gasped in disbelief. "My clothes!" she cried, rattling through shoes, make-up and hairbrushes. "They're gone!" Spotting a bright pink envelope bearing her name in familiar, flowery script, she fumed, "NOW what!" as she ripped it open wishing it was a *familiar somebody's* throat.

"*Surprise!*" it said. "*Business is good and we don't need the Extra Change any more. How about you try on that pretty yellow number hanging in the bag behind the seat. Just your size and this one don't need buttons - it's got a ZIPPER!*"

Across the way, Esmeralda's kennel man, Jack Milliken, and his blonde wife, Faye, looked up from grooming Blanche's entry in the Open Sable class.

"That's odd," Faye said. "Wasn't Esmeralda wearing a white blouse?"

As he finished scissoring a perfect outline along the dog's ankle, Jack asked, "What are you looking at?"

"Over there, in the yellow dress. I think she's crying." Faye stood, hands at her sides, floundering for the right thing to do.

Putting down his scissors, Milliken squinted his blue eyes and straightened a cap on his dark hair. "Well, let's find out." Walking to the other side of his trailer, he called out to his young helper, a fresh-faced teenager with curly brown hair, freckles and brown eyes. "Nancy?" he said, as she busily fluffed and powdered the coat of a classy Sable and White pup. "You keep an eye on the dogs 'til we get back. OK?"

"Sure thing!"

As they made their way past rows of cars, house trailers, barking dogs and people scurrying to their classes, Faye remarked, "What would an attractive woman like Esmeralda have to cry about? Something's wrong, Jack."

"Maybe we should stay out of it."

"She's our friend."

"Everything OK, Ezzie?" Jack asked.

Startled, she jumped.

"Would you like to freshen up in the trailer?" Faye asked. "I have some lemonade. Or, maybe some coffee?"

"Oh!" Esmeralda said, wiping her eyes and running a hand through her hair. "I'm OK, really."

"Are you sure?" Faye asked.

Esmeralda nodded. "Well, at least I'll be OK if everybody who saw what happened in the ring just now can only forget."

"What happened?" Faye asked.

Nothing!

"Well, for something that was nothing, you don't seem too happy," Jack smiled. "Whatever it was, it can't be worse than the time my dog lifted his leg and took a piss on the judge's pants!"

Esmeralda grinned. "You never told me that."

"See?" Faye said. "You're feeling better already."

"Me name's Jack Milliken," he said, in a Blarney accent, tipping his hat and feigning introduction.

"Esmeralda von Havenburg," she answered, laughing at the playfulness of her own kennel manager pretending to be such a stranger. "I have Collies," she clowned, glancing at the dog by her side.

143

"So I've heard," Faye said, picking up on their game. "Why, I don't think I've ever seen a Collie so elegant."

"Thank you," Esmeralda said. "But, if you knew my friend Blanche, she wouldn't agree."

"Blanche Sheffield?" Jack asked, keeping up the facade. "Isn't she one of our clients, Faye?"

"I *think* so," Faye said, eyes twinkling.

"She is?" Esmeralda said, putting on airs. "Well, then you must be the ones making such a difference for her now. You know, she's just *raving* about you."

"Thanks," said Jack. "We have our own way of doing things."

"A good handler is more than a good groomer. You have to work with the whole dog," Faye said. "You should see Jack. He gets up early, around five and makes sure every dog on the place is walked – "

"Uphill is best," said Jack. "We have some great trails near our place. We live in a mansion, you know."

Esmeralda laughed.

"Oh, yes. Everything's perfect in our world," he smiled. "Nothing like a mountain trail to get a dog in shape."

"Physically and mentally," Faye added. "That's where it's at for us at Loch Ness-wood. Yes, up in the morning, work all day, work them doggies! And our boss; what a Monster!"

"Yeah," Jack pitched in. "That boss of ours. Talk about tough!"

"Is she looking for help?" Esmeralda asked.

144

"I don't know. She's pretty tight when it comes to a penny," he teased. "And don't go thinking you could get away with sleeping late - oh, no. The dogs need their morning exercise!"

"That must explain why I've noticed such a difference in Blanche's dogs lately. They're brighter; more interested in life." Esmeralda quipped.

"Because they're fit," said Faye. "Dogs are natural-born athletes. Do you play tennis?"

"Yes. I love tennis."

"Then you know what I mean."

"Oh, I understand very well. I just don't see why I never related it to my dogs."

"Lots of people don't think their dogs need exercise," Jack said. "But, if you touch the average show dog raised by somebody who just feeds him and lets him lay around the house, then put your hands on one of ours - a dog we've fed and worked and conditioned ourselves - you'll feel the difference right away."

"Can you show me?" Esmeralda asked, enjoying their farce.

"Sure," Faye smiled. "We can even let you see one of Blanche's dogs if you want to. Come on over to the trailer. We're right across the parking lot."

Clicking to the dog beside her, Esmeralda followed them to the trailer, surrounded by grooming tables, crates pinned with ribbons and exercise pens.

"We're back, Nancy!" Jack called out.

"Oh! Hi, Esmeralda!" Nancy hollered from where she was working.

"What?" Faye laughed to Esmeralda. "You mean someone here knows you? You're not an abandoned dog show child?"

"My cover's blown," Esmeralda said, wilting as she accepted a glass of lemonade.

"Oh, we knew it all along!" Faye said, still having fun. "Better now?" she asked. "And, by the way, where'd you get the pretty dress?"

Esmeralda sighed. "Blanche made it."

"Should have guessed."

"And I'm feeling much better now, thanks," Esmeralda said.

"It's almost time for the class," Nancy reminded everybody and pointed to the pup she had been working on. "Did anybody see the scissors for trimming whiskers?"

"Nancy, you should have done the whiskers last night," Jack said, handing over a pair.

"I did. But, I guess I missed a few."

"Well, hurry up," he said. "And don't make a mistake and cut into the hair. Class is in just a few minutes." Turning to Faye, he asked, "You takin' him in or am I?"

"I will. Unless Esmeralda wants to?"

Esmeralda shook her head and stepped back. "No, I think I've had enough of the ring for today, thank you."

"Well, how's he look?" Nancy asked, as proud as an artist unveiling her latest sculpture.

"Like a million," said Jack. "Nice job."

"I think it's that new conditioner you came up with," said Nancy. "It really makes the hair stand out when you spray it with mist. You ought to bottle that stuff and sell it. See?" she asked, spritzing her hair and primping.

"Faye's secret formula," Jack said, slipping a show lead over the young dog's lean head. "It sure makes a difference. Nancy? Can you bring out Blanche's bitch and get her ready for Veteran's?"

"He wants you to see her," Faye whispered to Esmeralda. "He's been trying something different with her."

Nancy disappeared to the other side of the trailer and returned with an immaculately groomed and well-mannered Tri-Color, about eight or nine years old.

"What do you think?" Jack asked. "Have you ever seen her looking so good?"

"Cookie?" Esmeralda asked, with genuine surprise. "Is that you?" If dog tails were helicopter blades, Cookie would have lifted off the ground. "She's gorgeous!" Esmeralda exclaimed. "What have you done?"

Faye stooped down and wrapped both arms around the dog's ruff. "Jack's been doing some reading and we've been trying out a few experiments. You've been busy and we didn't want to tell you until we were sure. Run your hands over this dog, Ez. Feel how rich her hair feels? How thick? Did you ever feel such a strong back on a Collie?"

"I see what you mean," Esmeralda said, surprised.

"Now feel your own dog. Feel how soft his back is and how easy it is to push down on him? You can't do that with Cookie. And Jack's only been working with her for about a month. She's as tough as a wolf."

"Her hair feels so stiff. What's the secret?"

"Secret? Feeding, for one thing. Jack's been feeding her fresh meat, vitamins and vegetables."

"Vegetables?"

"Green beans, spinach. Whatever she wants. You'd be surprised. She loves it."

"Raw meat? Won't a dog get sick? Salmonella?"

Faye scoffed. "What do you think they eat in the wild? *Fresh* meat?"

"Well, I never thought about it that way. So when were you going to tell me? I mean, if it's working for Blanche's dogs, what about our own?"

"She swore Jack to secrecy. You know how she gets."

"But, Jack's on OUR side!"

"And he always will be. But, he isn't going to miss out on *anything* that can give our dogs an advantage, you can bet your life on that. We had it all figured out. Her dogs were a test. We were going to talk to you about it, and I just did, right now, didn't I?"

"Well, how many of her dogs are on this diet?" Esmeralda wanted to know, curious.

"Just Cookie here, and the male Nancy's working on over there. That's Cookie's grandson out of Ch. Blanche' Beige."

"Oh, well," said Esmeralda. "We're a team, right? Anything one of us figures out, the rest of us end up doing, too. Blanche probably wanted to be sure it worked before all of our dogs went on the same plan. So, we switch over tomorrow - right, Faye?" She paused and reconsidered. "But, what about Blanche when she finds out?"

"It was Jack she swore to secrecy, not me," Faye smiled, as they both laughed. It was fun staying a step ahead of Blanche and her tricks. Feeling much better now, Esmeralda busied herself helping Nancy trim whiskers as Jack shuffled around for an armband. "Faye, can you give me a hand with this thing?" A few minutes later, a kiss for good luck and he was on his way.

"How long have you and Jack been married now?" Esmeralda asked.

"Five years," Faye said.

"Any plans for a family?"

"Hopefully soon," Faye smiled.

"Something tells me Jack'll be pleased about that."

"Oh, I know he will. He'll make a great father and he can't wait. Can't you just picture Jack with a little boy or girl in his arms? We've been trying, but no luck yet. Sunday's our Anniversary. I

149

want us to have the whole day to ourselves. A nice dinner, candles; a whole
day just for Jack and me."

"I'll have the gardener put a *Do
Not Disturb* sign on the cottage door,"
Esmeralda giggled. "And I'll supply the
champagne!"

Prelude to Disaster . . . There's
*nothing quite like a winning day to put
everyone in good spirits. By early
evening, Blanche' and von Havenburg Collies had cleaned up. The young Black and
White Springer, the White Miniature
Poodle and the female Pomeranian Jack and
Faye had brought along as favors for
other members of the Kennel Club had done
just as well. Laughing and swapping a
whole new arsenal of new battle stories,
everyone packed for home. It was magic!
It was as if everything they touched had
turned to gold. It was PARTY TIME!*

Popping open a bottle of '42 Dom
Perignon, Esmeralda giggled and smiled at
everybody. "I was *mortified!*" she said,
pouring freely as Blanche held out two
glasses and loudly made a toast. "And,
Honey, *that* judge'll never forget you!
Here's to friendship. An old Irish saying
I picked up somewhere – 'Here's to you
and here's to me; *May we never disagree.
And, if we ever disagree, then to Hell
with you,*" she drank, 'Here's to me!'
Like the dress, Ezzy?"

"Love it, Blanchie."

"Thought you would. Hey, did I show you my latest?" she asked, fumbling through a cardboard box of leashes, bows, doggie barrettes and rhinestones. "Get a load of *this!*" she said, tossing a beaded collar and barely missing Esmeralda's head. "Here! Put it on! You can wear it like a headband, or wear it around your neck and I can make one for your dog, too. I can even make a matching leash. It's a whole new direction for me. I'm really excited about it. What do you think?"

"Very Chi-chi. Where'd you get the idea?"

"Just came to me, Honey. Just came to me. When you're an artist, you never know what's gonna happen next."

"Hollywood doesn't know what it's missing."

"Well, Hollywood's gotta wait. I got myself a goin' business now and a string of champions. You oughtta stop over more, Ez, you really should. I don't know why you stay away like you do. Robert would love to see you around more."

Unable to help herself, Esmeralda flinched. Why did it feel as if her voice defiled him every time Blanche said his name?

"Yeah, he was askin' about you just the other day," Blanche fluffed her hair, running a pinkie finger back and forth across her lower lip to be sure the bright red color was evenly spread. "I said, I just can't figure Ez out some-times; that's what I said."

Esmeralda handed the collar back and looked away. "It's very nice, Blanche. Can I order half a dozen in black?"

"Honey, you can order as many as you want. Black? Why don't I spice 'em up a little for you? I know! I'll put some feathers in 'em, or bead 'em around a silk bandanna. I have some of the sheerest silk. I can wrap a string of beads around it and really make you something special. I'll even put sparkles on it. How's that?"

Esmeralda nodded and picked up her drink.

"Aw, Ez," Blanche said, slipping her arm through Esmeralda's and standing beside her. "I know. I know. Don't think you can hide it from me. I know how you still feel about Robert. It ain't no secret and, believe me, he's worth loving. Boy, is he worth loving. But, you can't hold a torch forever. You gotta face it. He made his choice and that's just the way it is now. It's not the two of you anymore. It's Robert an' me. That don't mean we can't all be friends. *We are!* Nothin's ever gonna stand between you and me, Ez. Nothing! That's a promise. No man. Not even Robert. Hey," she said, pinching Esmeralda's cheek. "Come on. So I'm the one who got the points today. So what! Next weekend's another show. Wanna help me pack up?"

Wrapping all her beads and paints, taking down shelves of leashes and collars, and loading up her truck could take Blanche hours.

"I think . . . I think I'll have a little more champagne." Esmeralda said, picking up the bottle.

As grooming tables were folded, dogs were locked in their heavy crates, and entries for the next show were checked and checked again, Jack stepped into his trailer and found his wife.

"It's getting dark," he said. "We'd better head on out if we want to feed on time back at the kennel. Everything buttoned down in here?"

"I think so," she said. "Shall I strap the crates together?" she wondered.

"No, they'll be all right," he said. "We won't be driving over any mountains or anything." He glanced over his notes and hung the clipboard on a nail. "Six Best of Breed, two Best of Opposites, a Best of Winners and Best Veteran. Good day."

"Happy owners," Faye said.

"Between Blanche' and von Havenburg, those girls could take their dogs all the way to the top if they wanted to. A lot of people are taking notice."

"They're noticing you as a handler, too, Jack. If you ever want to, you could go pro."

"Fun, if you like living in a truck and trailer. Wouldn't you miss our cottage?"

"As long as I'm with you, Jack, I'm home."

Hugging her, he smiled. "I'm so lucky I found you."

"You can say that again. I'm the brains of this operation. I was really pitching for you today. Esmeralda was excited about the new training program. She could hardly believe what you've done with old Cookie."

"I'm surprised, myself," he said. "That raw stuff had me scared at first. I kept thinking she might choke on the bones, you know? But without that and all the uphill work, she wouldn't be near as good."

"Don't forget my coat conditioners." Faye reminded him.

"Faye," he said, with every compliment and tone of respect in his voice. "I don't know where you came up with that stuff, but, I'm *tellin'* you."

"Sure you do. From my Grandma, remember? She made it for our hair when we were kids. I don't know why I never thought of it for the dogs before. Tell you the truth, I thought it was only *supposed* to be used for kids," she laughed.

"Well," he said, looking around at the dogs in the trailer, "if you think about it and stretch your imagination a little, maybe you weren't too far off," he chuckled.

Stepping close and wrapping her arms around him, Faye kissed his neck gently. "Oh, Jack. We'll have babies. We just need some time alone," she smiled, as a dapper Robert sauntered across the parking lot in his tweed jacket, tipping his hat and giving friendly advice along the way.

"Next time, give your dog more lead. Just a little, so he can stretch out and show what he's got," he said to a couple from New York with their Old English Sheepdog. "Nice dog. I just couldn't give him the points because I couldn't see him move."

Promising to do better, they waved good night. Maybe their dog wasn't so bad after all.

"Esmeralda!" he called, seeing her. "What are you doing out here? It's going to rain," he said, glancing at the darkening sky and taking out a cigarette. "Party over?"

"Just thinking," she said, pouring herself another glass. "Want to join me?"

"Can't. Gotta get back and feed the dogs. Aren't you supposed to be helping Blanche?" he asked, shielding the lighter's flame from the breeze.

"Break time," she said.

He took a drag. "She'll be tied up a few hours."

"I know. But, all I want to do is get out of here and go home. If I have to stay here another minute, I'll die. Robert?"

"I'm here."

"Can you take me home?"

Tapping cigarette ashes onto the gravel, he looked at her, so vulnerable, so sad. "Sure. Happy to, Ez. I'm parked over there, he said, pointing to a green DeSoto a few rows away. "Give me a few minutes," he said, tossing the cigarette and taking off toward the vendors' row.

"Need some help, Blanchie?" he asked.

She looked up from stacking boxes in the back of her truck. "No, I've got it, Hon. Anyhow, if you give me any help, it'll take me twice as long to re-pack everything. You gotta get back to the house and take care of the dogs. Jack an' Faye are gonna follow you. I'll be another hour or so."

"Good show?"

She smiled big. "Got us another wholesale account. A pet shop in New York. She loves my new idea."

"Another brick in the foundation of your empire," he said, pleased for her. "Want me to pick up something for supper on the way?"

"There's a casserole in the 'fridge. You can heat it up in the oven. You seen Ez?"

"Out in the parking lot. She's ready to go home. Should I give her a lift?"

"Do that. But, just remember she's feelin' kinda funny and I don't trust it when she gets that way."

"I'm a big boy."

"That's what I'm afraid of."

He grinned. "Sure you don't want me to stop and get you anything on the way?"

"Nah," she said. "Hey! You know what I'm hungry for? A great, big sundae. Hot fudge and lots and lots of peanuts an' sprinkles. Why don't you swing around by Mt. Gretna and get me one?"

"One hot fudge sundae coming up."

"An' whipped cream!" she hollered after him. "Put it in the freezer 'til I get back!"

Jingling his keys, Robert made his way to the car. Things were looking good, he thought to himself. Blanche was starting to get somewhere with her dog show business; his weekends were almost filled with judging assignments now; and, thanks to the Blanche' and von Havenburg Collies, his bloodline was finally on the comeback trail. A little more of this and he'd soon be able to quit working as a house painter. Life was good. Life was very good.

When he got to the car, Esmeralda was waiting. "Does she know you're taking me home?" she asked.

"All clear," he said. "We're stopping for a sundae."

"With . . . sprinkles," Esmeralda added, not having to guess and pouring another glass of champagne. "Here," she said. "Celebrate with me."

Beside her like this, the two of them alone, Robert's ears felt warm. "What are we celebrating?" he asked, shifting into neutral and starting up.

She held the champagne bottle high. "1942," she said. "The year we met. Don't you remember?"

His upper lip, where he wondered if a mustache would make him appear more dignified, felt damp and he wiped it dry with the back of his hand. "I'll always remember. You know that," he said, shifting into first.

"Something else, we're celebrating, Robert. Can you guess what it is?"

As a flood of cars and trucks crowded toward the exit, Robert pulled up beside Jack and Faye's trailer. "No, I'm not sure I can," he said, opening his door and stepping out.

With a quick knock, he opened the familiar trailer door to find Jack and Faye embraced. "OK, love bugs; ready to go? I'll get my car out of here and wait for you about a mile down the road. Flash your lights when you see me."

"OK," Jack said, giving Faye another kiss.

"Sure you don't want to ride up front in the car with me?" he asked her.

"No, Connie's dog didn't take the ride so good this morning. I'll keep him company back here. Besides," she snuggled against his chest. "I like it when you miss me."

Back in the car again, Robert started up and jockeyed for position in the exit lane of the farm show grounds. Beeping the horn as they passed Blanche, he waved. Arms full of bags and boxes, she laughed as the dim figure of Esmeralda slid across the seat to brush dog hair off Robert's shoulder, and looked away. Always clowning, that Esmeralda.

"Have you guessed yet?" she asked him, glancing back to make sure Blanche had seen her.

"Still working on it."

Things so important to a romantic and so disregarded by everyone else, she thought. "Let me give you a hint,' she said, sensing a game. "It has something to do with you and me."

Robert sighed, though whether to think better or relax himself one couldn't tell. "You and me," he said, pulling off to the side of the road.

Though she had finished brushing off his jacket, she hadn't slid back across the seat. "That's right," she said, studying his face. "You," she poured another glass, "and me. Don't you just love the way champagne makes you feel, Robert? Don't you love the way it makes nothing else matter but right here, right now? It's a wonderful friend, champagne."

"Friends can be unpredictable."

"Do I ever know." She shook her head from side to side. "I know all about friends like that." She stared at him and smiled. "Oh, no you don't, Mister," she said, wagging a finger. "You're trying to change the subject! You're supposed to tell me what we're celebrating. Remember?"

"What if I can't? What if I don't know?"

"Then, I'll have to punish you, Robert. I'll have to think of something really bad and punish you." She drew back and looked at him sternly, almost wildly. "I will, you know. I'll think of something very, very bad."

Robert sipped from her glass. "Then I'll need your help to save myself."

"Why should I help you? You don't love me."

"But, I do," he said.

"Love me? Prove it," she said, as headlights flashed in the rear view mirror. "Prove you love me."

Sensing her challenge, he cursed Jack for bad timing. "I'm married, Ez. You know I can't do what I want to," he said, starting the car again and pulling back onto the road.

"I know! I know and *I don't care!* She doesn't love you, Robert. She doesn't!"

"You know her that well, do you?" he said, implying just the opposite.

"YES! I know her better than anyone! I know something about her even you don't."

"I'm her husband. I should know her pretty well. I sleep with her, don't I?" Did he have to sound so angry when he said that, he wondered to himself?

"*DON'T!*" she choked, pressing both hands against her ears and spilling champagne on her new dress. "I don't want to hear it!"

He looked straight ahead, both hands on the wheel.

"Do you think she's better than me? Do you?" she demanded.

"I wouldn't know."

"Yes, you would," she said, her voice bitter. "You found out." Putting a hand on his leg, she ran her fingernails up and down across the fabric. "We're alone, Robert."

Gershwin's "Rhapsody in Blue" began to play; Robert didn't move.

"I love you. I still love you, Robert. Say something! DO something. ANYHING but sit there and not look at me!"

160

As the music built, the only thing for him to say was, "If I look at you, I'll never be able to stop."

"Robert!" she grabbed his hand and pulled it against her breast. "Robert -"

"I've remembered that night a thousand times. I've kissed you everywhere. *Everywhere.*"

"Robert," she whispered, squeezing his hand tighter.

"I've pushed into you and felt a hungry, pulsing whirlpool swirling, pulling me, sucking me deeper than any man has a right to hope for. Don't make me look at you. Not now."

"Robert, come away with me," she said, hushed, barely able to hear herself saying his name.

"What about *Blanche?*"

Her throaty sob.

The fleshy sting of her hand on his face.

The roll of his neck backwards.

"*Damn!*" he hissed, rubbing his cheek where she had slapped him. "Maybe she isn't the greatest," he said, talking faster now. "Maybe I could have done better. Hell can't be any worse than the price I pay sometimes! But, damn it, *she was there! She was there for me when you left without even saying good-bye!*"

Spilling her drink as they rounded a curve, Esmeralda almost choked.

"*Wasn't there!* I almost missed my train to New York waiting for you! You never came! I sailed for London sure I had disgraced myself and you never wanted to see me again!"

"Blanche said you were gone. She said you had left. You abandoned me. I never felt so alone," he said. "Or so foolish."

"Alone? Is that how you felt, Robert? *Alone* is what every woman in this world is running away from!"

"Well, I'm running, too!" he said, lighting another cigarette and taking a puff. "I gave up everything. I gave up every hope I had for happiness and settled. I'm running, Esmeralda - you'd better believe it! *I'm running away from my life!*"

"I can't go on like this!" she said, snatching the cigarette from his mouth and flinging it out the window. "I can't stand it! You can't do this to me! You can't make me stand by and watch her ruin you! I love you! I love you! Don't you dare run away, Robert! Not unless you're taking me with you!" Overcome, she grabbed for the steering wheel.

"What are you doing!"

"NOW! We have a car. I've got money. Let's get out of here - right now!" she said, trying to drive.

"Esmeralda!" he hollered as the car swerved again. Shaking, overcome with emotion, she threw herself at him.

"No!" he cried, blocking the onslaught of her blows to his arms, his chest, his face.

"You!" she screamed, pounding harder. "*YOU!*"

The car barely missed a mailbox.

"I can't drive!"

"You don't understand!" she hissed, oblivious. *"You don't know what it's like!* I'm living in Hell! Ripped open! Every time I have a chance to get on with my life, I think of you and I'm bleeding all over again! *Bleeding! Burning!"*

An oncoming car blared its horn and whipped past them.

"We'll be killed!" Robert hollered as the skies opened up and heavy rain began to fall. Cursing, he switched his windshield wipers on to high.

"I don't care! What does it matter, Robert. I'm already . . . dead." She moaned, slumping in her seat. "Tell me you love me," she said as Edith Piaf's passionate "La Vie En Rose" began to play.

"You know I do," he said.

Giving up, she held her glass of champagne so the bubbles could catch the headlights behind them, each pearl-like strand of bubbles seeming to dance with a mind of its own; dancing, leaping, bursting. "A thousand bubbles," she said, her dark eyes dreamy. "One for every time I've thought of you and every time you weren't there. Such wicked, wicked thoughts," she murmured. "I dare you to say you love her. You don't love her — not now; not ever." With all the fury of a raging animal, she lunged at him once more. *"I HATE HER!"* she howled, threatening anything that stood in her way. "Say it, Robert! Say it NOW! Go ahead! Say it right now — right to my face! *Marriage?* I SPIT on your marriage! *She lied to you!*

She lied to me! *She TRICKED us! I HATE HER!*" she screamed, flinging the bottle

"*We're gonna hit!*" Robert shouted, guilt and fear overcoming him as he threw himself over her - and the car spun off the road in a blur of crunching metal; rolling trees; jagged branches, spattering rocks and dirt. Insane, tumbling lights! Glittering shards of glass . . . *Screeching breaks - screeching brakes - screeching brakes . . . ! The cursing of a man as his car and trailer of howling show dogs tore into the rear of Robert's DeSoto . . .*

The trailer; the trailer pivoting sideways, snapping the hitch, rolling - sliding - rolling!

"What's happening! Help me! No! Oh, God, no!" Faye shrieked under an avalanche of metal crates, dog food and grooming tables. "Jack!" she sobbed, under the wicked blare of a horn as yet another car ripped into the side of the trailer; viciously throwing its young driver and passengers into the night.

Save me, God! Faye thought. Oh, please! Please God, no! What have I done with my life? Is it over, she asked? Oh, precious Lord . . . It all went so fast.

Esmeralda awoke, her body twisted among blankets, dog show flyers and what she knew was Robert's arm across her chest. Searching her mind for pain, she opened both eyes to nothing but blackness.

I can't see, she thought! Oh, yes, it's night. It's night. Yes, yes, I remember now.

Noise.

A horn? A car horn? What happened?

Robert!

He's not moving. He's so heavy. Is he breathing?

Am I paralyzed?

Please let me still have children.

Bones.

Broken bones?

What's that I feel on my neck? It's wet. I'll faint! I'll faint!

Please, God, let me still have children, she begged in the personal prayer of those facing death.

My hand.

I can still move it. Thank you, thank you! Hold my breath.

Robert . . . so heavy.

Is he dead? Please don't be dead, Robert. . . *I've done this, she thought . . .* Oh, God, *I've done this to him!*

My back. My back.

It's OK. It's OK. How can it be OK? Robert!

He's still not moving!

Move, Robert! They can't find us like this.

It's my fault! My fault! My darling, darling Robert. If I've killed you, let me die now; I can't go on. *I can't go on!*

A man's skin had never looked so pale. His breath - he's breathing! He's alive! I'll take care of you - I'll take

165

care of you forever, no matter what! A man's breath had never come more shallow.

Odd, seeing him like this, under a veil of flashing red lights from the police car and approaching ambulance.

"Open your eyes, Robert! Please open your eyes!" she whispered. If he opened his eyes would he know her? Would he remember?

Oh, my love! *My love!* I can't live without you. I can't! I won't!

Cradling his head in her lap, she threw herself over him and sobbed. Such a waste. Such a stupid, stupid waste.

She lay there like that, wondering, hoping, praying for longer than she would ever know. Would she walk again? Would Robert live?

He was so still. So very, very still . . . .

Slowly, like a shabby drunkard waking up in a littered alley, Esmeralda pulled herself upright. It was blood on her neck, she realized. Not an artery, just a sticky, sickening patch of blood oozing to the back of her neck from the side of her head. She must move, she told herself. She must force herself to move now, before the pain and truth set in; before she knew how far things had gone; how bad it all was.

She must save him. She must save the man she loved.

"Help me, Robert. Help me just this once," she whispered softly. "It's my fault. My fault," she said, feeling for the steering wheel. "If you never help me again," she said. "If you go to Blanche and never speak to me again - whatever you do - *don't wake up just yet, my love. Not now!*" she gasped, her bloodied hand slipping as she fell back against the seat.

With all her strength, she willed herself to go on, pulling herself out from under him. Sleep, Robert. Sleep.

Heaving herself into the driver's seat, Esmeralda, shaking and weak, slumped in a wave of nausea from the smell of vomit; the stench of human Hell.

Sirens splitting the night; closer; closer.

Voices . . . *"QUICK! Over here!"*

Flashlight swords of light piercing the blackness.

It was bigger; bigger than both of them.

I can't let him take the blame for this, she thought. I can't. Touching his hair, knowing she would face the Lord of Darkness forever if it meant never feeling his arms around her, his hands upon her, his mouth to hers again, she whispered. . . "You never guessed what else we were celebrating, Robert. . . . The first time we've been alone since your wedding." Sobbing, she leaned over and gently kissed him; kissed his face, his hands, his mouth.

Chapter 4

It was early 1951. Dr. Jonas Salk believed he could develop a vaccine for polio and people were flocking to see Humphrey Bogart in "The African Queen." New York theater audiences applauded Yul Brenner in "The King And I;" Johnny Ray sang "Cry" on every radio in the nation, and at Madison Square Garden, another Boxer, this time Ch. Bang Away of Sirrah Crest, won Best in Show at Westminster. . . . .

Strategic Maneuvers . . . Funny, how you can live with someone and they don't know what you're up to; how your feelings have changed. She had tricked him. Just when he got wise to it and all the pieces of the puzzle had fallen into place, he was totally, completely at her conniving mercy. She fed him and took him for walks; scolded him when he was bad and petted him when he was good. What Blanche *had lost in the accident, she had more than made up for in the aftermath.*

As Robert mastered the use of crutches, there were no houses to paint; but plenty of time to think.

"*To me, a dog is like a ticket, Honey. The better the dog, the better the show!*" When pressed for an explanation, she had laughed and messed up his hair. "If all you want to do is hang around people in your own neighborhood, get yourself a mutt from the pound. But, if you want to spread your wings and make connections, you gotta get hold of the best dog you can and show it! I shouldn't have to tell *you* that."

Blanche. Irreverent, fun Blanche. A mistake, but he would miss her. "Hey, ain't you doing the show in Wilkes-Barre?" she had asked, as she puttered around the kitchen making breakfast. "I got my booth all paid for," she said, between flipping eggs at the stove and pouring coffee. "

"They made a change," he said, buttering a piece of toast.

"What for?" she asked, surprised. "We've got a feed bill to pay and I'm counting on that weekend to swing it."

Putting a plate in front of him, she said, "Here ya go, Sweetie. Just the way you like it."

"I guess the Club changed its mind about me," he said, taking a mouthful, chewing thoughtfully.

"What for?" she asked stirring cream into her coffee.

"I guess a lot of them are changing their minds," he said, showing her a stack of cancelled contracts beside him.

"But, why? Those things are legal aren't they?"

"Apparently, not as good as the paper they're written on," he said.

"The accident," she said flatly. "God damn it, can't they let it go?"

Could she, he wondered? Could she forget the dogs she lost? Could she forget Faye Milliken crushed to death in the trailer that night?

"Hey! I don't like what happened," she said. "Me an' Faye, we got along just fine. But, can't those friggin people get it through their heads it was an *accident!*"

"They don't care about Faye." There it was; he had said it.

"Hey, come on! I lost a couple of damn good dogs in that wreck. But, they're gone! Harpin' on it day in an' day out ain't gonna bring 'em back." It was the survivor in her. The thing he liked most.

"Connie Bentley doesn't feel that way." he said. "And she's not the only one. They want to see Esmeralda punished."

"What they want is attention," she corrected him. "It's show biz, Honey. Don't you know that? A big drama and they found a way to be in the center of it."

"Well, what are we going to do?"

"I'll tell you what we're doing. I'm your wife, you're my husband and we're goin' to that show, Robert. You're dressing up in your best suit and tie and I'm gonna smile as big as anybody ever saw me. Let 'em try an' kick *me* out of the show. I *paid* to be there!"

They had arrived at the show grounds before dawn that weekend. "What's the plan?" he asked, pulling up to a place in the grass marked "Blanche' Creations."

"Well, you just practice walkin' on those crutches while I set up the tent and tables," she said, scouting for somebody in charge; pouring them each a cup of hot cocoa. "And don't look so scared, Robert. You've got every right to be here."

"Obviously, they don't want me," he said.

"They don't want you to judge. That don't mean you can't be here helping me."

Reassured, he finished up his cocoa, tucked both crutches under his arm and found his balance. She was right. He would show more backbone, he decided.

Half an hour later, her tent in place, Blanche paused halfway between polishing a collar to lustrous sheen and pouring another cup of cocoa. "Hey, Baby," she said. "How 'bout helping me with this rack over here. I got a whole bunch of new stuff an' I want to show it off."

Obliging, Robert began hanging collars and leashes on the wooden racks he had built for her and painted her favorite hot pink. "How's that?" he asked, swinging out of the way.

171

"Nifty," she smiled, admiring her colorful exhibit. No artist in a Manhattan gallery could have done better, she thought. "Hey, this is kinda fun, you and me together like this, running the business. Don'tcha think?"

Merchants and food vendors laughed, joked and chatted as they raised their colorful banners and set out their wares. Show biz, she called it; theater. Circus acts roving from town to town. What a life, he thought. Being in charge was right for her; the only way.

"I just wish I felt better about being *here*," is what he said.

"Well, you don't have to fret about that for long," Blanche warned, pointing to about a dozen exhibitors and their dogs gathering nearby. "Get a load of Connie, over there."

"Connie Bentley?" he asked, spotting a Great Dane and the woman at the end of its lead.

"You know, she's askin' me if I'll go in with them on a lawsuit about the dogs. Everybody who lost their dogs is supposed to pitch in and file for damages. Remember, I said somethin' about that?"

"Too well. Thanks for not getting mixed up in it, Blanche."

"Well, I hate saying this, but as much as I love you, Robert, it's Ez I'm thinkin' about, and Jack. Some of the Breeders in the Club want to make this whole thing into a legal precedent. They want to establish a dog's value in a court of law and make it official. I see

172

their point. I mean, it breaks my heart that Puddin' an' Cookie and the rest of 'em died, and I know it must have been awful, the suffering an' all. But, like I said, my dogs ain't comin' back to me, no matter what I do. And Faye ain't either. No amount of *money* is gonna to make that happen. Money ain't the same as love," she said, "A lot of people forget that and it tells me how much they don't know about love in the first place. If love isn't based on money from the start - and mine wasn't - then money shouldn't have nothin' to do with it."

"Blanche, you astound me."

"Thanks, Hon," she smiled and pinched his cheek. "Now, brace up, 'cause we've got company." Slipping into character, she turned her attention to the group approaching them. "Connie! How *are* you this morning? Did that new collar of mine fit on Lulu?"

"Gave it to my handler," Connie said, nodding. "Got any more?"

"I'll see what I can find," Blanche said, scuffling through some boxes. "Say Hi to Robert!"

Connie barely nodded. "Aren't you supposed to be judging today?" she asked.

Did she have to be so smug about it, he wondered? "Apparently, there's been a change of plans," he said, unwilling to be drawn into conversation.

"So, you're helping Blanche out. That's nice," Connie said, dripping with sarcasm as she reached for the bills tucked in her brassiere. "My, how the mighty do fall."

Blanche stopped dead. "Excuse me?"

Pretending not to hear, Connie and her friends turned their backs and made small talk among themselves.

"Connie?" Blanche said. "Did you just say something?"

"It wasn't important," Connie smiled again. "Is that my collar?"

"Oh, but I think it was important," Blanche said. "It sounded important to me. It sounded like you were making a crack about Robert losing his judging assignment."

"Was I?"

"Yeah. I think maybe you were."

"Well, why don't we ask my friends, here?" Connie said, turning to the others. "Did I just insult anyone?"

"I didn't hear anything," said a white-haired man with a Wire Fox Terrier. "Did you?" he asked, turning to a beautiful young handler with long side-burns and a Dalmatian.

"I was looking at the rhinestone leashes," the answer came, with a sly grin. "What about you, Rita? Did you hear Connie say anything?"

The skinny blonde with a white poodle just rolled her eyes.

"Look," Blanche said, with both hands on her hips. "Will you guys just give it a rest? I have. And I lost some of my best dogs and a damn good friend. Don't you think that's a little bit more than any of you?"

"Well, dogs can't talk for themselves," the one with the Fox Terrier said. "And a lot of people are starting to feel the same way we do. You'd be surprised."

"Animals need a voice in things and nobody seems to care," a lady with a Cocker Spaniel pitched in. "What's the matter with people these days? Don't they have any heart?"

"People got plenty of heart," Blanche said, shoving a bag toward Connie and staring down the rest of the lynch mob. "They just don't forget about their brothers and sisters."

Swearing under her breath, Connie took the bag; the group left.

"Thanks," Robert said, watching them go. "I wasn't sure what to do."

"I'll tell you what to do," Blanche said. "You go find a place to change into that nice suit of yours and you march right over to that ring. You take yourself a seat front and center. And you plant yourself right there for everybody in this damn Club to see. You let everybody there know what you think about the dogs they pick today. They want a show around here? We'll give 'em a show. We'll give 'em a show they won't forget. Now go on. Get that suit an' get yourself out of here!"

"Are you sure?"

"Oh, I'm fine," she grinned. "I just don't want you around when our friend Connie opens that bag and finds out what I went and did. While she was blabbin' off her mouth, I went an slipped her a muzzle!"

He had never been more surprised by Blanche than he was at that moment; never more sure of her. She loved him. He knew it. If only he could forgive what she would never admit; that Esmeralda had been waiting for him; that there was no baby. If only the master choreographer before him hadn't spun one too many lies in her dance through life, they could have waltzed forever.

Hawks and Doves . . . The Campelltown

Fire Hall has been the scene of many outrageous events in its illustrious history, but few have equaled the fervor and righteous indignation of the meeting of the William Penn Kennel Club that third Wednesday in September. That was the night when nobody had Bridge, nobody's kids were sick, and nobody worked late. Attendance? That night, it was about as close to a hundred percent as a monthly meeting ever gets. "Mercenary." "Bloodthirsty." Those are words that come to mind. Let no one underestimate the power of a Kennel Club gone mad!

"EVERYBODY! EVERYBODY LISTEN UP! You have to be here no later than 9 AM for your picket signs!" Connie said.

"I want mine to say *BURN IN HELL!*" shouted the Chihuahua Breeder.

A murmur went through the crowd and Connie tapped her gavel.

"Libby, we want justice for the dogs, but we don't want to be arrested," said the Club President.

"I don't know what's the matter with all of you!" said the Basset Breeder, standing up from his seat to be more easily heard. "This was an accident. A terrible accident that killed our good friend, Faye Milliken. Faye was one of the nicest, sweetest people I've ever met and most of us, I'm sure, would agree with that." Again, a murmur went through the room. "Faye Milliken would be *ashamed* of this club for attacking Esmeralda von Havenburg this way."

"So, how do you suggest we do it?" somebody smart-assed.

"*SIT DOWN, Ralph!* Nobody's forcing you to be part of it!" Connie shouted at the Basset man. "If we don't stick up for the dogs – and show the world their poor, defenseless lives are worth a damn, who will? Huh? *You tell me!*"

"Those dogs were about as loved and well cared for as it gets," Ralph said, popping up again. "Hell, Faye's the one who took care of them! It was an ACCI-DENT!"

A long-haired Brunette in the first row yelled, "Accident, SHIT! *It was MURDER!*" The Club erupted in shouts and accusations; one voice higher than the next; coffee cups and soda cans spilling.

"Order! Order!" Connie hollered, pounding her presidential mallet against the table like a cook in a greasy-spoon smashing cockroaches. "Settle down! *SHUT UP!*"

The meeting of the Kennel Club electrified the night as, across town, Esmeralda answered a knock at her door.

177

"Robert! What are you doing here?"

The months since the accident had freed Robert of his crutches, but not the cane that would be his for the rest of his life.

"I had to see you. I had to let you know I'm telling the truth tomorrow."

"What on Earth are you talking about? Come in! You shouldn't be outside at this time of night. I almost lost you in a car wreck; I'm not losing you to a cold!"

"I can't let you do it, Ez. I feel like a coward."

"Don't be ridiculous, Robert. I have nothing to lose. I don't have a career that depends on my credibility. We've been over this a hundred times."

"I know what you're doing and why," he said. "But, I couldn't live with myself knowing you took the blame for what I did. It was me behind the wheel that killed Faye. We both know that."

"I'll call you a liar. I'll go on the stand, Robert, and call you a liar. Nothing is going to stop me from this decision. Nothing you can say is going to change my mind. Nothing!" She stepped up to him and held his gaze. "If I live a million years, I won't regret changing seats with you that night. Never."

Setting his cane aside, he moved closer. "I've made every mistake a man can make. But, not this time," he said, holding her face between both hands and slowly kissing her. He kissed her mouth, her forehead and each of her closed eyes. First her left, and then her right. Feeling her relax into his arms, he slid his knee along the inside of her thigh. "I love you, Esmeralda," he breathed, pulling her against him.

They stood, looking into each other's eyes. Sure of himself, sure of her, he began unbuttoning his shirt ... unbuttoning her silk blouse . . . unclasping her brassiere . . . holding her breast.

"Robert . . . I'm afraid."

"Good," he said, holding the tip of a finger on her tightening nipple.

"I'm scared about tomorrow - "

"So am I," he whispered, kissing her softly. "It's bigger than us now; bigger than both of us. I'm asking Blanche for a divorce."

"She'll never give it. I know her."

"Then I'll steal every minute I can with you," he said, sliding the blouse off her shoulders; down her arms; kissing her skin all the way.

"Robert!" she sighed, throwing back her head.

Holding her hands, he licked each finger. Gently, he placed her hands on his chest and wrapped his strong arms around her. Smoothly, she reached behind her neck and carefully removed the delicate gold necklace, light as a feather, which she had worn since it had been given to her. Running both hands down his shirt, eyes trusting his, she slipped it into his pocket and pressed herself against him. They stood like this, holding the moment, rocking gently side to side;

dancing to music meant only for them. "I can feel your heart beating," he said.

"I haven't died and gone to Heaven?" she asked.

Lowering her to the Oriental rug beneath them; stroking her tummy, he answered, "If this is Heaven, you've met a nasty angel."

"*My turn to say good*," she moaned, losing herself in his warm mouth.

He pulled her closer. Again, he kissed her forehead, then her lips, the ticklish place on her neck . . . circling her nipples with his tongue.

Slowly . . . ever so slowly . . . he slid to the valley of her navel . . . through musky smelling grass . . . slipping into waters never tasted by any other man, ever before.

"Where ya been?" Blanche asked. "It's late."

"Painting the Rossiter's living room," he lied. "Took longer than I thought. I changed in the truck and went out for a bite," he said, tossing his clothes and standing naked in the darkness. She liked it when he stood naked in front of her, loose; without modesty after a day's work.

"Come here," she said, pulling aside the covers. "I want to practice something new."

"Then I'd better shower."

"What for? I know what you smell like."

He smiled. "I feel dirty."

"You should see what's goin' on in my mind if you want to feel dirty."

"Tell me about it," he said, standing there. Why did he feel so strange? This was his wife. And yet, there was something wrong about it now.

"Closer," she said.

He laughed and crossed his arms. "Why do I feel like you're up to no good?"

"Because I am," she said, tossing off her covers and sitting up. "Come here. I want to bite you."

"Bite me? Where?"

"All over."

"I have to pee," he said, gathering up his clothes and heading for the bathroom.

She almost surprised him in the shower, but thought better of it. Let him wash. There wasn't much he wouldn't do if they were clean.

"Looking for a playmate?" she whispered, as he slid next to her under the covers.

Your Witness . . . "Cheese sandwich and soup to go, please," said Jim Rychart, shifting his briefcase to the other hand and fishing for his wallet.

"It's her lawyer!" a picketer shouted as Jim left the Red Rose Diner. "What's a smart guy like you doin' defending von Havenburg!" somebody hollered rudely. *"She's a murderer!"*

181

Months of turmoil from the community had accustomed him to hecklers from the local kennel club. Facing them, he wrestled with his conscience and PR savvy.

"The charge is involuntary manslaughter, folks, not murder," he said, just as he had repeated countless times to unforgiving accusers. Too bad it wasn't only Faye Milliken they were talking about.

"What's the difference?" hollered a man carrying a sign on cardboard. "She's gonna get off anyway, with all *her* money!"

"Lighten up, fellas," said Rychart.

"Hey! I take exception to that!" said a woman in a fringed jacket with a Great Dane pin on the collar. "Do I look like a fella?"

"Connie, ain't nobody ever gonna make *that* mistake!" a guy said to her chest. "How 'bout dinner tonight? I'll have some roast beef, mashed potatoes and beer!" he laughed.

"You're cookin'?" she fired back. "Sorry, I've got other plans."

"You tell 'im, Kid," said a heavyset man in suspenders, patting his Doberman Pinscher.

Jim raised his hand to cool the scene. "Listen. We're here for the preliminary hearing. My client is very upset. She's innocent until proven guilty."

"And just how long's it gonna *take* for the prosecutor to *prove* it?" somebody asked, to a round of hard laughter.

It wasn't easy smiling and gritting your teeth at the same time, Jim decided. "What makes you think they won't find my client *innocent?*"

"Come on, Jimmy. It's open and shut! Faye's dead and the dogs with her."

"Open and shut? I don't recall the police saying any of you were at the scene of the accident."

"Mr. Rychart, I'm Connie Bentley," the woman with the Great Dane stepped forward. "We're members of the William Penn Kennel Club." She elbowed the guy pushing in front of her.

"Ow!" he yelped. "My ulcer!"

"When I'm through with you, Bill, you're gonna have a lot more than an ulcer. Outta my way!"

"You wanted to say something, Miss Bentley?" Jim asked. "I only have a minute."

"Thanks. At least somebody's a gentleman around here," she said, turning around to make sure everybody heard. "We're doing this because we want to know what's going to happen about the dogs that were killed."

"Tell 'im, Connie!" an older woman with gray hair and a Schnauzer hollered.

"I'll handle it!" Connie told everybody as she faced Jim again. "Dogs are property, Mr. Rychart. More than property. I mean, how can you replace a valuable friend? An important show dog? How do you ever replace the genetic potential such a dog has to its kennel's breeding program? Does the law care about that?"

183

"Of course," smiled Jim. "We'll look into it, but, like I said, in this case I believe my client's innocent."

"She was drunk!" somebody hollered.

"Can you prove that?" Jim fired back.

"*Drunk!* And she didn't give a *damn* about those dogs! Blanche lost her best dogs! Champions! She had a pup that was gonna clean up! What's she gonna do now?"

"*Esmeralda was jealous!*" a woman hissed. "She wanted Robert Sheffield *and everybody knows it!*"

"Enough to cause an accident taking the life of her own friend, Faye Milliken?" Jim asked.

"She don't care! *She's rich!*"

"*And drunk!*"

"*Jealous!*"

"Can money make you forget? 'Cause if it does, I'll need a lot of it after this!" Rychart laughed, laying a five on the counter. It was a joke that fell flat.

"You ain't hurtin'" somebody scoffed. "You're a damn *lawyer!*"

Grabbing his briefcase, he headed out the diner scarfing his sandwich. Hurrying into the Courthouse, he left the picketers behind, marching in their solitary circle. "*Rich! . . . Drunk!*"

Jack Milliken sat in Court looking straight ahead. Twirling his silver wedding band, a habit intensified since Faye's death, he studied the flag hanging limp in a corner. *Like my life*, he thought. *Wilted. Useless*, he told

184

himself, as Nancy Godfrey, only nineteen, hunched her shoulders. Pulling her cardigan sweater over the sling in which her bro-ken arm still rested, she shivered. "I'm scared, Steven," she said to her boy-friend.

"Me, too," he said, holding her hand; wondering how his life had been spared that night.

"What are they going to ask us? I just don't remember a whole lot. I'm try-ing to forget," she said, as Robert Shef-field, seated at the end of the row in order to navigate more easily, propped his cane on the bench beside him. He would have done anything in his power to change things. Had he only said, no. *"No, Esmeralda, I can't take you home. I shouldn't tonight. I'll meet you anywhere you say, anywhere. Tomorrow . . . I'll meet you tomorrow."*

Seeing her there, alone in the Courtroom now with vile protesters jam-ming the corridors and the street outside was almost too much for him to bear. What kind of man allows this to happen to the woman he loves, he thought? She saved my reputation. How can I just sit here, watching? Watching her be ridiculed, hu-miliated right in front of me like this? Knowing she'll never escape the rumors, the gossip; not for as long as she lives. I have to tell the truth. I have to tell what really happened! I could always go away. I could go away and start all over again, he thought, as Jim Rychart ran his fingers over his tie, a nervous habit picked up during his college days.

Scanning his notes, Rychart wondered how a woman's friends and neighbors could turn on her so completely and with such cruelty. So kind to a dog, they were; so unforgiving to a woman. She trusted him; trusted him to guide her through this like a child holding his hand as they stepped timidly through a minefield. One more step; one more day; just one more, Esmeralda. If we're lucky, it won't be the last.

Mean-spirited, this town; cold. New Yorkers raved about its quaint architecture, its family-owned shops, its dichotomy of modern life and religious subcultures frozen in time. But, to him, Lancaster, Pennsylvania was an emotionally isolated place; a brick and cobblestone island floating in a sea of rolling green farms patrolled by an Amish armada. Nice? His face stoic, he turned around and pretended to search for someone he knew. No, this wasn't a nice place. In a few years it would be as concrete and lost in anonymity as Any City, USA. No better, no worse. In a few years, these people wouldn't even be memories.

Esmeralda wasn't moving. She was as still as if her spirit had transported itself to realms no one could touch; the heart he knew must be withering and growing cynical. That's the crime, he thought; theft of the heart. How could they expect people to pick up and go on after being hurt this way? More souls were degraded than ever comforted or inspired, in a Courtroom. Like the town, it was a self-righteous, cold place.

"Are you OK?" he asked her.

She didn't seem to hear him. Like Madam X in the Lana Turner movie from long ago, she sat there, staring, her skin pale, her eyes remote, her spirit distant. Was her heart seeing the years ahead?

"Esmeralda. Are you OK?"

Startled, she blinked and nodded. "They hate me," she whispered. "Blanche was right. I never believed it. I never felt it before."

"They don't know you," he said. "We'll change their minds."

In her simple tweed suit, white blouse and pearls, she appeared as frail as a winter sparrow in the snow.

"I'm scared, Jim." Eyes wide, she said it again. "Scared."

"*All rise for the honorable Waynette Hinter.*"

As the room swelled with power, the prosecution presented its case - sarcastic, accusatory, unforgiving: Esmeralda von Havenburg, haughty rich girl, partying away the night in diamonds and fur. How dare she think she is above the law! How dare she go unpunished for the crippling of others; for the death of young Faye Milliken!

To the emotional echoes of the prosecution's dramatic blame, Jim Rychart asked, "Have you ever done something you would give anything - anything you have - to change?" He paused. "Not money. Not a fine house, or a - " he seemed to grasp for the right words, "a boat or any such riches - and we all have our riches,

187

however humble they may be. Have you ever done something that no riches in this world could change? No riches in this world?" He touched his heart. "Have you ever done something so bad, so shameful, that no matter what happened, no matter what anyone said, thought, or did, you – you, yourself – would never forget it for as long as you walked the face of this Earth?"

Taking a slow breath, he nodded his head slightly and searched the room as only a man of clear conscience can do. "No matter if she rots in jail or walks away from here and never looks back, there will be no escape for Esmeralda von Havenburg. No matter what you decide, it will never erase the stigma she must carry wherever she is, and wherever she goes in this world, for the rest of her life." He shook his head and lowered his eyes. "Forever."

"*Officer Thomas A. Newton to the stand. . .*"

"*Your witness.*"

"*No questions, Your Honor.*"

"*The State calls County Coroner Edward Blakey . . .*"

"*Your witness.*"

"*No questions, Your Honor.*"

"*The State calls Dog Warden Thomas Billings. . .*"

"*Your witness.*"

"*No questions, Your Honor.*"

"*The State calls Steven Baumgartner . . .*"

"*Your witness.*"

"No questions, You Honor."

"The State calls Nancy Felty . . ."

"Your witness."

"No questions, Your Honor."

"The State calls Jack Milliken."

"Your witness."

"No questions, Your Honor."

"Your Honor, The State calls Robert Sheffield . . ."

"Your witness."

Jim Rychart stood up.

"No!" Esmeralda whispered, her voice trembling. "You can't."

"We have to."

"No!" she hissed. "You promised."

"My duty is to protect *you*; not anyone else. Trust me."

Steadying himself, Robert faced the Court.

"Mr. Sheffield," said Rychart, "how, exactly, would you characterize your relationship with the defendant, Esmeralda von Havenburg?"

"We're close. I've known Esmeralda for about ten years now."

"The prosecution has suggested there was more than friendship between you and Miss von Havenburg. Would you say there is any truth to that, Mr. Sheffield?"

Robert leaned forward. Looking at Esmeralda, searching for her eyes, he said, "I believe I've answered that."

"Are you married, Mr. Sheffield?"

"Yes. And my wife and Esmeralda have known each other since they were in their early twenties."

"Friends?"

189

"Yes."

"Best friends?"

"Yes."

"So it wasn't unusual for you and Miss von Havenburg to be alone that night. Is that correct?"

"It wasn't unusual, no. We had just finished a dog show - Harrisburg - and there was a lot to talk about. Blanche -"

"Your wife knew you were together?"

"Yes. Blanche - "

"Your wife?"

"Yes. Blanche was packing up and didn't want any help. Esmeralda had gone to the show with her, but wanted to get home, and I had driven my car separately, so, I offered her a ride."

"You offered her a ride. *You* . . ." the attorney said, pausing for dramatic effect, "offered her a ride. That means you were driving, does it not?"

"I drove the car out of the parking lot, yes."

"But, the police report states that, at the time of the accident, Miss von Havenburg was behind the wheel," the attorney said, and waited for an answer.

"Yes," Robert said, filling in the expectant silence. "I believe it does."

"*Believe* it does, Mr. Sheffield? I have a copy of the report right here if you'd care to look at it to refresh your memory."

Shaking his head, Robert declined. "That isn't necessary," he said. "I know what it says. But, I'm telling you I was driving the car."

Esmeralda slapped a hand to her mouth and a buzz went through the court-room.

Judge Hinter pounded her gavel. "Order!"

"Your Honor, may I have a moment to speak with my client?" Rychart asked. "Esmeralda," he said softly. "I won't hurt you on this," he said. "I promise."

Hurt me, she thought? Doesn't he know he's destroying me?

"Did anyone see you driving the car?" Rychart asked. "Were there any witnesses?"

"Yes. My wife."

"Thank you. No further questions, Your Honor."

"Re-direct, Your Honor!" the District Attorney said, seizing an opportunity to hammer one more nail in the coffin. "Mr. Sheffield, do you understand the punishment for perjury?"

Robert looked him in the eye. "I am not lying, sir. I know I drove my car out of the parking lot."

"Why didn't you tell this to the police?"

"But, I did tell them."

"Mr. Milliken has testified that you drove out the parking lot and that the plan was for you to pull over and wait for him. Is that true, Mr. Sheffield?"

"I don't remember."

"Isn't it true that you were tired and exhausted?"

"I don't remember."

"You don't remember getting out of the car to change places with the Defendant?"

"No, sir. I don't remember."

"Do you remember any other events of that evening?"

Robert looked at Esmeralda. "No," he said. "I don't. I'm sorry."

"Your Honor," the D.A. said. "I have here a medical report showing that Robert Sheffield suffered hip and head trauma as a result of the accident." Facing Robert, he said, "In other words, Mr. Sheffield, for all you know, Esmeralda von Havenburg, in an inebriated state as the Police Report says, and to which she, herself, has admitted, could, indeed, have been driving the car that caused the accident resulting in the death of Faye Milliken the night of April 19."

Could he look at her, he asked himself? Could he? All he had to do was say yes. That's what she wanted him to do; she would deny anything else he might say; she had said so.

"Mr. Sheffield?"

Answering softly; looking at the floor, the solemn faces staring at him; anywhere but at the woman he loved, he heard himself say, "It's possible."

"The Court can't hear you," the lawyer persisted, making sure every soul present would hear and remember. "Would you please answer the question louder?"

"*Yes!*" Robert said, pouring his gaze over Esmeralda with all the suffering of a man who knew, by uttering these chilling words, that he would never; could never; see his love again. "It's possible."

An evil rumble filtered through the crowd all the way to the back row, where a full-figured blonde dressed in a flashy pink suit and hat caught her breath. Rising to her feet, she silently exited the Courtroom and did not look back.

"You may step down," the judge said.

Steadying himself on the edge of the witness stand; sure that his heart could never recover now, he reached inside his jacket for what he knew would be the last chance to reach her; to tell her she was loved.

Limping past her; searching for the eyes that would not meet his, he briefly took her hand, then walked on.

He was leaving her, she knew. He was leaving and would never come back. Helpless; helpless to cry; to scream; to call his name; she knotted her fists . . . and felt a crumpled piece of paper.

Exhibit A. . . Funny, how you can believe you know a man so well, Blanche thought, mulling over what she had just realized.

It was one thing. loving a man openly, for the whole world to see, and something else entirely to pretend you didn't. All her life, she had been strong, independent. Never needing anyone, or anything. Until Robert; just a trophy at first, won, perhaps, through

193

devious means; a trophy prized more deeply than she had ever thought herself capable of feeling.

In the kitchen, she poured herself a glass of milk and downed half a pack of cookies before heading for the living room. Picking up a New York fashion magazine, she scanned the pages until the sound of familiar steps echoed on the front porch. Arms suddenly weak, stomach falling like a high-speed elevator ride, she dropped the magazine to the floor.

It was him. This was it.

"So what's the verdict?" she asked, following him into the bedroom.

"We don't know yet," he said, taking off his jacket and tie.

I can tell you what the verdict around here is, she thought. *Wanna hear it, Mr. Big Shot?* "Who makes the final decision?" is what she heard herself saying instead.

"The judge, I guess. This isn't a jury trial, unless he decides it should go that far."

"Do they have all the facts?"

"All they need to know."

"Are you sure?" she asked.

"What else could there be?" he wanted to know.

"Oh, maybe a little technicality it took me a while to figure out."

"Technicality?"

"Oh, I felt stupid, not figuring it out right away. I mean, who would know better than me when it comes to Ez? But, today, when they got to asking what you did and didn't remember – "

"You were there?" he asked, surprised. "I didn't see you."

"Back row. And from where I was – even without my opera glasses – I could see the horns growin' right out of your head!"

"Blanche!"

"This whole thing's phony and I say you're smack in the middle of it!"

"*Blanche!*"

"I can't believe you'd do this! Ez! My best friend! *How could you?*"

"How could I what!"

"LET HER TAKE THE BLAME!" she screamed.

"Take the blame?"

"Oh, Robert. *ROBERT!* Don't you know when a man lies to a woman he'd better make it *damn* good? You insult my intelligence! Ez never drove that car, Robert, and you know it."

"How do you know?"

"I know Esmeralda like the back of my hand."

His silence filled the room. "She's doing it for us," he said. "Trying to save the business and my reputation both."

"For us! Give me a break!"

"You've seen the members of the Kennel Club! They'd tear us apart."

"Is it worth it? Is it all worth it, Robert?"

"It's my *life*, Blanche. *Our* life!"

"Not any more, it ain't," she said, after a long and dangerous pause. "What was it, Robert? What was it! Pity sex you gave her? A last fling before she goes to jail? Of all the women you could have – just by snapping your fingers, Robert – why would you go after the one woman in this world I care about – my closest, closest friend!"

"I don't believe this," he said, looking around the room for a clue. For something, anything, that might have stirred her up like this. "You're making this up."

"Am I? Then explain *this!*" she said, holding forth a thin, delicate necklace. "She never takes it off, Robert. Never! *Not since the day I gave it to her when we made our first sale.* She's not like me, you know. No other woman is. She don't know men and she never did. If a man pays her any mind, it's all she can do to keep from fainting. You? She's loved you as long as I have – only for different reasons. The noble kind! You need a woman like me, Robert Sheffield. You need a woman who's tough, who can keep up with you in bed and every place else; who can push you and guide you. After I get done tellin' the cops, I hope you can find one."

It was the shirt; his shirt from the night before, crumpled up on the floor beside the chair instead of in the bathroom hamper where he'd put it. "Blanche – "

"*Don't touch me! Don't you dare touch me – ever again!*"

Chapter 5

Late 1951 found scientists about to
understand the structure of DNA, half of
Hollywood was being called Communist and
moviemakers were dreaming up "The Greatest Show on Earth." On Broadway, theater-
goers were buzzing about the revival of
an American opera called "Porgy & Bess."
As a small, but growing audience of television viewers watched "Your Hit Parade,"
Kitty Wells didn't know she'd win a Gram-
my for "It Wasn't God Who Made Honkytonk
Angels," and those "in the know" were
saying a Doberman Pinscer named Ch.
Rancho Dobe's Storm was a shoe-in for
Westminster.

Search and Seizure . . . There are
those who say Esmeralda bribed the judge
and others who say she paid a local pow-
wow woman to cast a spell. Either way, it

didn't get her out of paying a stiff fine, giving up her driver's license and, as Rychart said, carrying the shame of Faye's death everywhere she went. Of course, there were witnesses like Jack to think about, and young Nancy Felty. But, there are those among us for whom Fate has a convenient way of re-arranging what it does, and doesn't like. Announcing her sudden retirement to Havana, Cuba, Mrs. Harrington, who had been studying Spanish via Berlitz phonograph record lessons, kissed her duties good-bye and took off for her new villa.

As for Jack, thanks to an anonymous bequest and the magic of multi-level marketing, the loyal kennel man found himself with a home for life and the sole source of amazing, patented grooming products that worked on every breed of dog. As they say, an estate is a big place with plenty of room for secrets . . . and for those who promise to keep them.

Frantic, Esmeralda, half-dressed, threw clothes out of her closet. Skirts, coats, pants lay scattered all over the place, still on their hangers. "I can't find it!" she screamed. "*I can't find anything!*"

Hearing the commotion, Nancy Felty came running. "What is it, Esmeralda? What's wrong?"

"My black slacks! It was in my black slacks! He said he loved me! I can't find it! I can't find it! It's lost! My love! Lost!" she cried, falling down on her bed.

"Are these what you're looking for?" Nancy asked. Sliding her hand inside a pocket, she pulled out a note. Esmeralda stopped bawling, looked up and desperately grabbed the paper.

It wasn't easy being a housekeeper at Lochwood, Nancy thought. How had Mrs. Harrington done it?

"Give me those!" Esmeralda snapped. Clutching the slacks, she finished dressing and headed to her desk. Pressing the intercom, she paged the kennel cottage. "Jack. Are you busy? Bring the car around, please."

"Where am I taking you?"

"Blanche' Kennels."

Noticing how firmly she said it, emotionless, he asked nothing more. Something about her bearing, or the tone of her voice when she said "*Blanche'* Kennels" knowing full well what she really meant was, the Sheffield farm, made him think better of it.

"Happy to," he said, before finishing the pedigree notes he was making for the kennel files. While they were driving, he could ask which matings she had in mind for the two coming in heat.

"Breed them both to the Arrowhill dog of Florence Cummings," she said, on their way toward Hershey and North on Route 39. "I like him. A little cheeky, maybe, but great movement and he'll throw more coat on our pups."

Wondering if that's all she had noticed about the dog, he mentioned that he'd been up against the Arrowhill dog in the ring and beat him, not once, but several times. "Don't you think he's a little short in the neck?"

"Pull his neck higher in the ring. But, that coat! The coat! Have you ever seen such a coat on a Collie before?"

Admitting she was right, he hadn't ever seen better, he closed the subject. "Then, the Arrowhill dog it is."

"Good, Jack. Good. And we'll keep the best for the show string next year."

She went through her purse, more than usual, he thought, for lipstick and mirror; face powder and eyeliner. Were they picking up Blanche and going somewhere?

"Wait for me, Jack. This won't take long," she said, as he pulled into the lane and parked. He hadn't seen Blanche since the Hearing. Not long, but long enough to wonder if she would still be doing shows now that her best dogs were gone and how uncomfortable they all felt about it. Time would heal things, he thought. His grandma used to say that. Time heals all wounds. He glanced in the mirror to see Esmeralda walking to the front door, and wished Faye would still be here with him

"Wait for me," she had said. He would wait. Whatever she had come here for was the only thing on her mind right now. For a woman who seemed strangely in control of herself these past few weeks, Esmeralda was losing it, he thought; pounding on the door like she was thrashing out for a lifeline.

Inside, Blanche put down the bottle of hair color, as she sang, "Jum-ba-laya

. . . crawfish pie-a . . . and be gay-o .
. . for tonight I'm-a-gonna-see my
muchera-mio . . . "

Boom! Boom! Boom!

"Fill fruit jar . . . la, la, la .
. . mio-myo - "

Boom! Boom! Boom!

"ALL RIGHT!" Blanche hollered,
realizing it was somebody pounding on her
door and not the drummer for Hank Williams. Wrapping her hair in a stained
bathroom towel, she took both hands out
of her rubber gloves.

"I HEAR YOU! Wait a goddam minute!"
Hustling to the door, she bumped her hip
on the corner of a table and cursed. "Now
look. Black and blue!" Ready for bear,
she slung open the door and felt her head
go faint.

"WHAT THE HELL - Ez! *What are YOU
doing here?*"

"I've HAD it! I'm sick of you hanging onto this drama! What good has it
done? Look at yourself! Look at your
life!"

"What the Hell - "

"Where's Hollywood, Blanche? Are
you taking the scenic route? When's the
last time you took out your sketchbook
and whipped up a creation for Elizabeth
Taylor or Marilyn Monroe?"

"What's with the third degree all
of a sudden!"

"Robert!"

"Ha! I figured it would get down to
that."

"Where is he?" Esmeralda asked,
pushing her way into the house, rushing

to the kitchen, the living room, the bedroom. "Is he here? ROBERT!" she shouted.
Turning to Blanche, knowing he was gone,
she cried out, "You messed it all up! *You
messed up everything!*"

"What do you care? He's MY husband!"

"Only because you tricked him! You
tricked him into marrying you - saying
you were pregnant when you knew you
weren't! You KNEW it!"

"All's fair in love and war,
Honey."

"Speak for yourself!"

"GLAD to - a lyin' CHEATER is what
he is! Or, should I say a *layin'* cheat! I
sent his cheatin' ass back to Canada is
what I did!"

"NO!"

"And I'd do it again!"

"Oh, no! When? WHEN DID HE GO!"

"Who cares! The sooner I forget
him, the better!"

"Oh, God! Oh, God NO! You've RUINED
MY LIFE! I HATE YOU!"

Esmeralda didn't expect the slap to
her face; or how fast her own hands yanked off the towel wrapped around Blanche's
head and grabbed her by the robe. "Get
out of my way, Bitch!" Esmeralda screamed.

"*I heard that!*" Blanche screamed
back at her, stumbling as the towel fell
and quickly regaining her balance. Spinning around, hair color spattering the
walls, the pink whirling dervish headed
straight for Esmeralda, who made it to

the liquor cabinet and poured herself a quick one.

"Just when I thought I'd seen everything," Esmeralda said smugly, raising her glass.

"*You just called me a BITCH!*"

"And that's the LEAST of it, my dear!" Esmeralda needled calmly. "You should know what I called you in the car! Here's to the Queen of Fashion!" she laughed, downing a shot of whiskey, unwilling to let Blanche see her grimace.

"You break into my house and call me a Bitch! I want to know what this is all about *and I want to know now!*"

Setting down her glass in a standoff, shuffling through her purse for a make-up compact, Esmeralda smiled coldly.

"Oh, Blanche," she said sweetly. "You're not really a bitch. You'll have to forgive me. Will you? Can you?" she asked, powdering her nose as if to leave. "See, a *Bitch*," she said, with a cool smile as she calculated her distance to the door; "*a real one, my dear,*" she said, turning the mirror of her compact for Blanche to see her own reflection, hair dried into spikes of bright red and her face smeared with dye . . . "would do THIS!"

"*GET OUT! GET OUT OF HERE!*" Blanche screamed, slapping the compact out of her hand, flinging open the door and shoving Esmeralda outside. "I KNOW you weren't driving that car! *I know you weren't!*" she sobbed. Wringing her hands and wiping away tears, she hollered, "What are you doing it for? WHAT? You love him? YOU

203

LOVE HIM THAT MUCH? Well I *DON'T!* I
don't! *I hate him.* HATE HIM! You . . .
crazy . . . stupid . . . lovesick . . . *I
KNOW, EZ! I KNOW ALL ABOUT THE TWO OF
YOU! THE BIG AFFAIR! THE BIG SECRET!"*

Rushing to the car, Esmeralda flung
herself inside. "Get me out of here,
Jack. HURRY!"

Struck, spellbound, Jack wasn't
moving. "What's going on? What's she acting like that for?"

Esmeralda looked away; she looked
away and didn't answer. "Go, Jack! Hurry!
Blanche is making a fool of herself.
She's being ridiculous!"

Facing her now, his eyes filled
with questions, he said, "We've had e-
nough happen around here. Too much. We
don't need anything more. Go back, Esmeralda. Go back and make up."

"No! Get me out of here. *Get me out
of here NOW!"*

Cursing, Blanche turned and spit.
"GO AHEAD!" she screamed as the car ripped away. "LOVE him! Love him with all
you got! You're stupid. You don't know
nuthin' – *NUTHIN'!"* Shaking her fist at
the car as it roared off, her stare colder than a heart should know, she went
inside and slammed the door. If she never
saw Esmeralda again it wouldn't matter.
Nothing mattered after this.

Inside the house; a house so empty
now; a house without a husband and without Esmeralda, she heard a flutter in the
birdcage across the room. Bird cage, bird
cage, my life is a bird cage, she
thought, not knowing some day a movie

would be made of the same name. Staring at her mother's parakeets, one green and one blue, she had tried so hard to breed, she saw only herself and Robert; two people trapped behind bars, only one of them had just flown away. You left me — you left me! NOBODY leaves me! "Shut up," she said, reaching for a pack of cookies. "SHUT UP!" If she never spoke to Esmeralda again, it would be OK. It would! What was the matter with her? Why was she doing this — why was calling Esmeralda suddenly the only thing that mattered now — oh, God! She picked up the phone and dialed.

"Nancy? That you?" she asked, trying to be cool. "Yeah, it's me," Blanche said. "Ez home yet?" . . . pause . . . Well, when she gets back, can you have her give me a call? Yeah, I'll be up," she said, fighting back shame/guilt/love; fighting back things she couldn't understand, and all of them pouring over her, through her, at once.

"I'll be up all night. Yes, I will. All night — have her call me. Promise? You do? Well, I'll be waiting."

If she never spoke to Esmeralda again as long as she lived, it would be OK.

Yeah, right.

Robert. It was all his fault. If he hadn't been so . . . sure of himself; so . . . strong when he wrapped an arm a- round you and ran his knee up your leg; if he hadn't smelled so good when you snuggled into his chest. Hell, why did he have to smell so good? What was the matter with her? Loving was bad for your health, she decided. If she ever got out of this mess, she'd never love again.

She thought of the cute ice cream man at just about every dog show she went to and how his body wanted to bust out of those tight tee shirts he always wore. She wondered if he gave everybody else free sundaes the way he gave her. Taking a deep breath, she decided next time she saw him, she'd ask. It wasn't easy being a woman desired by every man she met. It was a big responsibility. She turned to the mirror with a satisfied smile - gasped - and almost fainted.

River of Tears

Can the night ever be colder than when we're lonely? Esmeralda stared at the ceiling, studying tiny, geometrical designs in green, yellow and blue as they floated in the blackness around her. Did anyone else ever see them, she wondered? If she ignored them, would they go away? She closed her eyes and opened them again, in the private game she had played since a girl. Still there. A zillion squares, triangles and circles, filling the air like colored packaging material filling up a box. A box that held something important, something worth protecting, like her life and the most important thing within it: Robert.

Robert. A man like no man she had ever known before. How could anyone be so handsome and still be of this Earth? His body . . . his mind. How many times had she lost herself in those eyes and bathed in the sound of his voice? How many times had she been naked with him, touching him, feeling him all over her, and he had never known? Until that first night. That one night when they had finally - simultaneously and without thought - rushed into each other like two storms, two hurricanes; two forces of nature.

Tears. Tickling, irritating, embarrassing tears oozing down her face, catching at her nose. Go away, tears, she thought. You won't bring him back to me.

Night moon, hurry! Dress yourself for morning. Bring a lantern of sun to light my way. Illuminate the path. The flagstone path leading from the kitchen to the cottage where I can find truth. Truth? Why do I ask for truth. Why do I seek it? How is it possible to find answers of love from one like Jack, who only knows animals? Why was she thinking of Jack?

Because, he, too, had lost, she thought, wrapping the blankets tight around her neck, knowing Robert wouldn't come back no matter how much she wept.

Where was he? Why did he go? Couldn't he have waited just another hour - another day? Didn't he know? Didn't he know how much she cared? Didn't he know how much she needed him?

Didn't he love her?

Of course he did!

He left because of Blanche. She drove him off. She didn't appreciate him. She didn't understand his fine nature.

She kicked him out and didn't care what happened to him.

Where did he go?

Canada, probably.

He went back to Canada where he knew people, had family and where he could make a whole new life for himself.

Go for it, Robert, she thought. Make that new life of yours. I wish I were part of it. I wish we could find a place to live and laugh and raise Collies, just the two of us. I'd be the best student you ever had. I would! I know I would. I'd do anything you say - anything! We'd raise the best Collies ever, and show them all over the world if you wanted to. Everyone would know Robert Sheffield and his beautiful champion Collies. If only we were together. If only. I'd hold you all night! I'd kiss you everywhere. I'd run my fingers through your hair and run my tongue across your eyebrows and nibble on your ears. You'd laugh and tell me no, but I'd do it anyway. Robert! Robert! Isn't my life supposed to be part of yours? Wasn't I born for you? Why am I living if you aren't here with me? Why?

"Esmeralda, do you want any breakfast?" It was Nancy, still awkward about her new position as housekeeper, knocking at the bedroom door. How could she even think I'd want food at a time like this, Esmeralda wondered, rolling away on the bed without an answer.

"Is that a yes I hear?" Nancy asked. "I brought you some juice and toast," she said, entering the room and placing a silver tray on a table near the bed. "There's honey and butter, too."

Still no answer.

"Do you want me to pull the drapes?"

"Remind me to tell you, you're taking this job too seriously," Esmeralda mumbled in morning-face numbness.

"It's what you're paying me for. Rise and shine at six, just like you told me. You said not to listen if you say otherwise. Don't you remember?"

"I must have been out of my mind. Don't they have any heart where you come from?"

"I come from here," Nancy said. "We've got lots of heart. Scattered all over the place 'cause half of 'em are broken."

"You're making me cry. And I've already cried so much this whole place is going to float away."

"Shall I build a raft?"

"Better than drowning," Esmeralda said, sitting up and pushing her covers aside. "I thought you said you brought me some juice."

"Right here," Nancy smiled, handing her a glass of tomato juice with a slice of lemon.

Esmeralda wrinkled her nose. "Lemon!" she said, gingerly picking it off the edge of her glass and tossing it on the tray.

"Don't you like it?"

"Sure, if you want to shrivel up your mouth," Esmeralda winced, setting down the glass.

"I'm sorry. I'll remember next time."

"Next time, I might not be here."

"Oh? And where are you going? I'd hate to think I'm losing a job before I've hardly even started."

"Drifting away. . . drifting away like a feather."

"But, you can't go anywhere, Esmeralda. You lost your license, remember?"

Esmeralda bit into a piece of toast. "That's what they think. I can go anywhere I want to, as long as nobody around here tells." She looked at Nancy, standing there in her simple dress, with her hair pulled back in a pony tail. "You wouldn't tell on me, would you?"

"If you finish breakfast, carry the tray downstairs and wash the dishes, I might consider. . . "

"You mean, you have to think it over?"

"Well, lying to the authorities could get me in a lot of trouble."

"Not sticking by your employer can get you in a whole lot worse."

Nancy smiled with mischief. "Make your bed and we'll talk."

Talk? Talk was something people did too much of. And if anybody thought she was going to bother making a bed on a day like this, they were sadly mistaken. Hurrying to the bathroom, Esmeralda slammed the door. Pouring a hot bath she squirted blue-green soap into the steaming water and smelled the fresh bubbles rising like foam on the crest of an ocean wave. Hoisting her nightie, she sat and peed. Hadn't Picasso done a painting called Peeing Woman? She wondered how long the woman had posed like that for him, wondered about the relationship between the great artist and his model, whom she knew to be his mistress, Jacqueline. Hadn't they had children? Would she ever have children? She stripped off her nightie and studied herself in the bathroom mirror that was just big enough to reflect her breasts, nothing lower. Too bad, she thought. How was a woman supposed to evaluate her figure if she could only see half? Maybe that was OK, she thought, pinching her nipples to make them hard. She didn't really want to see her tummy.

Hot water melted away goose bumps as she slid into the tub. Reaching for a wash cloth, she snuggled her face into its warmth. Is this what a man feels when he kisses a woman between her legs? Is this what Robert felt? She could have drowned him that night. She wanted to. She would have. She reached for the soap . . . as Nancy prepared her own breakfast downstairs . . . .

"Ah!" Nancy said, surprised, as she looked up from the dishes to see Esmeralda coming down the steps. "Sleeping Beauty finally arrives!"

Finding an apple in a fruit bowl on the kitchen table, Esmeralda bit into it with a crunch and a grin. "Playing with the dishes, I see. Who's telling what you might be playing with next if I hadn't walked in!"

Laughing, Nancy offered a chair at the table and poured them both a cup of coffee. "Hey," she said, sitting down and propping her chin in her hands. "It gets lonesome sometimes."

"Steven, you mean?"

"Yeah."

"Any letters lately?"

Nancy shook her head. "I'm worried."

"What about his parents? What do they say?"

"They say I'm darn lucky to be living here at Lochwood instead of on the road in motels like he has to."

"But, you love him. Would it matter where you lived? As long as you were together, I mean?"

Nancy rolled her eyes. "That's the thing. I've known Steven ever since we were kids. We grew up together. We went to school together, church, everywhere. I can hardly even think of being with anyone else, and I'm sure he feels the same way."

"Then why are you lonesome? I'd think you'd feel like the luckiest woman alive. I mean, at least you know there's someone who cares about you, and counts on you as part of his life. It's a big world out there, Nancy. I know; I've seen a lot of it. The Riviera is beautiful, Cannes is classy, the Alps really are as high as they say . . . and yet, sometimes

I think the biggest place of all," she gestured to her heart, "is right here."

Sighing, Nancy smiled and finished her coffee. "That's what I like about you," she said, standing up and rinsing her cup in the sink. "You've got a way of making people feel good."

"Think so?" Esmeralda laughed. "Usually, I'm called self-centered."

"Makes you wonder, don't it?"

"About what?'

"People, and what they think they know," she said.

"What's this leading up to?"

"Hey, you don't think I go dustin' off all the book shelves in that big library of yours without readin' a title or two, do you?"

"And what do you see when you're in there reading on my time?"

"'*Cosmic Consciousness*,' '*The Master Key*,' '*Yoga And The Soul*' - just to name a few."

"Ah! And now you think you know my secrets, do you?"

"Getting close, I'd say."

"Well, most of those books belonged to my mother. Her family is from England and they're a strange bunch."

"Fruit doesn't fall far from the tree, I've heard."

"If you're asking what I think you're asking, the answer is, yes, I do believe in a lot of what those books say. It certainly makes more sense than a lot of other things I've been told."

"I see Jack coming up from the kennel. He probably wants to know if I put in the order for the meat and vegetables he wanted." Opening the kitchen door, she called out. "Jack! In here! Come, get yourself some coffee and warm up!"

"I just want to know if you got the order in!" he hollered back.

"You can pick everything up this afternoon!" Nancy said. "Don't forget to bring the bill back with you this time, OK?"

Waving a hand, Jack turned and headed back down the path to the kennel.

"Hmpf!" Nancy said. "Guess he doesn't like my coffee."

"Seems in a hurry," Esmeralda said, watching him through the window.

"Last time, he forgot to give me the bill and when I placed the order, they reminded me," Nancy said.

"Got to keep our suppliers paid if we're going to stay in business," Esmeralda said. "Speaking of business, I hope Blanche remembered to order that new – "

"Oh! I forgot to tell you – she called."

"When?"

"Yesterday. Then again last night, before you got home. Then, again this morning."

Ignoring the subject, Esmeralda asked, "Hey, what do you think about some of the new pups?"

"Pretty nice," Nancy said, pouring them each a fresh cup and taking her seat again at the wide oak table. It was a cozy kitchen, for being so large; plants on every window sill catching the warm sunlight; pots and pans hanging over the stove, where they hung on wooden pegs that had seen many a social event since the mansion was built in the 1750s. "Jack thinks they're the nicest litters we've ever had. Have you seen the one he calls Copper?" she asked, stirring the last of the sugar into her coffee, breaking up the lumps.

"The Red Sable? Yes. He could be a sire prospect."

"Have you ever seen such a beautiful head?"

"Nancy, I know this is hard to believe, but a head is only one part of the dog."

"But, it's the part with the Expression."

"Ah, yes. The all-important Expression," Esmeralda said. "The thing we hear about over and over again until we're sick. Well, expression comes from attitude. Attitude is conveyed in how a dog feels about itself and carries itself. And carriage is only as good as what the body can deliver."

"Meaning?"

"Meaning, *movement* is the thing," Esmeralda explained. "Even a judge doesn't always realize that."

"And where, exactly, do you come up with that theory?"

"I guess I've had good teachers," Esmeralda chuckled.

"Jack and Robert, I'd guess."

"And a lady called Life."

"Re-fill?" Nancy asked, getting up and heading to the pantry. Pulling the string for the light, she spent several minutes sorting through the shelves of brightly colored boxes and cans. There it was, she thought; sugar. Everything organized just like it was supposed to be; just like Life wasn't.

"None for me, thanks," Esmeralda said, standing to leave and still looking at Jack through the kitchen window. "I think I'd better go see those pups we were just talking about."

Loves Me/Loves Me Not

His back was turned to her as she made her way through the garden path winding alongside the red stone of the mansion. Spicy boxwood, like natural perfume, reached her nose. Breaking off the delicate end of a branch and crushing its green leaves between her fingers as she had done since she was a girl. She breathed in the scent. The bushes, gnarled and untrimmed, had once been the manicured pride of the mansion's original owners, who had brought them by ship from a trip abroad. The greenhouse, where her mother's roses had bloomed even in the coldest winter; not for her, roses. For her, it could only be wild flowers. *So long ago now . . . so very long ago . . . .*

"He loves me, he loves me not."

"What are you doing, Esmeralda?"

"Searching for truth," she smiled, plucking the petals of a daisy. *"Loves me, loves me not. . ."*

And he had suddenly rushed to pick her a whole bouquet.

"Here," Robert had said, handing her Queen Anne's lace, snap dragons and violets. "As long as you live, may every one of them say he loves you!"

So long ago now . . . so very long ago.

Jack; she looked at him now. Strong, dependable Jack when he had first started working for her father at Lochwood. Until then, she had never studied a young man so closely before. There were no brothers, no cousins for her to grow up with. And, being privately tutored, no schoolboys for her to observe. Boys in church were only a fleeting vision. Church was a place seldom visited and much avoided by her father, whose understanding of power over others could not allow himself, or his daughter, to be dominated.

Jack; Jack with a heart so simple, so confident; knowing what he wanted in life, where he wanted to go. He had grown up loved, she was sure of it. He was important to someone. Was it her imagination, or could one really tell when somebody else had been loved? By the way he walked, maybe? The way he combed his hair and always smelled so clean? When he had first come to their place, she would peek around corners just to see him, drink him in. He sang to the dogs. That was the first thing she noticed. And the dogs would sing back to him. They would line up for him and yowl as if they, too, were singing. None of her father's dogs had ever done that before.

He would arrive early, with his mother. From her room, now her office, Esmeralda could see them walking across the field. Every morning, no matter how cold or rainy, they would trudge through win-ter snow, laugh in the Spring mud, wear a trail in the Summer dust and hurry through Autumn leaves. His mother, carry-ing sandwiches and cookies; Jack calling out to a young pup taken home for mending the night before, striking weeds with a stick, tossing rocks into a stream to see how far he could pitch. He liked women, she knew. And they liked him just as much.

When he got his first car, he was rarely without the blonde neighbor girl, Faye Dougherty, beside him. And he never noticed the others after that, not even the shy girl who had snapped a picture of him and kept it safe under her pillow, in her purse, in her pocket. He would have laughed, she thought, if he even suspect-ed his affect on her.

"Esmeralda!" he looked up from raking the grass now, propping his hat back just a little in a familiar gesture like the one Robert often made. "And, I thought I was the only one here, on a nice day like this."

You should never be the only one anywhere, she thought to herself. And you won't be. Someone will find you. A friend; a relative. Love will find you again, Jack. No, a man like you won't be alone for long.

Good thing others can't hear what we're thinking, she decided. "I wanted to take a look at the pups," is what she said.

"Good," he nodded to a golden-colored spirit, about six months old, adoring him from the kennel nearby. "I was just now getting ready to work with Copper, over there. You can help me."

"Hello, Copper," Esmeralda greeted the young dog with a sing-song lilt in her voice. "Aren't you beautiful?"

"He knows," Jack said. "Don't remind him."

She laughed. "What are you making here?" she asked, noticing the pattern he had raked in the leaves. "If I didn't know better, I'd say it looks like a show ring."

"I'd say the same thing," he laughed, slipping a collar and lead out of his jacket and over the pup's lean head. "Always knew you were a smart one."

"But, not smart enough," she said quietly. "Right?"

"What's that, young lady?" *Young lady* is what he called her, had always called her, when asserting his authority.

"I said, not smart enough."

He looked her in the eye. "To drive stick shift, you mean?"

She froze. *He knew! He knew about the car that night.* If Jack knew, then how many others had figured out she couldn't, never had, and probably never would be able to drive stick shift.

"Esmeralda, only you can say how far you'll go for love. But, let me tell you something. If Robert Sheffield loved you even half as much as the rest of us do, he never would have let you take the blame for what he, himself, had done."

"But – "

"Enough," he said, handing her the lead. "I want to see if you can take this pup around, then stack him up for me so I can see him. When this whole thing blows over, you'll have to go out there again in front of everybody. You can't hide forever."

"Is that . . . is that what you think?" she stuttered.

"Aren't you?" he asked.

"You think I'm hiding?"

"Why else haven't you sent in the entries?" he said.

She looked away.

"We can sell von Havenburg Collies for years if you want to, just on the kennel's good name. But, guess again if you think we can afford not to show the dogs for very long. We need the Collies to keep this place going. You know that. And the show circuit is our best advertisement."

"I can't face people. Not yet."

"You'll have to. We have a business to run. Do you think Blanche Jacobus is holding back? She's out there cleaning up. From what I hear, everywhere she goes, she's getting the points."

"They feel sorry for her, that's all."

"We gotta fight back," he said. "Where's your fire? Your guts!"

"They won't even look at me when I go out, Jack. They won't!"

"Well, *I'm* lookin' at you, ain't I? An' if Faye was here right now, she'd be tellin' you the same thing."

"Would she? Would she, Jack?"

"I know she would," he said forcefully.

"You miss her," she said.

To the pup's delight, he messed with Copper's soft ears and turned him loose. "Very much," he said. "Very, very much."

"I'm sorry about everything," she said, as the pup scampered off. "You know I am."

He nodded. "It was an accident," he said. "Regardless of who was driving. I just have to accept it, that's all. I have to accept what I can't do anything about. I can't bring her back," he swallowed, fighting the lump that still rose in his throat whenever he talked about it. "I know that." His whole body seemed to shudder, like one who is giving up. "I know I can't. But, I try. I try! I keep trying to understand *why?* Why her! *Why Faye?*"

Taking a deep breath, she slipped an arm around his side. "Jack. My dear, dear friend. If you only knew how many times I've asked myself the same thing."

"Makes you wonder if God even wants us to know," he said. What kind of God would ever have been so cruel? He could only trust; only trust that One seeing things from a higher standpoint, with a wider view, could know what he, himself, would never understand.

"Yes," she said, wiping away a tear. "I feel so helpless sometimes. So tiny, like nobody cares. Like when I was little, and Momma wasn't there for me because she couldn't be. And Daddy was away on business. Know what?" she brightened and smiled quickly. "Know what I used to pretend?" she said, facing him. "I used to pretend someone - a handsome guy with curly hair and blue eyes like yours - would take me far away and make me the most important girl in the world."

"And how would he do that, Esmeralda?"

"By loving me. Just me. Not Esmeralda von Havenburg, the richest girl in town. Just me."

"Esmeralda," he said, holding her safely, "if I was him - the one you're talking about - I would do that."

Something about him then, maybe not any other time, but then, made it feel OK. Gently, shy as a foal seeing its master for the very first time, she kissed his hand. With a question in his eyes, he searched her gaze for a moment, understood, and laid her down in the leaves.

Chapter 6

It was 1952. The world's population was 2.635 billion; Albert Schweitzer won the Nobel Peace Prize and a young woman named Elizabeth II became Queen of England. As Ernest Hemingway counted sales of his masterpiece, "The Old Man and the Sea," Jonas Salk developed his polio vaccine and "The Today Show" premiered on NBC. Fred Astaire was putting the finishing touches on a jazz album for Mercury Records, and, yes, the Doberman Pinscer did win Westminster.

Invasion   No, I will not talk with her," Esmeralda said, from an overstuffed chair in the library.

"But, it's her sixth call today," Nancy countered. "She says it's important."

"She should have thought about that before she messed up my life. I'm through with her!" Esmeralda snapped as she returned to the latest issue of the Collie magazine she was reading and Nancy left the room.

"I'm sorry, Blanche," Nancy said. "She won't come to the phone . . . yes, I understand . . . . Do you want me to tell her in exactly those words? No? OK, then. Good-bye, Blanche."

Nancy turned to see Esmeralda standing in the doorway to the entrance hall.

"What did she say?"

"You don't want me to repeat it."

"That bad, huh? Well, at least I know she's her same old self."

"Same old self, only a whole lot madder," Nancy said.

"Well she can just cool down," Esmeralda said, plunking herself back onto the chair. "What's she got to be mad about, anyway? Huh?" she said picking up the magazine again. "I'm the one who should be mad," she said, rifling through the pages. "I spend my whole life looking for a man who can take the place of Robert Sheffield and she - *the one who's got him* - goes and kicks him out of her life like a bum! Mad? You bet I'm mad. I don't know where he is or where I'd be able to find him even if I did. *You bet I'm mad!*" she hollered, tossing the magazine across the room.

"Well if you feel that way about it, why don't you go back over to her house and ask her where he is yourself!"

"Oh, she'd never tell me. Not now, she wouldn't."

"Then send Jack. He'll get her to tell him. Anyway, she likes Jack."

"Everybody likes Jack," Esmeralda said, pulling her sweater tight. "Don't you know that?"

Nancy smiled. "You bet I know it. If I wasn't married, I'd be after him myself."

"Well, forget it. I won't have any cheap romances going on around here under my roof - or NOT under my roof, whichever the case may be. Do you understand?"

"I understand," Nancy said, like a scolded school girl. "But you've got to admit, he's good looking."

"Jack? Good looking?" Esmeralda raised an eyebrow in surprise. "Why, I've never noticed."

"Never noticed! Why, I can hardly believe that. Didn't you see that man - in those pants of his - when he was cutting down those branches last along the driveway? If he'd been sweating any more, who knows what else we'd have been able to see."

"I didn't see anything."

"A body to die for, you said! Must be all the work around the farm, you said!"

"I don't remember - "

"The heck you don't! You talked about it for a whole week!"

"I did not."

"What! You asked me to take him some iced tea from the 'fridge and when I did, you just looked at his pants and stared."

"Nancy!"

"Don't tell me you didn't. I saw!"

"You didn't see anything. I was just making sure he had something to drink, that's all."

"Then why did you ask me if I thought '*it*' was real?" It was a question Esmeralda would never have to ask again.

"*Nancy!* Finish the dusting and water the plants. And when you're done with that, empty the garbage. And when you do, think about all the garbage you just said!"

"Come on, Esmeralda. Admit it. Jack's a good lookin' man."

"And burn the trash!"

"Any woman can see how good lookin' Jack is - she'd have to be blind!"

"Wash the laundry!"

"He's got to be lonely by now - "

"And hang it up to dry - "

"Don't you think he's lonely?"

"Outside! Hang it up outside!"

"All Jack needs is a little lovin'."

"*Outside!*"

A little lovin' was all anybody needed, Esmeralda thought, as she rescued the Collie magazine from a lamp shade before it caught fire; found what she had been looking for, and melted. There he was: *Ch. Von Havenburg Red Sunset*, sire of their new hopeful Copper; Jack Milliken in suit and tie right beside him. She had picked the suit herself. He wanted to wear the brown one Faye had bought for him, but he looked so good in navy blue. The hat was her finishing touch. . . .

"I can't go out-shining the dogs this way," he had said.

"The judge won't know who to look at," Faye smiled.

"Precisely the idea," Esmeralda teased.

They had taken Best of Breed that day, and a Group II besides. Only the German Shepherd was better, handled by a young Jimmy Moses.

"Nice dog, Jimmy's got," Jack admitted about the man who would go on to become one of the most recognized names in the sport. *"Wonder who his client is?"*

"Whoever it is, they're not paying Jimmy enough," Esmeralda said.

"What about you, Jack? Are you being paid enough?" Faye asked.

Smiling, he kissed her and she smacked him playfully.

"Sometimes," he said to Esmeralda, *"I think I could do better. Then, Faye, here, says where else could I have such a good time? No, Lochwood's my home,"* he said. *"Now and always."*

She could hear them now; see it all; she thought, glancing away from the pages, to the phone. The world - the whole world - was breaking apart around her, no matter what she tried, no matter how much she wanted it not to. But, von Havenburg Kennels was strong; here to stay, no matter what people thought; no matter what they said; no matter what they did.

And she - no one else - was von Havenburg Kennels.

"It's Blanche," Nancy said, breaking Esmeralda's concentration as she entered the library.

"I didn't hear the phone ring," Esmeralda said.

"That's because she didn't call," Nancy said.

"You mean she's here in person? After all this time? The Queen of the World deigns to show up at my door in person? Tell her to go away," Esmeralda snapped, the small veins at her temple pulsing. But, with a dramatic flurry of self-importance, Blanche strutted into the room, tossed Esmeralda's broken compact on a table and took charge.

"Your phone ain't working!" she smirked, throwing her coat and purse on a chair and helping herself to a dish of chocolates. "Somebody should report it . . . . "Well?" she looked at Nancy, shooing her away. "Run along! We'll be all right in here – just as long as you don't have any sharp knives layin' around. Right, Ez?"

The silence was deafening. With a question in her eyes, Nancy stood firm. "Should I go?" she asked Esmeralda.

If silence could be loud, Esmeralda's was like sitting next to a pair of clashing cymbals.

"Oh, come on, Ez," Blanche said. "Don't keep the poor girl waiting. You know we gotta work this out one way or the other. Let her go and let's get it over with," she said, pushing up her sleeves. "Come on! You an' me, Ez!"

228

"Since when did we start letting the scum of the Earth in here?" Esmeralda asked Nancy.

"See!" Blanche smiled brightly. "I told you we'd be OK!" Fluffing pillows and looking around with an air of comedy, she asked, "Now where'd you say you hid those knives?"

"GET OUT!" Esmeralda screeched, throwing her magazine.

Dodging like a prizefighter, eyebrows wide, Blanche picked up the pace - "Here," she said to Nancy, shuffling her across the room and glancing back anxiously over a shoulder. "Let me show you the door!"

Wondering if she should wait outside or get busy, Nancy went to the pantry for a mop and bucket. "Come on, mop," she said to a can of floor wax, "You an' me got a date with the front hallway."

The sound of shattering glass against a wall stopped her. There goes the Steigal vase on the coffee table, she thought, reaching for the dustpan and brush.

Muffled hollers - First Blanche, then Esmeralda.

What were they saying, she wondered?

The rip and crash of a curtain. Well, she wouldn't have to worry about pulling the drapes any more, she decided.

"BITCH!"

"I told you never to call me that!"

More splintering glass! The ash trays? Please don't let it be the Hummel figurines.

Slap!

Another slap!

Who needed soap operas in a house like this, Nancy thought? How much could they take? How much could they give! *How long could this go on?*

Sudden silence. . . .

More silence. . . .

Please, God, don't tell me they've killed each other, Nancy prayed. Should she knock on the door; call the police?

The calm voice of Esmeralda on the house intercom decided for her. "Nancy?" she asked sweetly. "Would you bring us some tea, please?"

Shaking her head with silent exasperation, Nancy answered, "I'll be right there. *I'll be right there!*"

Knocking on the door before she entered; prepared to duck anything - insults or unidentified flying objects hurling through the air - Nancy hunched her shoulders and gingerly entered the library.

"Paris! Oh, I love Paris," Esmeralda was saying, paying no attention to Nancy crunching her way over brittle shards of glass.

"Switzerland?" Blanche asked. "I think I've got relatives there."

Placing the tray on a small table, Nancy quietly surveyed the room she had so carefully maintained. "Your tea," she said. An ant on the floor, a bit of dust behind the sofa, couldn't have been more insignificant to the two women sitting there, laughing and paging through a stack of travel magazines. *So much alike,*

230

Nancy thought to herself. I wonder if they've ever noticed.

"Oh, the fashion houses . . ."

"Have you seen the swimsuits they're wearing on the French Riviera?"

"Honey, I hear they don't even bother!"

"Italy! . . . *The men!*"

"Madrid - *Matadors!*"

"England - *Buckingham Palace!*"

"Forget the Palace, Honey, when do they hold *Krufts?*"

Miles to Go

Funny, how we can be in one place, totally unaware of what anybody is thinking about us, somewhere else. Have you ever wondered if we can mutually feel such moments on some level? While Blanche and Esmeralda sipped tea and nibbled on crackers, surely Robert was asking himself what had gone wrong.

Why had he ever left Canada, Robert wondered, as he hiked through the woods that day. Was the sky really more blue here? Were the people in those houses of the village below kinder, gentler somehow? From here, on the trail that wove itself across this side of the mountain, he could see as far as a lifetime. Why had she done it, he asked himself, as he had asked so many times before. She didn't have to; it was, after all, an accident.

The Sable Collie at his side, Ch. Sheffield Excaliber, caught the sound of a startled deer spinning in the leaves and took up the chase. Deer and Collie, different creatures sharing the same world, and, for the moment at least, rushing in the same direction. Follow that dream, he thought. Go for it. Maybe you'll call me when you get there.

What about his own dreams, he wondered now? He was Forty, in his prime, with no prospect of a family. Most of his friends, those he had grown up with outside of Montreal, were celebrating anniversaries, buying cars and paying mortgages. He was still renting.

What was he afraid of? Catching those dreams?

He thought about his prospects of earning a living. Things had been good before the accident. During the week, there was enough work painting houses to pay the bills and set money aside. On weekends, there were shows; lots of them. He liked a good show dog. He liked the feel of being around perfection. He understood what it took to guide the development of a bloodline, and bring forth beautiful animals.

The Collie came back to him now, panting and falling into step at his side. Reassured that Robert was still here, he looked up at the man standing between him and life's uncertainties.

"She got away?" Robert asked about the deer. With his mind somewhere between Pennsylvania women and Canadian solitude, he said, "It's OK, fella. We've got miles to go."

Robert wasn't the only one with a few miles to go.

In a sudden flurry of bulging steamer trunks lashed with VH Belting straps from the factory; alligator skin suitcases, fur coats and high heels, the two power mongers had joined forces once again.

Swearing off men on Valentine's Day, armed with enough lipstick, cigarettes, false eyelashes and lingerie to make even Jayne Mansfield blush, Blanche and Esmeralda asked what in the world had come over them and booked a cabin on the very next departure of the Queen Mary. As they waved bon voyage from the highest deck, through a blizzard of confetti and a forest of streamers; bidding farewell to no one in particular, but everyone who mattered; there are those who say Blanche was seen winking at a well-dressed passenger who slipped her his stateroom key. But, how could they see? Esmeralda, toasting New York Harbor with champagne, had packed the opera glasses.

"HAVE ARRIVED LONDON (STOP) OVER SEA SICKNESS (STOP) BLANCHE GONE ALL NIGHT (STOP) ALL IS WELL. EZ."

"London," Jack said. *"Esmeralda's Mum. How long are they staying?"*

"Until the Queen throws them out!" Nancy laughed.

"With Blanche, they won't have time to unpack their bags!"

London was great. Esmeralda's mother loved Blanche; shopping was grand at Harrod's; Westminster Abby bored them to tears, and one particular guard at Buckingham Palace shall never forget one particular Tuesday when a brash, Blonde American gave him a hip-check and flashed both tits for a Royal smile . . . . Oh, yes; Krufts was good, too.

The Plot Thickens

"Oh, I'm so glad they're having fun again," Nancy said, shaking her shoulders with delight over a letter from Madrid.

Finishing a jelly roll, Jack nodded. "It sure feels better," he said. "Ever notice how a person doesn't even have to be around, and you can still tell a difference?"

She knew what he meant. The whole place seemed lighter. "Easier to breathe," she laughed. "What do the dogs have to say about it?" she asked, wanting him to stay; wanting to talk.

"Love it! Every one of 'em. The only thing is," he teased, "a few of them couldn't sleep last night."

"Oh?" she asked, picking up the basket of fresh-picked tomatoes and peppers he'd brought in from the hot house; washing them in the sink.

"Yeah, they say there was quite a commotion coming from over here. It got pretty loud."

"That's funny," Nancy said, her back to him as she diced a pepper for an omelet. "I didn't hear a thing."

But, he kept on. He could feel it crawling all over him like a suffocating, smelly sickness. "He's back, I take it?"

"I picked him up at the bus station last night," she said quietly, unable to face him, though why his opinion should matter she couldn't tell.

"What happened to his car?" Jack asked.

"The company's," she said, and in the tone of those simple words, Jack heard all he needed to know. "So, we'll be seeing a lot of Steven for a while," he said.

She nodded, and scrubbed the last plate for what seemed like the hundredth time. *Don't make me turn around, Jack, she thought. Don't you dare keep standing there, waiting for me to turn around.*

"Well, I guess I'll be going then," he said, standing his ground.

She rinsed the pan, slowly and began washing it again.

"Yep," he said, "Guess I'll be going."

"See you around," she said.

"Yep. See you later," he said.

She stood there as if both feet were stuck in cement. Pushing aside the frilly curtain of the window above the sink, she took in the view of the shady lawn, sloping to the cottage and kennels below. Even from here, between the branches of the oak trees, she could see him; Jack, in his rumpled white shirt and Stetson hat, going about the kennel gathering up dog food bowls and rinsing them for the next feeding. Life would go on, she thought. Life would go on as long as there was Jack and the kennel.

"*You seem so far away,*" she had said to Steven as she rubbed his smooth shoulders during the night. "Everything OK with your work?" He had been gone so long, it was almost like being with a stranger; spicy; stimulating to every scent, every nerve, every crevasse of her imagination.

"Yeah, Babe. Everything's fine. Don't you worry," he smiled, reaching around for her and rolling over on his side. "Hey," his eyes twinkled, "when are we gonna have a baby?"

"I don't know," she said, stroking his belly, pulling at the hairs, a shade darker than the sandy-blonde of his head. "You're away so much – "

"Well, that's gonna change," he kissed her. "Starting right now, I'm gonna be home every day."

"Every day?"

"Yeah!" he smiled, hugging her. "Every day."

"But, where?"

"Where, what?" he asked.

"I mean, where are you going to stay? I just have the one room here, and – "

"And what?"

"Well, what is Esmeralda going to say about it?"

"Who cares?"

"Who cares?" she asked with a note of disbelief in her voice.

"Yeah. Who cares what she thinks?"

"Well, I do. Esmeralda's my boss."

"You mean I'm your boss, don't you? I'm your husband. Is she your husband? Did you go and get weird on me while I was away? Come on," he said, sliding a leg over her and pulling her hips to him. "You ready? You want that baby? Let's make a baby."

Moaning how much she wanted their child, wondering what their daughter, their son, would be like; wondering if she could find them in a crowd, a crowd of unborn children waiting to be chosen. Wrapping both arms around him; kissing his neck; she circled her tongue around his Adam's Apple and nipped playfully.

"I love when you do that, Baby," he whispered, as he pressed and rubbed between her legs. "Love it."

"Mmmmmmm," she moaned. "I've missed you. I've missed every, every part of you," she whispered, reaching down, pulling his swollen cock, cupping his balls in her hand.

"Make it up to me, Babe," he said, his voice thick. "Spread 'em. Real wide. Let me look up your hole."

"They'll hear us," she said.

"Who's gonna hear? Jack's outside and ol' Ezzie's away. Ezzie the Lezzie," he smirked. "Can she do this for you, huh?" Crouching on his knees, he pulled her lower on the bed and spread her legs. Bending down, he blew warm breath between

237

her legs and licked inside her thighs. "Can she do this?"

"Steven!" She grabbed his hair.

"*What!*" he hissed.

"It's wrong."

"Wrong!"

"You know how I feel when you do that and kiss me right after."

"Don't you like it?"

"It's not - you know - clean."

"So, take a shower! Take a bubble bath!" he said, pulling away; sulking. "I'm not ashamed of you."

"That's not what I meant. I mean -"

"You mean you don't like it," he said. "I can make you like it. You know I can. *I can make you love it.*"

"That's not it . . . "

"Then tell me! Tell me what am I supposed to do if my wife won't do it with me the way I want? What am I supposed to do, Nancy? Huh?"

"It's OK," she said, quickly, spreading her legs apart; pushing her pelvis at him. "Do it, Steven. Do anything you want," she said, closing her eyes. "*Just don't kiss me after.*"

"Whatcha doin, man?" came the question that morning.

Jack turned to see a sandy-haired, blue eyed fellow in T-shirt, khakis and shades.

"Steven," Jack nodded, keeping his distance.

"Need any help?" the young man asked. "I was just walkin' around, thinkin'."

238

"I can handle it," Jack said, with a close-lipped smile, filling up the last water bowl for the dogs.

The young salesman trying to make his way in a world owned by others lit up a cigarette and crossed his arms. "Got in last night," he said.

"I heard," Jack said quietly, standing his ground.

"Yeah, Nancy an' me, we ain't seen much of each other this last month or so."

"*Your work,*" Jack nodded, like one who had heard it all before.

"Yeah."

"*With the company,*" Jack said, still nodding, but offering not the slightest praise.

"Yeah."

"*Just how is* the music business these days, Steven?"

Steven took a long drag. "Great," he, too, nodded his head. "Great."

"Good," Jack said. "Well, I'd better be brushing up some of these dogs, after the rain and all. Nothin' worse for a Collie than mud."

"Yeah. Sure. Well, nice seein' ya," Steven said, as Jack walked away.

Jack; always busy, always walking away. . . .

"He don't like me," Seven said, later, as Nancy poured him juice to go with the omelet. "That guy never liked me."

"Sure he does," she smiled. "He just doesn't understand your life, that's

239

all. He doesn't understand something as glamorous as the record business." The way she said "record business" left no doubt as to the high regard in which she held the industry and all its players. It was a regard not in small part cultivated by Steven, himself.

"Pretty big misunderstanding if you ask me," Steven scoffed.

"For a pretty big guy," she said, punching him playfully on the arm. "Last night was fun."

"Yeah? I wasn't so sure."

"Well, it was. I just . . . miss you so much, Steven. I don't know what to do sometimes. I don't know how to act. Were you telling the truth last night?"

"About what?"

She stared at him with scolding in her eyes. "About a baby."

"Oh! Yeah. Yeah, I was tellin' the truth."

"You really want us to have a baby," she said, making sure.

He wiggled his tongue at her and pulled her to his lap. "If it'll make you happy."

"It's not just me," she said, catching his tongue between her fingers; holding it gently, her eyes studying the rosy color of his mouth. "A baby isn't just for me."

"Yeah," he said, slipping his tongue from her fingers. "I know. I'm sorry, Nancy. Us. I mean, a kid for us." He scratched at a scab on his arm. "Any jelly around here?"

"What kind?" she grinned. He laughed; neither one of them spoke; each remembering the night before. "Steven?" she asked. "Can we afford a baby?"

He sat down his glass and just laughed.

"Steven?" she asked, again.

"Hey . . . Babe . . . " he said real slow, playing with her top button. "Didn't I tell you? I got somethin' big cookin'. Real big."

"Can you tell me about it?"

"Well, I'm not supposed to. If I do, it could cost me my job."

"Give me a hint," she said, cuddling close.

He leaned his head back, sized her up and squinted his eyes barely enough to notice his pupils, pretending to decide if she qualified.

"Come on, Steven . . ." she pleaded. "I'll let you do it again."

Easy enough.

"Alls I can say is, there's a new singer comin' out and we gotta get him."

"Man or woman?"

"A guy. I met him at a promotion party last month in Philly."

"What's he like?"

"Hot. Him an' his producer are workin' it. They're trying to get him on Bandstand with Clark."

"Exciting!"

"Like, big time," Steven said, warming up now. "If we could sell enough records, my cut would be enough to get you out of this place and get us to New York. We could have it made the rest of our lives – you oughtta see this guy! You oughtta see the girls go crazy!"

"I'll bet there's lots," she said, knowing Steven wasn't the kind to resist temptation. But, she wouldn't think about that; she would put the idea of Steven and other women out of her mind.

"Screaming their heads off!" he went on, oblivious to her mood.

"More juice?" she asked, pulling away.

He shook his head and pulled her back. "The thing is, this guy's with some rinky-dink label nobody ever heard of. He's almost twenty-five. If he don't get signed pretty soon, he'll end up dyin'. He belongs with RCA, but this producer he's got says our guys already know about him and this new song he wrote. He says if RCA wants the song, they gotta take the artist, too, or no deal."

"Is the song any good?"

He laughed in disbelief. "It's great! It's worth millions. But, the singer, himself, is worth more. His pro-ducer says he's got more material like what they're pushing now. You ought to hear it, Nancy! It makes you wanna *beat your feet*, you know?"

"Well, why doesn't RCA want him, Steven? Why don't they snatch him up?"

He paused. "They got their reasons, Babe. We got a singer of our own who wants the song. If I told you his name, you wouldn't believe me, but he's kind of special to the head of A&R."

"There's something else," she said. "Isn't there, Steven."

He hesitated. "Too smart for me, that's what you are. Hey, I could really use a cup of that coffee."

She got up and poured him a cup.

"Thanks, Babe. Well," he took a sip, "me an this producer, we get to talkin' and before I know it, he's tellin' me the only thing standin' in the way of him makin' a deal is this same guy in the A&R department, who I happen to know. He takes one look at me and says if I could change the guy's mind it could swing the whole deal!"

"Well, could you?"

"Sure."

"Well?"

"It takes blonde hair and blue eyes," he said, holding her gaze; knowing she wasn't picking up on it. "And pants," he finished.

"Pants?"

Nursing his coffee while the idea sank in, he waited.

"*Steven!*" she said, incredulous; he would never do such a thing – would he?

"For us? For our future, Babe?" He sat her on his leg again. "I'd do anything for us."

"I don't know." she said, feeling dizzy, unsure of his hands upon her now. Where had those hands been? She had never thought about that before.

"What's it matter?" he asked. "That kind of thing's nothing – nothing! I'd do anything to get past a secretary. Who wouldn't? Who cares?"

"I do," she said. "I do, Steven."

"*How the hell else am I gonna to get anywhere, Nancy!*" he said, raising his voice in the way of one who has examined every prospect, every hope and come up empty. "I got no college - no money. I'm not some company president or some smart inventor. I come from nuthin'. *I AM nuthin!*" What am I supposed to do!"

"But, you don't have to - "

"*How do you know?*" he pressed. "*How do you know* I already don't? Can you prove it? Can you prove it by the people I know? Who I hang around with? Do you know what it's like out there? *Do you?* You're livin' here, in this place - all private and safe. What do you know about life in the city, hearin' cuss words everywhere you go, sellin' records and pitchin' to DJs. It takes a lot more than a record jacket to get 'em to listen, Nancy. There's tons of guys like me out there; every one of 'em pushin records."

"Don't yell," she said, touching his face, running her hand through his hair. "How could I? How could I know? You never say anything. You never tell me."

"Why should I? It's bad enough for me to worry about! Jobs are hard to find, Nancy. Damn hard! Selling is all I know. You want me to get a job at the Belting like everybody else? Work in a factory and if we're lucky end up owing the bank the rest of our lives for some row house in town? Is that what you want? *What the Hell am I supposed to do!*"

"But, to - "

"What? Use my body? It's just a piece of meat, Baby. A piece of meat."

"Steven!"

"What!"

"Don't say that!"

"A piece of meat? Come on, Baby. Dick's just a way of gettin' around in the business, that's all."

"You never talked like this before," she said, the skin on the back of her head getting tight.

"It's not important, that's why. What's important - *the only thing that matters* - is how we get from here," he slapped one of his legs, "to here," he slapped her butt and smiled.

She had never seen him like this before. Where was the one she had grown up with? What was he telling her now? Men? Had Steven really been with men?

"Steven," she asked. "Have you - "

His eyes met hers, completely innocent to what she wanted to ask; forcing her to say it.

"Have you ever been - " but, she couldn't finish. If she asked, he might tell her; if he told her, she would have to make a scene; if she made a scene, she would lose him; if she lost him, there would be no baby. Maybe he was right. Maybe it didn't really matter. Maybe, like he said, sometimes his dick was, after all, just a piece of meat.

"Steven," she said, wrapping her arms around his neck; running both hands through his hair now; is that how you feel with me? You know, when we're," she looked upstairs, "like it's nothing?"

"*Oh, no, Baby!*" he said, hugging her close, pulling her to his chest. "No, no! *With you* - with you, it's like nobody else ever. It's like I'm home, where I belong. *The way it's supposed to be.*"

It was good enough. Good enough for now; good enough for always.

"So," she said now, understanding, "If you can get this guy in the company to like you, he might forget how much he likes the other singer."

"And if he forgets about the other singer," Steven finished the plan, "he's gonna sign our artist."

"Is it over then?" she asked. "Is it over then, Steven?"

"*That?*" he asked, surprised. "Sure, Babe!" he said, kissing her, knowing what she meant. "The last time. As soon as we get a deal."

Jack pitched another shovel of fresh gravel into the wheelbarrow and glanced down the long driveway. Was somebody sitting down by the road, at the estate's entrance? Probably a bike rider taking a break, he thought, as he returned to the job at hand. A layer of fresh stone dust from the local quarry made a good base for the kennel runs. Most kennels had dirt runs. A few of them poured cement, but he didn't like the idea of raising the von Havenburg Collies on cement. It made for sore feet and legs in his opinion, which led to bad joints over time. Sure, it helped to keep the nails short and was easier to clean and cement runs could be hosed down in just a few minutes. But, he could trim a dog's nails with a file and didn't mind the extra time it took picking up a dog's droppings if it helped give the von Havenburg Collies an advantage over the competition.

He pushed the wheelbarrow to the nearest run, dumped the gravel and spread it evenly with a rake. The stranger was still there. Curious, he set aside the rake, hiked to the mansion to check in on Nancy and found her in the kitchen with Steven.

"Sorry to interrupt," he said. "Anything for the mailbox, Nancy?"

Smiling, she went to the spice rack on the wall beside the cabinet where she kept canned goods and pulled out a letter.

Tucking it in his pocket, nodding to Steven, he tipped his hat and left.

"Told you he doesn't like me," said Steven, as they heard the pickup engine start. "He can't even hardly speak to me."

"Hush," she said, with a big, wet kiss. "Tell me about your artist," and with that, he knew she was with him, supporting him, believing in him no matter what it took.

"Well, that could be another problem," he said. "Him and his producer? They're both Black."

"But, that didn't stop Johnny Mathis or Nat King Cole, did it? Or Lena Horne or Eartha Kitt did it?"

"No, but it might stop our A&R guy."

"But, it's you he'd want," she teased. "The *bad boy*."

"Not that I want to be," he caught her eye.

"No. Of course," she agreed.

"Only 'cause it's the only way."

"Right," she said, almost a little too enthusiastically now, which he noticed. Women, he decided. He'd never figure them out.

"There's something else," he said.

"More? I'm not sure I can take it."

"This guy, the singer?" The plot thickened. "He's blind. He's gotta be led on the stage, he can't see where the mic is. Aw, Christ, this is stupid! It won't work. I finally get a chance to make somethin' of myself *and look what I'm gonna have to do.*"

"But, if it has to do with talent, who cares what color he is? Who cares if he's blind? Why should it matter? Does he have to go on stage? Does anybody have to know? There's a way, Steven. You know that. There's always a way."

He sighed. "Nancy, what am I gonna do with you. Am I gonna holler and scream or am I gonna just thank my lucky stars that you're in my life lookin' out for me. You're my angel," he said, hugging her.

"Well, I'll always look out for you. You know that."

"Good," he said. "You know, you're right. There is another way. I mean, maybe I wouldn't have to do what I said before. You know; let him do whatever he wants to with me in his office an' all. There *would be* another way, but, I just didn't think there was any chance of it, so I wasn't even gonna bring it up."

"What, Steven? What else could we do?"

"Well, if we could pull together enough money, this producer thinks he could buy us a few favors, you know? Hey, it's just business, remember? But, if we could; if we could get the cash; well, he knows who to take care of . . . "

"How much?" she asked. "I have some money saved up."

"Five thousand."

"*Five thousand dollars!* Maybe the first idea was the best one. Five thousand dollars. Why so much?"

"Because of what the deal's worth. This producer is so desperate to get a deal with RCA he'll give me a cut of every record the guy sells, every appearance the guy ever makes, every dime he makes for the rest of his whole goddam life! We're talkin' a shitload, Nancy. A shitload!"

"Steven, I don't like it when you swear like that."

"Hey, it don't mean shit. Everybody talks like that."

"Not around here, they don't."

"It's the business."

"I find that so hard to believe, Steven, when I think of Rosemary Clooney and Bing Crosby."

"Would I lie? I've told you everything. Put all my cards on the table. Would I lie to you now?"

She thought before answering. "Glad you added that last part," is all she said.

"Look, I gotta make some calls today," he said, knowing there was a slur in there someplace, but unable to find it. Do you think anybody'll mind if I use the phone? And I'm gonna need someplace to spread out my papers."

"As long as Esmeralda's away, you can make yourself at home. You know that. I mean, I can't see why not."

"Great," he smiled. "So what do you think?"

"About what?"

"About me asking Esmeralda for the five thousand?"

Parking his truck fifty feet or so from the entrance, Jack got out and waited. The unexpected visitor didn't move. Who could it be, he wondered?

"Hello!" he called out. "Do you need any help!"

No answer.

"Can I help you!" he hollered louder.

Still no response.

Hairs prickling on his arms, and along both sides of his head, Jack approached the figure slumped against the gate post. Dead, he thought. Why here? Who could it be?

"Are you OK?" he called out one last time before discovering the scare-crow effigy of a woman bearing the word *"Murderer"* painted in red across her chest.

250

Cursing, he yanked the dummy away from the gate and searched the driveway for nails. Good thing Esmeralda isn't here to see this, he thought, picking up the stuffed dummy and tossing it onto the floor of his truck; wondering how long it had been sitting there, for the whole town to laugh at.

"They thrive on it!" he said, throwing the scarecrow down on the kitchen floor. "They're a bunch of parasites living off crap!"

"Well, you're the kennel man around here," Nancy said, frightened. "You're the expert on that. Don't you have something for parasites?"

"The only cure I've got for creeps like this is buckshot."

"That'll send them flying," Nancy said.

"I mean, where are they, Nancy? Where's their guts!"

"Scattered all over the place, if you have your way," she said. "When do you think it happened? Last night? I didn't hear any dogs barking."

"You couldn't have heard anything over the screaming and carrying on from you and Steven," Jack said, with perhaps too much anger.

Her ears hot, glad Steven had gone back upstairs, Nancy said, "We're married. It's legal, and we're over twenty-one. And *you* aren't supposed to be listening!"

"Then shut the window. What's Esmeralda going to say when she comes home?"

"I don't know. I'll - I'll have to talk with her."

"Be sure you do. Mr. Steven seems to be making himself right at home."

Was it Steven who bothered Jack, or the idea that she and Steven made love? It was love, wasn't it? If it wasn't love, she decided, it was something close enough. Anyway, they were trying to have kids and this is how you did it.

"Remind me, sometime, to loan you our copy of the *Kama Sutra*," she heard herself saying, unable to resist. "THEN, we'll see who does the screaming!" she laughed and smacked him on the side of the head. "Now, finish up your coffee, tell me about this dummy paying us a visit and leave a grown man and his woman alone!" Gee, she thought. Where'd that come from; I sound just like Blanche.

"I refrain from comment," Jack said, slathering his toast with jelly. "There's so much I could read into your remarks it's embarrassing. Now," he said, "let's talk about that dummy."

This time, she really walloped him.

"*OK! OK!*" he almost choked. "I'm going back to look for footprints."

"Good!" she said. "Get out of my kitchen and take your dirty mind with you!"

"Glad to," he said, rubbing his head. "But, don't tell them about any of this in your letters, OK?"

"The private affairs of a man and wife?" she asked smartly, "Or, scarecrows with *Murderer* written all over them? No, I wouldn't *dream* of telling them," she

252

said. "We'll just put it on the list with all the rest of the stuff - creepy phone calls, dogs being turned loose, tires slashed. What's next, Jack?"

"I don't know. But, tonight, I'll be ready."

"They'll expect that," she said. "If you were them, wouldn't you want to keep us up all night? *Don't go there, Jack,*" she warned. "Don't you even try."

"Wouldn't *dream* of it," he said, in a mocking tone. "But, we can keep them guessing, can't we? Want to guess how much buckshot I've got around here?" Laughing, he gave her a wink, went out the door and hurried off to the kennel. It was good hearing Jack laugh again, she thought, even if the reason made her uneasy. Wiping up the kitchen table, she wondered how long it had been since she had heard Steven really happy.

"He's worked it all out," Nancy said, as Jack tidied up the kennel's grooming room later that afternoon.

"That so?" he said.

"He's got a plan, Jack. This time, he's really got a plan."

"And what kind of a plan, Nancy?"

"There's a new singer and he's made a deal with the guy's producer. It'll mean lots of money, he says."

"What kind of deal?" Jack asked.

"Oh, he'll get his regular commission on record sales, like he is now. But on this particular artist, he's going to get more. So, that means anyone who invests in it with him is going to get a share of that, too."

"Well, how much is he looking for?"

"Five thousand," she said.

Jack whistled.

"Oh, it's not as much as it sounds," Nancy said. "Not when you consider everything else. I mean, when you think that it could be worth millions with all the record sales and concerts and song royalties, I mean, five thousand dollars doesn't sound like so much when you look at it that way."

"It's a lot of money, Nancy. What do you know about this producer fella? Have you met him? Have you heard this singer?"

"No, but Steven says – "

"Steven's blinded by dollars."

"Jack, that's not fair. You might not like Steven, but you know he knows the record business."

"He's been knockin' around it long enough."

"Jack – "

"I'm sorry, Nancy. It doesn't feel right to me."

"Jack – "

"Nancy, I don't have all the answers when it comes to business. Faye's products are pretty simple as far as that kind of thing goes and without Esmeralda's office at the factory, I'd be lost in all the paper work. But, I do know when I don't feel right."

"Sorry I mentioned it," she said, stomping off. "Just forget I ever asked, OK?"

Why didn't people give Steven a break, she wondered. Why didn't they trust him, she asked herself, as she heard him on the phone in the study. Nobody worked harder than Steven did. Nobody.

"Everything OK, Babe?" he asked, his hand covering the phone.

"Just hunky-dory," she said, on her way down the hall.

"Great, Babe. Great . . ."

That night, as he stripped for bed, she couldn't take her eyes off him. Was it the sense of adventure? Knowing something about him would always be untamed?

"You were on the phone a lot today," she said.

"Business."

"I missed you."

"I missed you, too, Babe. You know that."

"How bad did you miss me?" she asked.

"This bad!" he smiled, pulling his hard cock straight up and laughing as he jumped at her, threw her legs high and kissed her between the cheeks. "Bubble bath!" he said, surprised. "Mmmm-mmm!"

She squealed; he laughed, and the stars twinkled just a little brighter.

In his cottage, Jack shut the window he always kept open just a crack and turned up the radio. Finishing his soup, he reached down and petted the Sable Collie beside his table. "Well, girl, what do you think?" he said.

Basking in the attention, Blanche' Beige, dam of champions, whimpered softly and wagged her tail as Jack stood, found a leash and slipped a collar over her head. "Let's go," he said, with a gentle tug, and they walked into the grooming area. They were met by a large Sable male, one of the von Havenburg champions. Filled with joy, the dog arched his neck, raised his tail and pranced in frantic circles.

"He's courting you, Girl. What do you think? Ain't he handsome? Oh? You've met each other before, you say? Well, now I believe you're right. In that case, what I'm going to do is just let the two of you alone. I hope you like the music I'm playing for you. OK, fella. Get the girl," Jack said, patting Beige's back. "Come on! Get the girl!" he coaxed.

He needn't have coaxed too much. After a few sniffs and close inspections, the male eased his chest and front legs up onto his mate's back and, balanced on his hind feet and began swinging his hips. "Good boy! Good boy!" Jack praised. Suddenly, the stud found his mark. Plunging deep, he pumped faster as Jack got to his knees, shoved an arm underneath the bitch's hind legs, felt to make sure the dog's penis hadn't slipped out, and wrapped his other arm around the stud's rump.

They remained like this, on the floor, both dogs and the man who ensured the conception of the von Havenburg champions, for several minutes.

"Good," he whispered. "We're in. Now, easy does it," he said, easing the stud off Beige and reaching for the dog's nearest hind leg. Carefully, ever so carefully, Jack lifted the leg up and across the bitch's back, until both dogs, still locked tight, stood facing away from each other. "It hurts me more than it hurts you," he said, "just thinking about it."

A half-hour later, their sexual grip relaxed, the male slipped out, walked slowly off and Jack hurried Beige to a nearby crate. "Good, girl!" he said. "Very nice. Now, if everybody's in the mood, we'll try again day after tomorrow and see if we made puppies. Oh, they'll be beauties."

He talked like this to the dogs. He had always talked to them. Not to do so would have seemed, well, cold somehow. Did they understand him? Of course they did. They understood him and they needed him. Without someone to care for them, the von Havenburg Collies would be lost. Without someone to handle the breedings planned so carefully by Esmeralda, the von Havenburg Collies would be no better than Collies anywhere else. Turning off the radio, he opened the window and put on a record of "Body And Soul," by Coleman Hawkins. The mansion was quiet now; the trees, the flowers, the garden were still. What do you see in him, Nancy, he wondered? What do you see?

Diaminds and Deception   Three
weeks in Spain took The Girls from bull-

fights in Madrid to the waterside res-
taurants of Seville, to the colorful ex-
citement of Barcelona. Along the way, in
the interests of cultural refinement,
Blanche met a man who insisted he was a
nephew of the great Picasso. No proof was
ever found of that, and, due to circum-
stances beyond her control, to the amaze-
ment of others, herself most of all, she
was not tempted to sleep with him.

"Steven? Come back to bed," Nancy whispered. He had been distant since returning from Philadelphia this time; unwilling to talk.

He stood by the window now, his naked back to her, his body bathed in sweat and moonlight.

"Steven?"

"I lied," he said, suddenly.

"Lied?"

"My car didn't break down; the company took it from me."

"I knew that, Steven," she said softly. "I knew something was wrong. You can't hide things from me."

"You knew?" he asked. "Then, why did you let me go on pretending?"

"Because I love you," she said. "And I understand."

"Thanks," he said. "It helps. I wish they did; but, no. That would be too much to ask." His voice fell low and soft. "Everybody else does it, and I get the blame."

"For what, Steven?" she asked. He was her husband. She must know. "What happened?"

"I got caught, Nancy. I got caught slipping a few bucks to a DJ."

"Why were you doing that, Steven? Why were you giving him money?"

"So he'd spin a record."

"But, why did you have to pay him to play a record? I don't understand." She sat up now.

"Nancy, you just don't get it, do you. This ain't the sweetest business in the world I'm in. I don't care what you hear 'em singin' on the radio. Those stations are playin' what we feed 'em, that's all. And how we feed 'em ain't always pretty."

"I know," she said. "You told me, remember?"

"That?" He cursed. "That's *nothing!* What I'm talkin' about is an investigation, Babe. Guys like me - we make gifts to the right people so they work with us, you know? But, we can't get caught, because it's not always legal."

"What's wrong with giving presents?"

"It's the kind we're giving, Babe. And what they agree to do for it."

"Steven, how did you get mixed up in all this stuff?"

"It's part of the job, like I said. You want me to keep my job, don't you? Well, this time, I got caught, Nancy. It was a new DJ and he was a plant."

"A plant?"

"He worked for the Feds."

"What exactly were you giving him, Steven?"

259

"You don't want to know," he said. "Trust me."

She dropped her gaze and let him finish. You don't want to know? How could he ask that when knowing the truth was all she wanted!

"There were cops and everything, so the label dropped me. They had no choice. And now, the Feds want me to give 'em information. They want me to tell everything I know. If I don't, Nancy, I go to jail. Like on that game you like - straight to Jail, don't pass Go."

"I can't believe this. What about everything you said before - the new singer. The money you need. What about us having a baby and a house of our own, Steven? Were they lies, too? Were they?"

"No! No, Babe; I meant it. I meant it all. This deal - this deal's my only chance now. Can't you see?"

"But you've been fired, haven't you? You said the label can't do business with you now. How are you going to get around that, Steven? How can you even get in the door?"

He sighed and dropped to the floor. "I gotta come up with that money, Nancy" he said, laying there. "I've got to!"

"And if we can't?"

"If we can't, I'm a goner. I'm scared, Babe. I'm scared. When's Esmeralda comin' home? I don't know how long I can hold this thing off. I don't know how long the producer's gonna wait for me. Alls I know is the record business. It's the only thing I know in the world. And I can't help the Feds on this payola thing.

I can't! If I turn in the guys I know, I'm screwed. I'll never work in the business again!"

"And if you don't, Steven? If you don't turn them in?"

"I'm counting on this deal to see us through. 'Cause if I don't talk - and I don't plan to - I'm goin' straight to jail, don't pass Go, don't collect nuthin'."

By morning, he was still there; asleep on the floor, naked. During the night, she had tip-toed across the room to where he lay and spread a blanket over him, kissed his forehead and his cheek, run a finger down his flat belly. "Steven," she thought . . . "My Steven . . ."

Grateful for the daily chores that forced her to get up and about, she went to the bathroom, washed and dressed. His mind was made up, she thought. He was going away. There wouldn't be a house of her own; there wouldn't be a family, not a real one. She knew it.

In the kitchen, she went to the sink, ran a shallow layer of water in a fry pan and brought it to a boil. Cracking a couple of eggs into the pan, she tossed the shells and watched the whites bubble and the yolks start to poach. She poured herself a glass of juice and popped a piece of bread in the toaster.

What was he going to do, she wondered?

He didn't hear her footsteps as she came back up the stairs with his breakfast; didn't sense the drop in her stomach when she found him gone.

Setting down the tray, she checked the bathroom. Had there been time for him to dress and leave the house? If he was still here, why was he hiding? It was a game.

Quietly, she went down the hallway past each door and then she knew.

He stood there; his skin golden, his back to her, the cheeks of his ass as innocent as a child's. Odd, that she would think of innocence just then. Odd, that Esmeralda's bedroom would seem like a shrine; her bureau its altar.

Should she speak? Should she walk away and pretend she never saw? Can't somebody tell me what to do, she pleaded to the walls, the ceiling, the very soul of the house she suddenly knew had become, would always be now, her home?

Where does a naked man put something like that? she asked herself, not wanting to know.

Without turning to face her, sensing her presence, he straightened. "She doesn't need it," he said.

"It's not yours. None of it."

"She'd never miss it. Not even one piece."

"We'd both know, Steven. You and me."

"I can pay her back. As soon as we get the money."

"Steven, no. Don't do it."

262

"Diamonds," he said, fondling neck-laces, bracelets and pins. "She doesn't need them," he said again, clasping a bracelet on his wrist, then another and another.

"Don't!" Nancy cried, afraid to go near him, not knowing why. "Steven, stop it! I'll call the police!"

But, he didn't hear – and she knew. She knew if she didn't turn and run down those stairs, run right now, run as fast as she could, she would lose him. She would lose him, their house with the white picket fence, their pretty baby; she would lose everything.

"*Jack! Jack!*" she screamed, running across the lawn to the cottage; her body, the world, in slow motion. Hurry, she thought, seeing it all slip away. *Hurry!*

"Nancy!" Jack looked up from the whelping box he was building.

"It's Steven!" she sobbed. "I can't stop him! *He's stealing Esmeralda's jewelry!* Oh, God!" she hollered, looking back at the mansion. *"He's taking my car!"*

"Call the cops!" Jack ordered, running past her to block the lane, know-ing Steven would never stop for him.

"Don't!" she grabbed his arm.

"Let go, Nancy!" he tried shaking her off.

"Jack!" she cried, but he was too strong for her. Pulling loose, he lunged for the driveway, threw himself at the car and grabbed the passenger door hand-le; slammed his hammer into the wind-shield.

"No!" she screamed. "*Oh, God, no!*"

Again, Jack struck the glass; his body dragging in the stones, his hand twisted and caught in the metal handle.

Not once did the car swerve; not once did it slow down. As Jack dropped to the ground and rolled in the dirt, the car sped off and she ran to him. Ran with all her heart, all her soul, all her being. Like a wildcat clawing for life as a pack of stray dogs tear out the hair on her back, she ran and fell to her knees beside him, saw blood, and hot tears of shame washed over her.

Top Secret Untouched by events of which they had no hint, The Girls moved on. The Swiss Alps may be fine for those into winter sports, but Blanche and Esmeralda preferred their ski instructors by the fireplace. Cozy and warm, they dallied in Geneva; basked in health spas and partied into the wee hours. But, it was under the blue light of Paris that Esmeralda found a charming apartment near the Rue de la Montmartre. Cafés, art galleries, the Eiffel tower . . . she was in her glory. Couture; handsome men; women adorning their bodies as passionately as the great Edith Piaf had ever sung, "If you Love Me" . . . Blanche clung to the fashion capitol of the world with both hands and every painted red fingernail. Days in Paris had a way of becoming pages in a book; a book with a plot; and Esmeralda's began to unfold.

Blanche would hate her; never for-give her. She thought of Robert now; so far away, yet in her every thought; affecting her every decision; affecting her life this way. He didn't know; per-haps would never know; what she planned. She would do anything for him; always love him, no matter where he was; no matter where he would ever be. Would Robert thank her some day, or hate her, too? Only time would tell.

At first, it was nothing but a vague possibility; could she do it? Get-ting Blanche this far had been easy. Could she take the next step; make the arrangements so Blanche would never know; could she get away with it? It was worth a try. If she didn't try, she could never forgive herself. If she died never telling anyone – not Robert, who left; not Blanche, who cared only for herself – it was worth everything she had; every-thing in the world, to take the risk. Life was too precious; too spectacular; too short. She must do this – she must!

A few inquiries here; a gift of cash there; yes, she was told. It could be done. Someone could be found; com-plete confidentiality assured; the terms, agreeable. And Blanche would never know.

Even Esmeralda was surprised by how easy it all was. Amazing, what the right money in the right hands can do.

"I Love Paris," the song said. From now until forever, Esmeralda would love Paris.

"Have you ever seen The Riviera, Blanche?" she asked, when all was as it should be. *"You seem tired. I think it's time for us to see the Riviera."*

The sand pulled away from under their feet as Esmeralda and Blanche walked the beach of Cannes that night. "It's beautiful here," Esmeralda said. "Being so far away like this, nothing seems as important as it did back home, you know?"

"Makes you want to stay away forever," Blanche sighed, stopping to roll her pant legs higher.

"Do you want to? Would you like us to, Blanche? Would you like to start up the fashion business again?"

"Nah. They'd miss us back home. Anyhow, I got myself some good ideas from the shops. I'm gonna come up with some of the fanciest dog stuff you ever saw!"

"I have no doubt," Esmeralda said, lost in thought.

"What is it, Ez? What's the matter?"

They stopped and let the ocean water take the sand away as if saying everything you depend on, everything you believe, everything you think you know, is changing . . . Should she tell her, Esmeralda wondered? Was it time? Or would Blanche be angry it had taken her so long to reveal something so important?

"Stand still," she said, taking hold of Blanche's arms. "See how long we can stand up."

266

"Whoa!" Blanche laughed; swooping backward slightly and shifting her footing as the waves pulled away the sand beneath them.

"See what it's like?" Esmeralda said. "Everything's changing. Everything around us. What we believed; what we saw. I wonder what's ahead for us?"

"We'll get older. We'll get wiser. We'll get . . ." she paused, took in the hotel and streetlights beyond the shadows of the deserted beach "prettier," she laughed. "Yeah, that's what. You an' me? We'll get prettier." She shook her head to fluff out her hair and raised her hands high. "We're it, Ez! *We're it!*"

"It?" The sound of waves and deep, swirling water washed over them.

"Yeah, you know! It! The center of everything! We're the girls from America! Everybody wants to be with us!"

A pair of lovers passed them in the darkness.

"Hey!" Blanche called out to them. "Where ya goin!"

"I guess they don't know us," Esmeralda said.

"Well, they should," Blanche pouted. "We're a hell of a lot of fun!"

"We're fun all right," Esmeralda said, wondering about tomorrow. "Are you ready to go back?"

"Yeah," Blanche said, wrapping her loose shirt tighter around herself as if to fight off the growing chill. "Yeah, I'm ready."

The weeks that followed for Blanche and Esmeralda were lived like all of us live our lives: Wondering how things pass us by so quickly; wondering where it all went; wondering if any of it was fair. But, what are you going to do about it? Especially when you've got it.

The Girls returned home from Europe in a flurry of packages, smiles and twice as many suitcases. "You didn't think we'd go all that way and forget you?" they said. It was a grand thing, with gifts and souvenirs for everyone. It was the return of two friends, refreshed from their travels; bound by new secrets; oblivious to the darkening waters of discontent around them. . . .

"Well, Nancy! I think I'll just pack my bags and go back. Everything looks so good. You've done a marvelous job, taking care of things while we were away." Esmeralda spun around the room and smiled. "Doesn't the place look great, Blanche?"

"Too great," she frowned, running a finger across a tabletop and checking for dust. "This place looks like it was cleaned up only yesterday."

"Ladies," Jack said, amused. "It's good to have you back home again. Where do you want me to take the suitcases?"

"Oh! Upstairs to my room," said Esmeralda.

Nancy glanced quickly to Jack.

"Don't you want to see the dogs first?" he asked.

"Oh, I can't wait to see the dogs! Let's go!"

A few minutes later, gathered around a nest box beside the fireplace inside Jack's warm cottage, they watched a litter of seven puppies nursing from their dam. "I know I took a few liberties with this," Jack said, as Blanche and Esmeralda sat quietly. "But, with you being away and nobody being able to reach you, things were pretty much up to us around here, right Nancy?"

She nodded.

"When Beige, here, came in heat while you were away, Blanche, I remember-ed it was one of our studs you mated her to for that young champion of yours we lost in the accident."

"A repeat breeding," Blanche said, understanding him.

"What do you think?" Jack said, proudly.

"What do I think?" Blanche asked, glancing at Esmeralda, who was beaming with delight. "I think . . . they're beautiful!"

"Look at this one," Jack said, handing her a plump, sleepy male with a broad, white collar around his neck.

"He looks just like your other dog," Nancy said. "The same, exact mark-ings. Maybe it's true, Blanche. You know, what they say? Maybe he came back to you." She paused a moment while Blanche held the puppy to her cheek.

"Hey . . . what's this?" Esmeralda asked. "You're supposed to be happy."

"I am," Blanche sniffed. "I'm happy. I've never felt so happy in my whole life. It's just . . . "

"Just what?" Esmeralda wanted to know.

"It's just, I've never felt so happy and *alone.*"

"Will you be staying for the night?" Nancy asked after dinner. "I can get a room ready for you."

"No, I want to sleep in my own bed tonight," Blanche said. "Jack'll drive me home. Won't you, Jack?"

Yes, he would.

"You sure?" Esmeralda asked, her eyes saying "Are you all right?"

"Yeah," Blanche smiled as one does with those who share secrets, as she put a hand on Esmeralda's shoulder. "It's time."

Time; the one thing Esmeralda couldn't buy. She could buy the finest cars, the most valuable dogs, and make any financial arrangement she wanted to. But, she couldn't buy one more minute of time. Deadly terms life exacted in its deal with you, she thought. Unfair, she thought. Let those next in line wait just a little longer.

"Go, then," she said. "It's been good."

Tossing back her head with a laugh, Blanche, as svelte as she had ever been, asked for her coat and purse. "Hey, guys," she quipped. "I dumped a *husband,* remember? *I lost a lot of weight!* See this?" she said, picking up a suitcase.

"With a little work, *this is gonna be my new Fall wardrobe!*" Her laughter covering a tinge of regret, she smiled to herself. "Come on, Jack. Take me back to that place I call a castle. I want to see if the Queen sent me a little present, like a certain, *particular* guard of hers! Or, maybe one of those bullfighters we saw in Spain. Right, Hon?" she winked at Esmeralda. "Loved those pants. Say," she said, eyeing Jack. "You know, you ought to think about that sometime . . . " and out the door into the night they went.

As they stood, waving good-bye, Nancy took a breath. Sooner or later, she'd have to let Esmeralda know about the jewelry. Later would be better, she decided. "Welcome home," she said.

"It was nice of you and Jack to do what you did for her," Esmeralda said, quietly.

"The puppies," Nancy said. "It seemed like the right thing to do."

"She almost cried," Esmeralda said. "She's been very sentimental."

"I noticed. I never pictured Blanche Jacobus as the weepy type before, know what I mean?"

"There's a lot about her that people don't know. And they never will. Privacy is important to a person, you know. Especially an artist."

Nancy waited for more, but there was none forthcoming. "Can I talk with you?" she asked; knowing, like Blanche had said, it was time.

"Sure, Nancy," Esmeralda returned to her seat at the table and gestured to the chair beside her. "Is everything OK?"

Nancy sat down, held her breath and sighed. "Not really, no," she said.

"What is it, Nancy? Can I help?"

Why is it that words get a life of their own when you need them most? Why couldn't she just say it? She had practiced for weeks. She and Jack had gone over every comment Esmeralda could make until she was ready for anything Esmeralda might do. "If she starts hollering, Nancy, remember she usually hollers at first. Ever since she was a kid, she hollers when she finds out the news. But she usually settles down, then. All you have to do is sit still and let her get wild. Then, if it goes the way it usually does, she comes to her senses and never says anything else about it. Kind of like those people who flip out and come back to their senses without ever knowing what they said or did."

"I know what you mean," she said.

"Well, don't let it scare you."

"Jack, I wish I didn't have to do this!"

"Do you want me to tell her? Do you want me to say you wouldn't call the police? Nancy, she's going to find out."

"I know . . . I know."

And now she sat with her boss, and there was nothing to say. She was wrong to think she'd be able to handle this. "I . . . I changed my mind," she said. "It can wait."

"But, I can't." The way Esmeralda said it left no room for doubt or evasion. "What happened, Nancy. Have you found other work? Do you want to leave? This is a big place. I know it's a lot of responsibility. Is it too much?"

Nancy shook her head. "Nothing like that. No. I love it here. I love my job. But . . . "

"But, what?"

"Something happened while you were away."

Esmeralda nodded. "Which is what you want to tell me."

"Yes. I want to tell you. But, it's not easy. It's the hardest thing I think I've ever done and I don't know how I'll ever be able to make it right. It's my fault it happened. Really. If I'd been thinking, if I wouldn't have been so caught up in things - "

"Nancy," Esmeralda said, taking control. "If you don't spit it out, you're fired."

"*No!*"

"Right here. *Right now!*"

"I found him in your room -"

"Who?"

"Steven."

"Steven? What was he doing in my room?"

"He called from the train station in Lancaster and asked me to pick him up."

"I thought he had his own car."

"Company car. It belonged to the record label."

"Did anything happen to it?"

"They took it away."

"What for?" Esmeralda asked. "How do they expect him to get around? Are you asking for a loan?"

Nancy became quiet. It would have been that easy, she thought. All they would have had to do was ask for a loan. "They dropped him," she said.

"I'm sorry to hear that. Can't he find other work?"

"Not around here," Nancy said, looking across the room at nothing in particular. "In fact, I don't think Steven's going to be around for a long time."

"You sound very sure of that," Esmeralda said.

"I am," Nancy said with finality. "You'll know why after I tell you."

Esmeralda listened quietly, as Nancy unfolded the events which had bought her to disgrace and self-doubt. To Nancy's surprise, there came no outbursts of rage, no admonishments of sin, no accusations. Had Jack been wrong or was the news so shocking that it hadn't sunk in.

"I said, he stole your jewelry and I didn't call the police."

But there was no response; no evidence of loss from the woman to whom every piece of jewelry had a name, a story and value beyond that of mere diamonds, rubies or pearls. Parting her lips just slightly, turning her head sideways just a bit, Esmeralda seemed curious; intrigued.

"All of it?" she asked.

"No. Not all of it," Nancy said. "Just what he could get away with before I ran to the kennel and got Jack."

"Which pieces did he take?"

"Three bracelets and two necklaces that I know for sure. Some pins are probably missing, but I don't know which ones."

"My mother's jewelry? Diamonds?"

Nancy nodded. "Yes, I believe so."

"Good choices," Esmeralda said. It was an odd remark for one who had been robbed. "When did it happen?"

"About three weeks ago."

"I assume that's what really happened to Jack's hand and he didn't get it caught under a rock, like he told me?"

"He didn't get it caught under a rock, no," Nancy said, shaking her head.

"Well! What do we do now?" Esmeralda asked, straightening up in her chair, ready to start.

"I have to make it right," Nancy said. "If it takes the rest of my life, I'll pay you back. You can keep my pay – all of it! I'll work for nothing, just a place to stay and food. But, I'll pay you back, Esmeralda. I will!"

Diamonds lost and golden opportunities found, Esmeralda thought!

"Let me think it over," she said. "You know, I trusted you, Nancy."

Yes, she must admonish Nancy; that much was expected.

"I trusted you with my home; I don't know how this makes me feel," she said, shaking her head, hoping she was being convincing enough. "I'll have to think about this. Now, go. Get some rest and I'll see you in the morning. Thank you for telling me. I think I'll go the study and get a book for a while. I need to unwind," she said. "Go."

Upstairs, Nancy remembered Blanche and the puppies. What was it she had noticed. Something – an invisible something passing through Blanche like a vapor when she held the puppy Nancy had handed to her. What was it she had said? *"I've never felt so alone?"* How well she knew the feeling.

Alone was waking up to no one; having dinner with no one else; living for nothing but the TV set. Alone was hoping, praying you'll smash head-on into somebody who thinks you're the greatest thing they ever saw and swoop you off your two, sore feet. Alone is what most people spent their whole lives trying to escape, even if it meant running with all their heart, all their soul, to others just as lonely as they were, pretending not to know it.

Alone sucked.

Nancy pulled the blankets back and sat on the edge of her bed. Gently, she traced the wrinkles of the covers the whole length of where he had been, where his legs had been, his hip as he laid on his side, his chest and folded arm on which his head rested without a pillow. Steven, Steven, come home to me . . . Steven, if love is as strong as they say, then why aren't you here, why can't you find work here in this town and stay with me? I love you, Steven. I've loved you ever since we were kids in school. I don't want anybody else. Do you? Do you, Steven? Do you sleep with other women, kiss them, laugh with them and never tell me? I'm growing old wondering about that. I never ask. I never ask.

She slid between the sheets, her nightie bunching up between her legs where his hand should have been. Oh, his hands. The things those hands could do; had done! Over and over again, ever since they were sophomores in high school; in the back seat of his car, the living room sofa when her parents were away, in the woods when they told everybody it was just a picnic. Love? Love! She knew it. She knew love so fierce if any woman ever dared take him away from her, she would ruin him - ruin him - so no other woman would ever want him as long as he lived. But, she knew she wouldn't. She couldn't. She couldn't hurt someone she loved. *Steven, come back; come back to me!* If you come home, I'll kiss your mouth, your belly, everything that makes you a man. My man. My man, Steven. Wherever you are tonight, she thought, clicking off the light beside her bed, you're mine.

Remember that.

Esmeralda sat there a while, then headed for the study and stood at the door, looking in. Even with the lights out, you knew when a place was empty, she thought, breathing in a silence not unlike the after taste of a party. Would Blanche tell Jack about their trip, she wondered? Would she tell him everything?

"But, Esmeralda, why?" Blanche had asked her in this very room. Their words were real; painted on the walls, suspended in the air. "Why should I take him back – I don't want to! You of all people should know why I shouldn't take him back – ever! EVER!"

"Blanche, I love you. You're my best friend. My best friend in the whole world – "

"THEN WHY DID YOU DO IT! WHY! I just . . . want to KNOW!"

"Blanche – "

"I have to know," Blanche wept softly, in a way understood only by women. "I have to."

There had been no answer. How could there be? How could she have asked Blanche to understand what she, herself, didn't even know?

"I – don't know what you want me to say," Esmeralda whispered, embarrassed. "I don't know what to . . . do."

What could she do. Did life want her to deny the man she loved – knew she loved beyond any possibility of doubt? Would always love?

There had to be a way. There had to be a way for her to make the biggest mistake of her life right again. If only she knew how. If only she could think!

"Blanche, I know it was wrong. I know it. I know! But – "

"But what?" Blanche asked, her eyes overflowing with sadness. "What can you ever say to me."

Esmeralda braced herself for anything – a slap, a fist, an insult. "I can't say anything, Blanche. *But, if there's a God in Heaven, I'll find something I can do to make this right."*

It was a promise not unlike Nancy's tonight, she thought, as she went to the shelf where her mother's books were kept. At least, he didn't get you, she thought, standing there. What was the saying? Don't cast pearls to swine? At least the swine didn't get these, she thought, touching them.

One by one, she removed them. The beautiful books; haunting books; books holding the secrets to her mother's wisdom, and now her own. As she set them aside, she saw it: The narrow drawer so neatly hidden; and, from her hair, she removed a delicate bobby pin onto which had been welded a tiny key.

Carefully now, Esmeralda slipped the key into the drawer latch; turned; and revealed the private safe-deposit box. Opening it, she smiled. There they were, every one exactly as she had left them; as undisturbed as the day she had put them there, herself.

Had she made a mistake in Paris? Had she been wrong going behind Blanche's back? What would Blanche say; what would she ever do if she found out?

She wouldn't find out. She mustn't. No matter what it took. No matter what she must do, Blanche must never know and Nancy was going to help her now. In the morning, she would say after thinking it over, she had decided not to press charges against anyone. She would thank

Nancy for the unselfish offer, but gracefully decline imposing such a hardship on anyone. After all, it wasn't Nancy's fault she had fallen in love.

You don't feel right about it, Nancy? You still think there's something you must be able to do to make it up to me? Well, there could be . . . perhaps; from time to time . . . certain things may need to be done; certain favors, perhaps; things that need to be kept in the strictest of confidence. Business things, shall we say?

Nancy, can you keep a secret? You can? Oh, if you could; if I truly knew you could do that, I would be ever so grateful . . . .

She wondered now what Steven would think when he discovered life wasn't always what it seemed and everything, every last bauble in her jewelry box upstairs, was paste.

Chapter 7

As 1952 rolled on, Gen. Dwight D. Eisenhower was mucking up after the Black Angus cattle on his Gettysburg farm; Harry Truman announced he wouldn't run for another term, King Farouk of Egypt was overthrown and The Jackie Gleason Show started a twenty year run on NBC. In Hollywood, Humphrey Bogart and Kathryn Hepburn won Oscars for "The African Queen;" and the very same Doberman Pinscer stayed on the campaign trail to compete a second time for Westminster..

Mutiny   "Another letter from Paris?" Nancy placed the airmail envelope on top of the day's newspaper, dog show notices and bills. "That's three, so far this month. Left somebody special behind?" she asked; a note of friendly suspicion in her voice.

"Thank you very much!" Esmeralda said, taking the mail, hoping Nancy would leave quickly and explaining no more. Nancy pulled a dust cloth out from her apron pocket and began looking around.

"You won't find any," Esmeralda said.

"Oh? You mean, I already dusted in here?"

"This morning, yes."

Stuffing the dust cloth back in her apron, Nancy walked to a corner of the study and bent over beside the urn from which a luxurious fig tree and vines reached almost to the ceiling.

"If you give that tree any more water, it'll drown," Esmeralda said in monotone, her eyes riveted straight ahead.

"Oh?" Nancy asked, the same as before, pretending to inspect for dead leaves. "You mean, I already watered the plants, too?"

"If you pick off any more of those leaves, the poor thing'll be naked."

"Mustn't have a naked tree around here," Nancy said, dropping her hands and stepping back. "Well, I guess if you won't be needing me, I'll be on my way then."

Her face holding a forced smile as Nancy turned to leave, Esmeralda tore open the letter. . . .

Jack pushed the wheelbarrow along-side the row of kennels. Calling every Collie by name, he petted and fussed over each dog as he served their morning meal.

282

"Looks like we need to do some brushing here," he said, to a big-coated female with a distinctive broken collar and four white feet. "You want to be brushed, Maggie?"

The dog wagged her tail and made a "Wooo-wooo" sound that never ceased to amaze him in its similarity to the pitch and tone of his own voice. "If you could talk, you'd be the gabbiest one in town."

"If she could talk, she'd ask how come you got in so late last night again," came Nancy's remark behind him.

"Spying on me?" Jack asked, scooping out feed into the bowls.

"Nope. Esmeralda just wanted to get me out of the house a while," she said. "A letter she didn't want me to see."

"From overseas?"

"Yup. Same as the week before and the week before and the week before that. Just like clock work now, every Wednesday. Curious, isn't it?"

"Sounds like she's got herself a boyfriend."

"Nothing wrong with that. Right now, she needs as many friends as she can get."

"And then some," Jack said. "This thing with the kennel club is getting nasty."

"Any more scare-crows hanging around the front gate?"

"You don't know the half of it. I came out this morning and the side gate was wide open."

"Forgot to shut it last night, you were in such a hurry?"

Reaching inside his jacket, he handed her a broken lock. "I found this."

Suddenly, she dropped her line of questioning and switched: "What are we going to do?"

"Well, for now, we keep it to ourselves. No use getting Esmeralda all worked up."

"When are you going to tell her about the other stuff, Jack?"

"If I can help it? Never."

"But, don't you think she ought to know?"

"Maybe. But, on the other hand, if she did, what could she do about it?"

"Well, there has to be something she could do," Nancy insisted.

"That's what I'm worried about," Jack said, glancing around the kennel. "I know her. I've known her since she was a kid. When Esmeralda gets something in her head, there's no stopping her and if she decides people are out to get her, she won't be fit to live with."

"Well, what do people want? What do they expect from her, Jack?"

"You know what they want. They want her to suffer."

"Like the dogs did," Nancy said, remembering Faye and wishing she hadn't mentioned it. "Sorry."

"You don't have to be," he said. "Me an' Faye know what you meant."

"Well, does Faye think we should we be worried?"

"Depends on who's behind it and what they're after. I know I won't be sleeping without a loaded gun at my bed any more."

"I don't have a gun," Nancy said.

"Let's hope you don't need one. Hey," said Jack, trying to lighten things up. "Are we gonna stand around all day like this, or what?"

"Just figured I'd come down and see the puppies for a while," she pinched his cheek. "Guess I'll go back now."

Pushing back his hat just a little, he smiled. Was Nancy flirting? He gave a knowing laugh. "You're welcome any time, Kiddo."

She liked when he called her that. It made her feel young. She always liked when he called her "Kiddo."

"Jack Milliken," Faye had said to him one morning. *"When I'm dead and gone, promise me you'll find someone to keep you laughing."*

The thought of losing her had never occurred to him before.

Throwing a dirty towel at him, she said, "'Cause you're *Hell* to be around when you're serious!" Always the joker, he thought. Where was she now? Stuck half-way between rainbows and fire for all the mischief she, herself, had pulled?

"Blanche cut all the bristles off your dog brushes, did she?" she said to an exasperated Esmeralda. "That's nothing," quipped Faye. "Wait'll she sees the hairdo you an' me are gonna give those boxwood bushes in her front yard!"

"But, I don't want to do anything to the bushes in her front yard," Esmeralda said.

"No?" Faye held up a scissors. "Well, girl, you should give it some serious thought!"

Faye, he smiled now. Good old Faye. "You still with me, darlin'?" he said, out loud. "Well if you are, and it's just 'cause I can't see you, then maybe you can help the Big Guy up there keep a watch over this place, OK?" He considered what he'd just said and made a correction: "That is, if you happen to see him one of these days."

Later, at the staff meeting where Esmeralda gave out the paychecks, she briefed everyone on their weekend duties.

"We have buyers coming in from New York for puppies and a family from Maryland looking for a horse their son can ride. Let's make the place look spic and span." She paused, gathering her thoughts, and continued . . . .

"On a more serious note, we all know there have been some problems around here. Those problems seem to have intensified while I was away. She glanced at Jack. "I'm talking about what some of the people in town are saying about . . . " she looked down for a second, but only a second . . . "me. Well, I apologize for that. It's not, and never was, my intention to do anything that would frighten you or cause any harm here at Lochwood, ever."

Looking around at the small group of people needed to run the estate, counting on her, depending on her, feeling, for the first time, that she hardly knew some of them. "You must believe that," she said, going on. "I just want to say, in case any of you want to leave, for reasons of safety or family, you can do so, now, with full pay and no hard feelings."

At first, no one moved. Maybe it was the shock of it; the idea that Esmeralda von Havenburg, symbol of privilege and power, would yield to anything outside her realm. Then, one by one, eyes averting her, they began to leave; gardener, cook, the farmer and his two helpers from the barn.

"What about the cattle? The chickens?" she asked them. "Who's going to milk, and collect the eggs?"

"I'll show somebody what they need to do," the farmer said. "I can stay another week."

"Only a week?" she said. "But, you've been here for years, Chester."

"It's not me, it's Debra," he said. "They're not makin' it so easy for her at church."

"I see," Esmeralda said, nodding. "I'm a woman of sin. Well, mustn't disappoint them," she smiled bravely. "Tell Debra, yes, I've loved; and my love brought unhappiness, to all of us, I'm afraid. I'm sorry about that. I'm sorry to see you go, Chester."

Did the flicker of his eye mean he might change his mind? Like most of the farming people in this part of Pennsylvania, Chester Zartman was a quiet man, not a brave man, and couldn't do much better than the angry woman who had done him a favor by marrying him. At least, that's what she had told him often enough and what he had come to believe.

Nodding, he simply turned and walked out the door.

"Gone, Jack," she said, after the last of them were out of earshot. "They don't believe in our dreams." Still seated at her desk, the same wooden desk her father had used in the ritual of handing out pay and punishment, she gathered up her notes and closed her checkbook ledger. "What now?"

"I don't know about you," Jack said with a twinkle. "But, I say the rest of us better start learnin' how to milk cows!"

"I'm afraid that isn't the only bad news," Esmeralda said, tapping her pen on the desk. "The feed supplier called. They won't be making deliveries any more and I'm supposed to send a check along, every time we pick up."

"For feed and hay, both? We get it all from the same place," Jack said. "Did they say why?"

"Austerity move." She tossed her pen across the room. "At least that's what it sounded like. Things aren't so good out there right now. For anybody."

She looked down at her desk, and the delicate papers there seemed to be the heaviest weights in the world. Sunning on the beach at Cannes is where she

288

should be, she thought. Why had she bothered coming back. She could have sold everything and lived the rest of her life in peace. But, there wouldn't have been any peace for her, she thought, in France or anywhere else in the world. A restless mind knows no boundaries.

"Esmeralda?" Jack asked, yanking her back to Lochwood as he bent over and picked up her pen. "Do you believe in, like they say, an Afterlife?"

"It's getting through this life I'm worried about," she sighed, reaching out her hand and thanking him. "Why do you ask?"

"Because I have the feeling sometimes that Faye's still around. But I can't see her."

"What do you think she's doing?" she asked, rolling her chair away from the desk; facing him.

"Oh, she's busy. She's probably in the kennel right now, with the new pups."

"They're very nice ones, Jack. Blanche was very touched." She stood and crossed the room to a tall, stately window from where she could see the kennel and barns.

"Yes, they are. I guess we should go ahead and fill out the paper work for the AKC then." He headed for the door.

"I'll be down later and sign the litter application for you. They're Joe's pups, right?"

"Every one of 'em. What are you going to do about the stud fee?" he wanted to know.

"We'll let it go this time," she smiled. "It's good having a litter around. It gives me hope."

"I know what you mean," he said, opening the door to leave.

"Jack?"

Their eyes met.

"About what happened between us, you know, last Fall."

He smiled, remembering their romp in the leaves.

"Well, a lot of things have happened since then," she said, "and . . . "

"And you'd rather not do it again," he finished for her.

She sighed. He was a wise one, this man. "Thank you for understanding."

"No problem," he said, stepping back, folding his paycheck and sticking it in his pocket. "It was just one of those things," he said, putting on his hat.

"One of those crazy things," she sang the tune wistfully.

"One of those wild things," he said; waiting, as he knew she wanted him to.

"Wild. Yes, that's what it was." Suddenly, she rushed to him and hugged tight. "Oh, Jack! Jack! I'm scared. I'm so scared I don't know what to do! Why did the feed store do that? Why? In town, why can't people look at me any more? Why are they so mean-spirited - so nasty!"

Cradling her, rocking her side to side, he kissed her hair and breathed in the natural scent of her skin. "If Faye was here," he said, "she'd tell them all to come to their senses."

"But they won't, Jack. They won't! People take forever to forget. Especially dog people!"

"Well, I wasn't going to tell you. But, we've been having some trouble around here you don't know about." He filled her in about the gate being open, names painted on the mail-box, the scare-crow dressed in a woman's clothes.

"So that's why nobody would stay," she said, pulling away and pacing the room. "They're scared, too. I knew there was something. I guess I stayed away too long."

"Well, you're back, now," he said. "You're home. And we're getting through."

"But, how, Jack? How? Everywhere I go; everywhere I turn, somebody's point-ing at me. Oh, they're not pointing their fingers, no, but I can feel it. I hear the whispers.

"They blame me for everything! And the worst of it? The worst of it, Jack?" Her shoulders shook and she hung her head. "They care more about the dogs than anything else. Like it didn't matter Faye was killed that night!"

For a second, so slightly that only the most perceptive student of human behavior could have detected it, he shrank as if his heart had been impaled.

"She was worth more than any dog, Jack. Any dog!"

Shaking his head at the very idea of such a comparison; at the humiliation of anyone thinking Faye's life and a dog's were anything close to being equal; he asked himself if he would ever understand human nature.

"They're insane, Jack! Insane! We've been to court. We've paid the price and they still want more! They want to drive us into the ground! *They want to ruin us!*"

"They can't ruin us," he said. "We're strong. And they're fools. They don't know the first thing about dogs if this is how they act. Dogs are about love, not hate. Dogs forgive. They forgive over and over again if they have to. If more of us were like the dogs we claim to love, then none of this would be happening. None of it."

Perhaps it was his common sense that pulled her together; perhaps the inner strength of knowing if he, of all people, believed it, then no one else had a right to feel otherwise.

"You're right," she said, standing beside him now. "You're right. I don't know what came over me. We'll pull through, Jack. I know we will," she said, pulling a handkerchief out of her pocket.

"That's more like it," he smiled, putting an arm around her shoulder.

"And if the feed supplier or the church or anybody else wants to make things difficult," she said, blowing her nose, "well, we can deal with it."

"You bet," he said, wondering if any of them would feel the same way after milking all the cows.

Nancy pulled in the lane, drove past the kennel, and up to the mansion. Parking in her usual spot near the back entrance to the kitchen, she gripped the steering wheel until her knuckles turned white. The second time this week, she thought. First, it was the bookstore, when she stopped by for office supplies: "I'm sorry. There's a balance on the account. We can't give you credit." Was that a hint of smugness at the corner of the cashier's mouth?

"How much is the balance, Florence?"

"Sixteen dollars and twenty cents."

Nancy swayed with disbelief that a store where the estate had a standing account would deny her credit.

"Sixteen dollars," she repeated what she could hardly believe.

"And twenty cents."

"And twenty cents." Nancy added. "Are you saying I can't charge these tablets and pens because there's a balance of sixteen dollars and twenty cents on the account? Is it overdue?"

"That's not for me to say. I just have my instructions," the woman said, glancing over Nancy's shoulder to her boss.

"Ed?" Nancy said, turning around. "You told her to do this?"

"Store policy now," the young man answered, almost proudly.

"Ed Cranston, I used to baby sit for you," she said, cutting him down to size. "Your policy or your Momma's?"

"Just," he said, his voice shaky, "store policy."

"Well, I'll tell you what: I've never been so insulted by a store in all my life!"

Cursing, she pulled out a twenty, crumpled it and threw it at the cashier. "There!" she said, slinging tablets and pens on the counter, cursing and stomping out.

"That'll be another five bucks for damage!" she heard the young man holler.

"Clean it up yourself - like I used to wipe your butt!" she fired back from the street.

Stopping by for a few items at the grocery store, she had stood in line only to be asked to wait before being rung up. "'scuse me a minute," the girl had said before seeing the manager.

Returning, she smiled politely, totaled up the order and bagged the groceries. "Tell Miss von Havenburg I said hello, Nancy, OK?"

"What's going on?" Nancy wanted to know.

The girl shook her head and pinched her mouth. "Don't ask," she said, reaching for the next customer's eggs and celery.

But, Nancy didn't have to. Clearly, the town had made its own judgement of Esmeralda and those who believed in her. Well, she could shop in the next town if she had to, but it was thirty miles away.

She sat there now, resolved to dealing with it. Esmeralda had been gracious enough to give her a home; to forgive Steven the unforgivable. Nancy wouldn't worry her with this. She would go inside, cut potatoes, put a beef roast in the oven with carrots and onions and make the best supper any of them ever had.

"Mmmmm . . . smells good," Esmeralda said, coming in to the warm kitchen for a break from her office. Nice thing about kitchens, she thought. They always felt cozy. "Roast beef and, tomorrow, beef stew?"

"One of our favorites," Nancy said. "I figured, if we're going to be operating at half-staff, I'd better feed everybody extra good."

"Good thinking," Esmeralda smiled, looking for the crackers and pouring herself a glass of iced tea. "Any brie?" she asked, looking in the refrigerator.

"Second shelf, behind the juice bottles."

"Keeping it out of the reach of invisible children, I see," Esmeralda said, pushing aside jars of relish, mustard and bowls of leftovers from the night before.

"Dangerous stuff, that brie. Speaking of which, I almost didn't get any today."

"Oh?" Esmeralda asked. "Why not?"

"Something goin' on at the store," Nancy said, catching herself. She had sworn she wouldn't say anything; too late now. "I couldn't tell, exactly," she said, wondering what Jack would have done, if he had been with her.

"Hmm," Esmeralda said, picking up a butter knife and spreading brie on a cracker. It was time to ask, she thought. "Nancy?"

"Uh-huh?"

"About those diamonds." Three words loaded with the power to make Nancy's heart freeze. Had she been wrong to think the subject would never come up again? Esmeralda hadn't actually said it wouldn't be forgotten. All she'd really said was, she wouldn't press charges.

"Yes?" Nancy asked, her voice weak.

"I've been thinking. I've been thinking there might be something you could help me with."

Nancy rolled her fingers against each palm.

"The letters I've been getting?" Esmeralda said. "The ones from Paris?"

"The ones you don't want me to know about, yeah."

"Well," said Esmeralda, "You might be seeing a lot of them from now on."

"I thought so," Nancy grinned, saying it with a sense of fun.

Allowing the young woman to think whatever she wanted to, Esmeralda made herself another cracker. "When you see these letters, Nancy, I want you to put them in my middle desk drawer. Don't ever open them." She looked Nancy directly in the eye. "I'll know if you do."

"I wouldn't. I wouldn't do that, ever."

"I'm counting on that," Esmeralda said, a certain tension in her bearing. "And if I ever ask you to mail something to the same address for me; whatever it may be; you must promise always to deliver that package without opening it."

"Well, that would be dishonest of me, don't you think?"

"Yes," Esmeralda said. "It would be. Almost like stealing diamonds."

The daggar had plunged and twisted.

"There's more, Nancy. If I should ever get an overseas call from a Dr. Philippe Barbeau, you must put him through to me immediately - no matter what I'm doing, or wherever I might be. Agreed?"

"Yes," Nancy assured her, sensing the urgency in Esmeralda's voice. "I promise. Dr. Barbeau. I'll remember."

"Write it down," Esmeralda advised. "You mustn't ever forget."

"I promise," Nancy said, going to a cabinet drawer, pulling out a notebook and writing down the name. So, she was right. Esmeralda had made a friend while she was gone. But, why the secrecy? A growing shadow of dread suddenly came over her. *Esmeralda was gravely ill and she didn't want anyone to know!*

No, she thought. She was just reacting to the incident at the store this morning, at the town turning its shoulder. But, would it ever go away, she wondered? Would things ever be happy again. She thought of Steven. Where was he? How far away did he get? Quietly, she closed the drawer.

"Good," she heard Esmeralda saying now, relieved. "I'm pleased. Well!" she clapped her hands together as if a matter of vital importance had just been resolved. "I guess I'll be getting back to work! I must fill out these tax papers for the factory accountant. Have you seen Jack?"

"He took the new pups to the vet."

"That's funny," Esmeralda said. "Doesn't Dr. Taylor usually make house calls?"

Jack held a puppy in each arm and sat in the waiting room, surrounded by white walls trimmed in blue wainscot. An abundance of Dr. Taylor's inexpensively framed prints of dogs and horses made the room appear lively, though crowded. The piercing smell of alcohol, linaments and salves gave testament to a lifetime of dedication to the healing arts. Dr. Taylor was a popular vet, and the only one in town.

"Oh, they're so cute!" a woman with an elderly Boston Terrier on a leash said. "Are they Shelties?"

"Collies," Jack smiled, proudly.

"Oh! Like Lassie. We just love that show. My kids never miss it."

"Bring them out to the kennel sometime. We like visitors," Jack said.

"Really? Oh, that would be nice. We'd like that," the woman smiled. "Did you hear that?" she asked her husband. "He said if we want to bring the kids to see the Collies, we can go out and visit their kennel."

The husband nodded silently and returned to his magazine.

"Where is your place, exactly?" the lady asked. "Do you have certain hours for visitors?"

"Well, usually, most people show up on Sunday afternoons. But, it has to be at a time when we're not away at a show."

"You show your dogs? Well, they must be very fine Collies."

"We think so," Jack smiled and looked at the pups. "Future champions. You hear that fellas?"

Placing them gently on the floor to let them romp around, he laughed as they slipped on the linoleum but quickly got their bearings. "It doesn't take them long to figure things out," he said.

"I can see that," the woman said. "You know, maybe we should think about getting a Collie after . . ." She nodded in the direction of her poor dog, its eyes glazed over, in the kind of understanding shared by dog owners.

"Trouble?" Jack asked.

"Blind," the woman said. "And her kidneys. The doctor thinks it won't be long now. She's such a love. Such a love - " her voice choked up, she shook her head and looked away.

"You know," Jack said, watching the goldfish swimming in their bowl on the receptionist's desk, "I think it's the lady who gives advice in the newspaper. Doesn't she say the best medicine for losing a pet you love is to go right out and get yourself another one?"

"Works for people, too, I've heard," the woman added, noticing the wedding ring now worn on Jack's other hand.

He nodded; for people, too, he thought. *Is she right, Faye? Is that what you'll be wanting for me? You want me to go places and have a good time? You want me to go out and dance again?*

How could he do that? How could he say to God and all the world that his life with Faye was replaceable? How could he put her away, like a treasured heirloom, and pretend she never existed? How could his heart bear that. He had always thought people who married again had never known real love. How was it possible for them to do such a thing? If they had known real love, true love, they would never want anyone else. He thought of Esmeralda. She loved Robert Sheffield and everyone knew it. He thought of Blanche, who could snap her fingers and have any man she wanted. He thought of Nancy; ashamed of the man she had married and questioning whether she had really loved him, really ever known him, at all?

"Jack?" the receptionist said. "You can go in now."

On the way home, Jack went over a mental checklist of everything that had to be done for the weekend. Customers visiting the kennel must only see the best.

"Everything must be perfect," Esmeralda said. "It has to be a dream come true for them. Lochwood has to be the place where everyone wishes their puppy could be born." It was an image carefully, intelligently cultivated.

Advertised in all the right magazines, pictures of the immaculately maintained estate, home of the von Havenburg Collies, were seen far and wide. Shows in which the dogs were exhibited to the public were, likewise, selected with the utmost consideration.

"If we're going to send the dogs away to a different town each month, they might as well go to the shows that draw the biggest crowds," Esmeralda decided. "And take plenty of business cards with you, Jack. Always."

It was an order; an order faithfully obeyed. Always.

"You've changed," he said to her.

"And why not?" she asked.

"Where's the Esmeralda who grew up here, chasing butterflies and pretending to fly?" he wanted to know.

"Half of her died of humiliation and the other half? Still in Paris," she sighed.

"That doesn't leave much," he said.

"No," she said. "It doesn't."

She was tired, drained of spirit, exhausted; as if the hope of ever reaching life's promise was unattainable. She would throw herself into her work now, he knew; into the estate, into the kennel, just as she had once thrown herself into catching butterflies to avoid the haunting loss of a mother who ran back to England; and a father too busy for love. Perhaps that's why she needed her first puppy. Perhaps that's why she needed a whole kennel full of dogs so beautiful, so perfect, everyone else wanted them and every one of them loved her.

"How did things go at the vet's?" Esmeralda asked.

"Passed with flying colors," Jack said.

"Sable and White," she smiled, playing with seven bundles of fluff. "These pups are really nice. Don't you think so?"

"Yes, I've been thinking so, myself," he said. "Something clicked in that mating."

"Lucky Blanche," she said. "Are all the dogs groomed?" she asked Nancy, who was brushing away with a mountain of soft Collie hair at her feet.

"I don't know how much more my arms can take!" Nancy said, standing back from a grooming table and shoving a brush into the back pocket of her jeans, handle first.

"Well, they look beautiful. Our visitors will be pleased," Esmeralda smiled. "How many do we have right now, Jack? What's the count?"

"Fifty-six here in the kennel; another seventeen on the road with handlers."

"How many litters do we have coming?"

"Three due in a month or so."

"Good," Esmeralda said. "Blanche is picking up hers in a little while. You know, they're so nice I feel like running an ad featuring them. Do you still have that photographer friend of yours?"

"Sidney? You bet. Last I heard he's on assignment for that billboard company he works for."

"When's he available for pictures, Jack?" Nancy asked, making a face and clowning around.

"I'll be sure to let you know!" he laughed.

Reigning them in, Esmeralda continued. "Call him, so we can set aside a day here and get some good shots for the ads, OK?"

Good photography could make or break a kennel, she knew. Robert had taught her that. The right angle could make a dog's shoulder look as if it could give the dog extra grace of motion; likewise, the wrong angle could make it's gait seem as if it must be short-strided and choppy. She thought of these things and the man who had shared so much with her. Would he be proud of her now? Knowing she had done the matings he suggested, had improved the quality of the von Havenburg Collies with each generation, would he smile at her and say. "Well done, Esmeralda. *Well done, my love.*"

She lifted her chin and straightened the posture that she had been trained to believe said so much about one's state of mind. If she projected confidence and strength, she could inspire Jack and Nancy now that life was going to be more difficult for all of them. True, she had said so before; but for the first time since the accident, she was uneasy on a level far deeper than merely reacting to an occasional insult from the townsfolk. Something was happening around them; something far more significant than outrage and punishment from a local dog club. Why had members of the kennel club made the death of the dogs so much more important than the death of Faye Milliken?

They want to get rid of me, she thought, with a chill that had haunted her since appearing in court day after day. *They hate me. They won't be satisfied until I'm wrecked the same as the cars that killed Faye and the dogs.* Well, she wouldn't be wrecked. She would hold her head high and stay in the game. Dog show judges could overlook her, people could snub her, employees could leave and suppliers could refuse to sell her feed. But, they couldn't defeat her. She had the kind of dogs the public wanted; and as long as she could get them out there for people to see, von Havenberg Kennels was a force to reckon with.

Shaking off the grip of such thoughts, she asked Jack to see the puppies once again. They had grown considerably in the weeks since she and Blanche had returned from Europe.

"They're different from other pups their age," she said, picking up the closest one and cupping its face in her hand. "Do you see it?"

"I know what you mean," he said, tossing a ball. "Notice the way they carry themselves; use their necks?"

"You've seen it too, then," she remarked, watching the puppies play. "They arch their necks like sea horses. Where did I see that before?"

"I only know one other dog that carried himself like that," Jack said, tossing the ball again. "Beige is out of Cookie, right, who died in the crash."

"Yes, she is."

"Blanche bred her," he said, considering the possibilities.

"Yes, she did."

"Well, didn't Blanche buy herself a daughter of Ch. Braegate Model of Bellhaven once?"

"*That stinker!*" Esmeralda exclaimed, the full impact of what he just said suddenly hitting her. "We've never seen the pedigree on this bitch. When she brought her over for breeding, she forgot the pedigree, remember? *That's why she bred Beige to our stud* – he goes straight back to Model! *She's line breeding on the Bellhaven dogs!* There's no telling how much Bellhaven Beige, here, has behind her, Jack. *These pups could trace any number of times to Model!*"

"I thought Blanche didn't like the Bellhaven dogs."

"That's what she's been telling us! I knew there was something better about these puppies. All this time, she's bad mouthing the Bellhaven dogs to me and line-breeding on them behind our backs! *I love those Bellhaven dogs!* She knows that! But, all she can talk about is out-crossing! Who ya gonna breed to now, Ez? You've got to out-cross for vigor, Ez!

305

You've got to out-cross for health, Ez! Well, sure, our litters are healthy. But, these pups look every bit as healthy as ours, don't they? And every one of them looks like a champion!"

"And after all the favors we do for her!" Nancy pitched in, sweeping up Collie hair from the kennel floor. "We'd never catch up this way! Would she really do that to us?"

"If it meant knocking us out of the game?" Jack asked, repenting for a few late night trysts now. "Come on, this is Blanche we're talking about."

"Doesn't she know how much it's costing us?" Nancy asked, in disbelief.

"*All these years!*" Esmeralda said, her face pale, "we've been out-crossing our stock *all this time* and she's been sitting back laughing! Damn, Jack! *DAMN!*"

"What are we going to do, Esmeralda?" he asked.

"I don't know. But, I'll tell you one thing. I promise, you. I promise you both and every dog in this kennel -- Blanche Jacobus is going to regret ever tricking me this way - and she's going to regret it for a Hell of a long time!"

En Guarde The line had been crossed!

Like the dogs who love them, Breeders can forgive many things, but one thing they can not stand - the one thing they can not abide - is faking pedigrees! Once again, Blanche had tricked her. Once again, the sanctity of their friendship

306

had been crunched and twisted into dust by a pair of fancy high heels that surely matched the black heart of Esmeralda's scheming nemesis.

She wouldn't take this — she mustn't! After all she had done for Blanche — after all they had been through together! Would this battle of wills never end? Well, Blanche could win her battles. She could win and laugh all she wanted. But if it was the last thing she ever did; once and for all — even if it took a lifetime — Esmeralda must find a way to win The Blue Ribbon War!

Checking her makeup once more and putting on her sunglasses, Blanche smiled as she pulled in the long lane of Lochwood. The puppies were seven weeks old now and ready to come home. It had been nice of Ez to insist that they stay with Jack until weaning, generous of her to pay for the vet check, shots and worming. *"We don't want to do anything that might disturb Beige's milk supply,"* Esmeralda had said. "You know how the slightest thing can upset a nursing mother and we don't want to risk anything happening to her puppies. Do we? Especially a litter as nice as this. *I think they're the best you've ever produced, Blanche.* Really, I do."

"Well, it's all right with me, as long as you don't mind," Blanche had said, thinking what a relief. Much as she liked them, puppies in the house made a place stink. "Sure, Ez. That's OK with me. I'll pick 'em up as soon as they're ready."

Seven puppies; every one of them a beauty. Perfect markings, perfect ears, perfect structure. How would she ever be able to pick the best one? She could almost cover her eyes with a blindfold, stand back and point. Life was grand.

"Hey, Jack!" she waved, as she pulled up to the kennel, parked and sauntered to the nearest run. Greeting Beige and her litter, she said playfully, "You guys ready to come home?"

"Oh, they've been waiting for this," Jack smiled confidently.

"Where's Ez?" Blanche asked. "I thought she'd want to be here, you know, to say good-bye to my future champions?"

"In the house," he answered. "Some office stuff she had to take care of for the factory, I think." He was smiling when he said that.

"OK. Well, load 'em up! I've get the crate."

Swinging open the back doors, she pulled out a crate. "Beige can sit up front with me," she said. "Us girls gotta stick together. Hey!" she swung around after they loaded up the last puppy. "Ain't there supposed to be seven?"

"Seven?" he asked.

"Yeah. I counted seven before."

"Oh. You must be talking about the pup for the stud fee."

"Stud fee? Nobody said anything about a stud fee."

"Sure," he said. "Esmeralda made her pick and you take the other six.

That's how it usually goes, right?" he asked, his gaze steady in a way that she knew left no room for discussion.

Knees rubbery, ears suddenly warm, Blanche studied the puppies, paused and faced him. "The one she picked. It wouldn't happen to be the big Sable with a real wide collar and two full-white front legs you showed me, would it?"

"Come to think of it, that does sound kind of familiar," Jack said, standing his ground. "You know, if I didn't know better, I'd say he reminded me an awful lot of one of the Bellhaven dogs."

Slamming the truck door shut, Blanche cursed. "Well, tell her I hope she's happy, ruining my coming home PRESent! *And thank YOU, Jack,*" she shot him a look that could wilt any man. "*For EVERYthing!*"

From upstairs, Esmeralda let the curtain fall back in place at her office window overlooking the kennel and the grounds below. Doesn't she look ridiculous, she thought, as Blanche slammed the back doors of her truck and spun her wheels on the gravel. Well, you spin your wheels, Bitch, because that's exactly what you're going to be doing for as long as I have anything to do with it. You thought I started with the best puppy? Wait until you see what the von Havenburg Collies become now.

Poor Jack, she thought, even though he seemed quite amused as Blanche drove away. Away? As in out of their lives? Hardly, she thought. There would be time, and time again, for Blanche to get even.

And, she would. But, not now. For now, I have *everything* that matters to you; whether you know it or not; whether you find out on your own or not; *whether I choose to tell you or not*. Any one of them could give you love, Blanche; *and I can hold out. I can hold out forever.*

Chapter 8

NEWSREEL: 1955 . . . Argentina ousts
dictator Juan Peron; West Germany becomes
a sovereign state; Rosa Parks refuses to
give up her bus seat in Alabama and
Churchill resigns in London . . . . As
Count Basie & His Orchestra play "April
In Paris," Author William Faulkner wins a
Pulitzer for "A Fable," Albert Einstein
and entertainer Carmen Miranda say good-
bye to this world; a horse named Swaps
wins the Kentucky Derby; the Brooklyn
Dodgers defeat the New York Yankees and
crowds at The Garden cheer for Dr. John
A. Saylor's Bulldog, Ch. Kippax Feamought
as he proudly wins Westminster.

In a moment of truce, Blanche, as a
friendly gesture, stops by just as Nancy
is about to go into town on the morning
errands and offers a ride. Excusing herself first to use the powder room, she
bolts through the house changing every
clock causing Esmeralda to miss an impor-

tant auction for a rare porcelain figurine that would complete her Lladro collection.

"Of course, I'll accept," Esmeralda says, a few weeks later, when Nancy shows her the pink invitation to the cocktail party at Blanche's house for the Kennel Club. "I'd love to go," she smiles sweetly, slipping something into her purse. . . . While the gracious hostess is otherwise occupied, Esmeralda spikes every open bottle of liquor from gin to scotch with a helping of Chanel No. 5.

Ka-CHING!

NEWSREEL: 1960 . . . As Bobby Darrin sings "Mack The Knife," recorded by Louis Armstrong & The All-Stars just five years earlier, JFK is elected president, Harper Lee's "To Kill A Mockingbird" is in all the bookstores; Alfred Hitchcock's "Psycho" is terrifying movie-goers; Emily Post bids a polite farewell to this Earth and a classy Pekingese belonging to Mr. and Mrs. C.C. Venable wins Best in Show at Westminster. . . . "DOROTHY JACOBUS STRICKEN!" screams the Havenburg Gazette; "HEIRESS BRINGS FLOWERS!"

As the battle of The Blue Ribbon wages on, Esmeralda asks Blanche to transport two of her Collies to the Delaware Valley Kennel Club show. She and Jack arrive late, open the crates and find both white ruffs doused with blue food coloring. . . Esmeralda, not to be outdone, takes off for the local grocery store, buys out the school supplies shelf and mixes white, water-base paste into

the jar of grooming cholesterol Jack ap-
plies to all of Blanche's dogs . . . .

As Brenda Lee sings "I'm Sorry" on
the radio, Esmeralda is definitely not.

Ka-CHING!

NEWSREEL: 1965 . . . In a country still
spinning from the assassinations of John
F. Kennedy, Bobbie Kennedy and Martin
Luther King; still believing it was lied
to about the death of Marilyn Monroe,
"The Sound of Music" premieres and
America marches into Vietnam. As Malcolm
X is shot to death in Harlem; 34 are
dead, over 1,000 injured and nearly 4,000
arrested in Los Angeles riots. Consumer
advocate Ralph Nader steps up to the
plate and the Dodgers defeat Minnesota in
the World Series; Lucky Debonair wins the
Kentucky Derby and, sure enough, it's
another Scottie, this one belonging to
Mr. and Mrs. Charles C. Stalter bearing
the lofty name of Ch. Carmichael's
Fanfare, that wins the highest honors at
Westminster. . . . Headlines in Havenburg
cry, "VH BELTING FACES BANCRUPTCY! TOWN
FEARS MOST WILL LOSE JOBS! HEIRESS VOWS
TO DO ALL SHE CAN."

Two days before the Northern Jersey
Kennel Club Show, Esmeralda calls in a
panic over her entries. "Where are they?
I can't find them! Weren't you going to
take care of them for everybody in the
Club?"

"What a shame," Blanche says;
"Must've forgot. And it's a major."

Ez and Jack, both squeaking rubber
toys, are seen at the show creating a

313

ruckus outside the gate just as Blanche leads her dogs into the ring; totally breaking her "concentration" . . .

    Ka-CHING!

NEWSREEL: 1970 . . . Simon & Garfunkel sing "Bridge Over Troubled Water," Blood, Sweat & Tears sing for Columbia and Miles Davis is laughing about "Bitches Brew" . . . As the Beatles break up, George C. Scott refuses to accept the Oscar for his role in "Patton," American troops invade Cambodia and students at Kent State are murdered by National Guardsmen during a political protest. Author Maya Angelou releases "I Know Why The Caged Bird Sings," and IBM introduces the floppy disk. Jimi Hendrix, Janis Joplin and Sonny Liston say good-bye forever to their fans; the average household income is $8,734; Dust Commander wins the Kentucky Derby and a flashy young Boxer named Ch. Arriba's Prima Donna, wagging her tail for owners Dr. and Mrs. P.J. Pagano and Dr. Theodore S. Fickes, wins Westminster. . . . The business page of the Havenburg Gazette, thinner now, reports, "BANK CALLS LOAN! HEIRESS SELLS OFF LAND TO COVER DEBTS!"

    Blanche, after years of being sickened by the statue of a Jockey outside Esmeralda's stable, comes over and paints it with black and white polka dots . . . Esmeralda buys out the local auto supply store and sprays Blanche's whole front lawn – hot pink.

    Ka-CHING!

NEWSREEL: 1975 . . . The Watergate cover-up is big news; George Carlin hosts a new show called "Saturday Night Live;" people can identify with "One Flew Over The Cuckoo's Nest," and Barbara Streisand sings "The Way We Were." As Aristotle Onassis sails off into the sunset, Siagon surrenders; Andrei D. Sakharov wins the Nobel Peace Price and Barbara Vanword's Old English Sheepdog, Ch. Sir Lancelot of Barvan wins Best in Show at Westminster. . . . "JACOBUS CLOSES FAMILY BUSINESS: OWNER SAYS, 'I'M A DOG SHOW QUEEN NOW!'"

Well into their second decade, The Blue Ribbon Wars find Blanche writing a letter to the editor bemoaning the fate of Richard Nixon. Esmeralda puts down the paper, picks up the phone and sends her a complimentary weekend stay at The Watergate Hotel . . . together with a pass to the hearings and later that year, an autographed copy of William Safire's "Before The Fall."

Ka-CHING!

NEWSREEL: 1980 . . . Ted Turner launches CNN, John Lennon is shot to death, and President Jimmy Carter sees Ronald Reagan win The White House. Genuine Risk runs for the roses in the Kentucky Derby; Pittsburgh beats the Rams in the Super Bowl, and the average household income is $17,710. As "Kramer vs. Kramer" gives the legal system something to talk about, Mae West cracks a few jokes with St. Peter and bargains for the Pearly Gates. As the crowd goes wild at The Garden, Kathleen Kanzler presents her Siberian Husky, Ch.

Innisfree's Sierra Cinnar in New York and takes Westminster . . . . "LOCHWOOD MANSION OPENS DOORS AS BED AND BREAKFAST," announces the Havenburg Gazette. "Public Invited."

As the War rages on, Blanche proudly goes to the Reagan inaugural on the arms of the next Secretary of State whom she meets while waiting outside the building at the aforementioned Watergate hearings . . . . Calling in a favor, Esmeralda digs up Steven-the-Thief, now a successful record executive with his own company, makes her own version of "What A Fool Believes," and dumps a thousand 45s outside Blanche's front door.

Ka-CHING!

Chapter 9

It was 1985. The Reagan administra-
tion took power; Mikhail Gorbachev became
ruler of Russia, and scientists reported
a gigantic hole in the Earth's ozone
layer over Antarctica. As Tina Turner
growled, "What's Love Got To Do With It;"
Hollywood toasted "Out of Africa" and
mourned the AIDS death of mega-star Rock
Hudson. In New York, Sonnie & Alan
Novick's Scottish Terrier, Ch. Braebum's
Close Encounter won Westminster and, like
everybody else, Esmeralda was asking herself, "Just what is it about those
Scotties?"

Diversionary Tactics . . . Esmeralda
closed the book she was reading and
tossed it on the table with the rest of
her paperback novels. Settling in at her
desk, she wrote out a few checks and
slipped them into envelopes for Nancy to

drop in the mailbox on her way into town. She always went into town at this time of morning, with the bank deposit. Pushing aside the curtain, she looked outside at the snow and could see Nancy, bundled up in her black coat, scraping off the windshield of her car. Beyond her, somewhere on the lawn, she could still remember Robert, laughing off his birthday, vowing always to stay young. She saw him this way, had seen him this way, every November 16 in the years since he had gone. All those years. So hard to believe.

All those years of love! She had been holding onto it, saving it for no one else. Time? She had been hoping; believing it would stand still. Why couldn't it? Why couldn't they be the first ones it happened for? Why couldn't the woman inside, the one laughing with Robert out there in the snow, be the one everyone else could see? If anyone had told her she would feel this way after thirty-three years, even a little bit, she wouldn't have believed it.

"Are you OK, Esmeralda?" It was Nancy, back inside for her shopping list and purse. Nancy; grayer now, more serious, as they all were.

"I'm all right," Esmeralda heard herself saying, but knowing so much better than that. Funny, how we lied to reassure others that we weren't, as the doctors had so often warned those around her, going off the deep end. "I'm just looking at the pretty snow," she said.

318

"Do you want anything in town?" Nancy asked.

Esmeralda returned to her desk, a desk devoid of factory business now, and gathered the stack of envelopes. "Could you just mail these for me?"

"Of course. Are you sure there isn't anything else?" Nancy asked, noticing the familiar letter going to Paris. The address had changed again, as it had throughout the years. But today, as always, she didn't ask; didn't pry.

"Has Jack let Kane out for his morning run?" Esmeralda wondered, tidying her desk.

"Oh, yes," Nancy smiled, putting on her gloves. "I had to chase him away from the garbage."

"Did you give him some leftovers from last night?" Esmeralda asked, taking all of the pencils out of the glass on her desk and rearranging them one by one. Why couldn't anyone remember that she liked all the points of her pencils sticking up, so she could see if they needed sharpened?

"Yes. You know I did." Intrigued, Nancy watched as Esmeralda ran a finger across the spotless desktop as if feeling for dust.

"Be careful about his teeth; are you stopping off at the butcher for bones?"

"Top of my list," Nancy smiled, waving the piece of paper in her hand.

"Well, please say hello to Mr. Shaw for me. You'll pick up anything we need for our guests?"

It was always like this; Esmeralda always reminding Nancy of what she had never failed to attend to on her own. Tonight's meal for the guests would be the same familiar Pennsylvania Dutch cooking tourists expected while lodging at Lochwood Inn.

"And, this is Tuesday isn't it?" Esmeralda asked, looking around the room as if the walls were speaking to her.

Nancy nodded. "Roots' Sale," she said, about the weekly farmer's market held every Tuesday outside of East Petersburg.

"Can you stop over at the pet food dealer and get a bag of that new kibble?" Esmeralda asked, picking out a sharp pencil as if to make a list. "You know, the organic kind Jack told me about? I want him to give it a try. Oh! And don't forget wheat germ oil from the health food store. OK?"

"Anything else?"

"Damn!" Esmeralda spat, breaking the tip of her pencil; quickly recovering her composure. "No . . . no, you'd better go now," she said, her shoulders slumping.

"Do you want me to bring Kane in for you?"

"That would be nice," Esmeralda said, burying her face in her hands.

"He's covered with snow, but I'll brush him off quick," Nancy said, allowing Esmeralda her emotional privacy; putting down her purse and starting for the door. Esmeralda didn't move. "Are you sure you're OK?" she asked, changing her mind about the privacy. "Do you want to come with me on the errands?"

"Oh, Nancy!" Esmeralda sighed, shaking her head. "I don't know what to do!" she suddenly broke down, sobbing. "He's alone - all alone, And that horrible Blanche! That cruel, horrible woman!"

"What do you mean, Esmeralda? Who's alone? Kane?"

"*He's dying!*"

"Who's dying?"

"*WHO DO YOU THINK!*" Esmeralda screamed, as if she was surrounded by idiots; grabbing a delicate Randolph porcelain vase filled with fresh roses; flinging it outside, flowers and all.

"Keep them AWAY from me! I can't stand them looking at me, so fresh and PERFECT! Everybody and their perfect, perfect lives!"

"But, they're from - "

"I don't CARE who they're from!" she hollered, snatching up her paperback novel again and plunking herself down on the couch. "It's gone, Nancy. Everything I have, everything I've built. What was any of it worth?"

Skillfully, the faithful housekeeper took off her coat, busied herself with the grandfather's clock and a bit of unnecessary pillow fluffing. It was early. Esmeralda would read for a while, she told herself, make a few calls to friends, laugh, perhaps cry. Before lunch, she'd check the guest list, make sure all the rooms were ready, walk down the path to the kennel, and go over the latest dog show results with Jack. By noon, she'd be in the greenhouse cutting fresh flowers herself, asking if it's possible to replace the Randolph vase. Impossible, Nancy would say. Deborah Randolf hasn't made her translucent porcelain vases in many years. Esmeralda would remember, shake her head and disappear for the remainder of the day.

That's how it would be. Another predictable day at Lochwood, now known, according to it's attractive sign by the road, as "Lochwood Inn."

"I'm OK, Nancy. I'm sorry for that," Esmeralda said, coming to her senses. "You go and take care of the errands. I'll be all right."

Knowing she'd better go while she could, Nancy gathered her coat and purse once again. "Well, I'd better hurry," she said. "The car's running. I'll let Kane in the wash room and give him a quick brushing."

Outside, the magnificent Collie saw Nancy and came running. Without a word, because no words were necessary, Nancy walked around the house to the kitchen door and he followed. Inside, she reached for the dust brush of her sweeping pan and held his immense ruff as she flicked off the snow in which he had been playing. "Good, fella," she said after a while, opening the door to the hallway that led to the rest of the house. "Now, go in and make Esmeralda feel better."

Wagging his tail, off he trotted to the library.

"Kane!" Esmeralda said with a smile, as the great dog trotted to her. Burying her hands in his thick mane, she pulled him close and kissed the top of his noble head. "Where would I be without you? You loving, loving spirit. Here, boy," she said, pulling him close beside her and telling him to sit. "Let me get that nasty stick out of your fur."

The alarm of twenty collies barking from the kennel announced Nancy's return. Minutes later, arms full of grocery bags, she made her way up the path to the back door and into the kitchen. Kane, ready to play with the giver of all special treats, greeted her with a dog smile.

"Hey fella! You gonna help me put away the groceries?"

His manner clearly said all he wanted to help with was a bone from the butcher.

"Give me a minute," Nancy said, as she pulled off her boots and went into the hallway to hang up her coat. "Esmeralda? Are you here?" There was no answer. "I guess she's busy," Nancy said, knowing Esmeralda never answered when she was busy. It broke her concentration.

In the library, Esmeralda was closing her book and sitting thoughtfully, ghost like; here, but not here. Reaching for the phone, her hand lingered. Then, standing to her full height of five feet and two inches, and wrapping her nightgown around a body plumper these days than she liked, she fluffed her hair. Blanche, she thought furiously. *No wonder Robert left that woman!*

"Are you hungry?" Nancy asked, on her way upstairs.

Esmeralda blinked, but did not answer.

"Would you like me to get you anything?"

Suddenly, Esmeralda seemed to realize she wasn't alone.

"OH! No! No, I'm fine, Nancy. Really. I shouldn't have done that. Thrown the flowers out, I mean. They were pretty flowers, really. Who were they from?"

"Well, the card said they were from Kane. Just to make you feel good, because you've been so blue."

"What a clever gift, Kane. Thank you!"

Pleased with himself, and not knowing why, the great dog moaned and groaned, as Collies do when trying to speak.

"I threw your flowers away? What a bad Momma I am. Oh, I wish Momma hadn't done that." Facing Nancy, she said, "Imagine how it must feel to be loved as much as Kane is. Do you think he knows?"

"On some level, I'm sure, he does," Nancy said, assured now that all was well and turning to go.

"Wait!"

Fidgeting with her pearl necklace, Esmeralda seemed suddenly frail; vulnerable. "I wonder, Nancy; I wonder if you could tell me – "

"Tell you what?"

"If ... if we could do it over again, if we had the power," Esmeralda

324

fumbled to express herself correctly, "do you think, if we knew then everything that we know now - right now - do you think most of us would ever listen to other people's advice? Would we hold back? Would we live our lives differently, no matter what others said, any of them? No matter who they were? Would you let other people decide your whole life for you?"

Their eyes met.

"Wouldn't you have done everything in your power to keep him here and never let him go?"

"Him?" Nancy asked. "Steven, you mean?"

Esmeralda blushed. Even now, such things were like standing on a cliff; closing her eyes; swaying in the breeze. "Yes! Yes! Steven! That's what I want to know," she said. "If you could do it over again - change things, make them right and do it now - this instant! - would you bring him back? No matter what I said, police, or anyone else around you?"

For a moment, Nancy considered the question that had never been asked aloud before and their eyes met again. "Yes, I'd have done anything - anything! - to have him with me for just one more day. One more hour!"

Dropping her gaze, Esmeralda turned away. "Anything... Yes, I knew that. Anything." She thought about this and the necklace fell to her chest once more. "Because you loved him!"

Nancy smiled gently. "If you hadn't let me stay, I don't know where I'd be today. Maybe I don't have Steven, but we've got our own kind of family here, don't we?"

Esmeralda nodded. "Yes. Yes, you're right. You don't ever have to thank me, Nancy. We all have each other and we have the dogs. They'll never leave us. They'll never go away." Suddenly, she stepped forward and almost fell.

"Esmeralda!" Nancy reached out to steady her.

"Oh, Nancy, she never deserved him! It was me he loved!" Blinking against the sting of tears held back for so long, her eyes drooped at the thought and she half-sobbed. Suddenly, taking a deep breath, she straightened up. "Life can turn out so different from what it should have been. Isn't that true? But, it was a long time ago. Like everything. Life goes on, Nancy, and we get over it. Life just goes on no matter how important we think we are. I never heard from him after that. Not really. Not in the same way. Oh, maybe a Christmas card or two. Birthdays forgotten. I never forgot his birthday, oh no. November 16. But, I guess we, we all make our own decisions about these things and, I guess, he made his and I ... I made mine."

She knew she hadn't. Speaking as if what happened so long ago was as fresh today as if she hasn't made a decision at all, she made a fist. "Maybe I'll go away for a while. Yes, that's what I'll do! I'll take a trip and forget. I'll forget everything. I'll close my eyes and smile and dance all night long! Do you think I could ever forget, Nancy? Do you?"

Placing a reassuring hand on Esmeralda's shoulder, Nancy spoke softly. "What about Westminster coming up? That always takes your mind off things."

"Oh, there's plenty of time. And if there isn't, how many ribbons can somebody win?"

Esmeralda missing Westminster would be like a train not showing up at Grand Central.

"I'll call you!" she said. "Don't worry. I'll tell you everything. I promise. I'll tell you where I'm staying, where I'm going, who I'm dining with. You'll see. I'll have fun! Lots of fun! Oh, I can't wait! I can't wait!" Dancing around the room, she appeared lighter somehow. Esmeralda - dotty, plain Esmeralda seemed almost beautiful.

As the rain splashed against her windows that night, she put on her favorite record, "Anything For Love." As the record spun, she remembered the years that had gone by like music since Blanche had spun out of her life. Well, not out of her life, really. But, no longer the close friend she had once been; should still be. Funny, how people feel about their dogs, she thought. But, not much of a surprise when you didn't have any kids. Why had she taken that puppy, thirty-three years ago, knowing full well he was the best; knowing, after that, Blanche would have to fight with everything she had to defeat von Havenburg with such a winner?

Why? *Because Blanche deserved it.*

Opening shoe boxes filled with ribbons, she lovingly turned the pages of old dog show magazines and scrapbooks filled with newspaper clippings. With growing excitement, she reviewed the years of her champions. The years of fighting Blanche at every turn.

"How can you do this to a friend?" Nancy had asked. *"After all you've been through? I mean, the trial and everything you've both been through? Europe; staying away so long, then coming back and, that quick, you're not even speaking to each other? Why?"*

"She tricked me, Nancy. The same as she's always tricked me. And I'm through with it."

"But, over a puppy? You've got a whole kennel full of dogs. What's one puppy to you?"

"It's not about the puppy," Esmeralda said. *"It's not. She's been lying to me about her whole breeding program and tricking me into going in the wrong direction. I'm the one who always liked the Bellhaven dogs - ME! But, she pushed me away from them. Deliberately! All those times we talked about our kennels, and the precise 'look' we were both after. All the breeding plans we made! You don't know how often we talked and all that time, she was faking her pedigrees to me. No wonder she never bred her dogs to mine!"*

"What's going to happen now?"

"Well, thanks to you and Jack, we've got ourselves a start back in the right direction. If we manage things right, we can take this pup and turn the whole bloodline around. Just a pup? No, he's not just a pup," she said, leaning over and scooping the Sable puppy into her arms. "This is von Havenburg's next champion. This is the great, great grandsire of my dream Collie. Three or four generations from now – or if it takes me ten generations or a hundred! – I'll be holding the pup that's going to make von Havenburg the most exciting kennel in the world!"

She had that dog now. She had Kane.

She thought of Robert. Why had he left her? Kane wouldn't leave her. Why hadn't Robert loved her enough to wait just a little while longer? An hour; a day, to find out the truth? Would it have killed his spirit any faster than marrying Blanche had done?

She remembered his dark hair, flashing eyes and broad shoulders; his smile that caught the attention of anyone in its way. What fun it had all been. What fun! Pulling another photo from her scrapbook, she tossed it into a cardboard box on her bed.

"I've never forgotten you, Robert. Not once, not for one minute of all the minutes in all these years. I don't care what the doctors say, you're mine and I'm yours for as long as we have together. Come home with me. I'll bring you home. Don't be afraid of what happened. It was so very long ago, Robert. I'll take care of it. Let Esmeralda take care of everything."

Folding shut the box, she tied a blue ribbon around it, over which she slipped the first rosette Robert ever awarded her. "I've saved it all these years," she thought, "Along with my love."

Closing her suitcase, she glanced in the mirror to pull a curl down on her forehead. Turning to survey her room one last time, she snapped off the light.

As was her morning ritual, Nancy went through every room, drawing the drapes and pushing open windows to let in the morning sun. Putting out the cat, she went to the greenhouse for fresh flowers. Back inside, she picked up a vase in the entryway, headed for the kitchen to dump the water and replaced it with the fresh bouquet. Setting out a breakfast tray, she brewed fresh coffee, made toast, prepared oatmeal with fruit and poured coffee into a small thermos. Across the plate on the tray, she lay a fresh flower and headed upstairs.

"Esmeralda?" she knocked on the closed bedroom door. "It's after seven. Aren't you getting up this morning?"

Fighting back a feeling of growing unease, she knocked again, harder. "Esmeralda!" she called out. "Wake up and have some breakfast. I've got juice and toast!" But, there was no answer. No irritable command for her to leave the tray; no imperious demand for her to go away and leave the sane to their sleep.

Turning the brass handle, prepared for anything, she opened the door. There was the bed, pristine as the day before when she, herself, had made it. Hand shaking, she reached for the note pinned to its covers. Outside, a dove startled from her nest in a Cedar tree, fluttered away.

"Jack! Jack!"

"Over here, Nancy!" he hollered from among the kennels, a snow shovel in his hands.

"She's gone! She's not in the house and the car's gone. Did you see her leave? Did you hear a car last night?"

"Which car did she take?" he asked, as if that might give a clue.

"The green Jaguar."

"The Jag?" he said, leaning the shovel against a tree. "Then it wasn't for dog business. If it was, she'd have taken the Jeep or the Pick-up. Did she take anything with her?"

"A suitcase. I checked for that right away."

"Just one?" Tipping back his hat and rubbing his neck, he said, "Short trip. Anything else?"

"Nothing that I could see, no."

"Well, how was she feeling yesterday? What was she talking about?"

"Moody's the best way I'd describe it." She handed him the note. "I don't think I've ever seen her that upset since the accident."

"What does she mean, here, 'If I don't come back?'"

"That's what gets me," Nancy said, as Jack took her arm and led her back to warm kitchen.

"It's cold out here," he said. "You're not dressed for this."

"She was nervous," Nancy said, as if she must talk quickly; tell him everything. "You know, how she gets when she doesn't know what to do? Fixing papers, straightening pencils, that kind of thing? I knew something was wrong. Then she got all quiet and strange, like it was OK now; she'd made up her mind. She said something about taking a trip, but I didn't think she meant disappearing like this. I thought she'd have me pack her bags for a few days in the Bahamas or Rio, like she does sometimes. I figured I'd be calling the airport for her today. But, this is different, Jack," Nancy said, pouring him a cup of coffee. "It's Robert Sheffield. She said he's dying."

"That's bad news. That could really throw her," he said, pouring milk into his cup and stirring.

"It did. I could tell. I never would have left her alone if I thought she was so upset. She fooled me, Jack. That old girl fooled me." Taking his spoon, she stirred sugar into her cup and tossed the spoon in the sink.

"She's pretty good at fooling people when she wants to," he said. "Where is Robert these days? Did she say? Does anybody know?"

"Blanche would."

"That's how she found out?" he asked. "Damn that woman! Always upsetting

Esmeralda. And with the biggest show of the year coming up. How long do you think she'll be gone?"

"How would I know? But, she said she'll let me know where she's staying so nobody worries."

"Take her at her word. Whatever's eating her, she wants to deal with it herself. She'll be all right, Nancy. Every once in a while, you gotta let a bird spread her wings."

"It's serious, Jack. She was crying."

"Rightfully so. When things don't turn out the way you want 'em to, it don't matter how much else you've got going. You can have a hundred champions in your kennel and spend your whole life trying to get back the one that got away. Robert Sheffield was the love of her life," he said. Then, changing the subject, he asked, "Did she get the roses?"

"I put them right in the study, where she wouldn't miss them."

Fool's Errand

Heading North, the custom-made, dark green Jaguar with its soft leather upholstery and satin-like cherry wood interior, purred its way across a map of towns, fields and forests. Like a luxurious time machine, the car passed through hazy possibilities of what might have been and the vividness of what was. If only he hadn't been afraid, she thought. If only he had known and understood. Canada? She would have left Lochwood, her father's company and all it stood for if it meant being with the man she loved.

What was he like now, she wondered? Not a day had gone by that she hadn't asked herself that question. What had life done to him? Had it turned out anything like what he had once hoped for? Whatever it cost her, however long it took, this time, she would find out.

She remembered the dog show; overhearing Blanche remark that Robert was terminally ill as she was selling a bag of doggie rubber bands. Had she been able to speak, to think, she would have asked how Blanche knew? Who had told her such a thing? That's what she would have asked, when all she really wanted to know was, had he married?

Was he married to a woman prettier than she; more intelligent, more graceful? It didn't matter. He would toss her aside and come back to Lochwood. They would rush into each others' arms with all the fury of a force of Nature -- no woman could love Robert more than she did! Not in a hundred million years.

She thought of his occasional picture in the dog magazines. Though it had been a while, she would know him anywhere. Though she hadn't heard his voice, felt it pouring over her, through her, for so long; she would never forget its power.

Did he have a family now; children; grandchildren? No! Please don't tell me he has what we should have had together!

Please don't tell me he has people who love him - yes, I hope he does. I truly do. But - oh, God! - can't he see how much I want him!

"But, people don't belong to us," Nancy had said when Esmeralda had asked why she didn't fight for Steven.

It wasn't the same, Esmeralda told herself. It wasn't the same. Poor Nancy. Steven wasn't the kind of man worth fighting for; slithering, slimy Steven.

"It's Steven! He's calling from Miami!"

From prison, Esmeralda thought, and she said so.

"No!" Nancy said excitedly. *"He's calling from his office. He's got his own office!"* Putting a hand over the receiver, she whispered loudly, *"He's with a new record company - they made him vice-president in charge of sales. He's met - "* Suddenly, her face went slack.

"Yes, Steven," she said. *"I understand. Yes, I know how long it's been. I . . . I guess I just thought . . . sure . . . sure, I will. Sure. Take care, Steven . . . Bye, Steven."*

Funny, what you think about while driving; what you remember. Nancy had never spoken another word about it; tried pretending he had never existed; had never been. Steven was gone. Jack was there. Steven and Nancy; Nancy alone; Nancy and Jack . . . The green Jaguar with the automatic transmission purred on.

Montreal greeted her with the homogenized savagery of any city, any-

335

where; a starving, gargantuan organism sucking in cars, airplanes and busses and spitting them right out again.

"Well, you won't spit me out," she thought. "I'm going straight through your heart like an arrow and taking what's mine."

Straight into the center of the city . . . past bunches of people huddled against the morning chill as they waited for busses . . . past stores and eateries and theaters . . . shoes for sale, clothing, law offices, Chinese food, TV stores and adult entertainment of every kind. Safe in her time capsule, she floated past hope, anger and desperation; past laughter, shouts and tears; all to the clash of horns, sirens and graphic curses beneath the dignity of any human mind.

How can they live this way, she wondered, knowing she never could, but understanding that many had known no other life and never would. Had any of them ever walked on a garden path and picked wild flowers? Had any of them ever heard the sound of nothing in the air but birds and insects on a summer day that held you in its spell like a loving mother?

Had they ever seen a newborn foal or held a wet puppy just whelped and taught it how to nurse? Or bottle-fed it when it couldn't?

An angry woman driver hollered at a man who cut in front of her. "*Asshole!*" she said in French. Perhaps the woman needed a colostomy to hold that part of her body in less contempt, Esmeralda thought. Or a hemorrhoid, to learn what sensitive creatures ass holes can be. Why not call him an arm? A foot? Why hold any part of the human body in contempt?

Working herself closer to the other car, Esmeralda amused herself by deciding the woman must be a pillar of success on her way from the hairdresser to a Board of Directors meeting and certainly never missing church on Sundays. With a better view at the next corner, she cringed.

The wasted, defeated woman driving that car, waving her arms and talking furiously to no one but herself, wouldn't know a hairdresser if somebody walked her into a beauty shop and strapped her down. Feeling herself being stared at, the young woman looked around, made a face and gave Esmeralda the finger.

They wouldn't have to strap her down. She was already strapped.

Through town, out the other side and into the country. Again, Esmeralda breathed a sigh of relief, then gasped. There it was, the road she was looking for. The road she had driven all this way for; waited a lifetime thirty-three years over for. It was his road. The road he drove back and forth on, time after time; the road . . . too much traveled.

Hands shaking, she found the mailbox; the brick house with white trim, and, from somewhere, strength. His home, she thought. If only I could have seen it in the spring. Maybe she shouldn't do this, she thought suddenly. Maybe it was a mistake! Oh, God, what if I'm making a mistake. What if he doesn't know me, she thought, with a chill jagging all the way down her arms. She could still turn away from this, let him die without her and preserve their memories forever. She could do that for herself. It was safer than pressing on; jumping off a cliff of her own making and falling into the waters below. But the cliff wasn't of her own making. It was a cliff of life's making, craggy and worn from the wins, the losses, and the nagging sense that every fragile weed she had ever hung onto had pulled her up only to make it that much farther for her to fall. Driving past the house, she thought how easy it had been finding his address, once she really decided to. A member of the Collie Club of America, on a trip North, she had said; when did their Breed Club hold its meetings in the Montreal area? She would love to meet some new Collie friends on a trip there. What kennel did she say, they asked? "The" von Havenburg Collies? Yes, Esmeralda had said, pride detectable in her voice. Would she give a talk at their meeting, they wanted to know? Oh, yes, she would be glad to talk. Pictures? Oh, yes, she could bring lots of pictures along to show them; lots of pictures.

She thought of those pictures now. Funny, how so much of one's life could be condensed into the space of a simple cardboard shoebox. It was only then that she noticed the sticker on the side of the shoebox, saying "Blanche' Creations."

Oh, it's a Blanche' creation all right, she thought. It's because of you we're all in this mess. It's because of you I'm coming all this way to straighten out what should have been put right thirty years ago. What were you thinking when you threw him out, Blanche? What in God's name? Or, *had* she thrown him out? In all this time, not until this very moment, had she considered the possibility that maybe it was Robert who had said good-bye that night and not the other way around. Feeling foolish, pushing away the possibility that she might not have it right, knowing it was too late; too late to take back all the things she believed about him; believed about Blanche, about herself, for so long. Gripping the steering wheel tighter, she turned on the radio and screamed.

Screamed like an ugly monkey jabbering senselessly in the jungle; her heart bleeding for mercy; her throat scratching like fire ants biting away everything it had ever said, every loving endearment, every passionate moan, it had ever uttered.

Screamed . . . tears of salt pouring from her eyes into rivulets of wrinkles; the woman she was, running away from the smooth, young girl she used to be . . . could have been . . . might have remained forever to the one she loved.

Should she? Dare she?

Did she have the right?

Struggling for breath, she slammed on the brakes. Turn around, Esmeralda. Turn around and go back! No. No, I can't. But, I must! I must find out. Even if it meant destroying the illusion? Even if it meant destroying his memory of her?

If she had cared about that - truly cared - she would never have left Lochwood. She would never have left, and would have spent the rest of her days locked in her darkened room, her curtains pulled shut tight against the world. She could have, you know.

She could have locked the gates, sent Nancy out for groceries and let Jack take charge of the kennel; let him really take charge. She could have soaked herself in champagne and washed away every last trace of the Esmeralda he once knew. He didn't love her; he couldn't love her. He had rejected her. He had left; disappeared. Nothing about the town; nothing about her was good enough for him to stay and fight for. Nothing. She could forgive; had forgiven; everything but that.

Robert, be kind when you see me again. Be kind when you see this woman from the past. I must find out. I must find out before I, too, die. Before we are lost in the darkness or the light, whichever force draws us most powerfully. I give you my every resource, my every hope, my every ounce of faith. I believe in you, always believed in you. I love you, Robert. And if there is truly a God, I will finally see. I will see God's power in your eyes, and feel it in my heart. I'll sense a future for us, if only for a day; I'll hold you in my arms as you say good-bye to this Earth and I will promise to know you in whatever adventure waits for us around the corner; waits for us next.

Robert! Robert! The one you knew is running, hiding behind the face of this woman you will see now; seasoned, tired. When I find you, the young man I remember will be no more. I throw them aside with no regrets. Don't turn me away, Robert. Oh, please. *Don't turn me away.*

He's dying, she reasoned. She must hurry! Nothing could stand in the way this time. Nothing! Parking now; turning the rear view mirror, she smoothed her hair, tilted her hat and rested a hand on the beribboned box at her side. This is it, she thought. Now, or never; and never meant spending the rest of her life without knowing. Picking it up, holding their box of memories like a shield, she made her way to the front of the brick house with its meticulously painted white trim, past remnants of flowers, withered and starved by winter's stingy portions of light.

Slowly, then gloriously, she walked. Could what started for them on a path among the wild flowers of Lochwood be ending this way, on a too-perfect side-walk of common cement? Casting aside pride, shame, and discretion - she pressed the door bell and knocked . . . .

"May I help you?" the man asked in a warm and familiar voice that even now made her weak. White hair, so unexpected, made him even more handsome, she thought. His eyes, brown-green and full of mis-chief, were still the eyes of a man with

341

whom everything was fun. His flannel shirt, unbuttoned at the chest, revealed a body honed by exercise, loved and well cared for.

"What is the lady selling, Robert?" a comfortable young woman in soft, shoulder-length hair and tight fitting jeans asked, as she joined him in the foyer and placed her hand on his shoulder. The way she said his name told Esmeralda all she wanted to know; more than she wanted to know.

"Oh! I'm sorry!" Esmeralda blurted. "I must have the wrong address!" It was all she could think of to say. He had changed. He didn't want her. He had forgotten all about her. *God, please help me out of this!* I don't want to see! I don't want to know! Stepping back without looking, she faltered and the box fell from her hands.

"I'll do it!" she hissed, disguising her voice as best she could as Robert stooped to pick up their memories. "I - I was looking for an old friend!" she said, apologetically, frantically grabbing photos, love letters and newspaper clippings at their feet.

"But, perhaps we can help you find your friend," the young woman said in her French-Canadian accent. "Perhaps your friend lives in the neighborhood?"

Hiding her face; looking down, looking away, fighting back tears, Esmeralda said, "No! I've made a mistake. *Please forgive me!* Please!" Pressing the lid back on the box, she held it to her breast and ran to her car.

"But, wait!" the young woman said. "You have forgotten this one!" But it was too late. The Jaguar was spitting out gravel and pulling sharply away.

"What scared her off like that, Kathryn?"

He stood still, his eyes following the car as it sped away, knowing, sensing. *Could it be? Could it possibly have been?*

Silently, she handed him the photo. "Robert? Is this not a picture of the man I love?"

"Harrisburg, Pennsylvania," he said, of the grooming tables, the Collies, the smiling faces. "I was just starting out. See that pup? I bred him."

He caught his breath; his skin prickling with a life of its own at the sight of the dark-haired young woman smiling so warmly as she stood next to him, as if it was the only place she would ever belong.

The screech of tires went through him like a hand piercing his chest and strangling his heart. The high pitched wail of tires skidding on a slippery road; the sickening, mundane thud; the falling dizziness of life being crushed out of his dream.

"*Mon Dieu!*" Kathryn screamed, as only a woman who knows what is happening without being there can do. "*It is her!*"

"*Get the car!*" Robert hollered, breaking into a run, his mind hoping, praying - *Oh, God, not again!*

Rushing into the house for keys, Kathryn grabbed a blanket and ran to the car. "Get in, Robert!" she hollered, pulling over and opening the door as she caught up with him. Saying nothing, he jumped inside and they sped down the road.

There it was; the beautiful car – its left side mangled, roof caved in; deep, ugly scars from metal scraping against metal, tail to front. Where was she? *Where was she!*

"Esmeralda!

"*Esmeralda!*" he screamed, throwing himself out of the car, running – tearing at the door that wouldn't give – smashing the window out with his fist – pulling the body slumped over the wheel to him. Pulling her through the window; running – running past courtrooms, jealousy, betrayal – for this to be how she fell into his arms again. Oh, no. Oh, no!

"*Find a phone, Kathryn! Call an ambulance!*"

Funny how the phone can ring sometimes and you just know it isn't good. Hesitating, Nancy answered in her usual way, though the quaver in her voice surprised even her.

". . . Who did you say this is?" she asked. "Robert? Robert Sheffield? . . . What kind of accident! . . . How bad? . . . I can't believe it," she said weakly, sitting down. "What hospital did you say?" Taking a handkerchief from her pocket and wiping her nose, she asked, "Can you spell that for me? In Montreal, you said? Do you have a phone number for them? Can I have your number, also? Yes,

I'll call her doctor. I'll call him right away. Yes, I'll ask him to call the hospital tonight."

Find the doctor's number. In the drawer - the address book - Hurry! *Work fast, fingers!* Stop shaking and dial!

"Not in? What do you mean he's not in - *this is an emergency!*" I'm Nancy Baumgartner calling from Lochwood. It's Esmeralda von Havenburg - she's been in an accident. Here - here's the number of the hospital in Montreal. Have him call there. He has to call tonight! Be sure to have him call!" Hanging up, she pulled her robe tight around her throat, slipped into a pair of boots and rushed down the garden path and straight to Jack's door.

"*Jack!*" she hollered, pounding. "Open up!"

"Nancy!" he said, surprised to see her there in her nightgown. "What's wrong?"

"They found her! In Montreal," she said, catching her breath. "There's been an accident - a truck skidded into her, but the driver took off and got away."

"Hit and run," Jack said. It was all he could manage to say. "Come in, come in! It's freezing - you'll catch cold!" he said, guiding her to a chair.

"It's bad, Jack," she said. "Internal injuries; head trauma. They said she's lost a lot of blood."

"How did you find out?"

"A call from - you'll never believe it - Robert Sheffield."

"Sheffield? Were they together?"

"I didn't think to ask. Oh, Jack – this can't be happening all over again!"

"A God wouldn't be so cruel," he said. "He couldn't be." He thought a minute, but only for a minute. "I'm going!" he said. "We can ask somebody to take care of the dogs."

"She's in a coma. You won't get there in time."

"Who says? Are they God?"

"No, but they're experts, Jack. They don't expect her to make it to morning."

Hospital waiting rooms; generic architecture; white on white on white. A person could die from boredom here, if nothing else, Robert thought, fighting the smell of sterility as he joined Kathryn in the waiting room. "I called her home," he said, handing Kathryn a white cup filled with coffee. "I spoke with her housekeeper."

"What did she say?" Kathryn added a packet of sugar to the tasteless brew.

"She was very shocked." Though whether Nancy had been more shocked by the news or by its messenger, he couldn't tell. "She promised to call Esmeralda's doctor," he said, as they were joined by a tall, lanky man with thinning hair, wearing an Irish wool turtleneck.

"Oh! Thank you for coming, Henri," Kathryn said to her brother. "It is terrible. A terrible thing! Robert's friend from Pennsylvania, she is hurt so badly."

Henri Moreau, an intelligent man in his forties, leaned over and kissed his sister on the forehead. "I came as quickly as I could," he said. "Robert? You are OK?"

"*Oui,*" Robert nodded, slumping somewhat.

"The mystery woman," Henri asked, pulling out change and crossing to the other side of the room. "Where is she?"

"Intensive Care," Kathryn said, sliding an arm around Robert's shoulder and leaning close.

"Who is this woman, Robert? How do you know her?" Henri asked, jiggling coins into the vending machine and pulling out a candy bar.

Kathryn looked to Robert as if asking his permission. "They know each other from a long time ago," she said, but no more.

"Ah! From the past! A friend."

Kathryn squeezed Robert's hand knowingly. "More than a friend, Henri."

"Then we must do everything in our power to save her. Everything!" Turning to Robert, he asked, "The doctors, they say she will live?"

Covered with sorrow, Robert looked up at his brother-in-law; his friend. "She is in a coma. They won't tell us."

"This is very serious. Does her family know?"

"There is no family," Robert said, his voice tinged with regret. "Esmeralda is the last of her family."

"You love this woman, no?"

Robert looked away.

"But, there is nothing to be ashamed of when it comes to love, my brother." He said, placing a hand on Robert's shoulder.

"Then I'm shameless forever, Henri. Help me save her."

Thicker Than Water   Red fingernails

on any other hand stirring cream into coffee might have worked. The white hair tucked under a gold turban made her appear taller, more commanding; or, at least as commanding as a reproduction would deserve. But, it was the eyes, with their triple pair of fake lashes, which gave the finishing touch; on the famous New York Sculptress Louise Nevelson, darling of the art crowd, the effect was glamorous. On big busted, overweight Blanche Jacobus, it was just too early in the morning. . . .

Setting down her spoon, she idly twirled the ears of the silvery, Blue-Merle Collie at her feet. "Such a pretty boy, Rocco," she cooed, or tried to.

At the sound of her curt, business-like voice, the earliest voice he could remember, the dog wagged his tail, then jumped up at the sound of the phone ringing.

Glad she had the sense to have a phone in her kitchen, Blanche reached over . . . "Hello? Connie! How ya doin', Kid? Paper? Sure I've seen the paper. Out in my front yard . . . You want me to what? Get my lazy butt outside and get that paper? No. Tell me. . . No, I'm not

348

goin' outside . . . No, I'm not runnin' around naked – I just don't want to. . . What? Well! . . . OK, fine!" she said, standing up now. "I'm goin' outside in the snow an' getting' the morning paper. I hope you'll be satisfied when I catch my death of cold, Connie, and you can pay the doctor bills." Setting down the phone, she found a pair of slippers and trotted outside. Finding the paper under a bush, she cursed the delivery boy, vowed to let him – and his whole family – have a piece of her mind and hurried back inside.

"Whew!" she said to Rocco. "Some people just don't give you any slack!"

Back in the kitchen, she picked up the phone. "Girl, this had better be good," she said, catching her breath. "Now, the whole damn neighborhood knows I got a hole in my nightie! . . . What? You want to know what I'm doin' still running around in my nightie? . . . I should ask you the same question! Yeah. What are you doin' HOME today? Isn't it a school day? Aren't you supposed to be drivin' the bus? . . . Oh. You called in sick. Somebody else is drivin' the bus. Pour myself a stiff cup of coffee and sit down? I am sitting down. Are you sitting down? My, but we're pushy today – that husband of yours holding out on you again? Got a headache? Men are such pussies!" she said unfolding the paper. "OK. So, what am I supposed to be looking for? Another strike at the factory? Well, there ain't no factory any more. Keep looking, you say. OK, I'm looking . . .

Esmeralda!" she gasped and spilled her cup – OH! OH! I spilled coffee on my leg!" she said, flapping her hand around for a napkin. "No! No, I'm all right. I'm all right! . . . Esmeralda! . . . Where? All the way up in Montreal . . . Connie, quit you're blabbin' an' let me read! It says she's hurt. It says critical!" No amount of bravado could hide the emotion in her voice. Was it disbelief? Was it fear?

Pushing the paper aside, Blanche twisted the phone chord. "Don't ask me! How the hell would I know what she was doing in Canada? But, with Westminster comin' up, it's gotta have somethin' to do with a dog. She shouldn't be driving, anyhow. She ain't never been a good driver. *Never!"*

Standing, nearly tripping over Rocco, Blanche stepped over to the counter beside the sink and poured herself another cup. "Oh, shut up with that – she doesn't tell me everything. Ez an' me haven't been that close for years. Oh, I guess I could find out. I guess if I called Nancy or Jack I could just about find out anything I want . . Is she going to live? You're asking me? Swear on my mother's grave, Connie, I don't know a THING!"

Hanging up without saying good-bye, Blanche headed for the garage. There, she took hold of a bag of dog food and ripped it open a bit too forcefully. It was just a joke, she thought to herself. *A joke*.

"Ez, you fool! It was all so perfect! The perfect plan! All you hadda

350

do was get outta my way a while. Why'd you go and get yourself in trouble like this? Now, you're gonna go and *die* on me!"

Scooping out a cup full of kibble, she hurled it carelessly into the dish, spilling half of it onto the floor. Dog food crunching as she went, she headed back to the kitchen. Pacing the floor, opening cabinets, slamming them shut, she circled the room.

"I told you not to buy that car! They're not safe. But, no! YOU had to have FLASH! You hadda have SPEED! Well, NOW look, Girl! Now look at the mess you got us into!"

Grabbing the phone, her mind made up, she dialed directory assistance – "Operator? I need help. I gotta make a call to Montreal! Yeah, Montreal, Canada. It's a big city. Didn't they teach you that in school? Hey! *Don't you hang up on me* – hey!"

Dialing again, she said "Operator! I need to get through to Montreal. Well, I have the Area Code, but not the number. Yes, can you? Can you dial it for me? I'm so upset, I don't know if I can dial it myself. Who do I need?" Holding the newspaper close in order to read without her glasses, she said, "The Medical Center – Montreal Medical Center. Yes, that's the place. HURRY! Thank you. Thank you, Operator."

Tearing the newspaper slowly, hands shaking, she sniffed and scrounged in her pocket for a hankie. "Don't die on me, Ez. Don't you DARE leave me alone and die on me!" Suddenly, she heard someone on the line. "English? You speak English? I'm calling about a patient? My friend. Her name's Ez. I mean Esmeralda... yes."

Rocco looked up at his mistress and didn't understand. Why was she slumped over? Why were her hands shaking?

Why was she crying?

Stroking her hair as she lay unconscious in the hospital bed, he kissed her; one of many kisses that should have been, but never were. Speaking to her now; hoping she could hear, could sense his presence; hoping she could hold on to a fragile thread of life; he rambled on . . . "You've been talking in your dreams, Esmeralda. Yes," he said, tenderly. "You were remembering a fashion show. You said you were as happy as you had ever been, getting ready for that show. I remember it, too. Oh, yes. I remember the department store in Philadelphia, and the one after that. I remember how excited you and Blanche were. How she pranced around in her fancy coat and dark glasses, smoking a cigarette like Bette Davis. She could be so funny back in those days. You were so happy then, both of you. So happy,

Don't take her away from me, he thought now, remembering all they had been through. No matter what happened; no matter what anyone else had ever be-lieved; I love her. I always, always loved her.

It had been like this, night after night. At first, Kathryn and Henri were there. After that, they took turns; now, it was only him. Only Robert beside her; stroking her hair like this, washing her face; wondering if she could hear of the stories he had locked away so carefully.

"Esmeralda," he whispered. "Where would you be if the fashion business had lived? I know where you would be. You would be far away; far, far away in Hollywood and I wouldn't be holding you in my arms." He would bring her through. No one could take her away from him now; no mighty God; no dark and merciless Devil. He loved her. If she never spoke another word, if she drifted forever in a world he could never know, he would take care of her; somehow.

She had lasted this long, hadn't she? Hadn't she made it through the first night, the next and the next? He would give her strength; he would give her breath; he would give her life. As long as he could touch her, stay here beside her, she would live. *She must!*

"Walk with me on the wildflower path," he spoke to her gently. "I'm picking you daisies, and snap dragons and Queen Ann's Lace . . . Here," he said, pretending to lay a flower in her hand. "It's a purple thistle flower, but I couldn't help it." And then he felt it. A quiver; just a quiver. But, enough to make him catch his breath.

Folding her hand shut as if pressing it upon a prickly thistle pod, he felt it again.

"Nurse!" he cried out. *"Nurse!"*

Filling the cottage with the warm, meaty smell of home-cooked breakfast for the Collies, steam rising around his face, Jack stirred a pot on the stove.

"Busy last night, were you?" he smiled as Nancy rubbed her eyes and bit into a piece of buttered toast. "Nice job you did," he said. "I always say half of being a champion is looking like one."

"The sun was coming up by the time I got finished," she yawned.

"Well, that won't get you out of your chores, young lady." He lifted the kettle lid and steam poured out like the love he felt for her at times like this. Faye would have approved of Nancy, he thought.

"There's rough times in life," he said, wanting her to know about him, following the impulse that seemed natural and important. "My father was a painter, an artist, back in the war days. Artists are funny people, Nancy. No matter what's goin' on around them, they don't seem to notice. They can't help it, that's just the way they are. See, they just can't help it. If you knew how hard it was for my Dad to find the right materials to paint with, digging for red clay in the stream; Burnt Umber from rotting walnut shells. You know what he used for green?"

Eyes soft, she shook her head. She loved knowing about his life. He so very seldom shared it with her, or with anyone.

"He'd crush tomato leaves for just the right shade of green," Jack said. Glancing toward the next room, he pointed. "See that painting there, over the fire place? My father painted that on a piece of sideboard from our old barn. We had our own farm, back then, just down the road. Oh, that was a cold winter!" he shivered; even now, he could feel it through his clothes.

"We were all out of coal. I don't know why I'm thinking about it now, but I remember it had been snowing for days. None of us ever saw so much snow around here before. All my aunts and uncles; my grandparents; none of us. We had already burnt up every stick and branch and dead tree in the woods around us long before, and were tearing down the barn for firewood."

"My God, Jack," she said. "You tore down the barn?"

"We were desperate," he said. "We'd already chopped apart a wall inside the house and some of the furniture."

"Furniture?"

"Wooden chairs; a table. There wasn't anything else left to burn. It was like God finally gave up on our family and he was going to put us out of our misery!"

"I'm glad He didn't," she said, coming to him; kissing him. "I'd miss you."

Hugging her back, he went on, his voice more urgent. "Mother used to save beans and tomatoes and dried apple slices from the garden and keep them in the cellar. This, we helped her with every year, us kids. Along with the eggs our chickens laid, and milk from our two cows, we always had enough. But I heard Mother and Dad that night. My brother and sister were asleep. But, I woke up. Mother was crying."

He looked away. "I can't go on, she was saying to my father. I can't. I don't know what to do. I pray, I pray all the time. I hope, I beg. Every day, I worry. There's no money left, John. We can't pay the bills. What's going to happen to us? What's going to happen! She was always worrying about what was going to happen. But, did it help her? Did it make her any happier? Did it give her even one more day of life? Or, stop her from dying?"

Lining up two rows of feed bowls, freshly scrubbed, he began scooping out the Collies' hot meal. "I guess it's you sneaking out of bed last night that got me thinkin' about all this," he said. "You know, remembering things. Anyhow, what got me started here at Lochwood is my mother cryin' that night." Clearing his throat, he looked at the painting and went on.

"I got out of bed, hoping my brother wouldn't wake up. I remember, he didn't. I wondered if we'd ever play and laugh again like we used to. If there was ever going to be grass and warm sun again. I was hungry; so hungry. I snuck downstairs and went to that cellar door, where I knew my Mother kept the canned food from the garden. And as quiet as I could, I opened it."

"What did you see?" Nancy asked.

Staring, once again the amazed little boy from so long ago, he answered in a soft voice.

"It was empty, Nancy. Dark and empty. The night before had been our family's last supper."

"What did you do, Jack?"

Taking a deep breath, he straightened up in his chair. "I came here, to Esmeralda's house."

"That night? In the cold? Did she know you?"

"Yes, that very same night. Esmeralda was just a little girl then, younger than me, and I didn't know her any better than any of the other kids in town did. Her mother was still living here then. I don't remember much about her."

"Weren't you afraid to go out? It was winter."

"Not just winter; it was the worst winter. The worst anyone could remember. Even now, I can't remember a winter being any worse. But, what difference was it gonna make if I froze right then or starved the next day?"

He didn't smile. Instead, he buttered a piece of toast and reached for the strawberry jam. "Good stuff, this. As long as you have butter and jam," he said, "you're safe."

"What happened that night?"

Jack bit into the toast and seemed to come to his senses. "Well, I was good with dogs, you know; with animals. Everybody always told me so. And I knew Mr. von Havenberg kept a kennel of Greyhounds. I heard he raced his dogs with friends of his in the next county and I knew a dog had to be in good condition to win. Running a dog makes it fit, and that meant somebody besides Mr. von Havenberg, himself, would have to run them because he was a big, heavy-set man who huffed and puffed every time he walked. It wasn't going to be him, for sure. If only I could talk to him – if only I could see him that night!"

Pushing up her sleeves, Nancy leaned forward, folding her arms on the table between them.

"Somehow, I got to the house," Jack said. "My hands were so cold, and I pounded on that door. I could hear dogs barking and I knew how warm it must be inside for the Greyhounds because a Greyhound has such short, fine hair. I longed for that warmth!" Shaking his head, he smiled for the boy he had once been.

"Mr. von Havenberg himself came to the door. Yes, he did. `Aren't you one of the Milliken boys?' he said to me. What on Earth are you doing outside like this? What's happened! Come in!"

Jack set his toast down. "He was a big man, and when he asked you something, you'd better answer. So, I told him. I told him everything. I said I had to find work. What kind of work can you do, he asked me. I can take care of your dogs, I said. I can make them the fastest dogs around. My mother can make the best dog food for them - meat and eggs and vegetables. She knows how, I said. She knew a veterinarian once and he taught her

358

everything. She can raise puppies good and healthy for you, I told him.

"I looked around the house and, everywhere I looked, I saw such fine, beautiful things. I had never been in such a fine house before. Things made of glass, and bronze metal and mirrors. It was so grand! And paintings. Paintings on every wall, Nancy! Every one of them framed!

"'My father's an artist,' I told him. I saw a vase near the door, a two handled vase that was set on the table and turned in such a way that one of the handles faced the corner. Why wasn't such a fine possession proudly displayed, I wondered? Why were they hiding it in a corner like that? Then I knew. That vase was broken! Beautiful as it was, too beautiful and rare to throw away, it was damaged. And in a fine home like this, I thought! 'My father's an artist and he can fix things' I said, as fast as I could!"

Curious, Nancy tilted her head sideways ever so slightly. Why was he saying this now? What was he getting at?

"Mr. von Havenberg had his driver see me home that night. I left as his new kennel assistant. And, along with my new title, I had a loaf of bread, a cup of butter, two jars of jam and that broken vase to fix. When I got home, I found my father in the kitchen, painting. While my mother slept, he had taken pieces of barn wood from the box beside our fireplace and with the last of his paints he made that very painting you see right there.

He made it, so, no matter what ever happened, we'd always have green grass, blue skies and flowers to look at. When I told him what I had done, he cried, and he gave that painting to me, Nancy. He had never been more proud of me than he was right then, at that moment. And, with that painting, I've held on to that moment ever since."

Pushing the jar of strawberry jam toward her, he said, "So, now you know a whole lot more about me than you ever wanted to."

She remained still, putting together the pieces. "And that's how your brother's antique restoration business got started?"

His eyes sparkled proudly. "That's right; his own business. We all helped out and the business is still going strong. We figured out how to get the work; how much time it might take so you could tell people how much it's going to cost to fix Grandma's favorite old tea pot; writing up the bills, paying the bills. Paying the ones who help you every week."

Nancy wiped her mouth and sized up this man she knew she couldn't live without; not for one day. "Need some help feeding the dogs?"

At the familiar sight of Jack and Nancy emerging from the caretaker's house with two kettles, which could only mean food, a joyous roar went up from the kennel. Collies of every hue leaped as only dogs who live for their masters can do; flexing muscle, bone and spirit with a fervor meant only for those lucky enough to truly know them. Tri colors, Merles, Whites and Sables all bore the unmistakable characteristics of their great sire, Kane, whose eyes were locked onto the one who cared for him.

"Well, look at that," Jack said. "He's a proud champion again."

"He's always a champion, Jack. Just like the guy who loves him. Wanna know how I got his coat so shiny?" Nancy asked, as their voices trailed off and they turned a corner.... Somewhere, Faye Milliken was smiling.

The Battlefront When you've got show dogs, weekly handling classes are one of those social gatherings one tries never to miss. Not exactly like going to church, but in the great temple of the Show World, about as close as one will ever get. There's a certain hierarchy to such events, cultivated in direct proportion to one's perceived standing in the greater arena of dog show world, itself; Conformation first, Obedience second. By the 80s, through sheer force of will, Blanche' and von Havenburg Kennels had either out-lived, out-foxed or out-numbered most of their competition in either category. With Westminster just around the corner, and Esmeralda now side-lined, which one of the two great kennels would take the Breed now was all the buzz.

As Jack took a striking young Sable male through his paces, Nancy turned to a brunette with Kerry Blue Terrier. "Jack says we have to keep the dogs sharp in case Esmeralda comes home in time for Westminster. He sent in all the entries, but only one of our dogs got accepted. So, we're doing the Collie Specialty in Jersey first with the whole string. Then, after that, Jack's going to handle our entry at The Garden. He thinks we have a real good chance of taking the Group!"

"Good luck," said the brunette, as Jack took the dog down and back for the judge and set him up for inspection. Patiently, as if born to the show ring, the young dog stood for the judge to check his teeth, run both hands along his back and sides, and down his tail. Nodding her approval, the judge stepped back. "Take him around," she said.

"What do you think?" Jack asked, beside Nancy when he joined her at the end of the line again.

"Great except for . . . I don't know. Something seems a little off."

"Nancy?"

"I don't know," she said, looking around at the dog to see how he walked. "Something about that left hind leg bothers me."

"He's been getting enough exercise. We're hiking him in the woods. Think he needs more? Here, switch dogs with me and you take him around, so I can watch."

"He's gonna look the same," she said, trading leashes.

"Maybe. Maybe not," he said, wondering what it was about the hind leg that bothered her, waiting for her turn and studying the young dog.

"I think I see what you mean," he said, when she finished her turn a few minutes later. "We'll change the angle on the treadmill tomorrow."

"What's that gonna do?" she asked, out of breath.

"If we're lucky, it'll build his thigh muscles enough to pivot the way his feet are hitting the ground."

"In time for Westminster?" Nancy asked, misting the dog's ruff and brushing it forward, into an Elizabethan collar effect.

Completely absorbed, oblivious to the stir of electricity around him, Jack said, "All we can do is try, right?"

"Well, try all you want, Honey!" Blanche smiled in her big way. "That's your entry for Westminster?" How they had missed her usual grand entrance astounded them.

"Could be," Jack said, playing it close to the vest. Where had she come from, out of the blue like that?

"What about Kane for Veteran's?" Blanche asked, on a fishing expedition.

"Off his feed," Jack said.

"Oh, yeah," Blanche said. "Esmeralda. Well, sorry to hear about that." She said, not meaning it. "Maybe he'll snap out of it. Give him some treats," she suggested. "Rocco, here, just luuuuuves his treats. Don't you boy?" she asked Rocco in affected baby talk.

"Soon as she's back, Kane'll be his old self again," Jack said. "You'll see."

"Can't wait!" Blanche retorted, leading Rocco around herself in tight circles. "God forbid what could happen if he never sees her again," she said, as if she cared.

"He'll see her again. We all will." Nancy said, hoping desperately it would be true.

Looking at her, but speaking to Jack, Blanche smiled. "Really," she said, her voice cold. "Well, that's marvelous. I guess then I can start believing in miracles."

"All right, everybody! Set your dogs up," the instructor said. "This is the real thing."

Instantly, everybody lined up, focused only on their dog. Like soldiers in a row, handlers placed their dogs square, heads forward.

"Come on, girl," Nancy said to the young female she was leading. "See the bait? Watch the bait. You like liver, don't you?"

"All right, boy. Show 'em what you got," Jack said, stepping back from the young male perfectly stacked and waiting. "Look smart!" he tugged the leash slightly.

"Rocco? Want a cookie?" Blanche asked, as Rocco stood to perfection. Turning to Jack, speaking just loud enough for everyone around them to hear, she said, "You're gonna have to do something about your dog's hind leg, Jack, or my Rocco's gonna be all the judge sees."

"I wouldn't be so smug," Jack said. "We'll do just fine."

"*Ha!*" she laughed, hard; mean. "At Westminster? If that's the best you can come up with, I won't be losing any sleep!"

"Take your sleeping pills, and don't forget none," Jack snapped. "Westminster is our show, it always has been and always will be."

"Without Kane? You don't stand a chance."

"Kane or no Kane, we can beat anybody out there," Jack said.

"Are you getting blind in your old age?" Blanche laughed again. "You must be. Look at this boy. *Don't you look away when I'm talking to you, Jack Milliken!*" she scolded. "LOOK at my Rocco! You're lookin' at Best of Breed at the Garden!"

"That's what SHE thinks!" Nancy whispered, under her breath. "Look at that mutt of hers. He's NOTHING compared to Kane!"

"I heard that!" Blanche shot a glare at Nancy.

"Well, he ain't so hot! This dog I got right here can move a hell of a lot better than *that!*"

"Yeah? And who's gonna lead him? You? I'd learn to dress myself before I'd run around in front of a crowd like Westminster," Blanche said, looking around for smiles of support.

"Don't let her shake you up, Nancy," Jack said. "She's just tryin' to rattle you before the judge comes. Oldest trick in the book. Lighten up, Blanche."

"What for?" she wanted to know. "She's gotta toughen up if she's gonna play the game. Ain't that right, Nance?"

"Lay off, Blanche!" Nancy warned.

"Oh! What have we got here? Miss Pig Tails & Nancy Drew Mysteries? Don't think I don't know you've been snoopin' around, askin' about me. Well, I can tell you right now, I got nothin' to do with ol' Ez takin' off like she did. As far as I'm concerned, she's a grown woman who can do whatever she likes. If she wants to take off before a big show like The Garden, hey, that's her business - not mine!"

"Not that YOU'D care if she ever comes back!" Jack said, throwing in his two cents.

"Can I slap this guy?" Blanche asked, looking around. "Let me slap him. Just once!" she said, as the instructor approached them.

"Are we having fun over here?" the lady asked, reaching down, taking the muzzle of Jack's pup in both hands and spreading the lips apart. "Nice bite," she said, running her hands along the dog's body, and straightening up. "Down and back please."

Again, Jack trotted his dog to a far corner, turned around, trotted back and stopped a few feet in front of her. "Ho, fella!" he commanded, as the Collie stopped perfectly and he checked to be sure Blanche was watching.

"Nice," the instructor said. "Now, can you take him around for me?" she asked, and turned her attention to Blanche.

"Very beautiful," she said, about Rocco. "He really is one of the nicest Blues I've seen."

"Thanks, Ethel," Blanche said, recovering from the imagined insults of Jack and Nancy. "Those von Havenburg people are so arrogant!" she huffed.

"Down and back, please," said Ethel, weary of the never-ending battle between the two kennels. If only they had picked different breeds, she thought. But, if they had, she reasoned, things might have been a little dull!

"My pleasure," Blanche smiled grandly.

Again, a perfectly mannered dog.

"Poetry in motion!" Ethel said, for all to hear, as Blanche gloated with pride.

"I sure hope Esmeralda makes it," Jack said on the drive home after a silence of a few miles.

"Two of us," Nancy said, deep in thought. "Did you see Blanche? She almost looked happy."

"Well, she won't be after we win at The Garden."

"I mean, she didn't sound sorry at all about Esmeralda," Nancy said, still thinking out loud.

"All she could think about was Kane and how he won't be at the show. You know, Blanche' and von Havenburg Kennels have been at each other's throats almost long as I can remember now. I can't hardly think of a time when her an' Esmeralda weren't fussin' about somethin' or other."

"It's such a pity. They used to be such friends," Nancy said, from the shadows.

"Well, there's friends and there's friends," Jack said. "Some are just people who know you, and others are people who'd die for you. Big difference, I'd say."

"Well, I don't think Blanche Jacobus would die for anybody. And only the good die young."

"She's as self-centered now as she always was. 'Course she used to be a lot more fun," he said.

"Was she? I don't remember."

"Well you didn't know her back then."

"I just can't get over how she didn't seem sorry about Esmeralda. She wasn't sorry at all, Jack."

"Stuck out that much, did it?"

"Who could miss it?" she asked.

"Did you see how perfect her dog was?" Jack said. "She must be spending hours and hours on him."

"Every tooth, hair and toenail is perfect on that dog," Nancy said, leaning her head against the window.

"And if it wasn't right to start with, you can bet it is now," Jack said, averting a skunk rushing across the road. "Whoa! Did you see that?"

"Glad you missed him!" Nancy laughed.

"Wouldn't have stunk any worse than Blanche and that dog of hers thinking they've got a chance at The Garden."

This time, they both laughed.

"Have you ever seen such ears on a Collie, Jack?"

"That dog looked up at her and his ears didn't even flop back!" Jack smirked, like a naughty schoolboy.

These were the good times, Nancy thought, when she loved him most. When they felt young together, like two kids.

"Blanche made his daddy a champion, his grand daddy, an unbroken chain of winners all the way back to the first dog she ever got from Robert Sheffield," Jack reminded her. "I heard it was part of their divorce settlement, she'd only show the dogs under certain judges and they'd always give Blanche' the points as long as she was on the lead, herself."

"She does always show under the same judges," Nancy said. "doesn't she?"

"Yeah, it gets her ribbons. But, how many other American kennels have dogs in the World Dog Show over in Europe, like we do?" Jack asked.

It was true. The von Havenburg Collies were sought all over the world.

"Jack? Can I ask if something else is true?"

"Fire away."

"Well, legally, can somebody own a dog that's born after they die? I mean, if Esmeralda's Will says all her dogs have to be put down when she dies, does that mean all the Collies she owns at the time of her death, or all the dogs in the kennel when the vet shows up to put them to sleep?"

Jack grew silent, then cleared his throat. "Sounds to me like you have a reason for asking me this."

"Maybe a big reason," she replied. "Maybe getting bigger every day."

"You're pregnant?" he asked with a grin.

"Wishful thinking," she said, slapping his arm playfully. "When are Annie's pups due, Jack?"

"Shhh!" he said, touching a finger to his lips. "We can't tell anyone! If Esmeralda doesn't make it, Blanche will push to see that the Will is carried out to the fullest extent of the law. *And those could be Kane's last puppies!*"

Odd, the kind of things one dwells upon after handling class, Connie thought. Every day she honked as he she drove the yellow-orange school bus past the sign in the front yard saying "Boarding Kennel." She honked every school day; her way of saying hello to the woman inside; a woman she had come to know better as time went by. How Blanche had ever managed to get over losing her best dogs in that accident, she would never know, but she had. People just didn't understand what a dog means, she thought. As for herself, she would never forgive.

A dog was a gift from the Angels. A dog could love you no matter what. A dog wouldn't turn you down because you weren't pretty enough; wouldn't laugh at you because you weren't good enough at baseball in gym class. She thought about how ironic it was that she had never escaped the very school she had grown up hating; how she drove the kids of her childhood enemies to school every day and knew the names of every one of them by heart.

She hated her job. The jacket she wore, the hat; every morning, she wrapped herself in the armor that somehow got her through the day and home again; home, to the dogs that depended on her. Life. As cruel as it had ever been; as bleak as she ever expected.

Her dogs depended on her. If she wasn't there, who would take them to the vet? Sure, somebody might see that they got their shots, got wormed. But, how many people would make sure they got everything they needed? How many people really cared? She knew from her own life how cruel people could be to innocent animals that have no voice, no representation, in this world; no one to stand up for them. If she got sick, if she was killed, who would take care of her dogs? Without her paycheck, how could they be fed? And so, she put up with the kids of those who had ridiculed her in school; had never married, and could count the days she had taken off work on the fingers of one hand.

She stepped on the gas and honked now, even though she had long since passed the house and no one would ever know. Blanche was lucky, she thought. Blanche had her own business. Esmeralda was even luckier. Esmeralda was just plain rich.

Them and their Collies; didn't they know a Dane was the most majestic dog of all? Great Danes were strong; noble. Collies were air-headed fluff. Just looking at a Dane, being around them, filled her with a sense of confidence and power. Who in their right mind would want any other Breed? Sometimes she couldn't even stand looking at other dogs. Why did some people even bother with them? But, then, "people" were what she didn't understand; not even herself.

Had she married, it might have been different. But marriage, the idea of asking permission to do what she wanted to do with her own money, having to consider somebody else's feelings in everything she did, wanted or thought? No, that wasn't her style.

A Great Dane wouldn't put up with that.

Blanche's place wasn't the kind anyone would call a clean house if clutter meant dirty. Canisters of flour, sugar and rice weren't exactly lined up neatly in a row. The spice rack might have been straighter and the refrigerator handle could have survived without the pancake mix stuck to it. Pfalzcraft dishes, leaning like stacks of quarters in a Vegas slot machine about to spill the jackpot, gave testimony to a master of creative thought. A thin film of grease on the stove and stains on the ceiling directly above revealed that a woman who cooked often lived here. The yellowed curtains and fly-spattered windows said she was a woman who didn't see the world as others do; a woman who didn't have time for household distractions. But it was the smell; the permeating, meaty smell of dried dog food coming from the storage room beside the kitchen that offended the nose of others and gave the house its distinctive odor.

"Did you hear that?" she asked the adoring Collie at her feet. "Did you hear Connie saying hello to you?" The idea that Connie was saying hello to her would never have occurred to Blanche. No, Connie was the mother of Axel, Alexis and Adonis. She was the mother of Rocco. It was through herself and Connie that their kids said hello to each other.

Not that she withheld her attentions from the other dogs in her kennel. No, it wasn't like that at all. But, if mothers were honest, there was always one who was extra special. She studied Rocco and handed him a biscuit.

"You are the *prettiest* boy," she said, admiring his thick coat with its cascade of black patches mingled among the silver. "But this bothers me." Reaching for a small bottle of eyedrops, she took hold of Rocco's head.

"Don't you pull away from me! You wanna win, don't you?"

The frightened Collie whined and twisted.

"Rocco, behave!"

The dog resisted, whimpered and fell limp like a rag doll.

"Rocco," she said, standing up, straightening her hair and turning the dog loose, "sometimes I don't know what to do with you." Shooshing him away with her hands, she scolded, "Go play then. Get outta here. I'll have that white haw of yours tattooed instead. That'll fix you, Mr. Big Shot."

Rocco scampered off as fast as he could, and Blanche studied him like a surgeon, taking in every curve and angle of his body in motion. She knew everything there was to know about this dog and his ancestors going twenty generations back.

"You're the best thing I got," she said to him, but really to herself. "That stubborn left ear. Cost me enough to fix, but look at those ears now, Baby. Gorgeous! And such color! Let 'em think it's the diet. They'll never know. Wouldn't the people at "Good Lookin' Hair Color" like to know what "Golden Sunrise Formula 8" can do.

"We're gonna make a fortune with your babies, Rocco. Everybody's gonna be talkin' about Blanche' Kennels. You wait. Little ol' Blanchie Anne from the wrong side of town is finally gonna show 'em. You bet! All we gotta do is take Westminster. I want a big, silver cup - right on my dining room table - and a big blue ribbon beside it. You gorgeous thing. *You gorgeous, GORGEOUS THING!*"

Back inside at her worktable, surrounded by piles of leashes and collars, and Rocco at her feet again, she paused. The glue she'd bought at a craft store wasn't drying quickly enough and her rhinestones wouldn't stick. She'd promised delivery of the matching leash and collar tomorrow and the customer would be furious. Sucking in a deep breath, she pushed aside her jar of glistening stones.

"Dogs!" she hissed. "Dog people!"

"You won't tell if I take a little short cut on this one, will you?" she asked Rocco, reaching for her beads and glitter, but passing over some of the best stones this time. "You won't leave me if you don't like something." Patting Rocco's silken head, she smiled as he slimed her hand with his nose. Just natural, she thought, as she admired her workmanship, and spread out the glittering collar to dry. "Such a beautiful thing," she said, before noticing the clock above her table.

It was almost time for her favorite Gospel hour. She looked forward to the music and the phone calls. It was fun trying to figure out who the voices belonged to, some of them filled with such joy and others so desperate. It was fun listening to the confessions of others.

She turned on the dusty radio among the scattered scraps of leather and string that had somehow become her life, her identity in the sport that was her world. "The Dog Game" was her stage. People knew her. She was a player. And yet, honor, that one invisible thing bestowed upon those who had also played the game, and not nearly as long as she, eluded her.

"It's his fault, Rocco! It's all because of him. Don't fall in love with a man, Rocco. Stick with Momma."

Looking at the dog with the ruthless eye of one who could have been more important in the show ring had she cultivated compassion rather than brute force, she considered the distance between his eyes. She studied the shape of his ears; the texture of his coat; the precision of his chiseled cheekbones and fullness of his muzzle. He was a fine specimen, Rocco was. And yet, in spite of his physical perfection, this dog, the best she had ever produced, lacked that unexplainable something that makes an enduring champion.

She clicked her tongue and Rocco's delicate ears lifted, tipping forward as she has trained them, with what seemed to her like a turnpike of tape and glue. Crafter's glue. The same crafty glue that held her life together.

"Rocco? Rocco?" she asked, with a lilt in her voice. "You could be so great. You really could. We got the judges in our pocket - well, almost. I know all their secrets, Baby. You betcha. Momma's got us covered. All we need is a shot at the Brass Ring. You know, Rocco? Why can't we? Why can't it be our turn?"

Purple Heart   *Funny, how each of us lives the same night in a different way. Annie and Kane curled tightly beside each other, their radiant coats heavy with mud*

*from the rains and clay of their large
kennel runs. Full in whelp now, it was
difficult for the young bitch to find a
comfortable position in which to sleep.*

*It was only a willow branch
scratching across the roof of the kennel
building. She curled tighter beside Kane
. . . .*

Inside her trailer, Connie flicked
on the TV and cleaned up the supper
dishes. Maybe the Tonight show would have
somebody important on, or someone beautiful. Some people had such interesting
lives. How did a TV show find such
guests? Wiping dry the last of her dishes, she put them away.

"Move over," she said to the broad
shouldered Dane stretched out on her
couch, as she lifted and folded a limp
paw out of the way. Reaching into the
basket on the floor, she pulled out the
latest grocery store tabloid and stared
at the pictures. . . .

Embraced in an armchair, Blanche
sat in the darkness and felt her chest
pull tight. Heart be still, she thought.
You've seen too much and have too far to
go. Bowing her head slightly, closing her
eyes, she saw beaches, heard the flowing
voices of foreign strangers and felt the
warmth of their curiosity.

*"We've got it, Ez. We're the girls
from America. Everybody wants to be
around us . . . ."*

In her bedroom of the von Havenburg
mansion, Nancy put down her glass of

water and turned the page of the paperback novel Esmeralda had been reading the day she left.

What did you find in this story that upset you so, she wondered? You promised to call. You promised to say where you were staying. You promised to tell me everything.

Reaching for her cotton robe, fresh from laundry that afternoon, she headed downstairs for the kitchen. She always headed for the kitchen when she couldn't figure something out. Flipping on the light, she gasped.

"Oh! You scared me, Jack!" The sight of him standing there like that, even though she knew he occasionally raided the fridge at night, caught her off guard.

"Turn off the lights!" he whispered sharply. "Quick!"

Instantly the room went black.

"What is it?" she asked, as quietly as she could.

He stood there, by the door, as if ready to lunge from a starting gate. She had never seen him quite like this before. "What's wrong?"

"Down there," he said, holding the door open just a crack.

"Shall I call the police?"

"Hurry," he said, hoping it wasn't too late. Was that a shadow he had just seen running past the barn? How many were out there - one? Two? He squeezed the cold rifle in his hands. *God help me, he thought, if I have to use this.*

"They'll be here," she said, returning from the hallway. "Can you see anything?"

"At least two," he said, under his breath.

"Where? How'd they get past the dogs?"

"Must have come in from the fields. They're at the barns."

"The stable?"

And then he saw it! "They're stealing the horses!" he said, his hand on the doorknob.

"Don't!" she hissed. "The cops are on their way!"

"But, they won't catch 'em. The cops can't drive back there."

"They can block the road," she said.

"Which road?" he asked. "We don't know where they've parked the trailer."

"But, what are you going to do?" she whispered, bunching her collar around her neck.

Knowing he couldn't shoot and risk killing a horse, he hesitated, didn't answer, and just slipped out the door.

"Jack!" Nancy hissed, running for her boots and a coat. *"Jack!"*

Crouching low, he took the path along the garden. If he could make it to the kennel without the dogs starting up, there was a chance. *Please don't bark, he prayed*, counting on a Collie's sixth sense to hear him, knowing the waking of the kennel would only force the thieves to move faster. Glancing over his shoulder, he could see a mare and her foal being led away just as he reached the first kennel, and Kane.

Still as the many times he had posed on Jack's lead in the show ring, the great dog stood; his unforgiving gaze fixed in the direction of the stable. *He already knows*, Jack thought, releasing the kennel latch. Without a sound, Kane tore off like a Greyhound out of the starting box.

It was the mare that saw him first; a mass of Sable and White anger hurling itself at the strange man taking her away; away from all she knew and into a destiny unknown. Raising his arm to protect his face; a scream caught in his throat, the man fell as the frightened mare yanked her head high and tore free.

Panicked by her mother's sudden whinny, the foal spun and ran; ran straight into the man behind them; knocking him backwards; her tiny hooves plummeting his legs, his chest in crazed innocence as she ran. "Ugh!" he moaned, grabbing at his crotch, struggling to stand, scrambling to run like a horse tortured by colic directly into the man and wolf creature before him.

Deaf to the roar of Collies from the kennel barking all at once, men and beast locked into a battle of the wills, but not a growl, not a sound came from the mysterious, crazed spirit standing between them and a clean escape. Trapped like one who has no understanding of the power of loyalty; no sense of how deep the bond between Collie and home may go, they saw the clear fields around them and the woods beyond. Perhaps that made it worse. They were trapped and they knew it; trapped like an animal whose foot is caught in a steel trap and surrounded by the fields and forest into which it can't escape no matter how much it tries - driven to chewing off its own limb to get away.

But this was no steel trap of man's making standing between them and a fate worse than either one of them wanted to consider. This was a king among Collies, harking back to the call of his fore-bears; rushing, circling, dodging in the fashion of his ancestors on the harsh and rugged Scottish highlands as they pro-tected the herds of their masters. Gone was the kind and gentle dog who graced Esmeralda's life and lay at her side as she brushed him hour after hour on the back porch since he had been a puppy. Nothing mattered now. Not the fists pounding at his ribs, the boots kicking at his back, the curses of two men a-gainst a force greater than both of them. Esmeralda was gone, gone from his life, and he must save everything that belonged to her.

Again and again, blinded by rage, he tore into the men. They would not pass him. As he fought on, a lone dog against two crazed intruders, outnumbered but not outwitted, he didn't see Jack running toward them with the gun; didn't feel the spotlight from the police car surrounding them; didn't know every pounding fist to his ribs had held a knife.

The great dog lay there, his white chest matted in blood; his heaving sides stained. This was his reward; his prize for being a Collie; a herding dog trying only to hold his world together. "Easy boy," Jack said, softly, tenderly, gathering Kane in his arms. "Easy."

Carrying the heroic dog past the policemen, past those who would have stolen from Lochwood its valuable horses, and with them, that much more of Esmeralda's joy, Jack almost stumbled. *Please don't let me drop him*, he said to himself. Not now. Not ever. Let me hold him as safe and high as a man can ever hold a friend.

"Jack?" Nancy asked, her voice quivering in the dark and, from his silence, she knew. There was no time to lose; perhaps no time remaining to them at all. "I'll call Dr. Taylor," she said, hurrying to the kennel cottage with him.

Inside, she found a blanket and spread it on the floor. "Is this OK?" she asked, knowing he wouldn't answer; knowing he was lost in healing. *Don't speak*, he would have said. *Don't break the thread; I have to concentrate!* And for those moments, those immediate, frightened moments of raw tragedy, she would remain as still inside as the night after the last howl of the last dog taking its last breath with Faye Milliken so long ago.

Is he going to live, she wanted to ask; she wanted to know. But she wouldn't. She wouldn't dare break the spell Jack was empowering to save the dog who symbolized all that was von Havenburg; all that was their dream.

"Whoooo, boy," Jack whispered in Kane's ear. "Whooooo."

Dr. Taylor would be there soon, Nancy told herself, listening for his car; why was everything so quiet in the kennel? Why weren't the Collies barking at the policemen; the lights; the horses still running loose outside? Why did she feel so haunted? The sound of a shingle flapping on the roof made her shiver as if she were outside in the sudden breeze. Esmeralda would be heartbroken if she were here, unable to bear it. "Is he still breathing?" she asked, and she knew the answer as Jack asked for needle and thread, antiseptic and his special healing salve.

Hurry, Nancy, she thought, bringing the first aid kit, clean towels and hot water in a bucket. *Hurry!*

Carefully, Jack cleaned the wounds. Tenderly, he petted Kane's face and kissed him. "Hold his head up," he said, "don't let him strangle."

Slipping her hand underneath, she moved closer and placed the head that had once been called the most splendid in the Breed on her knee. Touching an ear, severed to the base, she felt a hot tear at the corner of her eye.

"He's losing blood," Jack said. "We can't wait for Doc. I've got to stitch him up myself."

She was already on it. "Here," she said, handing him a threaded needle; holding her breath as Jack pricked thickening skin at the worst of the punctures. Pulling, tightening, he worked; as Kane lay in Nancy's arms.

"I hear Doc's car," she whispered. "I hope they tell him where we are, outside." Footsteps; a knock and push at the door; and Dr. Taylor was on the floor beside them.

Without a word, he placed the stethoscope against Kane's chest, barely moving now. Again and again, he listened for something, anything that might tell him the odds.

"So much blood!" Nancy said, her voice hushed, as Jack sewed shut another wound, and another as an eerie, mournful howl, different from any she had ever heard before, began rising from the kennels outside. First from Annie; then Collie after Collie.

"Jack," said Dr. Taylor, placing a hand on Jack's shoulder.

Another knife wound; another. Stitch and pull; stitch and pull.

"Jack," Dr. Taylor said again.

Stitch and pull.

"Jack. . . . Darling. . . ." It was Nancy now, placing her hand on his; taking away the needle and thread that could never create a design so perfect as a dog; could not hold together the life and body God had created, no matter how much he hoped; no matter how much he tried . . . .

Skin prickling, Esmeralda rubbed her hands up and down her arms as she lay there in the hospital bed. Had the nurse forgotten to close the window, she wondered? She glanced across the room, hearing Robert speak, knowing he was there; skipping the meaning of his words. No, the nurse had not forgotten. The window, opened at her request to breathe in the day's healing sun was closed now against the night chill.

"Are you sure you won't let me call anyone?" Robert was saying.

"No. No. I have a lot to think about, Robert. A lot to think about."

"What about the Collies? Who's taking care of them?"

"Jack knows what to do. He'll never let me down."

"Jack Milliken? Still with you."

"After all this time, yes. And I'd be lost without him."

"From what I see in the magazines, the von Havenburg Collies are doing very well."

"With Jack's help, yes."

"Hard to miss those ads of yours."

She smiled. "And, what about the Sheffield dogs, Robert? Are you still breeding?"

"On a limited basis, yes. Nothing like you and Blanche. But, Kathryn's a marvelous handler. As a matter of fact, that's how we met."

"Kathryn. The woman at your house?"

He nodded.

"This was a mistake," she said, looking away a bit too forcefully. "I shouldn't have come here - I didn't know - I didn't know any of this!"

"Esmeralda, why won't you look at me?" He asked, his hand touching her cheek.

"Don't! If I look at you, I'll never turn away. Not ever again, Robert. I'll be the woman who turned to stone believing in a dream that couldn't be. A fantasy! I've been stupid. I feel so damn stupid. I held on so long. So long!"

"Holding on too long can make your arms hurt," he said with a special grin.

"Night after night of emptiness can make them hurt even more, Robert." He couldn't know, would never know, how unbearably true that was.

He hesitated, not knowing what to say. Should he hold her; hold her so tight the tide of their hearts collided in the white froth of waters from the deepest realms ever known? Did she know? Did she know how much he wanted to wave his hands and find the spell that washed away mistakes, lost years and unholy regrets?

"I want to ask - I want to know - what brought you here?"

"Besides a car, you mean?"

"Besides the steel and speed of a car," he said, his eyes searching hers.

"When I go back, I'll have the rest of my life to figure that out. But, you can help me, Robert. You can help me know the truth. Don't let me live without knowing the truth."

The corners of his eyes crinkled in their friendly way she had always loved. "I'll do my best."

"How long has it been since you've talked with Blanche? Tell me."

"Well, I believe I saw her at a show in Quebec. I passed by her booth. I remember how surprised we both were. It had been so long."

Funny how you could marry someone, fight, cry, have sex, live a whole life and then pretend you didn't care about each other any more.

"Did you talk?" she wanted to know. "Did you have dinner? What did you say to each other?"

"Well, that's the thing of it, you know? You'd think we'd have a lot to say to each other. We were married ten years. But, I remember not knowing what to say at all. And she must have felt the same way, because neither one of us took it any further. I've heard that's how it goes. I never believed it. You'd think you picture each other naked, that kind of thing. But, I didn't."

"When was that, Robert? How long ago? Can you tell me? If you never tell me anything else, ever again, this one thing is enough."

"It's important?" he asked, fixing her pillows. "Is this better," he asked, pulling her up higher.

"It's more important than you'll ever know," she said, thanking him. "Especially now."

"You're going to be all right, Esmeralda," he told her. "The doctors say so."

"If you consider being in a wheel-chair for a while all right. I'll get

387

better a whole lot faster if you tell me, Robert, when did you see Blanche?"

"Well, I think it must have been about five years ago."

"*Five years!* But, it can't be! I've been unconscious five years? No!" What had happened? Lochwood! The kennel!

"No, no, darling! Calm down. You've only been here a few weeks."

"Oh . . . oh . . . but, but you said you saw her five years ago."

"Yes, that's true."

"But, I heard her talking about you just before I left – "

How, then, could Blanche have known he was dying? Standing there, so close, his hands, his arms so strong; he was the very embodiment of radiance. His vitality, his smell – was this the body of a dying man?

"No letters? No calls? You haven't heard from her in *FIVE YEARS?*"

He shook his head. "Swear to God."

"Robert. Are you seeing a doctor for anything? Are you OK?"

"Do I look sick? That's what I get for hanging around hospitals," he smiled and squeezed her hand.

"But, I thought. I mean, I was told – "

"You're getting tired. I should leave," he said, not understanding her anxiety and not wanting to excite her.

"No! Don't go, Robert. Not now. I have more to ask now. More than ever!"

"It can wait," he said. "We have time, Esmeralda. We have time."

"No! I've waited long enough. Wondering how you were after everything that happened and being afraid to let you know? I've wasted my life waiting, Robert. Wasted it!"

"Don't say that."

"It's true! I see that now, and what I see isn't pretty. Tell me, Robert - I have to know. I have to know this one thing. If you never tell me anything else. If I go. If this is it and we never see each other again, I have to know why. *Why, Robert? Why?*"

"You mean," he asked, his eyes roaming over her, nostrils flaring slightly even now, "why didn't the great judge end up with his pick of the litter? Maybe," he said, his shoulders drooping just a little as he said it, "Maybe because the pick of the litter deserved a better life."

"*Better life!*"

"She was the richest girl in town and he was just a common house painter."

"The best house painter around!"

"How could he have supported her?"

"She'd have followed him anywhere, Robert. Anywhere! She'd have lived in a hut and worn rags for a million years to be with him! Oh, Robert! Come home with me! Let's forget everything else. Let's forget time, and people, and what we're supposed to do and how we're supposed to live. Let's forget everything but us. Just us! I don't care what else is going on in the world. I don't care if the world is scrambling in war and they take every freedom we ever had away from us.

389

For once - just once before we turn the corner - can't we have something for ourselves, Robert? Something?"

"What about Jack? Your friends?"

"Jack isn't mine - he never was! Don't take away my last chance at happiness. I don't want to go. I have nothing to go back for! Nothing! Robert!"

"You have everything! You have every reason!"

"NO! No, I can't! I CAN'T go back, Robert. Never. Never again!"

"Esmeralda! You have to. You must."

"I told you NO!" she said, grabbing his arm.

"It's not Blanche you should be asking me about," he said, his heart breaking. "It's Kathryn."

"Kathryn! A convenience! A body to use."

"That body has a heart and soul. She's my wife," he said, looking into Esmeralda's eyes with no other words.

"Your wife." A stone dropping into the Grand Canyon wouldn't have fallen further than her heart. "For how long, Robert?"

"Long enough for the neighbors to believe it," he answered, "Even though, sometimes I can't," he said, holding her gaze.

"*NO!* It's me you love! I know it! *I know it!*" Clutching his arms as if shredding the barrier that separated them with her bare hands, not knowing whether to throw herself at him or hurl him away, she covered her face. Scratching at her hair - thrashing out with her arms she knocked a water pitcher over and sent it flying across the room.

"Nurse!" he hollered, throwing himself across her to hold her down.

"You left me, Robert! *You left me and you left Blanche and you never knew!*"

"Esmeralda!"

"Don't touch me!" she screamed suddenly. "Get away! *GET AWAY FROM ME!*"

"Watch out!" he hollered to the nurses who came running, as she struggled to throw him off her.

"You'll have to leave!" one of them hissed, slipping on the floor, and grabbing hold of the bed.

But Esmeralda had said it best: "*You left and you never knew!*" Letting go of her again would never banish those words from his life.

Phone wires stitching together members of The William Penn Kennel Club sizzled with the news. Kane, the Champion who had won more trophies than any dog any of them had ever known; the pride of his kennel and resented by all of them, had died defending Lochwood while Esmeralda lay on the brink of death in far off Quebec. Who were the robbers? What were they after, people wondered, recalling the scene in "Zorba The Greek" as the rich, old foreigner struggled on her deathbed surrounded by thieving neighborhood women coveting her treasures. Each time she closed her eyes; each time she gasped for breath, they scrambled; each time she opened her eyes, they froze.

*News travels fast in dog circles;
faster than . . . (You thought I was
going to say, "Faster than a Greyhound
leaping from the starting box)" . . . .*

"Blanche? You still there?" Connie
asked on the phone.

"Yes," she said, her heart almost
still; her mind thrashing for air. "I'm
here."

"I said, Kane's dead."

"I . . . heard you."

"Well, don't you see what this
means?" Connie asked, her voice light,
almost giddy. "It means von Havenburg is
out of business! The big star is *gone.*
You're it, girl. Blanche' Kennels is
finally on top! I've got pull, Blanche.
*You're in! You're taking the Breed at
Westminster!"*

As the horses murmured over their
fresh hay and grain, Jack went over the
events of last night. Who were those
guys, he wondered? Why were they after
the horses?

"A ring of thieves," the police
chief had said; transporting horses
across state lines and selling them at
out of the way auctions for a quick buck.

"They hit quiet, country places
like this and the owners never know until
the next morning. By then, it's too
late."

Too late for Kane, Jack thought,
setting down a scoop of sweet feed as the
anxious mare fretted. *Are you crazy*, she

seemed to be saying? *Can't you see I'm starving?*

He finished pouring the grain into her feed bucket and would have smiled; but, not today. Today, he couldn't even say a word. The emptiness; you could feel it. You could feel it all around, everywhere you looked. How would they go on, he asked himself? How was he going to tell Esmeralda?

"I can't believe it," Nancy said, beside him. "It just doesn't feel the same."

"Like a drunken dream?" he asked.

She had no answer. Drinking was something in which she never indulged. Not for her, the ravaged character of Anne Baxter's *Sophie* in Somerset Maugham's *"The Razor's Edge"* she had seen at Annville's Allen Theater. Funny, how movies could make you feel, she thought. But, this, now, was no movie.

"I guess I'll have to talk to Robert," he said, wobbling inside, trying not to fall off the circus tight wire on which he found himself so precariously balanced.

"I can make the call if you want me to," she said, sensing his fear.

"No, I can do it myself," he said. "It's not Robert I'm afraid of. It's what this could do to Esmeralda."

"Then don't tell her," Nancy said. "If you love her," she said, knowing he always had, always would, "spare her."

As the day transformed itself from morning, to afternoon and beyond, they worked; sometimes alone, sometimes side by side. It was the longest day she had ever felt, thought Nancy, as she lay beside him in his cottage now.

Rubbing a hand on his stomach, she found his belly button and pushed a finger in. "I feel that," he said, in the dark.

She kissed his shoulder. "I was just thinking," she said, loving how it felt to be so safe with him; thankful they had overcome the ghosts that haunted them both. "If those guys were part of a gang, is anybody going to come back?"

He had asked himself the same thing, over and over again. "I don't know," he said.

Her soul cringing, she wrapped her arm around him, tight. "Jack?" she said . . . "let's make love."

Life went on, as it somehow manages to do. People loving, people hating, people wondering where it all seemed to go. The thing about having a kennel full of dogs is, you never have to wonder what you'll be doing tomorrow. There's a sense of safety in that; a feeling that, no matter what happens out there in the big picture, you're OK as long as you take care of the things you can. Feed the dogs, pick up after the dogs, brush the dogs, take them to the vet. Jack pulled in the lane with a truckload of dog food and a few bales of hay. Was that Nancy flagging him down?

"She's coming home! I got a call! Just a little while ago!"

"Esmeralda?" he said, rolling down the window, knowing he didn't have to ask.

"They're releasing her tomorrow and she's arranged for a flight back." Nancy said, catching her breath.

"Harrisburg International? What flight?"

"She doesn't want us to meet her. She's already made arrangements for a limo."

"How did she sound," he asked.

"I don't know. It wasn't her I talked with. It was Robert Sheffield's wife. He's married," she said with a look they both understood.

Jack nodded and his silence said oceans, mountains, valleys and all the heavens. It also said, "How is she?"

"She has a way to go, Jack. We'll have to get used to a wheel chair around here."

His eyes met hers and all was understood. "Tomorrow?" He looked at her and thought about tomorrow. Esmeralda would want to see all the dogs groomed to perfection when she drove past the kennel, and all the runs perfectly clean. They would groom today and rake the kennel runs in the morning.

"What about Annie?" Nancy wanted to know. "Should we tell? She'll be so excited."

"When the time's right," he said. "Not tomorrow."

Tomorrow always comes, at least until we're gone. With mounting excitement, Jack and Nancy rushed to make sure everything was up to Esmeralda's standards. Windows sparkled; dishes gleamed; the dogs couldn't have looked more proud. Funny, how one gets to know the sounds of a kennel and what the dogs see. . . . .

"She's here!" Nancy cried, as the kennel sprang to life outside at the sight of a black limo slowly approaching the house. Together, not knowing whether to go outside or wait, they watched from the kitchen as a driver stepped out and, with the efficiency of one accustomed to the ritual, opened the trunk. But, it wasn't luggage he was getting. There were no leather suitcases or traveling bags. Instead, he set on the ground beside him a metal wheelchair, unfolded it, and proceeded to the passenger door. Pale and fragile, Esmeralda emerged from the limousine, seated herself carefully in the wheelchair, and waited to be pushed to the house. From a last, desperate flight for love, she had come back to the place where it all began, a wounded dove. Like the wheels on which she now depended, her life had come full circle.

"Oh, look at her," Nancy whispered to Jack as they hurried to help. "Is she on some kind of medication? They didn't say anything about medicine. Should I call the doctor?"

"She didn't even look at the dogs," Jack said, strangely. He was right. The ruler of von Havenburg Kennels hadn't even noticed.

"Esmeralda!" It was Nancy, taking over for the driver, who nodded solemnly and stepped back, customer delivered, job done. Tipping his hat, he turned and, sensing all was as it should be, left. "We've missed you so much," Nancy said.

"Welcome home," Jack smiled, or tried to. But, not a word, not a smile, not a gesture emanated from the woman they once knew so well.

Ever since she could remember; ever since she was a little girl, she had stared out the window overlooking the gardens and swimming pool. Beyond that was the kennel building, where she could see Jack now, bringing one of the Collies to the house. Touching the glass gently, then pushing away from the window, she wheeled herself to the desk littered with unopened mail, and searched for a pen and paper. She would write to him, make him change his mind. No, she decided after a while, crumbling the paper in her fist. There had been enough change for now.

The gentle knock on her bedroom door had never sounded so intrusive; the touch of her trusted confidante never more unwelcome. But there was no soft, *"May I come in?"* There were no manly footsteps reassuring her of his presence. Not this time; not now; maybe never a-gain. *Oh, don't leave me alone, she thought. Not you, too.*

Slowly, the door opened and the beautiful face of a Sable and White

Collie appeared. Quietly; as if sensing the despair and taking it upon herself, the graceful spirit took her place beside the woman on whom all life at Lochwood depended.

"Annie?" Lifting perfectly tipped ears at the sound of her name, or perhaps at the rush of spirit unseen but so real between them, the dog's eyes searched for understanding. Onto the knees of the one who decided everything, she gently lay her head. "Annie," Esmeralda said the name kindly, taking the Collie's thick ruff in both hands, choking back all the mourning for a love so great it had been worth everything; leaning over to kiss the simple dog who adored her. "We've lost them."

Blanche sucked on a slice of orange, bit into the pulp and peeled off the skin with her fingers.

"How am I supposed to know?" she said into the phone. "Alls I know is, she's back. My neighbor says she saw a big limo in town. Well, who else around here needs a limo? Of COURSE it's her. Trust me. She's back. And just in time for The Garden," she said, almost giddy. Covering the phone with her hand she hissed at Rocco.

"Let go of that pancake!"

Returning to Connie, she said, "That dog is always after my cookin'. You'd think he was a MAN or sumthin' the way he goes after my stuff."

"Hey, girl," Connie said. "Sounds to me like more than Esmeralda von

Havenburg's back. Now, this is the Blanche we all know and love!"

"Honey, when ya got it ya got it. Sex Appeal is sumphin' you're born with. Ask Sophia Loren. She said that."

"Well, maybe she can tell me if it's true what I hear about you and that All Breed Judge from Maryland."

"Honey, when that man comes to town, it's the whole Fourth of July!"

"Girl, you're a trip!"

"A trip an' a HALF, hon. A trip an' a half."

With Annie at her feet, Esmeralda steadied herself on the handles of her wheelchair.

"Don't get up, Annie. It's OK. I've been practicing." Slowly, carefully, she raised herself up and stood, shaky at first, then stronger.

As Annie watched, once again the woman she worshipped made her way to the desk, found some notepaper, and began to write.

"It won't be easy," she said out loud, as the curious dog wagged her tail against the floor. "But, I've got a plan."

A knock at the door stopped her.

Quickly, Esmeralda struggled back to the wheelchair and covered her legs.

"It's me. Nancy. Can I come in? I want to empty the trash."

No comment was made as Nancy pushed open the door, entered the room, and took the wastebasket. "Two more to go," she said. "Then it's the garbage. You know what they say . . . ."

"No. What do they say, Nancy?" Her eyes distant, and empty of fun, Esmeralda waited and both knew it wasn't the rest of the saying about a woman's work that she wanted to know.

"Ah. She wants to know the gossip. Can I sit down?" Nancy asked, knowing if they talked now or later, it really didn't make much difference.

Nodding in the direction of a nearby chair, Esmeralda said, "Please do." But, there was no smile, no warmth between friends. Holding the moment of suspense just a bit longer, she asked, again, "What do they say?"

"A lot of people are saying you deserve it."

"Deserve? How judgemental."

"They say the only reason you're still alive is to suffer and see what you've caused by everything you've done."

"A long list," Esmeralda said.

"They say Faye Milliken's ghost can never rest until the truth of that night comes out."

"I believe Faye knows the truth of that night better than anybody."

"They say Robert Sheffield is living here at Lochwood somewhere."

"I think we both know the answer to that."

"They say Blanche Jacobus is going to take Best in Show at The Garden," Nancy said, her eyes on the wheelchair.

"Do they."

"They're saying the von Havenburg Collies are finished now. They were saying all the dogs were going to be put down if you died and that it would be Faye Milliken's last laugh."

Standing to go back to her duties with a satisfied smile, Nancy picked up the wastebasket once again. She loved gossip.

"What about you, Nancy? What do you say?"

"Me? I'm stickin' around for the show. 'Cause I got a hell of a feeling there's going to be one!" she said, closing the door behind her. *That ought to do it, she thought.*

"Bitch," Esmeralda said with the first hint of a smile.

The door popped open, Nancy stuck in her head and winked. "Welcome back, Esmeralda."

Something about the cleansing ritual of burning the trash after dark felt right. In a paper world, it was oddly reassuring to know the simple stroke of a match could so effectively erase the day's score and clear the slate to start all over again. Nancy thought of the mythical Phoenix bird she had once studied in Latin class; the bird that died in flames and rose up again, renewed. She had always known the real message of the Phoenix was to reassure us that it was, indeed, possible to start all over again. No matter what happened to us, no matter how unbearable or final it seemed to be - even reduced to ashes -

it was possible to start again. She wondered what Esmeralda had really found in Montreal. She wondered if she would ever know.

It was the color of the paper, light blue even in the gold of the flames that caught her eye; a crumpled piece of paper fallen out of the incinerator, waiting on the ground; waiting to be discovered.

One in every crowd, she thought, picking it up; then recognizing it to be Esmeralda's personal stationary . . .

"Dear Faye," the letter started.

With a tinge of guilt at her intrusion into Esmeralda's private life, Nancy almost tossed the letter back into the fire. But, she couldn't. She must know; she must know why the letter, written on the same stationery as all those private letters to Dr. Philippe Moreau in Paris; was pulling her so desperately.

A letter to Faye. Was it possible? *Was Faye Milliken alive?*

Knowing if it was true, she and Jack could never marry, that he had been lied to; that all of them had been lied to; she remembered her promise. She had promised Esmeralda never to open such letters. But this was different; she hadn't opened this one. This letter had fallen right into her hands.

"I would never have considered myself capable of murder . . . " it said.

"I, delighting in each new life born here for as long as I can remember, am astounded at the absence of love in my heart at this moment. What have I done, Faye? What has happened to me? How could life pass me by so quickly? I have often wondered what others would do if given the chance to live it all over again. It's a foolish question, don't you think so? A question entangled with 'What ifs' and 'If onlys' as elusive as the mist of evening on Lochwood Lake for me ... until now."

Faye was alive and Esmeralda was going to commit murder!

She must find Jack. He must know! Gripping the letter in her fist, Nancy hurried to the cottage.

"FAYE'S ALIVE, Jack!"

"What!" What had gotten into her?

Showing him the letter, Nancy gushed, "All those letters Esmeralda's always sending? Faye's alive and Esmeral-da's gone crazy! And she's going to kill somebody! *Oh, my God, Jack!* What if she's already done it - *in Canada!* Maybe that's why she's acting so strange. Has anybody heard from Robert since he called? What if she killed him! He's married now. He told me. *What if she killed his wife!"*

"I can't believe that," Jack said, his hands trembling as he read the note and Nancy went on.

"She's writing to Faye," she reminded him, wondering why he was so calm at such a moment.

"I can see that," he said. "But, she believes Faye protects Lochwood," he said, sad at the desolate tone of Esmer-alda's words; understanding the pain with

403

which she lived; never fully realizing it until right now.

Surprised that she would seek comfort from one who had been a friend to all of them; that, like him, she would always want Faye to be there; that she would seek out Faye's loving advice in times of need, want out speak with her?

He wasn't surprised by that at all. "She believes in such things," he said. She was raised that way and, I guess it's rubbed off a little on me, too. No, Faye's gone, Nancy," he said, putting an arm around the new love in his life and kissing her forehead. "You're my girl now. That's how Faye wants it."

"But, she sends the letters to a doctor, Jack. A doctor in Paris."

"How do you know this one's going to him? It didn't, did it?" Well, he was right about that. She had to admit that. "So what if it's her writing paper?" he asked. "What else is somebody supposed to write on?"

"But, how do we know she doesn't mean it, just the same? She's different now, Jack! She's not like she was when she left. She doesn't care about anything. We really could be talking *murder!*"

"But, we know our friend," he said, and, at the risk of being gruesome, he added, "Nancy, can you really see Esmeralda hurting anyone on purpose? Other than Blanche, I mean."

She caught the joke. "Well, when you put it that way, how do we know that isn't who she's talking about?" she

404

asked, settling down. "God knows, Blanche has gotten her mad enough in the past. And, half the time, I wouldn't blame her if she finally did bump her off." She thought a minute. "Maybe it's awful of me, "But, can you see Esmeralda killing Blanche? Jack, *you know* she'd never allow herself to go to prison. I'd go upstairs some morning and find her dead with both wrists slit! Oh, what a horrible thing! Why did I think that?"

Jack shook his head. "Wouldn't happen," he said. "Faints at the sight of blood."

"All the quicker!"

"No, more likely, she'd drive the car off a cliff."

"In a wheelchair?"

"Temporary inconvenience. But, what she *could do*, is jump out the window."

"Hang herself!" Nancy said, brightly. "That's what she'd do. Or take all her pills at the same time. That would do the trick."

"Nope. You've got the key to the medicine cabinet downstairs. And she can't hang herself; what would she hang herself from? How can she reach up to tie a rope from a wheelchair? But she could set a fire and burn the whole place down."

"And mess up the trophy room in the house?" Nancy asked, incredulous. "No, I'm the one who shines those trophies every day. And I'm telling you, there's no way she'd melt them down."

"Well, then, how's she going to end it all?" he asked. "Drown herself?"

"How?"

"Bathtub?" he asked.

Nancy shook her head. "Forget it."

"How come?"

"Esmeralda would never let ANYBODY see her naked!"

Making no particular comment about that, he said, "Well, she could stab herself if she wanted to."

"I thought you said she couldn't stand the sight of blood. We've got to change her mind, Jack. If she hasn't already killed someone, we can stop her! We mustn't let her out of our sight!"

"Well, what are we going to do? How do you stop somebody if their mind's made up to commit murder, which I don't believe for a minute anyhow. Do we face her with it? Tell her we know? You know how she is about anybody snooping in her mail. We've been around a long time, but she's not herself right now. If she finds out you've read one of her letters - ."

"I didn't think of that."

"Well, you can start now, Nancy. Something happened in Montreal that we don't know about, and it happened with Robert. That's why she's writing this. It has to be. She needs something to change her mind - a reason to live." he said.

Nancy brightened. "Jack! She doesn't know! She didn't figure it out! There's no way Esmeralda von Havenburg wouldn't say something about it. I mean, we were in there, the two of us, just as catty as could be, and she never said a thing. Not one, single word! Annie!" she laughed and scolded the Collie playfully now. "You mean to tell me you spent the whole day with Esmeralda and she never found out your secret? Girl, remind me to let *you* know when I want to keep a few!"

"She hasn't asked about Kane," Jack looked away and sighed. "We'll have to tell her. We can't put it off any longer." They stood for a moment considering the impact; dreading what might happen, looking at each other.

"Can we come in?" they asked, knocking as they entered Esmeralda's room.

"I was just reading," she said, putting down her book as they made themselves comfortable.

"We need to tell you something," Nancy said, sadly.

Esmeralda hesitated. She had wondered when they would tell her; how they would say it. Even now, she choked back a sob at the thought that he would be with her no more; that her hands would never again touch his face. "I already know," she said quietly. "Kane . . . Robert told me. We shared a lot of things; after I threw a pitcher of water at him and a bed pan."

Looking for all the world like the outdoorsman he was, in his work pants, loose shirt and cap, Jack said, "Feisty, as always, I see."

"Just what you always liked about me."

She was taking it well, he thought; perhaps too well. "Esmeralda, I'm sorry," he said. "Kane was a great one."

"It wasn't your fault, Jack. I know that," she reassured him. "He was a king. He wasn't afraid of anything. The Alpha, remember? He was just doing what a Collie must do." She put her hand on his.

"But, there's something else," Jack said, with a twinkle in his eye. He petted Annie, who stood at his side on a short leash.

"We have a surprise for you," Nancy smiled.

"I've had quite a few of those lately," Esmeralda said, not knowing what more to say.

"A good surprise," Nancy added.

"Well, that's different," Esmeralda relaxed, as Jack gripped her hand and placed it on Annie's belly.

"If your heart is pure and filled with love, you can feel them."

"Pups," she said, smugly. "Yes, I know."

Nancy stepped forward and got on her knees beside the wheelchair.

"Not just pups, Esmeralda. They're *Kane's. Kane's!*"

As gently as they had come to her, they stood to go. Silently, they looked at each other, as Esmeralda said not a word. Was that a tear on her cheek? They must go; they must leave her alone now. Of course, she had known Annie was carrying pups. A Breeder all these years would never miss such a thing. *But, she had not known they were Kane's.*

And as they closed the door and walked away, they heard it. They heard the sobs; the uncontrollable, wrenching sobs; the cries of loss for what could never be again. But, it would be all right now. Everything would be all right.

"It's up to God now," Nancy said, once they were downstairs.

He took her hands, wrapped them around his waist and pushed against her. Kissing her on the mouth, he smiled. "That's what I love about you, Nancy. You always know the right thing to do."

Rubbing her hands up his back and along his shoulders, she whispered, "I'll meet you after I turn out the lights and lock the doors," she said. "Warm the sheets for me."

He kissed her again, kissed a hand, and left. A gallant man, she thought, watching him walk away; her man.

She unplugged the coffeepot, walked to the front door and locked it. Funny, how a house feels right again when its owner comes back, she thought. Funny, how you don't know "empty" until they're gone. Deciding to check one last time, she went upstairs, knocked and found Esmeralda asleep on the bed; Annie curled up beside her.

"Did I ever tell you how lucky I am to have you in my life?" Nancy whispered later, smoothing her hands over his back, as he lay beside her on his belly.

"It's me, who's the lucky one," Jack said, sliding a leg between hers. "I *guess*. " he teased her.

"You *guess?*" she asked, her fingers playing up and down the crack of his cheeks. "You're not sure?"

Rolling on his side, he breathed in her smell. "Your hair smells good," he said, playing with her nipple. "Did I ever give you a nipple kiss?"

"No," she smiled. "I don't think so."

"Well, first . . . " he said, sucking her nipple and twirling his tongue, "you do this."

"Mmmm," she smiled. "Don't stop."

"Your turn," he said, pulling back.

"My pleasure," she smiled, biting his nipple.

"Make it good and slippery," he said. "You'll see why."

"How's that?" she asked.

Feeling himself to make sure, he said, "Perfect. Now, lay still and don't move," he said, lifting himself above her, sucking her nipple again.

"Just checking," he laughed gently. "Perfect," he winked in the darkness. "Now, the trick to this," he said, lowering his chest, is not to let . . . anything touch except . . . " he blew a quick, sudden breath on her breast and their hard nipples touched.

"Ah," she whispered, fighting the urge to wrap her arms and legs around him.

"Nancy," he said, tensing his pecs, relaxing, tensing again, "I love you."

"I love you, too, Jack," she said, pulling his hips to hers and smacking him. "I love the way you kiss."

If night is for lovers, then morning is for good-byes. Pulling the

410

blankets up over his naked shoulder, Nancy left the bed and dressed. She hated leaving him this way, pretending; hiding their love. Some day, it would be different, she promised herself. Some day, he'd be ready and so would she. . . .

From the spacious kitchen of the mansion, she smelled hot chocolate.

"Would you like a cup?" Esmeralda asked from her seat at the table.

Hiding her surprise, Nancy took off her jacket and scarf and hung them on the coat rack. "Yes, please," she said. What else could she say? Esmeralda shouldn't be downstairs. She couldn't walk. She shouldn't even be awake at this hour.

"How did you - ?"

"Never mind me," Esmeralda said. "What I want to know is why you weren't in the house last night. Anything could have happened. Why, I might have needed you. I'm an invalid now. A cripple. There could have been a fire. We could have been robbed. Any number of things might have happened."

"I was . . . I was - "

"No need to tell me," Esmeralda said, putting up her hand for Nancy to stop. "I know where you were."

"You do?"

"Of course. You don't think I'm blind, do you?"

"No."

"I've known Jack a long time, Nancy. Long time." A distant smile crossed her face and she lowered her eyes to her cup. "Jack and I were lovers," she said boldly. "It was right after Robert left. I don't know what came over me. I should have known better, but I didn't care. All I could think about was how empty I felt. My life was over - the life I wanted. Nobody wanted me. Nobody!"

She caught her breath. Even now, she felt the world closing in on her. "There's freedom in love, Nancy. Remember that."

"He never told me," Nancy said quietly.

"He's not the kind who would," Esmeralda replied.

"How did it end?"

Esmeralda smiled wisely. "Nancy, love is a force of Nature," she said. "Like the weather, it has seasons. I'm not sure if it's love that has the season, or us. I've never had love long enough to know. But, I do know love is different with each one we might choose. And our hearts are much, much bigger than we've ever been told."

"You've been reading your mother's books again," Nancy said, feeling closer to Esmeralda that moment than she had ever thought possible.

"Go for it, Nancy. Move into the cottage. If I need you, you're as close as the phone."

"Are you sure?"

Esmeralda nodded. "We've got work to do."

"Shouldn't you be resting?"

"That was yesterday. We've got ourselves a job ahead."

"A job?"

"You'll see," Esmeralda said, with a grin. "Now help me upstairs. Pulling myself down those steps was hell on my ass."

A few hours later, Esmeralda sat outside in her wheelchair, bundled against the winter chill, as Jack ran the dogs through their paces. "Is this the last one?" she asked Nancy, standing beside her.

"Yes," came the answer. "Just the six."

"Which ones do you like?"

"The first one and the last two, I think."

"And Jack?"

"He saved the best for last," Nancy smiled, sure that Esmeralda could see the quality of the young dog being put through his paces in the training ring before them now.

"There's something about him," Esmeralda agreed. "Why haven't I seen him before?"

"You have. He's one we held back from the last litter because nobody wanted him. Jack thought he should have some extra time and maybe we'd sell him already started."

"You mean the pup with the hair sticking out all over the place? The one that looked like a possum?"

"That's him."

"Looks like Jack was right," Esmeralda said, as he slowed the pup down and stacked him. Like a pro, the young dog gave all his attention to his handler, ears alert, neck arched, focussing on the bait in Jack's free hand.

"He wants to know what you think," Nancy said, about Jack glancing over at them.

"I know," Esmeralda said softly, keeping her smile hidden. "Let's keep him guessing."

"Torture?"

"I'm good at it."

"Have a *heart*," Nancy teased.

"What for? He's stealing my house-keeper."

"Such a bad boy," Nancy smiled.

"Yes, he is," Esmeralda said proudly. Leaning forward, cupping her hands beside her mouth, she gave the command.

"Brush 'em up, Jack! *We got a SHOW to do!*"

"WHAT!" Blanche screamed into the phone. "I don't BELIEVE it. How'd you find this out?"

"I have my sources," Connie said. "You know I buy goat milk for my pups and they told me Nancy had been there just the other day. That means a litter. They said the pups are Kane's!"

"He's DEAD!" Blanche screamed.

"The bitch was already bred."

"Bullshit! That dog hasn't sired a litter in YEARS!"

"Well, do you think it's true? If it's true, Blanche, they'll be worth a fortune."

"And she KNOWS it! What does SHE need the money for! She just ruins it for everybody!"

414

"You're jealous! If you could get it, you'd charge every bit as much and more," Connie said.

"She doesn't need the money!"

"Well, do you want her to just give them away?"

"I'm SICK of it! Everywhere you turn - Kane, Kane, KANE! It's a publicity stunt. She'll do anything to stay on top and keep her bloodline going!" Blanche said, cursing and slamming down the phone.

Sabotage

Only weeks away from Westminster now, a new sense of determination and purpose took hold. There would be bathing, trimming; there were hotel accommodations to be made; packing for the biggest two days of the dog show year. This was it. This was the big time. This was what every dog Breeder in the country dreamed of!

"I want everybody in peak form," Esmeralda said, in the kennel building. "I want this place spit-shined! Nancy, you polish all the leather - every lead, every muzzle. Jack!"

"Yes?"

"You make sure to hike that new pup on the mountain every morning at 5:00 sharp. Not a minute later! I want to see him at breakfast every day, when I have my tea. Nancy? Make sure I have my tea and toast by 6:30 AM."

"Understood," Nancy said.

"Any questions?" Esmeralda asked. "We've got a business to run! Nancy, I want you to help me draw up an ad. We'll run it in all the magazines - the Gazette, the Bulletin, Collie Expressions - all of them! I want the world to know Kane's back and our bloodline's secure. This litter's the best thing that's happened to us in years!"

Nancy winked at Jack and smiled. The power behind von Havenburg; it's heart and soul; was back in the driver's seat. Maybe not a car this time, but a driver's seat nonetheless.

"Jack!" Esmeralda fired out. "When are these pups due?"

"Just about any day is my guess."

"Is everything ready?"

"All set," he said.

"I can hardly wait! Make sure you call me," she ordered. "No matter when. Day or night!"

"Promise," Jack said from a corner of the room where a young dog trotted on a treadmill machine.

"This sure brings back a few memories," said Nancy, trimming whiskers and nails.

Esmeralda looked up from reading a stack of Collie magazines and studying the competition. "You were one of the best groomers we ever had, Nancy."

"A dog's feet are the secret to good movement in the ring," Jack said, turning up the radio. "We've been walking the dogs on the road, Esmeralda, to toughen up their pads."

"That's one way to get attention," Esmeralda laughed. "Right, Nancy?"

"You gotta do what you gotta do," Nancy laughed.

"The cameras of the world are going to be on us this year. Did you know that?" Esmeralda asked.

"No! The dog show's going to be on TV?"

"Sure is," Esmeralda said, turning a page. "Ah! The Kilderry dogs. Now there's a line worth going up against. Do they have anything out there right now, Jack?"

"Kilderry Tycoon. A big Tri."

"I like the name. Who's the handler?"

"Bill Stanley, from what I hear."

"From Connecticut? The one who got suspended?"

"White hair to his shoulders, braid on one side, that's him."

"Handsome man," Esmeralda said.

"Didn't he used to work for the big kennel in California that belonged to that doctor?"

"The plastic surgeon," Esmeralda said. "Yes, that's the one."

"What happened?" Nancy asked.

"They got caught doctoring up their dogs," Jack said.

"What kind of stuff were they doing?" Nancy wanted to know.

"Besides ears?" Jack said. "Well, I heard they were pretty good at shaping a dog's eye if it wasn't right. Tails were no problem at all."

"I hate the thought of that," Nancy said.

"Simple cut, that's all."

Esmeralda butted in. "How about the metal plate everybody thought we put in Kane's skull?"

"That was a laugh," Jack said. "Where was the scar?"

"You think it'd show in all this hair?" Nancy scoffed. "Come on, Jack!"

"They were talking about a metal plate in the back of his skull. Now something like that would leave a scar!"

"Maybe," Nancy said, thinking about it. "But, I know I've seen some pretty poor dye jobs out there."

"On the dogs or the handlers?" Esmeralda snickered.

"Blanche uses it. I'm willing to bet."

"Now, now," Esmeralda pretended to scold.

"Seriously. That Rocco of hers? The Blue Merle? Haven't you ever noticed how perfect his black patches are around the edges?"

"Blanche is an artist. But, I'll bet you never knew about how she gets her ear sets. She has her vet make a slice on top of the head and pull them closer together. They make the incision length wise, so it doesn't mess up the lay of the hair. Throat latches, she does pretty much the same way. Remember that one Champion, Jack? The one with the great profile, but he never threw anything like himself no matter how close you bred to him? Chin implant."

"I remember," Jack said. "How about the water injections in the tips of the ears? Who was it who used to do that?"

"Helen Bartlett," Nancy said. "The same one who had the monorchid that miraculously grew another testicle when he was two!"

"And just in time for the National Specialty," Esmeralda laughed. "How about you, Jack? Think you could do something like that? And extra testicle?"

"Dog Breeders are a clever bunch," he blushed.

"They can be," Esmeralda said. "If they'd put as much effort into breeding right in the first place instead of faking it, we'd have a lot better dogs. Oh, I can't *wait* for this litter!"

"Well, it's good to hear you laugh," Jack said. "Welcome back to the game."

But, things were going too good. Somewhere out there; somewhere in the dark lived a plotting mind so fiendish, so desperate, so - shall we say the word? So jealous! - that nothing - nothing - was too low to dare. As the radio played and laughter pierced the darkness, the crunch of hesitant footsteps were scarcely heard outside. Approaching the kennel, they stopped outside the nearest chain link run; then another and another, until all the von Havenburg Collies had been visited . . . .

"Nancy, wake up," Jack said urgently the next morning.

"Oh, let me enjoy being in your bed," she moaned.

"*No! I need your help!*" he said pulling at the covers.

"Have mercy!"

"We've got a problem in the kennel," Jack said, his face white. "Big time! Doc Taylor's on his way."

At the mention of the veterinarian's name, Nancy's eyes flew open and she sat up. "What's wrong?" she asked, sensing his urgency, tossing off the covers and looking for her clothes. "That man's starting to live here – and at 82!"

"Doc's tough," Jack said. "And he's got help. But, I don't know what's wrong with the dogs. Something must have been wrong with the feed last night – all the dogs have the shits!"

"*All* of them?"

"*Every last one!*"

"Oh, God," she sighed. "Does Esmeralda know?"

"Not yet."

"Shouldn't we tell her?"

"Wait 'til Doc gets here."

They didn't have long to wait for the familiar gray station wagon to rumble up the driveway.

"I got here as fast as I could," Dr. Taylor said, gathering a few things from the back of his car and zipping around like a man half his age. "OK, show me what we're dealing with."

"Well, so far, it looks like they've all been affected with the same thing."

"What's this!" Nancy called out half-way down the first row with a shovel and bucket.

"Be right there!" Jack hollered, taking off at a run with Dr. Taylor not far behind him.

"It's a piece of meat," Nancy said, looking at Jack. "We didn't feed this to them."

"Poison."

"But, what kind?" said Dr. Taylor.

"Why didn't we hear anything?" Nancy asked.

"Last night, we wouldn't have heard a gun shot going off out here," Jack said.

"What time do you think it happened?" asked the vet.

"Well, we didn't hear anything after we went to bed, so it must have been before midnight," Nancy said. "Wouldn't you say, Jack?"

"Had to have been. Any later and I'd have heard something."

"Seven hours," the vet said. "Slow-acting for a poison. And all of them have it," he said, looking up and down the rows.

"Every last one except for Annie. I had her in the cottage."

"The one in whelp?" the vet asked.

"Due any day."

"Well, thank yourself for that," he said, kneeling beside the nearest dog and checking its heart rate. "Can you hold him, Jack, so I can get a temperature?" Doc asked, putting on gloves and pushing soiled hair aside. "Nasty stuff back here!" he said, holding his breath.

"And we had them all looking so nice," Nancy said.

"Wicked!" Doc said, standing up and breathing again. "Temp's normal, heart, too. It's just a guess at this point, but, once they get through whatever it was they ate, I don't believe they're in any real danger. I'll leave something with you to help. Aside from that, you might want to put everybody on rice and cooked hamburger a while, until things get back to normal. Can you do that?"

"I was just headed up to the kitchen," Nancy said. "I know I've got plenty of rice. I'll check how much 'burger we've got in the freezer."

A chill of terror went through Esmeralda and she clutched her nightgown. "Every one?" she asked. "They'll be off their feed now. They'll lose weight. They'll all have to be bathed again – every dog in the kennel. And right before the show ... *Blanche!* It's her! I know it!"

"I still can't figure out why they didn't bark," Nancy said. "They're usually so alert. I mean, *nobody* drives past the kennel without the dogs barking. Isn't that right, Jack?"

"But, would any of us have heard them last night?" he asked. "Somebody could have parked down by the entrance and walked in the lane; the dogs are always barking at cats and small animals, and we don't pay any attention. All they'd have to do is start tossing meat and the dogs would quiet down right away. What a dirty trick."

"I'm just glad we had Annie inside the house," Esmeralda said. "Is Doc sure they'll be all right?"

"Pretty sure, yeah. And I called the cops to report it."

But, what could they do - search for fingerprints? Did this mean guard duty every night? Living that way wasn't worth it, Esmeralda concluded in the days that followed. No one had to tell her who would have done such a thing. It was Blanche who stood to gain the most if von Havenburg didn't make it to New York for Westminster.

Big Dividends You can't keep a good team down. Kennels can be cleaned up and bellyache overcome. Life goes on; one day, one week, one generation at a time and nine squealing Collie pups were welcomed into the world . . . .

"Let me hold one," Esmeralda said to Jack, as she held out her hand.

"How about this one," he asked, picking a dark brown and white male, bigger than the rest.

"He's marked . . . he's marked exactly like Kane," she smiled.

"Acts like him, too," Jack said. "You ought to see that sucker push his brothers and sisters out of the way."

Kane would have been proud, Esmeralda thought.

"We'll tell everyone at the show next week," she said. "When they ask what we have at home, we'll say Kane puppies. The last of them."

The Blue Ribbon

It was show time! Across town, Blanche, phone ringing in the background, loaded up grooming tables, boxes and shelves for her booth; a crate for Rocco, and the obedient dog himself. . . . At Lochwood, it was feed bowls, bottled water, blankets and leather suitcases.

Every year, the same; every year, the finest dogs from across the United States descended on New York to compete at Madison Square Garden for the Best dog in the land. It was a power show. It was "The" show. To win at Westminster was the ultimate glory. "Make me proud, Hon," Blanche said, as she and Rocco headed East on the Pennsylvania turnpike. "It's your turn now." As if he understood, the dog settled down in his crate, assuring her that all was well . . . .

Arriving at The Garden, finding their places and setting up shop, Esmeralda and the von Havenburg entourage attended to the dogs, handed out business cards and fielded questions.

"I guess we're the old guard now, Jack," Nancy said.

He laughed. "Well, if you hang in there long enough, sooner or later nobody can remember when you weren't around."

They were interrupted by an attractive young foreigner.

"*Bonjour,*" she said in her French accent. "Would these be the von Havenburg Collies?"

"Yes," Jack said, handing her a business card. "They sure are."

"And is Miss von Havenburg here, please?"

"She's still at the hotel. Classes don't start until later," he said, intrigued, but not knowing why. Something about her, he decided; *something about her seemed familiar.*

"And which hotel, please? The New Yorker?"

"Yes," he nodded. "Just across the street. Does she know you?"

"She is expecting me, yes!" the woman smiled brightly. "*Merci, mon ami!*"

"Pretty," Nancy said, rubbing hair gel into the fur of a dog's white front legs and dousing them with powder as the young woman left.

"Yes, she is . . . " Jack said. "Do we know her?"

"Don't think so," Nancy said, hands busy and moving on to business. "When did you say the first class is coming up?"

"Half hour," he said. "It's never easy getting through this crowd."

"Ah, but that's the glamour of it," Nancy grinned. "You never know who you're going to bump into!"

She was supposed to be here by now,
Esmeralda thought, from her hotel suite.
What if her flight had been delayed? What
if she hadn't been able to find a cab?
What if she changed her mind?

She wouldn't, Esmeralda told herself. She wouldn't change her mind. Few
needs could be more powerful than to know
who you are and where you come from. Only
Esmeralda could tell her that. Yes, she
would be here. She would be here.

"Front desk," the man answered.

"Can you tell me," she asked, her
fingers playing with the pearls around
her neck. "Has anyone asked for me? Do I
have any messages?"

"Is this Miss von Havenburg?"

"Yes," she said.

"I thought I recognized your voice.
Actually, there is someone looking for
you." He glanced across the lobby, dec-
orated with its enormous chandeliers.
"But, she didn't want us to disturb you."

"She's early!" Esmeralda thought,
heart beating faster. "Can you send her
up, please?"

"Certainly."

Oh, breath! Don't leave me. *She's
here! All this way - all this time!*
She'll be beautiful. She'll be so beautiful. I want everything to be perfect,
Esmeralda thought, primping in the bathroom mirror. It has to be. It has to be
perfect. Oh, hurry. Hurry!

Unable to wait any longer - the
years had been long enough and she could
never get them back - Esmeralda wheeled

herself to the hallway to see the young woman walking, then running to her.

"Faye! *Faye!*" she cried, her body shuddering with hope; her voice lifting higher as she spread her arms wide with love. It couldn't be anyone else; it couldn't be anyone else in this world!

"*Ga-bri-elle Faye!*"

Back at The Garden, the classes wore on and the crowd deepened. Hour after hour, Collies from some of the greatest kennels in the country competed in a process of elimination leaving only the finest to vie for the Best Collie in the Best show in the United States.

Representing von Havenburg Kennels, Jack appeared dapper in his suit and tie; as he went through the paces beside other handlers and their dogs from California to New York leading the young pup he had raised with such faith. But it was Blanche, her big white hair dyed brassy yellow; proud in her pink dress with Rocco at her side, who the camera adored.

"Come on, Rocco," she cooed in her one-of-a-kind way. "The judge likes you. I know he does," she coaxed, as Rocco gazed up at her as if no one else in the world was more important to him at that moment. Following her every move; every graceful gesture of her hand, Rocco poured his attention on the woman he worshipped as if his very life depended on the piece of dried liver hidden between her long, red-painted nails.

"Around again, please," the judge said, in his black tuxedo. Around they went.

"One, two, three, four," he pointed, and Blanche, her heart leaping for joy, smiled as demurely as she could. Best of Breed was hers and Blanche' Kennels would now represent the Collie in the Herding Group. If she won that class; if she took the Group; then, after all these years, a Collie would finally be competing for Best in Show again.

"Congratulations," Jack said, exiting the ring.

"Thanks, Hon," Blanche smiled, smoothing her lipstick for the cameras. "Where's Ez?" she said, looking around the crowd. "I don't see her."

"She was watching the class from up there," he said, pointing to an upper level entrance behind the stadium bleachers. "She and a friend of hers," he added. "I don't know how they could see anything. Must've had binoculars."

"Opera glasses," Blanche said, remembering a time long ago and looking down at her nails. *"Fire engine red."*

"Are you all right?" Esmeralda asked, as she was wheeled toward the elevator.

"Oh, yes," Gabrielle nodded. "She is just - "

"What, Dear One?"

"So different from what I thought she would be, you know? I wanted her to be . . . different." There was a sadness about her now. A sadness in the words.

"Well, yes, Blanche is very different, if you really want to know. Why, no one in the world is as . . . creative . . . " Esmeralda felt her voice falter, and she cleared her throat. "And she . . . uses her creativity in so many ways. She does. Yes, yes, she does," she said, nodding to herself. "That's . . . that's one of the things I always liked about her best, if you really want to know."

"She's not what I thought she would be. How she carries herself, the way she moves," the young woman, so cultured and naturally graceful, imitated Blanche's style and it wasn't flattering. "And so fat!" She puffed out her cheeks and shook her head.

Esmeralda smiled politely. Did the impersonation have to be quite so cruel? "We must go back to the hotel," she said. "We have a lot to do before tonight."

And what a night it was. Lights! Camera! Action! TV crews; newspaper reporters; magazine writers covering the crème-de-la-creme of dogs showcased in New York City's hallowed hall of sports, Madison Square Garden.

As exhibitors fussed and primped their dogs in a cloud of sprays, cologne, and potions rivaling any hairdresser's convention, the crowds jammed the place in a rush of noise and expectation. As dogs paraded for the judges center stage on bright green carpet; in the very spot of concert performers, boxing champions and the foremost entertainment of a nation, row upon row of seats rose upward

in a sweep of faces. Applause! Whistling!
Laughter! Every seat in the house was
taken as the best dogs of the Herding
Group; German Shepherd, Bouvier de
Flandres, Briard, Shetland Sheepdog, Old
English Sheepdog, and all the rest
entered the ring . . . . .

Standing tall, Blanche held proudly
onto the delicate leash she had designed
for Rocco. Squinting her eyes against the
harsh television network lights, she considered the effect of the tiny rhinestones she had glued to his pink lead,
and the effect of the glitter in her
matching gown. Feeling all eyes upon her,
she took a breath; held it, and slowly
exhaled. This was it, she thought. The
big moment. With a dog whose pedigree
bore the names of generations for whom
she, herself, had personally planned the
birth, raised and cared for; all the way
back to the very first puppy she had ever
owned; Blanche' Kennels was representing
the Collie Breed to the world.

Blanche Jacobus had arrived.

Taking her place in the line up,
Blanche posed Rocco effortlessly, her
every move executed with efficiency and
style.

Graciously, she smiled for the
cameras, even while dreading the moment
when she must jog around the ring with
Rocco at her side. Making excuses for not
working out harder at the gym, she
dismissed the thought, as the elegant
judge in black approached them from her
right.

"Cookie?" she asked Rocco, who perked his ears and grew animated at the sound of the word and the chance to taste the bait with which she teased him. Swaying her hand above his face, holding her fingers so artfully, the voice he knew so well said, "Cookie?"

Like a living work of art, Rocco stood proudly as the judge searched for the most flawless body of the finest dog of the Herding Group. Rocco; Ch. Blanche' Big Shot; a dog who had never seen a farm; never seen a cow, a chicken, a duck or a sheep.

"Down and back, please," the judge said, emotionless.

As the deep voice of the Announcer echoed throughout the great hall, expounding on the Breed's great history, Blanche smiled and lifted herself into a swooping stride that would have been the envy of any ballerina. Around she went in a sweeping triangle, allowing the judge to see Rocco from all points of view. Her mind in slow-motion, she returned to the judge and stopped before him.

Once again, he examined her creation. Once again, he paused. Once again, she went over and over the list of all she had done for this historical moment.

"Around, please," the judge said, with a gesture of his hand as he stepped back for a better view.

Grandly, she obliged as the crowd applauded the silver-haired Collie from Pennsylvania. This was it, she thought to herself. Blanche' Kennels had a star.

As the Belgian Tervuren flinched when the judge touched it; as the Puli broke stride half way around the ring; as the Corgi charmed the crowd with its antics, Rocco remained secure and strong.

As he weighed his decision, knowing the impact of what he must do now, the judge faced the men and women lined up before him. Each of them had worked diligently to reach this pinnacle of achievement. He understood how long it had taken them; how much they had each sacrificed for this honor and recognition. The dog world had its favorites, this he knew. But, right here, right now, he was the judge. Upon him fell the responsibility of granting The Blue Ribbon to the greatest example of its Breed standing before him tonight. Steeling his nerves against the disappointment that must be suffered by those so urgently seeking his praise; desperate, himself, for the flood of approval on which his reputation must depend; he crossed the ring to his table, leaned over and scribbled a few notes. Returning to the center of the ring now; speaking clearly for all to hear, he pronounced his sentence.

"*The Collie!*" he called out, pointing one, two, three, four.

It's me! Blanche thought, suddenly unable to move. Oh, I can't remember how to walk! Oh, I can't believe this! Yes, I can! Yes, I can! Oh, I want to thank everyone who wanted me to win! I have to thank – oh, forget it, nobody helped me. Nobody wanted me to win – I did it all myself. I worked, I hoped, I prayed. I

*clawed myself up the ladder of success
and took every chance in the book to
build myself a bloodline. I married a
Collie man and learned everything I
could. Nothing stopped me - nothing! I
lost the best dogs I ever had and I
started all over again. I didn't go out
and buy Rocco from somebody else. I
brought him into this world, I raised
him, I trained him, I did it alone,
World, and here he is. Here he is - my
STAR!*

Shrugging as if all the credit
belonged to Rocco, the mastermind of
Blanche' Kennels faced the nation's television audience with a humble smile.

Slowly, calling upon the Blanche of
days gone by, the woman before them
transformed her bearing once again into
that of the saucy young girl within her
soul who had waited so patiently within
that razor sharp mind. Big hips swaying,
eyes searching the crowd for the one whom
her victory must surely hurt the most,
she sashayed to the judge and accepted
her ribbon. Triumphantly, gloriously, she
tossed back her head, laughed victor-
iously and held the ribbon high.

I did it! she thought, parading
Rocco around the ring to a standing ova-
tion of deafening applause. *I did it!*

*Had the night ended there, it would
have ended as perfectly as a dozen red
roses in a Randolf vase of translucent
white porcelain. As winner of the Herding
Group; the level of her game raised that
much higher; Blanche and Rocco would have*

left the ring in a blaze of glory. But,
Blanche had not seen her greatest rival.
In spite of all she had accomplished; all
she had proven to herself and the
international dog show community, the
face of the one person who could fully
understand; who had always been there
watching from afar; eluded her this time.
What did it matter, she thought, to
herself. What did any of it matter if
there was no one who knew how much it had
cost. Savoring every second as she ran,
beaming her best Hollywood smile, she
played to the cameras and they ate it up.

Here it is, Ez, she thought, waving
the ribbon for all to see. *Here it is!*

And then it happened. As dramatical-
ly as her face had conveyed the victory
of winning, the smile began to drop; the
eyes grew disbelieving; the complexion
beneath the Helene' Rubenstein makeup
went deathly white.

There, among the crowd, directly in
front of her now, sat a wheelchair-bound
Esmeralda. But, it was not her old friend
and nemesis who so shattered the woman
who would have given anything to bask in
the glow of praise just one moment
longer. It was something else.

Was it a trick? Was it her nerves?
Yes, that must be it; she was running too
fast. It was all too much for her!
Slowing now; coming to a complete stop
half-way around the ring and shielding
her eyes from the television lights, she
looked again. There they stood, directly

behind the one to whom she had not spoken in what seemed like a lifetime now.

Haunting; apparition-like; far more handsome than she remembered him, stood a dark-eyed man in a 1940's white blazer, navy blue slacks and tan hat propped back just a little.

With him; the very vision of herself so long ago, stood a curvy young blonde in a familiar hat and slinky dress of matching pink more beautiful than she ever remembered herself or the original Blanche' creation to be.

It wasn't possible!

Ghost-like, they stood there, mysteriously observing her from the past, making no comment; no judgement. Then, turning silently; certain she had seen them, felt them and taking it all away now; they faded into the crowd.

Picking up her pace; running with all her heart, all her soul, the proud woman of Blanche' Kennels screamed "Wait! Don't go! Come back! Oh, please - *please — don't go!*"

On she ran - across the ring; toward the crowd - oblivious to the cameras; unashamed of her weight, forgetting her newly gained status in the dog show world.

Nothing mattered now - if they got away from her nothing would matter any more, ever again!

"Don't go away from me!" she cried.

With all her heart; encompassing the agony the had hidden for a lifetime, she pleaded, "*STAY!*"

And, with that; with that one, simple, well-taught and never to be ignored command; all that remained of Blanche's dignity, if there was even a shred left to be saved after breaking dog show protocol in such an unseemly way, went down the toilet. For Rocco, obedient to the point of no longer thinking for himself, did exactly what his mistress commanded.

He stopped.

Chroniclers of "Most Embarrassing Moments" vary in their particular order of the events that followed. Some say the wig flew off her head first; others deny that and say, no, it was her shoe. Either way, both versions agree that Blanche crumbled to her knees and hit the floor slamming like a ball player sliding into home plate.

For an instant, the crowd held its breath as every paramedic in sight stood ready to rush to the stricken woman lying there in a glittering pink heap. Then, bravely, as if to let no one mistake that she was even then, and would always be, in charge of herself no matter what she had done in the past; no matter what she might ever do - and she would surely think of something - she stirred. Clawing her way back, first with one fist, then the other, she raised herself up. Shuddering, her great body steadied by ring stewards on either side, and judge alike, she rose, as the television cameras zoomed in for a close-up of the face of America's new darling.

"My baby!" she sobbed; her eyes searching the crowd; her voice lost in thunderous applause. "Oh . . . oh," she sighed, deep and mournful.

"My . . . Baby."

"It's OK," someone said, handing her the leash. "We got him!"

There are those who say success is the best revenge and for those who seek it - revenge - there can be no thrill quite as great. Gloating in her suite, Esmeralda burst open a bottle of champagne and poured her protégé another glass . . . .

"You were brilliant!" she said. "*Brilliant!* You followed everything I said perfectly - just enough; no more; the perfect mystery. If I only knew what was going through her mind when she saw you. *If I only knew!*"

"She was surprised, no?" the young Frenchwoman smiled.

"As if she saw a ghost!" Esmeralda laughed. Her sides hurt; but, oh, it had never felt so good.

"You are happy then? That is good! Auntie," came the unexpected question. "Did she really make the dress I wore?"

Esmeralda became quiet. "Oh, yes," she said, remembering. "She's very good at that. She and I were going to Hollywood - didn't I ever tell you?"

The young woman, looking so much like her mother tonight, shook her head. No, she didn't know about that. Esmeralda had never mentioned it.

"I didn't? Well, I'm very surprised," Esmeralda said. "We were in business together, Blanche and I. We had signed contracts with department stores for the Blanche' fashions. "But, then . . . " her voice faded.

"What happened then, Auntie? Tell me," the young woman coaxed.

"Your mother married. I went abroad and came home to find her married. She told him she was pregnant, and he married her. If she was really going to have a baby, I was never sure. That was long before you came along, of course. By the time they broke up, she really was pregnant . . . with you, my darling . . . *Gabrielle Faye Sheffield*. My little Faye," she said fondly.

Her eyes grew distant now; seeing places so very far away; seeing London, Madrid; the small apartment in Paris. The risk had been worth it. She knew that now. She had done the right thing. Blinking; taking a quick breath, she snapped back.

"Blanche wanted to be a fashion designer in the movies and I was her business manager. We were going to meet two handsome actors and live happily ever after." She laughed softly and shook her head. "It didn't turn out that way."

"But she was on the screen tonight, was she not? Your promise has been kept, no?"

"My promise," Esmeralda repeated, almost to herself. "All over the news, the mighty Blanche Jacobus brought to her knees." She paused; letting the impact of it all sink in. *Shouldn't it be more delicious, she wondered?*

"We leave in the morning," she said. "You must come back to Lochwood with me and get to know everyone, Faye. You can stay as long as you like."

"But, did I not tell you? I must go to Montreal. My father wants me to meet Kathryn."

"Ah!" Esmeralda nodded quietly. Could loneliness ever felt more cold? Letting the statement hang, the young woman for whom Esmeralda had done as much as she ever could, noticed a nearby table graced by a 1940s champagne bottle holding a bouquet of dried flowers.

"An old souvenir?" she asked, delicately.

"I take it with me to every show," Esmeralda said, bravely. "For luck! You know, that bottle once held a thousand bubbles for every minute of every hour I thought of a very special man. The love of my life," she said wistfully. "He picked those flowers for me."

Careful not to reveal his name; deciding to let their story bloom in its own, natural way, she selected a dried daisy, kissed it and placed it behind the ear of the one who should have been her own.

"There," she said. "A wild flower from Lochwood. May you be lucky in love," she smiled, knowing, after tonight, she would never see the giver of those flowers again.

"There's a path; it's such a beautiful, winding little dirt path where

he and I used to walk. It always felt
like being in an old Wallace Nutting
photograph. Have you ever seen them? Such
pretty pictures. Thin, dark frames; *de
riguer* of antique shops! Stately trees,
winding dirt roads, flowers in bloom."
She thought of their faded colors and
paused. "Well, things don't always turn
out the way we hoped," she said, "or the
way we're told they should be. You're
sure you've never seen them?"

Seeming to understand that their
time had come to a close now, her guest
smiled politely. "No, I have never seen
them. Perhaps, some day, when I come to
Lochwood, you and I will walk there, and
you can show this path to me, yes?"

For now, the path of her own life
was beckoning. "My father is waiting for
me," she said, with a kiss and a hug.
"Good night, Auntie. Thank you for
everything. So much fun! But, so naughty.
She will be all right? I will write to
you soon!"

It would be a long time before they
saw each other again, Esmeralda knew,
savoring the name *Auntie*; loving it no
matter how unconventionally it had come
to be. Hoping now for one last glimpse,
she rose from her wheelchair and crossed
hesitantly to the window. One last time,
she hoped, searching the streets below.
Let me see him just one last time.

She found him waiting by a taxi,
saw him opening the cab door for his
daughter; saw him smiling as she got in.
Suddenly, he looked up.

Does he see me, she wondered? Is he blowing me a kiss?

Waving; hoping; she caught his kiss, touched the window and felt the loneliness of it all. There would be no doing it over, she knew that now; no chance to try again. Time had run out. It hadn't stood still for her after all; not like she once believed it would. It hadn't stood still for any of them. Resolved, she picked up the phone and dialed.

"They're gone," she said, to the one who had waited a lifetime for the truth. "No, I couldn't get her to stay," she said. "Don't cry, Blanche. Don't cry."

Pausing, she let it wash over them like gentle waves on the Riviera sand at night.

"I know!" she said as brightly as those faraway city lights. "Why don't I order us sundaes? Would you like that? Do you want me to, Blanche? Mine with caramel and yours with fudge and peanuts and sprinkles the way they used to make them for us at the old ice cream parlor in Mt. Gretna. Remember? I have so much to tell you," she said, wondering if Blanche would ever believe it; any of it. Why hadn't she told her before? Why hadn't she told the truth when they had met in the dress shop that day?

Nothing - *no power on Heaven or Earth* - could have stopped her from finding out for herself what Blanche Jacobus was like that day; from seeing her face; knowing what her voice sounded like; hearing her laugh. After all these years, would it matter why Esmeralda had to meet the blonde girl Mrs. Harrington finally told her about after Jason von Havenburg's elaborate funeral?

Even now, she could see Mrs. Harrington telling of her weekly visits to Dorothy Jacobus's dress shop to deliver the sealed envelopes for Jason von Havenburg, returning home to Lochwood with snap shots, notes from school; crayon sketches of stick figures wearing bright pink dresses, fancy hats and high heeled shoes.

She touched the shoebox beside the dried flowers now; the Blanche' Creations shoe box she wouldn't drop this time. She must tell her now; she must tell Blanche everything.

"I know what!" she laughed. "Why don't you wrap your hair in a silk scarf, like the movie stars do, and put on your face. We'll pretend all the stores in New York want that sparkling gown you wore tonight. That was a beautiful number, Blanche. It really was. How many famous designers can say they had a national TV commercial like yours?" *Little Faye was right, she told herself. You did it, Blanche. You made it to the big screen.*

The torrent of wisecrack scolding?

She had missed it.

The recriminations? The tears?

She deserved them, she guessed. She hadn't needed to be quite so mean. Life had seen to that for both of them.

"Yes, Blanchie. Do bring the ribbon. I have so much to say; so much to tell you," she whispered, tears blurring her eyes now as she took the bouquet of wild flowers from the bottle. *Good-bye, Robert,* she thought, crushing them to dust. *If you ever loved me, I loved you more. Good-bye, secret child* she knew no better than her father had known a girl named Blanche.

It was 1986. "We Are The World" was playing everywhere. "The Oprah Winfrey Show" had just hit national television.

Life was the movie; we were the stars . . . and Ch. Blanche' Mr. Big Shot had almost won Westminster.